Hollow

Out of the Box, Book 12

Robert J. Crane

Hollow
Out of the Box #12
Robert J. Crane

1st Edition

1.

Jamal

Wi-Fi: Connected.

Messenger Status: Online.

Thirty thousand feet was a strange place to find myself into the biggest trouble of my life, but somehow I managed it.

Airplane etiquette dictates you should just lean your seat back, put your tray table to the down position, eat your snack, take the Coke or whatever it is they offer, then maybe go to sleep for a little while. Basically, hang out until you arrive at your destination. Right?

Well, not if you're me. My name's Jamal Coleman. I'm a hacker, and I was on this flight for a really good reason. I was following a guy named Caden Sims, and from what I knew … Caden Sims was some kind of trouble.

Let me start back at the beginning. I've been around for awhile, working in the background. Maybe Sienna told you a thing or two about me. I hope it was good. It could go either way, really. I've done some bad things.

Some … really bad things.

But following Caden Sims onto that plane? This time, I was really, really trying to do some good.

Normally, when I have to follow a guy, all I do is pull up his image on a surveillance camera and watch him from across the country. Because I can and because that's the safe, sensible way to do it. Not to book yourself on a flight, follow him through airport security, get on the same plane, and then sit there almost across the aisle from him, hoping he doesn't realize that you are actually following him in this confined space where neither one of you could escape.

Yeah, sensible. Not really my way of doing things this time.

I watched Caden Sims from the takeoff. He was engaged in slightly not normal activity—on his phone as he was boarding, took out his tablet the minute he sat down, played with it until after takeoff and until we reached ten thousand feet. Then, the moment the Wi-Fi turned on, he's got the keyboard attachment out and he's playing on his tablet, which he's now transformed into a laptop. Tapping away like he's hurrying to exorcise a demon from the net or something, big noise-cancelling headphones wrapped around his ears. The entire plane could've been coming down and he wouldn't have noticed.

I've been known to get that way myself. But it was good for me because he wasn't watching me at all as I snuck a furtive glance or two across the aisle at him, already playing with my own tablet. The drink cart came rattling by, beverage service now concluded.

I shook my head at the flight attendant when she asked me if I wanted the cookies. I didn't. I like the peanuts. She didn't have any of those, though. Allergies on the flight or something. Damn.

My stomach grumbled. Watching Caden Sims was an exercise in boring. All he was doing was tapping on a keyboard. If all you can do is watch a man tapping on a keyboard all day long, sooner or later you'll probably go insane.

I didn't have time to go insane, though. I had a suspicion Caden Sims was up to no good and this was the only time I had, ever, to get a shot at him.

About a year ago, I'd learned that someone had done a little experiment in my neighborhood, given people metahuman powers out of nowhere. Mine was power over electricity.

Most people I knew who had this power, like my brother's

girlfriend, Tanishia, used it to summon up a big old bolt of lightning. Fearsome thing, scary as all hell. I'm not talking about the lightning here, I'm talking about Tanishia. She's frightening. She could do things with her lightning bolt powers that would probably shock the hell out of anybody. No pun intended. She used it to defend Atlanta, to protect the people, do the usual sort of hero stuff.

I used mine to do a different kind of heroing. They call it hacktivism. And that's how I found Caden Sims.

I search the net a lot. It's what I do at night when I can't sleep. Hacktivism means you always gotta be keeping your eyes open for the next thing. A lot of refreshing to follow the flow on message boards, waiting for new content, fresh replies, the next part of the thread. Tying myself in on Messenger with groups that are always looking for the next thread to pull on, the next thing to go after. We always kept our eyes open, always talked about the next big thing. The next refresh of the page that would bring new data.

Someone once said that history doesn't repeat itself, but it echoes. Skimming the online communities I'm part of, you see a lot of echoes. Certain names keep coming up over and over again in the flow of uninterrupted knowledge.

Caden Sims's name was one of them.

When I looked into the guy a little deeper, I found a short bio—VP of Development at a tech company with three employees. Their mission statement was all generic corporate fluff, but the heads up I got that pointed me toward Caden Sims suggested he was anything but vanilla corporate. There were whispers of something deeper, traces of his hacker fingerprints from before he went to work for that company all over some malignant code that found its way out into the web.

That was enough for me to take a closer look at the man, but when I did ... I couldn't get into any of his systems.

Nothing. When a man lives on the net and you can't find any hint of what he's up to? That's a sign that he's taking a lot of trouble to keep his security airtight. Which, for a hacktivist ... it's like ringing the dinner bell. Challenge accepted.

Whatever he had, it had to be kept offline. I was good, but not good enough to access a system that had no connection to the internet. So that begged a question: what to do? It didn't have an easy answer.

Well, okay, maybe it did—you search for more info about the guy. Crack into the systems of every major airline to find his name in travel records. Which produces a record of a booking for a flight he was taking from Austin, Texas—near as I could tell that's where he lived, even though I couldn't find a record of his residence—to New York City. What was the likelihood that this man—a tech geek not unlike myself—would take that trip without bringing his computer with him?

So I caught a flight out of Atlanta to Austin and caught up to Mr. Caden Sims.

Caden Sims didn't look like much of a *mister.* He was twenty-nine years old. Not a skinny guy, but not a big muscly fellow either. Gym membership and general appearance suggested he kept in shape. Pale complexion, as some of my hacker brethren might tend to have. Not a huge surprise. Dark hair, mussed like he'd rolled right out of bed and gone straight to the airport. Wore a suit, but it was wrinkled. Long face, not quite horsey but definitely oblong.

I keyed my tablet computer into the plane's Wi-Fi, did a little bypass so I didn't actually have to pay for that Wi-Fi because, let's face it, $15 for a two-hour flight is out of control. You airline people are out of your minds.

Then I was in. All I had to do was figure out a way to finally get access to Caden Sims's information.

It's kind of technical and I don't want to bore you, so let's just say he had some firewalls up. If this was a man who kept most of his information offline, I doubted if he was going to make himself super vulnerable when he took a flight, even if he couldn't seem to keep his computer in his laptop bag. It was the equivalent of, "Dude, just keep it in your pants."

But he couldn't. And I couldn't blame him, because I couldn't keep offline for that long, either.

I went up against his firewall systems, my finger up to the power port of my tablet, using my electrical powers and pinpoint discipline. It took probably ten minutes before I finally broke through, careful not to trip anything to alert him. I kept stealing glances at his screen, not that it did any good. He had one of those protectors up that shaded it when you weren't looking directly at it. Even with my meta eyesight, I couldn't see what he was typing, just that he was still tapping away feverishly.

I just hoped I wasn't tipping him off. He didn't make any moves like I had. I maneuvered into the system, past his last safeguard, and boom. I was in.

The laptop had a pretty sizable amount of storage space, which was typical for these sort of laptop/tablet hybrids. I ran a program that did several things to make my search easier, especially since we were heading into hour two of the flight.

First off, it ruled out anything that was system related, i.e., vital to the computer's function. It was possible to hide stuff in the system, but I didn't want to have to go through the trouble to comb through that until later if the answer was obvious. Second, it skimmed his non-system files and compared them to one of his computers that was online but filled with nothing suspicious at all.

That took about two minutes—two long minutes during which I stared at my slowly ticking clock display—to finish. Once it was done, I was presented with the results—one file.

One file that wasn't part of his system and wasn't on his computer that was connected to the internet.

"Shit," I muttered under my breath. One lousy file? I'd gotten on two long flights and followed Caden Sims across the damned country for one lousy file? It was labeled, "Martha Hayman's Recipes."

This couldn't be it.

Could it?

I cursed again quietly, and figured I'd rule it out. If worst came to worst, maybe I'd get a cookie recipe out of the deal or something. I opened the file, and onto the screen sprang a spreadsheet that looked like a business's balance sheet.

I stared at the words, at the sums, and wondered why the hell he'd bothered to label what was obviously an innocuous

Excel document with a false title that made it look like a recipe file. It was just page after page of innocent charges, money to Amazon for purchases, money to a vendor via Paypal for some artwork he bought on Ebay, an expense to Etsy for an artisanal something or other.

I'd almost given up when I hit an expense that contained a familiar name … and I felt my blood go cold as it sunk in that whatever else he was doing on Amazon and Ebay and Etsy, this one little line item, hidden in the middle of his expense report, was the reason he'd named the file something other than what it was.

And this was the reason that I'd followed Caden Sims onto this plane.

2.

Sienna

Menomonie, Wisconsin (pronounced Meh-nom-un-ee, heavy on the *meh*) was a scenic thirty minute drive from Eau Claire, Wisconsin (pronounced Oh, Claire! Except that exhortation might have some passion in it; Eau Claire had pretty much none), an hour from St. Paul, Minnesota (pronounced *yawn*), and an hour and eleven minutes from Minneapolis (pronounced *home*).

Menomonie was a college town, home of the University of Wisconsin-Stout (yes, the name of their college was Stout. In Wisconsin. The beer jokes write themselves) which was part of its appeal to me, a young fugitive with the face and haircut of a college student but with far more interest in anonymity. Most people want to stick out of the pack, be noticed.

I was working really, really hard not to.

Okay. Maybe not *that* hard.

A scream tore across the quiet small-town street, causing me to jerk my head around. I was carrying grocery bags in either hand, my weekly trip to Dick's Fresh Market (don't get me started on *that* name) done. I was loaded up with enough to eat for a while, my head popped up for this visit (metaphorically—my hood was down and I was looking down as much as possible, because while it pays to watch for trouble, it doesn't pay to look like your head is on a swivel because it makes people suspicious) and ready to bury it back in the sand—or snow, as the case was.

Banks of frigid white a couple feet high lined both sides of the city street, but the sidewalks were shoveled. The old houses rose up under leafless skeletons of trees. A grey winter sky covered in clouds and blocking the sun with its thick, blanketed layers hung overhead. It reminded me of my old neighborhood in Minneapolis.

I cocked my head, listening to make sure I hadn't imagined the scream. It had been a while since I'd seen any action—of any variety, really—and part of me thought I was just hearing things, like a flashback to a past where I was relevant instead of irrelevant.

Another scream echoed down the snowy street as the wind picked up. It was coming off the lake hard this morning, and it rustled the boughs above me, causing them to clack against each other and dislodge a flurry of snow. I let my head swivel, now that there was a reason for an ordinary college girl to be looking around for a threat.

It didn't take long with my meta-enhanced senses to recognize that the screams were coming from one of the long driveways that ran to a garage. The garage was probably thirty, forty feet off the old street and almost out of view behind the house. The scream came again, high and fearful, and I dropped my grocery bags in the hardened snow bank and broke into a run.

I didn't run as fast as I could; I was still aware that the likelihood that this was a serious emergency was low. This was Menomonie, after all, and lethal danger didn't exactly lurk around every corner.

I wanted to fly, though, fly right toward the problem like the Sienna of old. I could swoop in, sort the problem out, and then zoom off like—

No. No, that wasn't my life anymore. And I kept a restraint on myself as I hurtled over the snowbanks with just a touch of levitation to keep myself from sinking into the fresh powder that had fallen during the night.

"AHHHHHHHHH!" The scream was deeper, more heartfelt, less echoey the closer I got. It sounded like a person in terror now, afraid for their very life. Or possibly arachnophobic and having just seen a big spider. Tough to tell sometimes.

I burst through the side yard of the nearest house and around, trying to hone in on the fearful sound as I tore through a clump of bushes, bare save for the accumulated snow, and burst into the backyard, trailing twigs, my coat ripping slightly. A fresh wave of chill rushed into the newly made hole, causing my skin beneath to ripple in the frigid air. "Yeeeeeeesh," I muttered, letting my teeth follow their natural instinct to chatter at the brisk outdoors. I believe it was ten degrees Fahrenheit. January in the Midwest is not for the faint of heart.

I looked down the alley, sweeping for some sign of trouble. I figured muggers, rapists, murderers … any one of them could be at play, though I kept that spider idea in the forefront of my mind as well just to be sure I didn't overreact and start hurling fireballs or anything. Trouble was everywhere in my experience, after all, but there were no points for saving a life and then getting the police to descend on me in the process. The last thing I needed was to clash with the cops and lose another hideout.

"Help me!" a high-pitched voice shouted, and then I heard an "OOF!"

I took off behind the garage in the direction of the voice, puffing as I stepped lightly—so lightly my feet didn't touch the ground, though I kept them close enough to the icy slush that covered the yard so as to make that unnoticeable to all but the most careful of watchers.

I came around the garage and skidded to a stop. Three figures huddled between the garage I'd just rounded and the house behind it. A secluded spot, cut off from easy view by old trees on either side. One of the figures was already on the ground, on his ass, hands help up in a pleading, surrendering manner, shaking with fear.

The other two were standing over him, menacing, classic bad guys lurking here in the space between. They wouldn't have looked out of place in any gangster movie, except that their heavy winter coats made them look a little like the man from the Michelin tires ads. They were both totally focused on their prey, clearly doing a little hunting, and as I came to an abrupt stop, it took me a second to size things up.

The prey in this case was a dude. A dude with a stocking cap and a very thin attempt at what I think was a lumberjack beard, but … it was a beard. Sort of. At least in the loosest sense of the word. He even had a little wax in his thin mustache. "Please!" He shouted, holding up a hand at me, as if inviting me into his little nightmare. "Help me!"

Both his assailants turned, and I raised my eyebrows high. By their girth and attire I might have assumed they were Russian mobsters or something.

They were not.

They were both women, both scowling, both with their hoods up, both looking like they wanted to disintegrate me with an angry look.

"What the hell is this?" I muttered, trying to reconcile my brain with the scenario before me. It's not every day you come running into an alley in small-town America to find a thin man getting smacked around by a couple of, uhm … larger ladies. They were both physically intimidating. If I'd been a normal human, I wouldn't have wanted to mess with either of them, and that was before they gave me the scowl of death, like I'd spat in their Cheerios.

"Get out of here, stick," one of them said, sounding like every dumb-witted guy who'd ever unknowingly threatened me without realizing who he was talking to. "Or we'll break your twig ass, too."

"Wait," said the other one. I couldn't really tell them apart, because they had their hoods up so I couldn't see their hair color, and their faces both looked blunt and red-cheeked, like they'd been out in the cold a while. "Give us your cell phone, first." She took a few steps toward me and thrust out a hand.

"Please," the guy said, looking at me like I was his last hope. I stared at him a little harder and realized the only dark spot in his beard was a trickle of blood where one of them—presumably—had given him a fat lip.

"Go on," the one with her hand out said, thrusting it at me again, and wiggling her fingers. "Gimme your cell phone. Wallet, too."

I was feeling kind of dumbstruck, but not totally dumb, and certainly not subservient. I didn't want to blow my cover, but a couple of months ago I'd let myself get tossed in a dumpster to avoid that exact problem and ended up getting my cover blown anyway due to, uhm … intemperance of personality later on. I blinked, looking into the beady eyes of the woman standing there expectantly, waiting for me to kowtow to her by handing over my stuff, and I said, in a calm voice, "No."

Yes, you tell them, Wolfe muttered in my head. *Kill—*

"No," I said again, causing beady-eyes in front of me to slump slightly in shock.

"Listen," the other one said, now turning her back on the man with the barely-there lumberjack beard and advancing on me, "we will break your stick ass to pieces and leave them scattered around the street." She threw her hands out. "Ain't nobody gonna stop us in time, neither. We will scatter you around this place in bloody chunks." She reached under her coat and pulled out a knife, a stiletto-looking thing that opened with a flick of her wrist. Apparently she hadn't felt the need to use it to cow the poor dude bleeding in silence in the snow. "So what's it gonna be, princess?"

I just stared at her and her equally badly-dressed compatriot, and laughed right in their faces.

Yes, that's excellent, Gerry Harmon said dryly in my head, *embrace the smug side of the force.*

"Shut up," I snapped at him, causing both of the women threatening me to go wide-eyed, apparently thinking I was talking to them. I took advantage of their stunned states to deliver my ultimatum. "Dumbasses, this is a small town. The cops are already on their way, so if you had two brain cells between the two of you to rub together, you'd already be giving up on us and running. But since you don't, let me say this—"

"Stick—" the one with the knife started.

"I appreciate the flattery," I said, dismissing her and causing her head to rock back in surprise, "but don't think that's going to save you." Nobody called me stick, at least not anybody with a reasonable grasp on the way my size compared to the rest of the population, but it felt like the best compliment I'd had in months. "Drop the knife. Turn. Run away." I made a shoo-ing motion at them. "Or else."

Oh, she drops the BOOM on them! Eve Kappler snarked.

Reminds me of those text-based RPGs I played in my youth, Harmon said. *You encounter a strange goblin in an alleyway, hissing and foaming at the mouth. What do you do?*

"I would kill you if you weren't already dead," I muttered under my breath to the former President of the United States.

The two big ladies stole a look at each other, one of total confusion, before looking back at me. The one with the knife, and apparently all the confidence, spoke again. "You must think we're really dumb—"

"Nailed it," I said. "Now go, before I begin a war of tit-punching you cannot possibly win." I nodded at their bulky jackets. "You're looking like a big target under all that padding. And I will get through the padding, I promise you. Walk away now and I won't leave you weeping in this alleyway, sucking snow through your nose as you cry about how much it hurts." I put some iron in my voice, hoping it'd be a good enough deterrent for Big Bertha and Slightly-Bigger-Bertha.

It wasn't good enough for either of them.

Bertha-with-the-knife's eyes flashed in rage, and she came at me. I rolled mine and caught her firmly by the wrist as she stabbed at me, then rolled around and captured her wrist with my right arm and put my elbow against her left as I spun her into my trap. I wrenched her arm, hard, and her scream filled the alley this time. She dropped the knife and I kicked it like a Hacky Sack, punting it onto the roof of the garage before thumping her gently on the back of the head and sending her into the snow face-first.

"Olé!" I shouted, because I suspected it had looked like a bullfighter whirling out of the way of a prized bull. The only thing missing was the promised tit-punch. I looked at the Bertha who remained and said, "If you don't run, I'm going to keep my promise to you."

"The hell!" she shouted, looking like another bull about to

charge. Her nostrils flared, her face flushed red in indignation.

Then she charged.

I'd done the jiu-jitsu thing to the first Bertha because it was plausible that a college girl could whoop the shit out of a bigger foe with that style of martial art, mostly because it hinged on using your foe's power against them.

It did not, however, embrace the promised tit-punch.

So instead, this time, I went low and belted Bertha in the gut with meta speed. I kept her between me and the skinny-jeans wearing victim so he couldn't give an account of what I was doing. Bertha exploded (not literally, unfortunately) as I popped her in the gut and caused her to expel all her air into the frigid morning. Her lungs were gonna ache when she managed to get her breath back, because sucking in this much cold air? It hurt.

Bertha halted right in her tracks, momentum stalled like she'd just hit an immovable object and realized she wasn't an unstoppable force. Her eyes were big as balloons, her arms were spread wide like she was reaching out for a hug. She wasn't; she'd just lost control of her limbs because knocking the air out of someone takes the fight right out of them and puts them in panic mode as they try and seize a breath in order to stave off that desperate, panicky feeling of asphyxiation.

With her arms wide and her balance gone to shit, I took advantage of her situation and punched her in the left boob.

Her already wide eyes locked on me, the panic filling them turning to pain as her nerves reported what I'd done. I didn't hit her hard enough to do any serious damage, like burst an implant (I doubted she had need of such things; she was a big lady) but I guarantee she felt it as she pitched over and landed in the slush that covered the driveway. I imagined the wet, cold icy mixture sluicing down the back of her shirt and smiled, my breath misting in the cold. "Ahhhhh," I said, feeling like I'd finally got some action I could enjoy. Really broke the tension.

"What … thank you." Skinny Jeans hauled himself to his feet slowly. He looked around, mystified, as though his brain couldn't quite put together his astonishment at what had just happened. "You … you … saved me from them."

"Yeah, that makes me sad for you," I said, going over to Bertha the first and hauling her moaning form out of the snowbank I'd left her in before she drowned in a combination of snow and her own drool. I tossed her on top of Bertha the second and then thumped their heads together, sighing. "What was this all about, anyway?"

"Well, I mean," Skinny Jeans started to look a little defensive, "they were … y'know … mad at me. And stuff."

"This wasn't a random mugging?" My eyes narrowed. "'And stuff'? What 'stuff' were they mad at you about?" I felt a little sick, but not too sick, since one of them had pulled a knife on me and the other had tried to rob me of my wallet and cell phone.

"We, uh," Skinny Jeans had a look of guilt in his eyes as he shied away from looking into mine while answering the question, "had a, uh … encounter—"

"Please tell me it was *this* kind of encounter, with knives and threats."

"—an, uh, intimate encounter—"

"With … which one?"

"Both of them." Skinny Jeans flushed. "At the same time—"

"Ohhhhhh, man," I moaned, covering my eyes. It didn't help with the imagery or the guilt. I'd just intervened in a personal squabble of the sort I wouldn't have wanted to touch with the ten-thousand foot pole I reserved for occasions with the ninety-nine hundred foot pole just wouldn't do. "This is what happens when you don't action for too long," I muttered to myself.

"Well, I mean," Skinny Jeans said by way of explanation, "there were two of them, it wasn't like this seemed like a bad deal for me—"

"Oh, good grief!" I turned away, shuddering. "Just stop! Keep your business to yourself!" I clapped my hands on my face. "Okay. Well. This has been … absolutely horrific." I spun on him. "You … call the police and sort this out for yourself."

He looked at me in confusion. "But, I mean … you just saved me. Shouldn't we talk to the cops together? I mean, they're gonna be on your side—"

"*I'm* not even on my side right now," I said. "For all I know, these women were perfectly within their rights to be pissed off at you."

"What?" He put a hand up to his heart like he was deeply offended. "I just—I mean—just because I didn't call them the next day or—or—or—or take their calls –"

"Stop talking," I said. "Stop talking—"

"—and just because I might have said some things that night in the moments before and—"

"Stop! Just stop!"

"—well, in the heat of passion—"

"SHUT UP!" I bellowed, and blessedly, taking a step backward in fear, he finally did. I exhaled mightily, and heard the first sound of sirens in the distance. "This your mess to clean up," I lied. "So … clean it up." I turned on a heel and ran off, wondering if I had time to retrieve my groceries before the cops arrived.

It didn't really matter, though, did it? Because once again, I was going to have to flee a town because I'd gone and stuck my nose in other peoples' business. "Stupid do-gooder," I muttered, sighing as I hoofed it down the alleyway and leapt a fence once I was out of sight of Skinny Jeans. With luck, I'd be out of town on a bus before anyone realized exactly what had happened.

"But where do I go next?" I asked myself as I came down in a backyard filled to the brimming with snow, snow and more snow. The answer might once have been filled with possibility—as a free woman I could have traveled anywhere, done almost anything. Like a normal person.

But I wasn't a normal person. And I wasn't supposed to be free. Not anymore. I was a wanted woman, the cops and the FBI still on my trail.

Which made the question of "Where do I go next?" distinctly less exciting, less invigorating … and much more disquieting.

3.

Jamal

"Sir, would you like anything else to drink?"

I blinked, the flight attendant's words jolting me out of a data-induced coma. I'd looked for the refresh button on my browser window a minute earlier, thinking maybe what I was reading wasn't the complete file. Maybe I'd just reload the page, like any other website, and find it changed, different, not the same as what I'd just absorbed.

Nope. It was a file, not a webpage.

"Uhhh …" I looked up at the flight attendant, a middle-aged dude with a smile and twinkling eyes. "Peanuts?"

His smile never wavered. "Not on this flight. Did you want something to drink?"

"Right." They'd announced that peanut thing before takeoff. "Uhhh … gin and tonic?"

"Sure thing." He disappeared up the aisle.

Yeah, I was sitting in first class. Had to be in order to be close to Caden Sims, who was still head down, noise-canceling headphones on, feverishly typing away at his computer.

I started to exit his system but stopped. What was he working on now, I wondered?

A few keystrokes—or a little voltage in my case—and I could know. So I stuck my finger up to the port and made the move.

My screen blurred, fritzed—it does that when I work

directly on the circuits sometimes, even with extremely low voltage—and then pulled up the file he was working on.

And if what I'd seen before wasn't enough to raise my eyebrows … this helped do it.

The problem with leaving things in the state they are, I watched the words scrawl across the screen as he wrote them, *is that the system is broken, open, and vulnerable. This provides opportunities for those who seek change. Our power grids are vulnerable, outdated, not smart. Our infrastructure is aging, and despite the low-tech approach to online security, with the proper skills and dedicated resources, even our nuclear infrastructure is vulnerable to attack.*

This is an opportunity, he tapped, the clicking of his keys like gunshots as he wrote these words just a few feet away from me, *and one we should exploit now, before anyone wises up and makes it more difficult.*

Sims paused, then straightened up, his nose twitching like he smelled something. He leaned in, staring at his screen, and I forgot for a moment that I had essentially mirrored his desktop just a moment earlier. I glanced back at my own screen and realized I'd totally missed the sudden pop-up window:

WARNING! INTRUSION DETECTED!

Oh, shit.

I shut my tablet case with a loud snap. Startled by the sudden noise, everyone in the rows beside me looked at me.

Including Caden Sims.

My heartbeat thundered in my ears like I'd gotten caught out in a lightning storm, and I stared at Caden Sims as he stared at me. Mere surprise at the sound of my tablet screen cover snapping down changed as he looked at me into … suspicion … and then past that into …

Aw, hell.

I panicked, throwing my tablet into my backpack. I snugged it tight, not really sure what I was doing, and then got up, throwing it over my shoulder. Sims was reaching over the seat in front of him, slapping some guy on the shoulder. I was already taking off down the aisle, but I threw a look back.

It was a bodyguard.

A big one.

I felt a little like a rabbit being chased down by a big dog, but I hurried my ass up and walked hard, almost running for the back of the plane. I didn't know what I was gonna do when I got there, or exactly what I was running from, but the instinct guided me. It wasn't so much as issue of "fight or flight" as it was just "flight."

Run away.

The big bodyguard followed along behind me, maintaining a reasonable distance, ambling along. He had a couple of feet of height on me, and he didn't look to be in a hurry. Maybe he realized I was running out of plane.

I got to the back galley and tried to decide what to do. The bathrooms were both unoccupied, not that locking myself in was a great course of action. My breaths were coming hard and fast now. I wasn't gasping, but the adrenaline was definitely surging.

The big guy was about ten rows behind me, no sign of a flight attendant back here, nor a convenient beverage cart to block his path. Nothing, really, except a bunch of rows of people snoozing or watching their tablets and phones and ereaders, and a big dude in a suit who was walking toward me with a blank, bordering-on-angry look.

Damn.

I looked at the emergency exit and ruled that out. I couldn't fly, after all. I looked at the other emergency exit just to be sure, like I'd gain the power to fly if I only hoped hard enough.

Nope. That wasn't going to work.

The fight or flight question rose again. I'd run out of room to flee, and the guy after me didn't look like he wanted to just talk to me sternly.

He looked like he was closing in for the kill.

My mouth was suddenly dry, and I was wishing I'd taken the attendant up on his pre-flight offer for another bottle of water. I stared at my pursuer in his dark suit, close-shaved head and flat brow making him look distinctly Cro-Magnon. "Uh, hey," I said, warbling in what I hoped was an amiable voice.

He didn't answer, keeping his head down, eyes on me like I was some kind of threat.

Which made me think … oh, yeah! I was some kind of threat.

I held up my hands. "Hey, man—don't come any closer—"

He didn't listen, didn't break stride. Just kept coming.

"Don't do this," I warned him. "It doesn't have to be this way—"

He didn't stop. Like the Terminator, he kept walking.

"You don't need to—"

He was within a dozen feet of me, and I'd been keeping my voice down. Trying to avoid letting the plane know trouble was going on back here. I wondered if he hadn't been hearing me, if the engine noise was keeping him from being able to.

Then he leapt at me, covering the ten feet between us in one step, and seized me around the neck.

And I knew he'd heard every word I said.

Caden Sims's bodyguard was a metahuman.

4.

Sienna

I was still cursing myself quietly as I stormed back into my apartment. I would have done it loudly, but people tend to notice someone swearing at the air in front of them if they don't have a phone up to their ear or a Bluetooth headset in it. I could have looked angry if I'd used the prop, but without it I would have looked like a crazy person, so I just steamed internally.

I'd completely blown out another safe house, and all because I'd gotten involved in some hipster player's husky three-way gone bad. Of all the stupid reasons to burn a town for myself, that had to rate way, way above trapping an aggravating woman in a Porta Potty and dumping her over to stew in her own juices. And those of others, I suppose.

Okay, maybe there had been more to that last one than just the Porta Potty incident, but still … this was getting ridiculous.

Face it, Gerry Harmon smarmed, *you're a violent criminal. You need the internal satisfaction of getting into a fight. It's like a drug for you, physical violence. I'd tell you to get laid, but frankly, since you're a succubus, that's violence of its own kind.*

"And you wouldn't want to encourage anyone to commit violence, would you, Mr. President?" I often called him by his title in order to be as much an asshole to him as he was to me.

His response came back as distinctly miffed. *Not for no*

profit, no. That would be pointless.

"If one of the parties is carrying a knife, trust me, there's a point," I muttered as I looked around my dimly lit, sparsely furnished townhome. "I only wish you had gotten a point so you could have bled to death instead of getting trapped inside my brain to taunt me for all eternity like some sort of ghostly, dickhead color commentator on my life."

That's a swing and a miss, Mike, Harmon said. *Maybe she'll do better next season.* He paused, as though reflecting. *Is that what the commentators sound like? I never had any patience for sports. They all seem the same to me; overmuscled men playing with balls. It's all very Freudian.*

"Another thing the smartest man in the room doesn't know." I didn't oblige him by admitting that my interest in sports was pretty flimsy and my experience with them was mostly limited to the time I'd destroyed Soldier Field. I pushed off the door and headed for the dresser in the bedroom to pack my things. "That's getting to be a hell of a list."

Hah, Wolfe crowed. *She has a point.*

"She has a point, *Mr. President*," I responded. That caused Wolfe to guffaw and Bjorn to chortle heartily. "You should always show proper respect for your fellow inmates, Wolfe, especially when they've gone from being the most powerful man in the world to an impotent shade of their former selves, not even the top of the food chain in my brain."

I could almost hear the steam coming out of Gerry Harmon's non-existent collar, but he didn't speak. Not a word. Blissful silence for the twenty minutes or so that it took me to gather the clothes I needed, a few wigs, and a couple other … unsanctioned items, plus some spare cell phones that hadn't been activated yet. I tossed them all in a duffel, slung it over my shoulder and was out the door into the freezing cold minutes later.

For all the times you insult my intelligence, Harmon said, *you don't seem to be doing a very good job running what's left of your life these days. I mean, really—*

"What's left of my life is more than what's left of yours," I muttered as I walked down a snowy sidewalk. I was going to need to catch a bus in Menomonie to get to the main station in Eau Claire. From there, I'd have to decide on my next destination. It seemed stupid to keep wintering in the upper Midwest when there were so many temperate places I could be. Florida, Texas, and Arizona came immediately to mind.

Someday you'll have to take responsibility for your actions, Harmon said. *They're not just going to forget about you. And they're never going to forgive you for what you've done. Running … it's a temporary reprieve at best. The world is getting smaller. Cameras are everywhere.*

"You don't have to tell me twice," I said, fishing an oversized pair of sunglasses out of my bag and putting them on. Fortunately, the sun was out from behind the clouds now and glaring off the snowbanks, making the day unbearably bright. I wouldn't have wanted to wear the sunglasses in the middle of a grey day, but they helped break up my profile so that facial recognition software couldn't find me as easily. The hoodie I was wearing beneath my jacket helped with that, too.

You'll have to pay the piper sometime, Harmon said. *You can't run forever.*

"My cardio is game is strong. I bet I can."

Harmon laughed, low and quietly. *All right, so let's say you can. What does that get you? You have no contact with your friends. That brother of yours was a piece of human shrapnel last time you saw him—*

"No thanks to you brainwashing him into doing terrible things."

Yes, it was almost like he was channeling you. Harmon's glee came through as he turned mocking. *But the point is … you've left these pieces of human detritus in your wake … Reed, Ariadne, the poor soul—*I seethed quietly; he'd erased me entirely from Ariadne's memory. Or so he'd claimed. I hadn't seen her to be sure. *All the members of your old team, left in the dark. They still believe in you, some of them … but you can't see them. Can't go to their houses for Christmas or Thanksgiving. Can't help them in their times of sorrow comes up, as we all have from time to time.* He sounded positively gleeful about it. *So tell me, Sienna … what kind of life are you going to lead here, on the run, sprinting from safe house to safe house? Putting your head down, ignoring the world around you until a* *scream sounds so close that you can't possibly ignore it?*

What kind of life are you living? He didn't wait for me to answer. *Less than a half a life. A life in darkness, always running, always afraid. And not afraid of your weakness … no, you're afraid of your power. You're afraid to step out and let the world know that the police, the FBI, the government—none of them could really hold you back if you made it your business to walk free. You're scared of the body count if you showed them all what you were capable of.*

"One of those bodies could easily end up being mine," I muttered.

And how much longer do you think you'll care about that? He was nearly crowing. *Living like you are … I give it six months before you stop viewing other people as human lives to be valued and start letting out this beautiful, festering resentment that's growing inside you like cancer. It'll come out in small ways at first; self-justifying ways. "I don't need to help that person, that city, those people … because it'll just expose me, make me run. Then it'll grow stronger with time and reinforcement … "To hell with them. They don't want my help anyway." And finally … "Screw them all. I don't want to help them. I want to destroy them."* I felt like I could see him leering at me in the dark of my mind. *I call it 'Global Destruction in Three Acts.' What do you think?*

I kept my head down, walking toward the bus pickup with my eyes fixed on the tree-line road ahead of me. "I think you're full of shit," I lied.

He knew I lied.

Everyone in my head knew I lied.

But Harmon was the only one to laugh as I walked along the dead, winter street of Menomonie, Wisconsin, hurrying to catch the next bus out of town. What else could I do? Whether he was right or wrong, I still had to leave. The police sirens still echoing in the distance were a constant reminder of that as I trudged along the sidewalk, avoiding the little patches of melted and re-frozen ice, and tried to ignore the truth that I'd just heard.

5.

Reed

The highways into Woodville, Texas, were surrounded on either side with brown grass, but only a few trees had shed their leaves. It wasn't a totally brown earth, looking down on it from above, not like you'd find north of here in Arkansas or Tennessee, or covered in desert plains like West Texas. Woodville was on the east side of the state, and wasn't all that different from Mississippi or Alabama, a far cry from what I'd seen all the times I'd been to Austin, San Antonio, El Paso …

When summer rolled around, it'd be a green land, hotter than hell and humid, but a fertile little stretch of glory in a state that was mostly imagined by folks who'd never been here as … not green. There was one key difference between it and the surrounding areas, though, one that almost no one—outside of perhaps the most intuitively predictive scientists at the NOAA—knew about Woodville, Texas.

That it was about to be hit by one of the most massive tornadoes in January ever seen in American history.

I'd been sleeping in the clouds over Boulder, Colorado, when I'd felt it. A stir in the fringes of my mind, a tingle of familiarity. It wasn't something I used to feel; it was something new to me over these last few months. I'd never been able to sleep in the skies before, cradled in the embrace of the clouds like a baby in a bassinet.

Times really do change, I guess. I know I've changed.

I could feel it a thousand miles away, that sense that trouble was coming. I'd felt it few times lately, here and there. I hadn't known what it was at first. I'd thought it was just a tingle in my mind, in my body, that feeling you get in your gut when you know something's wrong, that you've forgotten something but you don't know what it is.

I'd felt it for the first time a month ago, and led by that feeling, I'd ridden the winds to Metairie, Louisiana.

I'd arrived just in time to feel the funnel cloud forming. I couldn't see it, not hidden within my sanctuary of clouds. I could walk on clouds now, sleep on clouds. Hell, I could sleep on empty air, but it felt too exposed, so I always chose the clouds. They traveled with me, or I with them, blowing everywhere I wanted them to. I'd ridden my cloud formation right over Metairie in the midst of a December storm, and felt that funnel cloud forming, ready to reach down on a town, touch it with tendrils of destruction, ripping trees out of the ground and turning them into projectiles. A tornado could bury a toothpick in a telephone pole; imagine what it could bury in a human body.

I'd slipped out of the clouds and watched in horror as it started to descend, like an angry god reaching down to touch mortals with death, to bring them into its angry embrace.

And in that moment, I had known what I had to do.

I had found a purpose once more.

Now in the skies above Woodville, Texas, I had that same feeling, that same burning righteousness that I'd felt over Metairie, when I'd done what I'd done that first time. It felt like I'd been lost in the wilderness, abandoned, uncertain, unsure of where I was supposed to go, what I was supposed to do.

That day over Metairie, all that uncertainty vanished … for a little while. And ever since, I'd been chasing that feeling.

I dropped out of the clouds over Woodville as the funnel cloud started to form. It was a big one; EF-5, angry skies readying their vengeance on the still and unsuspecting land. It was as though they were resentful of the peace they saw below, not realizing how little peace there actually was on earth. The storm winds were already racking the city, rattling barns and buildings, threatening to tear off shingles. Hail was coming down, and a few stray pieces grazed me as they fell to earth. One of them hit hard enough to cut my forehead, causing me to bleed, a slow stream clouding my eyes.

I didn't care. I didn't need to see what I was doing anymore.

I could feel it.

The smell of the storm in the air mingled with the metallic scent of my own blood, thick in my nostrils as the cold rain washed it down my face. There was a rumble of hunger long held at bay in my belly, an acrid taste in my mouth from fasting for a month, sustaining myself on moisture from the clouds alone. The touch of the cold wind bit at my flesh, but I was long since used to it by now, and the roar of the storm around me was like a sweet harmony to my ears.

I reached out my own hand toward the grasping, falling funnel cloud, dropping to the earth, reaching out to touch. I could feel the swirl, the hard vortex, the power of that funnel. I held its image, its feel in my mind, pulsing air turned toward violent ends.

And I touched it with my power, unspooling the storm like I was unwinding thread. I tugged at the winds, reversed their course. Slowly at first, from bottom to top, stripping them away bit by bit until all that was left was a rumbling cloud overhead, drenching the earth with its moisture in the form of falling rain.

I let out a long breath of chill air. My clouds had passed on and I hadn't even noticed. I hung in the air above Woodville, staring down at the little town in the distance. I could see the path of the tornado in my head; it had been set to sweep the outskirts, would have rent a nasty trail of carnage through neighborhoods and farms.

I mopped the blood and rain from my brow with a ragged shirt sleeve. I didn't do laundry in the clouds, after all, and I hadn't set foot on the earth in a month, not since I'd realized I didn't actually need to eat, only to stay hydrated. The old me would have needed to, but that was before the former President of the United States had decided to experiment with my genetic code, turning me into one of the most powerful metahumans on the planet. Now I could probably even survive without oxygen for a few months, though the effect, based on what Sienna had told me of a few who'd experienced it, would be unpleasant.

My stomach rumbled again, as if trying to remind me that this fast I'd undertaken had its limits. Woodville was right there, and I was already exposed, my clouds moving on … I could catch them or call them back later. This need in my belly was growing too loud to ignore. I didn't feel weak yet, but that was because after thirty days, I'd gotten used to it.

Thirty days since my last meal, and it had been probably fifteen or so before that. I'd done the whole "human contact" thing sporadically of late, mostly because coming back to earth …

Well, it wasn't where I wanted to be right now.

I started to descend, dropping slowly to the green and brown land below. Cars streaked along the roadways in and out of town, oblivious to the fate that had almost befallen them.

Except for one line of cars—vans, mostly. They were going along the highway in a tight caravan. I almost chuckled in amusement in their predictability. Stormchasers. Clearly I wasn't the only one who'd detected the atmospheric conditions brewing around Woodville.

But I was the only one who could have done anything about it.

I ignored them as I descended toward the town, my work done. The rumble in my stomach from thirty days of starving myself had gotten to be too much. There had to be a diner or something, somewhere I could get a meal.

I caught sight of a Dairy Queen and a Jack in the Box and angled my descent toward them, the winds keeping me aloft gradually fading in intensity as I continued to descend. A burger might be nice. Ice cream would probably not sit well on my stomach after all this time spent not eating, but a burger …

My feet felt the rough touch of the pavement as I settled on the sidewalk. I blanched at the sensation. After a month of walking on air with bare feet, this was … sobering. I ran a hand over my ragged beard and through my hair, which was knotted tightly, and swallowed. Did I even still have my wallet? I felt for my back pocket and found it empty. I patted the breast of my jacket on either side; there was no lump indicating a wallet or identification there, either. "Shit," I pronounced. I'd had it when last I landed, hadn't I? This is what I got for sleeping in the clouds, I guess.

"Hey," a lady said, her car window open. She was the first in a line of vehicles, vans pulling up to the curb now, people stepping out, rolling down windows, craning their necks to get a look at me. The stormchasers had apparently abandoned the storm in favor of chasing me. Which was just as well, because the storm was over.

Or maybe the storm was me.

"Hi," I said, my voice scratchy and rough, almost unrecognizable after being unused for so long.

She was peering at me through her open window, her neck craned down so she could look me in the eyes. "Can I get you something to eat?" She had a faintly Spanish accent.

"In return for what?" I asked, my scratchy voice sounding like I'd gargled glass this morning. "A clear description of a vortex from the inside? It's windy. You're all set."

She frowned at me. "Helpful. But no, Mr. Treston. That's not what I'm looking for at all."

I stiffened. She knew my name? How would a stormchaser know my name? I mean, I was quasi-famous when I left the civilized world, but … not that famous. Not enough to be recognizable the way I looked right now. "Who are you?"

"My name is Miranda Estevez," she said, and for the first time I realized she was driving a new series Mercedes. That was not the vehicle of choice for stormchasers, not at all. "I work for your old employer, and I have a message for you …

"We'd like you to come back to work."

6.

Jamal

"Hey, man," I said as Caden Sims's bodyguard gripped me tightly around the throat, fingers poking against my jugular. I had to fight to get my words out. I landed a hand on his wrist, trying to loosen his grip. "What are you doing?"

"You're coming with me," he said in a dull, robotic tone. Big man looking all scary and huge.

"To where? My seat?" I asked, not resisting him much. I didn't want to give away the game that I was a meta. Not yet.

"Yes," he said, though his eyes were dancing around as he questioned that himself. "And then, when we land, you're coming with us."

I grunted against his grip. "You going to kidnap me right off a plane? Right out of the airport? In front of all these people? For what?"

He was thinking it through, blazing fast. "You're right," he whispered, coming to a conclusion I did not like. "I guess you can't—"

I mostly used my power to influence digital information, but once upon a time I'd used it to murder two men who'd killed my girlfriend, Flora. I didn't like using my power that way, delivering electrical charge to human flesh.

But I wasn't going to let some bodyguard snuff me right here in the back of an airplane without argument, either.

I zapped the shit out of Caden Sims's bodyguard, hit him with enough voltage to stop an elephant's heart. I was scared, afraid for my life, and I just let him have it. He jerked a few times and then went limp, and I caught him before he thumped to the floor. He fell against my shoulder and I held him there, staring back down the aisle to see if anyone had noticed our altercation.

They hadn't; not his massive twitching, not our words exchanged, and no one was looking at me now, cradling his corpse. They were all still looking at their screens, not taking any notice of our little scuffle. He exhaled his last breath and I forced the lavatory door open and dumped him onto the seat. He slumped over, head lolling against the bulkhead, and I shut the door on him and slipped the lock closed the way I'd seen the flight attendant do when they'd needed to close the door on a kid that hadn't known how to lock it. The little sign went from VACANT to OCCUPIED. I heaved a sigh of relief, then staggered back up the aisle toward my seat.

I slipped into my chair and caught the look of flat-out astonishment from Caden Sims. It would have been funny if I hadn't just electrocuted a human being and had had to turn my eyes away so I didn't see him look at me with his last, accusing look. My heart was pounding, my hands sweaty, and every breath I took felt like it was near impossible to draw in, like my airway had been crushed shut by my attacker.

I zoned out for the rest of the flight; like falling asleep but actually being awake the whole time. Caden Sims kept looking back at me, long face even longer because his jaw looked like it was on the floor. As if I was going to murder him next, like he couldn't believe what he was seeing when he looked at me. I stole a few empty glances at him, but my head kept going back to crazy paranoia.

What if someone found the guy I'd killed?

That thought hung on me like a weight on my chest throughout the rest of the flight, which felt like solid lead running through an hourglass, unmoving.

I heard the hammering at the lavatory door just before we came down for a landing. It stopped within a few minutes, and I had a suspicion that the flight attendant had found our passenger's body and was now keeping it quiet, the better not to worry the living cargo occupying all these seats. I couldn't tell, though, being in the front of the plane.

Paramedics came up the aisle when we landed, coming at a jog, their orange bags and a stretcher between them. The flight attendants told us not to leave our seats just yet due to a medical emergency on board. I listened, didn't pay any attention, but looked at Caden Sims, who looked back at me, mouth like it was zipped shut. Everyone else had their head turned, craning their necks to see what had happened in the back of the plane. He didn't say anything to me, nor to anybody else. Just sat there like a hole in the plane, empty, watching me.

I watched back, waiting to see if he was going to tattle on me. There wasn't anything else to do.

The announcement that we could finally deplane caused a wave of people to barge for the exit. I figured it was fifty-fifty whether they were going to assume foul play on this guy's death and have a whole flock of cops waiting for us, but I walked out into the terminal at LaGuardia to find no one waiting.

What was I supposed to do now? I caught a glimpse of Caden Sims running down the concourse ahead of me, hurrying like he was going to miss his plane, and I just froze. I could catch him if I ran, no problem …

But if I did … what was I going to do with him? Grab him by the back of the neck and march him off in a kidnapping? Kill him right there? Drag him into the bathroom for further interrogation?

I bumped along the concourse as he disappeared from sight, unsure of where I was going other than toward the baggage claim. I couldn't have done any of those things. Not one of them, really. I'd had a hard enough time electrocuting a guy who'd been about to kill me. We'd been so close, I'd seen his eyes. It hadn't been like that with the other two, the two I'd killed to avenge Flora's death.

Plotting a kidnapping or beating someone up or interrogating them forcefully or even killing them as they ran away?

That wasn't me. My hands were still shaking as I made my way out of the security checkpoint and toward the taxi queue. Honking horns sounded like distant noises instead of the blaring, aggressive sounds of a city known for its blunt ways.

I thought back to what I'd seen on Caden Sims's laptop, and felt sick to my stomach. The evidence was right there in what I'd seen. Something was happening here.

Something bad.

And I didn't know what to do. I couldn't imagine going after him myself, being willing to do the things it might take to drag the whole story out of him.

But I knew someone who did.

It didn't take me longer than a few seconds to connect to wi-fi, and then to search for what I was looking for. It wasn't easy, because she was pretty good at hiding, but I'd done the legwork recently and had a solid idea of where to look. It took me less than five minutes to find a number, one that was active and online right now, and I was dialing it up as I grabbed a cab to Manhattan. But the phone was still ringing when the cab started off, and I began to wonder if she'd even pick up.

7.

Sienna

I hate it when my phone rings. I never know if it's someone serious or just a telemarketer who's dialing every number in an area code one by one in hopes of selling me on consolidating my nonexistent student loan debt or lowering the interest rates on my credit card or pretending to be the IRS in order to scam me. Even with my unregistered phones, which nearly no one had the numbers to, it was those assholes—those scammy, telemarketing assholes—who called me almost all the time.

But a few times in recent memory … it hadn't been those assholes. It had been someone I actually needed and wanted to talk to.

And it was with that in mind that I answered the phone as I stood waiting for my bus, and said, "Hello?" instead of, "Go screw yourself with a jackhammer!" I could always say that second thing later, once I'd established they were trying to scam me or sell me something.

"Sienna." The voice was hushed and urgent. The sound of a car in the background was barely audible under the voice at the other end of the line and over the rushing of the wind past the overhang where I was waiting for my bus.

I froze—and not just figuratively, because it was damned cold in Menomonie. "Who is this?" I asked, almost afraid to move.

"It's Jamal," he said, and I felt a small rush of relief. "Jamal

Coleman."

"Dude," I said, "next time, say your name first, not mine. You scared the hell out of me."

"Yeah, okay." He glazed right past that. Jamal was a cool guy, like … ice cube cool, normally. Menomonie-in-winter cool. He sounded pretty close to panic, though, and that was enough to freeze me again, straining to hear him over a truck blowing its horn on the nearby freeway. "I got a problem."

"What is it?" I asked, kind of afraid of the answer I'd get. Jamal wouldn't call me for a small problem, like matching his clothes or something (which I would fail at, anyway).

"The kind you can't discuss on the phone," he said, then paused. "I wouldn't be calling if it wasn't important."

"I know that," I said, trying to defuse any insult he might be feeling at my brusqueness. I was still pissed at myself for getting involved in that stupid fight behind the garage, after all. "But … I'm not sure you want to be seen with me right now." Or ever, really, if he wanted to stay off the list of my Known Associates.

"We need to meet," he said. "This is … it's big. I need your help," he said, falling back to a hushed whisper. "This is outside my expertise."

I took a deep breath of freezing air and my lungs immediately regretted it. "Yeah. Okay," I said. "I can catch a bus to—where do you want to meet?"

"I know where you are," he said. "I'm in New York right now. I can catch a flight to Madison in a little bit. Meet you there?"

"Sure. That'll work." I cradled the phone next to my ear. "Is there anything you can tell me about this? You know, over the phone?"

"I'm in a cab right now," he said, "heading to Newark airport." He paused, and I caught the inference—the cabbie was listening even if no one was electronically eavesdropping. "But I ran across the name of a mutual acquaintance of ours earlier today. Someone you … encountered last time you were in Manhattan."

I frowned. I tended to encounter a lot of people in my work. Some of whom I killed. Mostly bad guys. "I don't suppose you could drop a name?"

"Just a hint, maybe," he said, "like … their handle. ArcheGrey1819."

I stood there in the cold, and took another too-deep and incredibly painful breath. ArcheGrey1819 was the name of a hacker who had broken into the US Attorney's Office and deleted digital evidence while in the employ of a psychotic Wall Street broker named Nadine Griffin. I'd walked away from that case seething, with Nadine Griffin receiving a burial at sea for her efforts to destroy an innocent woman in the course of clearing herself, but her hacker accomplice had vanished like dust in the wind. Even Jamal hadn't been able to track down ArcheGrey1819.

"You still there?" Jamal asked.

"Yeah," I said, stirred back to life by his words. "Was just … thinking about our old friend, and how nice it would be to … meet up."

"Madison," he said. "See you in five hours."

"I'll be there," I promised, and hung up. The clouds had blown back in and the skies had turned grey once more. In spite of all that, I smiled. I'd already been heading east anyway, and now I had an even better reason to go that way.

Oh, look at you, Harmon said. *Cheeks all aflush with the prospect of doing something marginally useful. Or is that the freezing cold? So hard to tell here.*

"You're from Boston, shut up," I muttered under my breath, clenching my jaw to keep my teeth from chattering. I should have waited inside. He wasn't totally wrong, though.

It did feel nice to have something to do again.

8.

Reed

You would think after thirty days of starving myself, I'd wolf down everything in sight, but that wasn't what happened. I chewed delicately on the burger from Jack in the Box, the mustard tasting especially strong. I'd been eating for five minutes and had barely gotten anything down. Miranda Estevez stared at me from across the table.

Her hair was brown with a few lighter, semi-blond highlights, twisted like she'd used a curling iron to give it some whorls. She had a little mole on her cheek, and watched me with deep brown eyes as I picked at my food. She was wearing a long, elegant coat over a smart blouse and skirt combo that was probably perfect for Texas winter weather on the days when they didn't have tornadoes.

Putting down my burger, I sat back in the booth and returned her look. I was afraid to delve into the curly fries, fearing that they might be too greasy for my stomach now that I was back to having something solid for the first time in weeks. "So …" I said by way of opening conversational gambit. She didn't bite, cocking her head and waiting to see what I'd say. I picked up and finished my thought. "… You work for my mysterious old boss?"

"I do," she said.

I waited for her to say something else, but she didn't, which was maddening. "And you want me to come back to work again?"

She looked at me coolly. "That is the message I was given, yes."

Having a conversation with her was starting to feel like pulling teeth. "Sienna *was* that team," I said. To hell with trying to drag something out of her; time to just say what I was thinking. "Without her … it's done."

"Not so," she said, reaching into the slender bag she carried with her. "Mr. Coleman and Ms. Forrest have already returned to work, and are engaged in an active training regimen once more. We've also recruited Veronika Acheron and Colin Fannon on a more permanent basis—" She showed me a shot of the four of them standing together, like something out of a CW series promo, "—and have reassembled the strike team Ms. Nealon put together before her unfortunate departure."

"Hampton back in charge of that?" I asked. She nodded but didn't expound as I picked up the photos, which, in a truly disappointing break from the noir-ish nature of our meeting, were in full color instead of black and white. I slid them carefully back across the table to her. Everyone looked happy enough and healthy enough. "Great. Well. Sounds like you have a good crew. I'm sure they'll do wonderful things—"

"We'd like you to come lead them," Miranda Estevez said, shutting me up mid-sentence.

I stared at her for a full five seconds before I snatched up a curly fry and slammed it into my mouth. It tasted good. Greasy, but good. "You can't be serious."

She just shrugged, not even deigning to answer my question with words.

I shoved another fry in my mouth, way too violently, smashing it up before I even chewed. I spoke through bites. "Sienna was the leader of that team."

"And now she's not." She said it so simply.

Why was this so difficult? I wondered. It should have been easy. She'd offered me something, I'd turned it down. I had important work to be doing, after all, keeping watch on the skies of America, making sure tornadoes didn't come sweeping down out of the clouds to destroy unsuspecting lives. It was the single best application of my new powers, a way to save lives that would otherwise be lost.

And, I was self-aware enough to acknowledge, it meant I didn't have to go home. Ever, maybe.

"I—I have things I need to do—" I started to say.

"Protecting the people, yes," Miranda said, nodding. "We wouldn't want to interfere with your new duties … but at the same time, tornadoes come very occasionally this time of year, yes?"

"Yes," I said lamely.

"And can you detect them from on the ground?" She leaned both elbows on the table, then lifted them up, apparently developing an unfavorable opinion of the staff's table-cleaning habits.

"Maybe," I said a touch defiantly. I could. I could feel a hurricane starting half a world away now, thanks to this broadening of my powers.

I got the feeling Miranda Estevez saw right through me. "Then there's no reason why you couldn't do both." She scooped the pictures back up into her bag, as though taking her offer off the table because she was done presenting it. "If you wanted to." That came out as a challenge.

"Maybe I don't want to," I said.

She stood up, gathering her bag, and looked at me with the same polite calm she'd exhibited since we'd met. "That's certainly your choice. You can continue to hide in the clouds and try and help people from afar. You seem to be doing quite a lot of good. But …" She slipped a thin manila folder from her bag and put it on the table in front of her. "… It's hardly giving it your best, don't you think?" And she walked right out, leaving me in the Jack in the Box in Woodville, Texas, with nothing but a burger, some fries, and a folder that I opened the minute she was out of sight.

After reading it for five minutes, I definitely didn't feel like eating the rest of my food.

9.

Jamal

I passed through security at Newark, got on my flight, and took off without a whisper of trouble. I'd done some looking around the net while I'd waited in the Newark terminal and found that Caden Sims's bodyguard was being preliminarily ruled a heart attack, not a homicide or an electrocution. I flagged the file, figuring that had the potential to change after an autopsy, but it gave me a little reassurance that at least for now, that particular albatross wasn't going to be hung around my neck.

I stepped off the plane in Madison and hopped a cab. I dialed up Sienna the moment I was clear of the airport, and she answered on the first ring. "Yeah," she said, simple as that.

"I'm in town," I said. "Where do you want to meet?"

"I'm at a sports bar right now. Why don't you come see me?"

I pulled my phone away from my ear and punched a button, then gave it a little touch of electricity, back-tracing her location. "I got you. Be there in ten."

I walked into the sports bar ten minutes later, cabbie paid and my backpack slung over my shoulder. I scanned the room, trying not to show my unease. Inwardly, I was bubbling with panic, not just because of what I'd learned but because maybe I hadn't thought things all the way through. Sienna was right; she was a wanted woman, and just because she'd done a damned fine job of throwing everyone off her track this long didn't mean a SWAT team wasn't going to come busting in anytime.

Meandering past the bar, I searched the dark corners of the room, looking for any hint of her. The place wasn't that full, TVs were blaring from where they hung on the wall. Lots of ESPN, the occasional news channel for variety, and dim lighting. There were a few people with their heads down in the booths along one wall, but the lunch rush had died off and left the bar empty, except for a woman in a business suit with long blond hair that went to mid-shoulder.

"Pull up a chair, have a drink," she said as I passed her. It took me a few seconds for it to register that she was talking to me and a few more to get my ass moving toward her.

"Sienna?" I asked, and she turned to give me a withering glare with bright green eyes. I blinked; her eyes had been blue when last I'd seen her … and her hair damned sure hadn't been blond, nor long, not even in the most recent surveillance photos. It didn't look like a wig, either. It was long and glossy and disappeared into her scalp seamlessly. Her business suit was a cut above, too, hiding her natural curves within their lines and making her look … taller, somehow.

"Shhhh," she said, tipping a glass of whiskey up to her lips and taking an almost imperceptible sip. I got the feeling she was working it more for the cover of having something in her hand at the bar than because she was serious about drinking; when she pulled her ruby lips back from the glass, the level of the drink hadn't moved. "Sit." She waved at the seat next to her. "And talk quietly," she said in a meta-whisper over the droning of a commentator talking about why the Cardinals were destined for the Superbowl this season.

I sat down, trying not to look her over too obviously. She looked way, way different than any time I'd ever seen her before. "No wonder you're evading the law so damned well," I said, taking her cue and meta-whispering.

"Is that a compliment?" she asked with a hit of acerbic humor.

"Uh," I said, glancing away quickly, "thanks for meeting me ..."

"Yeah, well, I found myself with a sudden opening in my schedule," she said, lips hidden behind the glass again, "and since the stupid bus routes don't run across the Dakotas, I was heading east anyway."

"I know," I said, pulling out my tablet and searching out the restaurant Wi-Fi. I connected and then activated my VPN. "I had your ticket tracked down about five seconds after I got the ping on your phone."

"It creeps me out that you can track me that easily," she said, still hiding her lips behind her glass. "What's stopping the government from doing that?"

"They don't know how you get your phones," I said, and she gave me a smooth, sidelong look, "or who you call with them." I'd just revealed that I knew one of her secrets, a big one, and one that I doubted my brother or her other friends had any clue about. "Once you follow that trail ... it gets easier. Lets me see the other things you do out of sight."

"I'll have to cover my tracks more thoroughly," she said coolly, then took a real sip of her drink. She didn't show it, but I had a feeling I might have rattled her a little bit. "You want to tell me what's got you so jittery that you got on a plane to Wisconsin in the middle of January? Because I know a Georgian like you isn't here because of the weather."

"Got that right," I said, shivering. I'd packed a coat for the flight between Austin and New York, but Wisconsin was a different level compared to NYC, even. And I hadn't planned to stay in NYC after I hacked Caden Sims. I'd planned to go home, not to Wisconsin. I pulled up a page on my tablet and slid it over to her. "Note on our friend ..."

She put down her drink and scanned the tablet, paging up when she needed to. Her nose wrinkled as she reached the bottom of the file. "What ... the hell did I just read?"

I stared at her. How could she not realize ...? "You don't ... you don't see it, do you?"

She held up the screen, which was filled top to bottom with HTML, flashing me an irritated look from between thinly slitted eyelids. "No, Jamal. I don't see it. I don't even see where the hell I might find it, whatever it is, between the backslashes and brackets and," she stared down at the screen for a second, "'a equals ref'—what the hell is this? Do you think I can read the Matrix?"

"It's code."

"And an indecipherable one, at least to me."

"Okay, it's basically—I just forgot to turn it back into plain text —" I tapped a few things on my tablet and the text formatted itself like it was a word processor screen. I handed it back to her. "Try it now."

She scanned down the tablet again, green eyes catching the glare of the screen and reflecting glassily on her contacts. I could see the text in her eyes as she scanned over it, staring, brow furrowed, trying to make sense of what she was reading. "Who is Caden Sims?"

"Some dude with more firewalls than a—"

"If this is going to be a conversation," Sienna said, stopping and turning to look right at me, those deeply disquieting green eyes locked onto mine, "we need to be speaking the same language."

"He's a tech … guy," I said. "Who's hiding something."

"Is there any other kind?" I stared at her. She looked soooo different, and I was trying to figure out what it was. She caught my stare. "What? Do I have whiskey on my face?"

"No," I said, still talking extra-low. "You just look … way different."

She looked around for the bartender, who had still not appeared. "I'm wearing makeup," she said, and I think she blushed a little under her concealer. Her skin was a shade darker, too, like she'd spray-tanned.

"Oh." I shifted on my barstool and it made a horrendous squeak. "Look, Caden Sims … the file says, right there," I pointed at the pertinent passage, "had ArcheGrey1819 construct some code for him. To do something he couldn't do on his own. Now, maybe it's innocent—"

"But based on our dealings with ArcheGrey," she finished for me, "you think not."

"He hacked the FBI and the US Attorneys," I said

shrugging in lieu of putting up a compelling argument. "Doesn't exactly scream 'White Hat.'" I paused. "That's a, uh, hacker who does, like security tests on networks and benevolent works. As opposed to a 'Black Hat,' who would—"

"I get it." She rattled her ice cubes. "So if this guy had ArcheGrey do some … coding … for him," she turned the word "coding" over in her mouth like it was poison, "and we don't know what he's up to—"

"We have a hint," I said, and scrolled the tablet to the bottom of the screen, where I'd captured the diatribe about crashing the system that Sims had written on the plane, "which is one of the reasons I freaked out and called you." I let that sink in. "Also, there's already a body count, and—"

"You figured you'd call in the expert on that sort of thing?"

"I've killed people before," I said lamely. Three of them, now.

She peered into my eyes. "Yes, you have. But somehow I don't think you enjoyed it this morning at all. Before, when you did it … it was at a distance, right?"

I turned away from her gaze. "Yeah."

"But today, it was up close and personal?"

"In an airplane galley," I said, staring at all the nicks on the wooden surface of the bar. "His hands were on my neck. Can't get much closer than that."

"You could have been having sex when you killed him," she said, staring straight ahead, then looked at me and shrugged. "I'm a succubus. It's an occupational hazard I've had to consider."

"Sex is not your occupation, so how – never mind." I felt immensely uneasy with the direction this conversation was taking, and worse about my blurted out reply. "Uhh, anyway. Caden Sims's scheme … I don't know exactly what he's planning to do, but I have an idea for where he's going next." And I tapped my hand on another item downloaded from his computer—his personal calendar, with one event on it.

"Javits Center, New York City," she read out loud,

frowning as her eyes traced along the screen. "Conference of Technology, Engineering, Communication and—" She stopped midway through and yawned theatrically. "I get it. He's going to bore everyone to death, but unfortunately he's failed to realize that everyone going to this particular conference is already immune!"

"Har har," I said. "He's at the Javits Center for the next week at this conference. Now maybe he's meeting someone there, maybe he's picking up this code ArcheGrey—"

"Couldn't they just email it or something?"

"Yes, but there's gotta be an exchange of payment, right?"

"Which could take place via … what do they call it? Bitcoin?"

"ArcheGrey didn't take payment in any cash form I could trace last time," I said, trying to hit the stride of my argument. "I don't think he works that way."

She sunk into silence for a moment and then took a long, genuine slug of her drink. "No other leads, and yeah, maybe this dude is up to some bad, especially if his bodyguard—what, tried to kill you?" I nodded. "Okay. I guess, New York City it is." She looked almost pleased, though it was hard to tell, because Sienna Nealon had basically one expression, and cross was usually it. "I could use a trip to the Big Apple."

10.

Reed

I strolled uneasily into the new headquarters of our agency/directorate/Alpha/whatever. I'd worked for so many para-law-enforcement and quasi-secret organizations that they'd all lost their mystique. I'd forgotten what the name of the most recent musical chair I'd sat down in was, probably because I hadn't bothered to learn it in the first place. It was an acronym of some sort that had been bent to mean something, kinda like SHIELD.

The welcoming party was, in fact, welcoming, which shouldn't have been all that surprising. "Bro!" Augustus Coleman said, rushing up to greet me from behind his desk when I walked into the bullpen. He clapped me hard on the back and held me in tight, like he might not let me go. I felt the strength of his embrace and hesitated.

It felt good, being touched by another human being after spending the last couple months away from all humanity.

"How you doing, Augustus?" I asked as we broke. My voice still sounded scratchy, especially since I'd flown here on my own ahead of Miranda Estevez. High altitude didn't do wonders for my throat, apparently. Kinda dried it out, and I hadn't had a lot of cloud moisture to offset the problem.

"Better than you," Augustus said with his usual levity. He was dressed crisply in a nice suit. "I like the *Miami Vice*-meets-Robinson Crusoe look you're rockin'. Except for the hair, dude." He gave me a look of mock seriousness. "You got an impending man bun, and you know how we feel about that around here."

"I'm so sorry to be treading so close to hipsterdom," I said seriously as I could. "I feel like I should commit ritual seppuku in apology."

"For having man bun hair?" Veronika Acheron stepped around a cubicle, the overhead lights catching her dark hair along with her immaculate pinstripe pantsuit. "I deem this penalty harsh, yet fair."

"And I deem your poetry the stuff of rejection slips from even the most hackish of publishing houses, Veronika," Colin Fannon said, zipping around a corner and blowing a half dozen papers off a desk. He gave them a brief look of distaste, though whether he was displeased about them being knocked over or that we didn't have a paperless office, I wasn't sure. "Pleased to see you again, Reed," he said, sounding a little subdued. "And ..." he messed with his beanie cap, "I just want to go on record saying that there is nothing wrong with a good man bun."

"I like a good man's buns," Kat Forrest said, slipping quietly out from behind another cubicle. She wasn't done up to the nines like when she was filming for TV, but there was no denying that Kat was a natural beauty. She smiled and caught me in a slow-moving hug that she wrapped tight around my waist.

"Hey, Kitten," I said somberly as she gave me a squeeze.

"We were worried about you," she whispered, more for the solemnity than secrecy; everyone could hear her, after all.

"I can't imagine why," I deadpanned, pulling back when we were done. I indicated my beard and my hair. "I bet you had your stylist waiting on call, ready to fix this impending fashion nightmare."

She let out a breath of a laugh, but her eyes stayed laced with concern. Despite the evidence to the contrary, she was no fool, that Kat. "Have you talked to—"

"So, I hear we're in the business of doing some good again?" I asked, like it wasn't the unofficial mission statement.

"Yeah, man," Augustus said, fiddling with his three-button suit. "New dress code. New staff. New lawyers. New management. I hear they were even looking for a new leader." He gave me a little look of significance.

"I heard a rumor about that, too," I said. "But I wouldn't get too excited." I spun around, giving the place a look. The bullpen was a good size, as big as the inside of a horse barn in Wisconsin where I'd once sheltered, but filled with desks instead. It was only a fraction of the office, too; I'd seen there was more when I came in. "After all, our last leader is currently a federal fugitive, so I can't imagine we're going to get much business right out of the gate—"

"We've got three manhunts pending," Augustus said, cutting me off. "Northern California, Eastern Alabama, and one in Orlando, Florida. All state and local level agencies looking to hire us to clean up a meta mess."

"Well, okay, then," I said, appropriately chastened. I'd seen some of the meta incidents I'd missed in the last couple months detailed in gruesome, living color in Miranda's folder. Trouble had risen while I was gone. "I guess people are more forgiving of my sister's … antics …" I swallowed another, more gut-level first response, "… than I would have thought."

Augustus gave me a look that was almost pitying, and then it was like a curtain fell down on his expression. It didn't take a degree in psych to realize that he was holding off on saying whatever he had to say to me regarding my sister. Probably something relating to the need for our help being greater than the sin of associating with her, or something. "How do you want to divvy this up?" he asked.

I blinked at him. I was in charge, wasn't I? "Uhm, well, I would say … you get Eastern Alabama, because that's close to Atlanta, right?"

He pumped his fist in victory. "Oh, yeah."

"Kat …"

She perked up. "Yes?"

"You and Colin take Northern Cali? It's not quite your home turf, but … you'll do well there." I stared off into space, then glanced at Veronika. "And you can go with—"

"You," Veronika said forcefully. "Since you didn't send me home to Cali, I mean, I might as well tag along to somewhere warmer than this. Alabama's not my speed, so …" She mimed freezing, putting her arms around her suit sleeves. "And I mean, really, who wants to live in this?"

"I don't know," I said, brushing off her comment and finding Augustus again. He was reading a folder and looked up when he noticed I was looking at him. "You won't have any backup in Eastern Alabama—"

"Sure I will," Augustus said. "I'll take Angel with me."

"You'll take … David Boreanaz with you?"

"He'll take Angel with him," came a soft voice from behind the cubicle in the corner, and a petite woman stepped out, her hair long and black as my iPad's screen border, and just as shiny. She was wearing a pair of tight jeans and a loose white blouse that wasn't quite buttoned to the top. She also had on a pair of glasses that bucked the trend—thin frames and very thin lenses. She stared straight at me and extended a hand. "Angel Gutierrez. I'm new." I felt like she'd already declared the place home, maybe even marked said territory a little bit. She reminded me of a pit bull for some reason, small and fierce.

"Nice to meet you, Angel," I said, trying to assimilate the fact that we'd not only hired three new additions, but that I'd never even heard of one of them. "I'm sure we'll, uh …" Words failed me. What were you supposed to say in a moment like this, new boss to new hire? "… Everything will go just swimmingly."

Yeah. That was lame.

"You want the deets on this Orlando situation?" Augustus asked, brandishing another folder.

"Hit me," I said. Angel Gutierrez faded into the background, but I could still feel her eyes on me, watching me with unflinching boldness. I was the leader; I guess everyone was supposed to look to me.

"Guy's out for a jog in a place called Lake Eola Park … who makes these names up?" Augustus just shook his head. "Suddenly gets accelerated to about a hundred miles an hour out of nowhere and ends up going shoulder-first into a tree.

Lucky he didn't go head-first, or we'd be looking at a homicide."

"Hmm," I said, putting on my thinking pose, fingers on chin. "He didn't just manifest himself, did he?"

"I doubt it," Colin said, situating himself in a pose like he was the traveling professor, lecturing. "When a speedster manifests, it comes on slow. He couldn't have zoomed up to a hundred miles an hour out of nowhere. Someone did it to him."

"One of your folk?" I asked.

"Maybe, but I doubt it." Colin shrugged. "If so … have fun catching them." He flashed me a grin. "Call me if you need me."

"Noted," I said, and nodded at Veronika. "I guess, unless we have any further business … we should get going?"

"Oh, now?" Veronika seemed a little surprised. "Sure. Okay. I'll grab my bag and meet you at the airport."

I cocked an eyebrow in amusement. "Airport?" I sent a little gust through the room. "How about I just see you in Florida?"

"You're high and mighty now that you've forgotten the FAA has ceased and desisted you from flying," Kat said.

I caught her gaze. "I've been up in the clouds for the last two months and they haven't come to complain. I'm starting to think they're not going to notice if I fly to Orlando."

"Yeah, but Miranda will notice," Angel piped up. She had her arms folded across her chest. "Trust me. Go commercial, it'll be safer for you. In all ways."

I gave her a probing look, but got little back in return. "Yeah," Veronika said, shoulder bumping me, "you're gonna leave a girl sitting by herself next to some rude stranger?"

What the hell was I supposed to say to that? "Aren't you usually the rude stranger?" I asked, causing Veronika to break into a grin.

"You think you know me, slick," Veronika said, bumping me again. "But I got a few tricks up my sleeve, you wait and see. C'mon." And this time she bumped me toward the door.

"What about tech support?" I asked, not resisting her pushes. "And a phone? Q branch?"

"You know who's in charge of all that," Veronika said, now pushing me toward the door. "And you can catch up with him via phone." She paused, opened a desk drawer, grabbed a phone out of a box and tossed it to me, along with a small bag. "This is all the gadgetry you get. Let's roll."

"What about clothes?" I asked, digging into the bag. It had a fresh ID for me, a couple credit cards, and a wad of cash. "A toothbrush?"

"And a haircut, and a new suit, and all that?" Veronika just grinned at me. "They have all that stuff in Orlando, champ. Let's get a move on. A minute ago you were ready to fly cross country on your own wings. Haste makes paste of us all."

"That doesn't make any sense," Augustus said.

"But it rhymed, and dust doesn't. I dunno, let's just go." And she pushed me again.

"Nice to see you all again," I called back to the others, watching us go. Kat, in particular, had a look on her face that suggested we'd be talking again, and soon. I didn't look forward to it. I looked at Angel. "And nice to meet you."

"Likewise," Angel called back as Veronika shoved me—lightly—out the door. I wasn't sorry to be going, but mainly because I really did want to get back out into the field, get on an investigation.

And I didn't want to be home.

Not yet.

11.

Sienna

I flew low and slow toward New York City, keeping just above the trees so radar wouldn't catch me, and slow enough that I might have been mistaken for a bird or a train or something. Real-time downlooking satellites could still detect me, but hopefully they wouldn't, because I was trying to avoid scrutiny, the government, and anyone else who might have had a beef with Sienna Nealon. It was potentially a very long list.

The clouds were covering the moon. I'd waited until after the sun had set and night had crept in before beginning my flight. Jamal had not waited, catching the next departure out of Madison for New York, and leaving me behind by several hours. That was okay, sort of. I couldn't risk taking a commercial flight at present—getting boxed into a plane full of civilians at 30,000 feet was worrisome—and I preferred this anyway.

No plane.

No worries.

All I felt was the peace of flying through the dark night, cold chill settling on my body. It had been a couple months since I'd flown—the last time being when I'd come back from sending off President Harmon to his eternal reward, which was apparently to irritate me endlessly—and man, had I missed it.

There weren't too many birds this far north in the winter,

so the skies were clear. The moon cast a silvery light from where it hid behind a layer of clouds, faintly illuminating the night in the spots where it wasn't shining. Some stars peeked out when I was between cities, but massive festivals of lights denoting human settlements were laid out above me on the clouds, working like checkpoints on my road to New York.

And the biggest point of light was coming up soon.

I rose in altitude as I grew closer to the coast. Soon I could see Jersey City as the darkness of countryside gave way to more and more development. Manhattan was ahead, and as I zoomed over the Jersey cliffs and down to the water over the Hudson, I felt a slight spray kick up from below, dotting my face. I adjusted my altitude to keep me off the waters; I didn't want to walk the streets of Manhattan soaked to the skin, especially in January.

I didn't know quite what to think of what Jamal had presented me with. He'd elaborated on some things—the fact that this Caden Sims had a meta bodyguard immediately made it my purview, along with the loose, dangling thread of ArcheGrey1819. I didn't like leaving troublemakers out there to make more trouble, even though I was nominally off duty at this point. Something about it just rubbed me wrong, like this unfinished business was my responsibility.

I swooped low and came in for a landing on a rooftop not far from the Javits Center. I was supposed to meet Jamal at one of the hotels nearby. He had texted me to inform me that he'd procured two rooms and was just waiting for me to show up. Probably nervously, because this type of operation, in spite of what Jamal had done in the past, was not really his thing.

He'd ridden with me once on a fight out in Nebraska against the Clary family and gotten wounded for his trouble. But what I really thought of when I thought of Jamal was the fact that he'd intentionally tracked down and murdered the two men most responsible for the death of his girlfriend. The negative always sticks up in our minds, and outweighs the positive.

It was the same reason America would probably always remember me revenge-killing M Squad, blowing up a square block of Eden Prairie, and whacking an endless stream of people on YouTube rather than, I dunno … saving the world.

We all had our crosses to bear.

I riffled around in my duffel and brought out my blond wig. Taking care, I attached it to my head again (I'd given up on stapling it to my forehead, because *owwww*) and then dropped down to the street as soon as it was clear, using the map of Manhattan in my head to make my way to the hotel.

12.

Jamal

Even though I knew she was close, I still jumped when Sienna knocked on the door. "Who is it?" I called, almost dropping my tablet on the floor as I scrambled to close the screen-protecting cover.

"NYPD Public Morals Unit," she called, "we're here because you're running an unauthorized massage parlor in your bathroom shower! Open up or we will continue to gently knock!"

"Oh, haha," I said, putting the tablet down. "Hold on."

"No, seriously," she called back, "the knocking will continue, all night if necessary. Very quietly, like Chinese Water Torture. You may be able to sleep through it, but it will irritate your dreams!"

I threw open the door to find her standing there, looking slightly windblown, makeup having run a little, blond wig in near-flawless form, though. She thrust out her hand. "Key?"

"Oh." I took a step over to the desk and nearly tripped over my own feet, fumbling for the little paper sleeve that held the keys to her room. "Here you go." I handed them to her as she came in, dropping her duffel as I closed the door. "Good flight?" I asked as she stood there, twisting like a snake, arching her spine like she was trying to pop it.

"It was good to be flying again," she said. "Sucked to be going that slowly, though." Her phone buzzed and she pulled it out of her pocket, looked at the screen and smiled before putting it back in and turning to me. "What's the plan for tomorrow?"

"Hit up the Javits Center," I said, matter-of-factly. "Find Caden Sims. Don't lose him."

"He knows your face, right?"

"Well, yeah," I said.

"Okay, so, I'm going to surveil him close," she said. "I'll need you in the building, though, trying to keep track of him and whatnot. Digital eyes on the man, because I can't get *too* close. You'll need to see what I might miss."

"I need to be in the building for that?"

"Yeah," she said. "What if he meets up with someone and we need to follow them, too? What are you gonna do, rush over there from here?"

"I could," I said. "Or I could follow them digitally—"

"No," she said, shaking her head. "No, no, no. I mean—yes, you should follow them digitally, too, with your cameras and whatnot, but nothing beats having eyes on your target as they move about their business. You can do the digital following act later, after the fact, right?"

"Probably," I said. It was true, I could likely reconstruct a person's trail later, if need be, but it was easier to follow them in real time. "I might even be able to do it from my cell phone, it'll just be a little more effort."

"Just make sure to keep your eyes up when you're out in the real world," she said, like some of kind of jaded professor teaching a newbie what to do. "Focus on your subject. Otherwise you might miss something important. But not too hard, or you'll tip them off by being creepy."

"Okay, got it," I said, nodding feverishly. "Conference starts at nine—"

"We need to be over there at eight or so. Get the lay of the land before everything starts, get a good idea of the most common exits, maybe a few of the less common ones as well …" She paused in thought.

"You mean in case Sims tries to run?"

She smiled. "I was thinking in case *I* need to run. The last thing I want is to get into a scrape with the NYPD. They're doing their job, and I don't want to leave them or the city in wreckage."

"Oh, right. Of course. So, uhh … what do we do about Sims? Are we gonna have to …" I made a motion with my hand across my throat.

"Cut off his head and use it to turn our enemies to stone?" She smirked. "Gosh, I hope not; I doubt decapitations are going to weigh well in my favor as my lawyers continue to try and get this indictment dismissed. But the answer to your question is … no, we do not kill Caden Sims unless we have no choice." She stiffened up again, as though her self-chiropractics had done nothing for her. "We need to stay in the shadows on this, and killing some dude in the middle of the Javits Center is not shadowy at all. Especially since it's like chopping off the tail of the snake as he's diving back into his hole; it makes a mess and doesn't kill the snake. If this Sims guy has got some evil plot, we don't know that just taking him out ices the plan. It could still go off without him, and that means we'll have murdered some sap for nada." She gave me a dark look. "You know I don't mind killing someone if it comes to that, but it has to be for a reason. Like saving your own neck, for example."

My collar felt suddenly very close to my skin. "Uhm, yeah. Of course."

"Good. Glad that's clear," she said, and hefted her duffel bag on her shoulder. She waved the paper sleeve with her room keys in it at me and said, "See you tomorrow, early. Get breakfast before we meet if you need it, because there's not going to be a lot of time to stop off for lunch when we're working."

"Good tip," I said, making a mental note to fill my backpack with food to graze on. The truth of what I'd done and what I was doing now settled in on me in a moment of silence. We were really in this.

I'd really killed someone earlier today.

"So …" I said, "this is it, then?"

She raised an eyebrow at me. "It's the beginning. Hopefully we'll see the end of it tomorrow, but who knows? Sometimes these things go on for a while, sometimes they're done in a jiff. No way to know until we dig in and see what gets turned up with the next shovelfuls."

"All right," I said, trying to project more confidence than I felt. "Tomorrow, then."

"Tomorrow," she said, nodding at me as she headed out the door. It pulled itself closed behind her, and I was left in the quiet of my room, wondering why the hell I was sticking my neck out like this.

13.

Reed

I wanted to sleep on the plane, but Veronika apparently didn't feel the same. She drummed on our shared armrest with her manicured nails, driving me slightly nuts. When she noticed me glaring, she smiled and said, "Sorry," then started doing it again thirty seconds later.

"Veronika," I said in a hushed whisper, prompting her to look over at me with curiosity, "would you mind not …?" I pointed at the armrest.

"Oh! Yeah, sorry," she said, pulling her hand off the armrest entirely and wrapping it around herself. "I just got distracted. Don't really like flying, you know."

I looked at the metal sarcophagus around us. I hadn't felt this way about flying before, back when it was the only way for me to effectively travel, but now? I didn't care for it, either. "I understand."

"So …" she said, "you just spent a couple months in friendly skies, huh? Talking to birds?" She grinned at me. "Preventing tornadoes and all that? Enjoying the benefits of fresh air up your kilt?"

I blinked at her. "I don't wear a kilt."

"You know what I mean," and she thudded the palm of her hand against my shoulder. It hurt a little. "You haven't been down in two months—"

"One month," I said, feeling pedantic. "I came down a

month ago in Kansas. Needed to eat something."

"Damn," she said, shaking her head. "What did you eat up in the sky? Raw pigeon?"

"I fasted. Drank water vapor and … meditated." I didn't really do much actual meditation in the sense she probably thought about it. But I did stay up in the clouds and just … stewed. Thought, I guess. Turned over my state of mind, then turned it over again.

"I've got a neighbor back in San Fran that would have really dug that kind of getaway." She was looking at me, all attentive. "What did you think about while you were up there?" She smiled in a kind of condescending way that suggested to me she knew exactly what I was thinking about while I was up there.

I looked at the seat back in front of me. "Do you know why I chose you for this assignment?"

"Good looks, mad skills, biting repartee, a great ass … that last one is technically grounds for sexual harassment since you're the boss, but I couldn't blame you if it was a key factor, because … seriously, have you seen this? And these gams, too?" She waved at herself from the waist down and smirked at me, clearly looking to push me. "I mean, who wouldn't pick me?"

I didn't laugh. "It was because I don't know you, and I was hoping we could just stick to the case."

She stared at me, wild amusement flaring in her eyes, and she snorted. "Oh … you wanted me along because you thought I wouldn't nose into your personal business or that emotional baggage you failed to check back at the terminal?" She laughed. "That was dumb."

"I'm starting to see that now," I said, assessing the gleeful look in her eyes. It was not reassuring.

"Look, slick," she said, taking on an air of patience with me that felt patronizing as hell, "if you don't want to talk about what happened right this minute, that's fine." She patted me on the arm like I was a dog. "But we're going to get to the bottom of this by the time our little adventure is over. Count on it." She smirked. "To be continued."

"Great," I muttered as she turned away and started tapping her nails against the armrest again. I couldn't help but think of the line from *Indiana Jones and the Last Crusade:* "He chose … poorly."

14.

Sienna

It was eight forty-five in the morning at the Javits Center, another beautiful, January, New York City day, with snow on the sidewalks and in the gutters, but fortunately I was spending it indoors rather than out in the freezing cold, where the icy wind came off the Hudson and sliced right through you. It was an improvement from Menomonie in terms of temperature, but the wind chill reduced the NYC advantage to zero. Lucky for them they still had the restaurant advantage. Cuisine in Menomonie was rather limited, Culver's and possibly a few of the local bars being the high points.

I was cramming the last of a bagel with egg, cream cheese, and bacon into my piehole when Jamal's voice crackled in my ear over my Bluetooth phone headset. I was dressed like a totally upright business lady, though my eating habits were probably undermining my cover. I had a Starbucks cup in hand and had crammed most of my necessities into a very professional shoulder bag. Hopefully I just looked like a woman in a hurry as I wolfed down my bagel and not like the partial savage that I actually was.

"Hey," Jamal said, catching me with my mouth full, "I'm set up downstairs. Flipping through the camera feeds now."

"Mm fmmm bmfmm!" I said, then took a moment to rapidly chew my bagel and swallow. "I mean … I'm outside meeting room A-1, waiting." I kept my finger off my

Bluetooth, kept my coffee in my hand, and fake laughed so I would seem like a normal person just doing … business or whatever. Planning my evening, which would probably include theater tickets, and vegan ice cream, and possibly sex. Whatever normal, non-fugitive, non-succubus New York City people did with their evenings.

"Yeah, I see you," Jamal said. "You're looking casual. It's good."

"Thanks," I said, and some dude with hipster glasses wandered close to me, looking me over. "What?" I asked him, an octave or two above my normal register.

"You look familiar," he said, staring at me like he was trying to work out a puzzle.

"Oh!" I laughed, mimicking Kat—basically doing something here that Sienna Nealon would never have done. "I was internet famous for a minute. A video of my misspent youth went viral." I winked at him.

"Ohhhh!" He smiled and nodded. "Yeah. Cool. Well, have fun …" And he wandered off.

"That was an interesting excuse," Jamal commented.

I turned away from the guy who'd thought he recognized me. "What? It's technically true. He was probably thinking 'porn' when they were actually snuff films, but that's not my fault."

Jamal snickered. "You got an answer for everything."

"Well, I have a lot of time to think lately," I said, sipping my coffee and heading toward the big doors to A-1, which were open. I paused in the middle of the hallway and acted like I was hearing something on the other end of the line, smiled, and fake-laughed again, cradling my coffee and then playing with my hair like I was smitten with whoever I was talking to.

"Why do you keep fake laughing at me?"

"Because it's a normal thing to do when you're on a phone call, to respond to whoever's on the other end," I said in a low voice but keeping my face in a smile as I answered. "If I was in hurry and didn't want to be bothered, then I'd feign being pissed, but airheading it seems like the way to go here."

"Unless it gets you the kind of attention from a boy who

takes a lot of interest in the idea that you might have been in porn back in the day," Jamal said.

"I suppose that's always a danger."

There was a moment of comfortable silence while I drifted near two guys who were conversing. Both of them were grade-A geeks, and one was clearly pitching the other something: "My idea is for an app that scans for your obituary, and when it detects it, it deletes your search history." He nodded, clearly pleased with himself. "Whaddya think?"

"I'd buy it," the other guy said, causing me to snort.

"What's up?" Jamal asked.

"That was a genuine laugh." I paused for effect. "All right, remember, we're in the real world here. Eyes up."

"Huh? Oh," Jamal said, and I could hear him moving on the other end of the line. "Okay. I've looked around and am now returning to my screen."

"What did you see?" I asked, pacing back toward the nearest wall. Standing in the middle of the hall wasn't great for keeping out of sight.

"I saw a bunch of people playing on their tablets, computers, and smartphones," Jamal said. "So … basically the same thing you see everywhere these days."

"You're blending right in," I said, putting my back to the wall.

"Yeah, maybe you should just stick your nose in a phone, join the modern age."

"Phones are terrible for situational awareness," I said in a hushed whisper once I was sure no one was in earshot. "Bury your nose in a phone, or worse, put on earphones and turn the volume up, and you can almost watch your life expectancy plummet, especially in a city, because you're completely blind to the myriad threats to your life that simply abound around you, whether it's a speeding car running you over or a robber who wants to see how shooting a person boosts his rep. And it's worse when you're in my line of work. Or … my old line of work," I amended, feeling a little embarrassed.

"Seems like you're still in that line of work," Jamal said,

but I could tell he was mostly being polite while focusing on something else.

"Yeah, well," I said, "I guess I'm too young to retire."

"Shit."

"In your pants?" I quipped.

"No," Jamal said. "And—no! It wasn't literal, it was—"

"I got it. What are you seeing?"

"Caden Sims just walked in," Jamal said, lowering his voice. I could tell he was concentrating really hard on something. "And he's not alone. He must have taken yesterday's loss real hard, because … the dude is in a sea of bodyguards."

15.

Reed

Sunny but cold. That was my first considered opinion of Orlando in January. I'd been to the city before ... I thought. It was hard to remember all the places I'd been. I recalled at least getting into a fight with Sienna against the forces of Century at the airport back during the war, but I couldn't remember if I'd been here before that, or if I'd toured the city or what. It was all a foggy blur, just another town I'd probably visited at some point in my illustrious career.

"Nothing wrong with this," Veronika said as we stepped out into the wind after parking the rental car. Lake Eola Park was pretty big, it seemed, and it had some kind of fountain going in the middle of it, like a layer cake of water rising up out of the pond. It was kinda cool looking, but a little ways out from where we were, which was next to the crime scene tape near a stone amphitheater.

"You must be Mr. Treston," a short, perky patrol officer said, extending her hand to us. Her nameplate read, "Borstein," and she had dark eyes and freckles on her nose.

"I must be," I said, and nodded to Veronika. "This is Ms. Acheron." I favored Veronika with a querying look. "Is it 'Miss,' 'Ms.' or 'Mrs.'"?

She graced me with a withering glare in return. "Ms."

"Mrs.?" I asked, needling her. If she thought I was just gonna let her poke at me like she'd vowed on the plane without any pushback, she was fooling herself.

"Officer," Veronika said, smiling sweetly and deliberately ignoring me, "what can you tell me and my personal jackass about what happened here?"

"You know, I am your boss." That didn't get anything from Veronika but a half-glare, half-eyeroll. A glare-roll.

Borstein took in our little spat with a wary eye but shook it off quickly. "This way." She steered us under the caution tape, holding it up for Veronika, but too short to get it quite high enough for me, even as I ducked. I folded nearly at the midsection in order to accommodate her and keep from breaking the tape with my forehead, and we proceeded onto a little squared-off area of grass next to a tree that looked like it had been traumatized.

"This is where it happened," Borstein said, hands on her belt, resting but ready to draw in that way cops stood. "Or where the vic came to land, anyway." She pointed at the walk we'd come up. "He was jogging there and suddenly, *whoosh!* Breaks his shoulder here." She nodded at the tree, and I took a closer look at the bark.

It had definitely taken a hit. There was an indentation where I suspected the victim's shoulder had made contact, and a slight crease where I guessed the rest of his neck and maybe collarbone had collided with it at high speed. There was a little blood, but not too much, and I wondered exactly how the vic had turned out, so I asked.

"About what you might expect," Borstein said. "Broken shoulder, collarbone, major bruising. About six inches to the right, and he would have a fatal skull fracture, according to the paramedic." She regarded the scene carefully, then looked at me with undisguised curiosity. "Is this normal for you?"

"People colliding with trees at high speed? No," I said.

"Oh," Borstein said. "I just meant … I've never seen a meta case before."

"Not a lot of commonality between them," Veronika said, giving Borstein a jaundiced eye. She was speaking like some kind of veteran in this. "One meta has the power to read minds, the next has the power to produce sweat on such a level you can't keep a hand on them. Lots of variety."

Borstein pondered that for a second. "Sweat … powers? Really?"

"It can be more fun than it sounds," Veronika said with the trace of a smile.

Borstein edged subtly away from her. "So … what does this one look like to you?"

"Could be a speedster," I said, still looking at the base of the trunk, examining the blood spotting there. "Though given how fast they can go, I would have expected a speedster to send this guy straight into the trunk and leave nothing behind that wouldn't fit into a pudding cup. Tell me about the victim."

"Sure," Borstein said, and scrambled to pull out a notepad, then read from it. "Thomas Inglered, age 45, jogs here almost every day, lives a few blocks over." She waved to the north. "He was a lead programmer for some app design company, something to do with a technical field, pumps or something. Pretty dry stuff."

"Interesting," I said.

"Really? Because it sounds boring as hell to me," Veronika said. "What about a significant other? Aren't they the ones responsible for most murders?"

"Says he doesn't have anyone," Borstein said, reading off the page of her notebook.

"Pfffft," Veronika said. "He has to be screwing somebody."

"Man his age?" I asked, standing up from where I'd been looking at the tree. "Maybe not."

"Feeling the strains of age, Reed?" She gave me an appraising glance. "The beard is adding years to you. Ditch it."

"Thanks for the advice," I said.

"So where do we go from here?" Veronika asked, folding her arms.

"Wait, don't you know?" Borstein asked, her mouth falling open.

"It's her first case," I said.

Borstein nodded. "Tough being the rookie."

"Yeah, we should get together over drinks later and talk

about it," Veronika said, going from zero to lascivious in the space of one sentence.

"We'll need to talk to the vic," I said, pondering what I'd heard so far and trying to change the subject when I noticed Borstein blushing, her freckles suddenly disappearing in the sea of her red face. "Maybe look at his place, too."

"Cool, I love snooping through other peoples' houses," Veronika said.

Borstein's blush faded, and her brow furrowed. "Wait, I thought you said you were a rookie. Have you done this before?"

"You don't have to be a cop to go snooping through peoples' houses." Veronika smirked.

Borstein's mouth fell open. I chose that moment to key my new phone and dial a contact that had been preprogrammed in. It got answered on the second ring.

"REED THE STEED!" J.J. yelled. "Thundering across the plains, the mighty man himself!"

"I don't think I'm doing much thundering at the moment, and if I did, it'd be across the swamps, cuz I'm in Florida. Plains are in short supply."

"Dude, either way," J.J. said, "it's damned good to hear from you. Glad you're back and *the man* in charge now. Well deserved."

"You got a problem with a woman being in charge?" asked a cool yet amused female voice in the background.

"Abigail, darling," J.J. said, "you know I don't, by personal experience. I'm just—"

"Yeah, yeah," Abby said, "and I'm just giving you shit, you pig."

"You two working together now?" I asked, rubbing my forehead as I listened to their back-and-forth. I hadn't known Abby for very long before President Harmon had shown up and brainwashed me into joining his merry band, but what I'd seen of her, I liked. She seemed pretty cool. The two of them together, though? A bit much.

"Partners in stopping crime," J.J. said. "So … Reed-man, what can I do for you on this finest day, to inaugurate our once again riding together as brothers, figuratively speaking?

Help get you back in the saddle."

First I was the steed, now someone was being saddled. Keeping up with J.J.'s metaphors was only slightly less exhausting than keeping up with my sister's. "I need you to gather some electronic intelligence on a Thomas Inglered. He's our victim down here, and I'm gonna have to have a talk with him in a little bit, try and establish some motive. Seems he's an app designer in a technical field, so … see what you can come up with?"

"I shall come up with every charge this man has ever made on every credit card he's ever owned, every bank transaction, debit card hit, his favorite porn sites … you name it, I'll get it."

"You can keep that last detail to yourself unless you think it really pertains to the case," I said. J.J. wasn't kidding about that, and in the past it had really hurt my ability to look people in the eyes, knowing some of the kinks they were into in their off time. "Like, if he's got a thing for people being thrown into trees for injury purposes, that might be important. If he's just into … I dunno, scat or something, you just button that away for eternity, okay? I don't need to know."

"Understood," J.J. said, sounding like he was either glowing or bursting. "Good to have you back, boss. We'll get right on it."

"Thanks, J.J." I raised my voice. "Thanks, Abby!"

"Later, dawg," J.J. said. "Hound 'em!"

"He's polite, I like that," Abby said as they hung up.

"What's our play?" Veronika asked as I sauntered back up to her and Officer Borstein, who was now blushing violently. I suspected Veronika had not played nice with her while I was gone. Veronika, for her part, was grinning widely, but Borstein looked like she was ready to run for the hills. Which would take a while around here, because the land was pretty flat. Not Iowa flat, but pretty flat.

"Talk to the victim." I was still puzzling over this one. Sienna had always talked about how she really wasn't an investigator, and that went just as true for me. We'd certainly done some investigating, but we were hardly the best at the trade, and had often talked about how we felt like amateurs in this part of the game. She'd always leaned on her ability to punch faces, and I'd followed in her footsteps in that regard, all the while declaiming that no, I was different, trying to read investigative texts and keep up on forensics and civil rights law and other stuff …

All of which flashed through my head as I stood there, realizing that, yeah … *I was in charge.* A sobering thought that made me want to go get a big, fat gin and tonic or something, to break my sixty days or so of unplanned sobriety in a big way.

"You sure about that?" Veronika asked, apparently amused at my indecision.

"Yeah," I said, nodding. I took a long breath. I was out of practice on this, and felt like a storm was rumbling through me, friction against my own waffling. Also, now I wanted waffles. "Let's go," I said, shaking off the thunderclouds for another time. It was a well-practiced habit for me by now.

16.

Jamal

"He's heading your way," I said as Caden Sims walked across the glass-covered lobby of the Javits Center, his six bodyguards in tow. They were scanning the room, subtlety clearly not their first concern. They had a job to do and they were doing it, partner, no damns given if they got seen. They were all wearing trademark scowls, too, the kind of the looks that discouraged anyone from popping up to say 'Howdy' to the body they were guarding.

"Yay for me," Sienna said, and then slurped coffee loudly over the microphone. "Any familiar faces?"

"Uhmmmm," I said, capturing the six bodyguards on a nearby surveillance camera and then taking clear frames of each of them to toss into a facial recognition database with the Department of Homeland Security through a backdoor I'd installed in their system a while back. "Not to me, but gimme a few and I'll let you know what the 'gubmint' says about 'em."

Sienna snorted. "Great. How long until they make it to me?"

"Five minutes or less. Hang out until then?"

"Sure," she said, and a bite of impatience came through. "But what will you do in the meantime?"

"I'm gonna try and dump the man's phone," I said, standing up and steadying myself, ready to follow along behind him and his entourage at a safe distance.

"Dump … it?"

"I'm gonna try and connect to it, either via Bluetooth or by piggybacking over the local cell tower so I can download his contacts, GPS, apps, email, everything he keeps on it," I said. I should have really done this yesterday, but I'd been so focused on getting his computer files that I hadn't followed hacker best practices and just grabbed everything on the man. Besides, depending on what kind he had, the phone might have been even more difficult.

I followed along behind the Sims entourage, riding up an escalator, walking under the shadow of an endless series of interior metal supports that allowed for the massive, hundreds-foot-tall open glass walls to the outside. It gave a nice view of the cityscape of New York outside, but it didn't give as much light as I would have hoped for today, what with the clouds covering every square inch of the sky.

"Feel like I'm reaching the point in our extended conversation where I'm going to have to either hang up or carry this into the bathroom," Sienna said, and I caught a hint of strain on her side of the conversation.

"Oh come on," I said. "You don't have to …?"

"I've had a lot of coffee this morning," she said tightly, "and of the many things my meta abilities give me, a meta bladder is not one of them."

"Can you hold it?"

"Uhmmm," she said, pondering it over. "No. But the good news is that you're still at least two minutes out and there's a bathroom right here. Be right back." The sound of her pace quickening made its way through the phone.

"Uhhh, uhhh, okay," I said, because what else could I say? I'd been watching the main entrance while she'd watched the hall because there were multiple ways Caden Sims could enter the building, and now that we had him, we at least knew his vector for the most part. Hopefully there wouldn't be any surprises on the way.

"For crying out loud!" Sienna muttered. "Always a damned line in the ladies' room. I bet the men's room is empty."

"It's a tech conference, so I kinda doubt it."

She made a grunting, growling noise. "EMERGENCY," I

heard her say, then somebody cried out in surprise at the other end, and a door slammed. "So rude!" someone shouted, and I could have sworn I heard a purse being slapped against a stall door.

"Yo, you there?" I asked when the hubbub settled down at her end.

"Shhhhhh," she admonished me, nearly whispering. "I'm muting myself now. Don't talk."

"If you're muting yourself, why does it matter if I talk?" I asked.

"Because I have shy kidneys. Now shut up!" And her voice cut off, along with all other sound at her end of the conversation.

I stared at Caden Sims's entourage ahead of me, walking along the corridor in a tightly knit wolfpack. I was far enough back and my face was mostly buried in my screen. I dodged behind groups of people every chance I got, threading my way through in a very leisurely manner, letting them get further ahead. I had eyes on them via the surveillance cameras in the Center anyway, so I could afford to give them some rope and let them run. I'd know if they made any abrupt moves.

A toilet flush sounded loudly in my ear, and then I heard the unmistakable sound of a zipper being pulled up. "You back?" I asked.

"Yesssss," Sienna said, sounding so relieved. A stall lock unbolted, and she said, "All yours."

"Thanks a lot!" someone said with all due snark.

"You're welcome," Sienna replied with a snotty lack of grace. Water sounds from a faucet came just as a hand dryer turned on the background. "I left a little something on the seat for her anyway, the cow."

"Hey!" someone shouted in the background, sounding pretty upset. "You pig!"

"You deserve it!" Sienna shouted back. "I should have left the seat up! I hope you fall in!" And then the background noise got a lot less echoey and turned into more of a dull clamor of voices as she presumably left the bathroom behind.

"You have a way with people, you know," I said, steering around a group of tech bros with their satchels slung over their shoulders.

"She deserved every bit of it," Sienna replied, chock full of hostile defensiveness. "I wish I had water powers, because I would soak her ass with toilet water. And the rest of her, too. Actually, I would do that to a lot of people."

"You should go absorb your ex, then," I said.

The conversation died in a hot second. "Yeah," she said, tightly, after a short pause, "everybody seems to think that's a good idea, but then you actually have to live with these people in your head. And they're like the worst roommates you've ever had."

"Uh, okay." I doubted that, but that was because Sienna had never actually lived with Augustus. My brother took up all the counter space in our shared bathroom. All of it. The man had more creams and sprays than should have been legally permissible to possess. If I ever needed to create a chemical weapon, I was starting with my brother's bathroom cache.

"They snark constantly. About everything, from your food choices to your wardrobe. They bicker among themselves. They actually have preferences for what I wear, and I get to hear them, low-level arguing, over even the most inconsequential stupid shit. Actually, they argue more about that stuff than they do the big things. It's like the worst family Thanksgiving you can imagine, but you get it twenty-four/seven/three-sixty-five. Sometimes they even wake me up arguing, though thankfully they've gotten better about that. And they have sex in my head from time to time, I found out recently—"

"Okay, you sold me on—"

"They used to hide it, but now that the news is out? Nope! I mean, I can stop it, if I catch it in time, but it requires me to lock them up in this little prison-y section of my mind, which feels a little cruel, but is honestly the only reasonable response to seeing Bjorn's ass in my mind's eye—"

"I don't need to know—"

"And the new guy? What does the military call it? FNG?

Yeah, that guy—you know who I'm talking about, right? He's the *worst.* The literal worst, worse than two serial killers and a whiny baby with combustion powers—shut up, Aleksandr—"

"Uhm—"

"Oh, whoops," she said, and her tone slipped to hushed. "I have eyes on target."

I was about to ready to thank the stars, because I'd heard enough about Sienna's headcase problems. I was suddenly really thankful I wasn't an incubus, because based on her description, I was not sure that sopping up powers like a sponge taking in water was worth it if you had to deal with people like that in your head.

"It was a compliment, Wolfe. You're better than he is," Sienna hissed. "You happy now? I said it."

It wasn't the first time I'd seen one of her in-head conversations break out into the real world. Augustus used to call it her "going creepy" moments. It was probably for the best that the press hadn't reported on that side effect of her abilities, because it kinda made her seem like a lunatic.

I was still working on Sims's phone, and it was proving to be a not-so-easy nut to crack. He was doing all the standard smart stuff, using a VPN, having serious encryption, making sure his Bluetooth didn't just pair with anything all willy-nilly, and didn't connect to random networks as it passed. If I could get at his GPS, though, I'd basically have a record of everywhere the man went for however long the phone kept records. That'd be a treasure trove of useful information, especially since I hadn't yet found his primary residence, but the contacts would be similarly useful.

"Whatever's going on in this hall is about to start," Sienna muttered over the line, her outbreak of crazy apparently silenced for the moment. "They're playing some music, and people are getting … well, about as excited as tech-conference goers probably get."

"So they're sitting quietly in their seats and staring straight ahead?"

"Looks about right. Also, someone's coming to the podium up on stage. Our guy is making his way in now."

"Cool," I said, probably a little less than a football field away from Sienna at this point. I took a breath of the heated air, that smell of a furnace running making it heavier and drier than usual. "Keep an eye on 'em?"

"Locked on," she said quietly, and the sound of music piped through my earpiece as she entered the hall.

"Welcome, welcome, welcome!" the speaker said at the podium. She started to speak, just a basic intro kind of thing, boilerplate, with a joke or two interspersed to keep things moving.

I slowed my roll as I came to the back entrance to the hall. "Am I clear to enter, or are his boys watching the door?"

"I count at least one girl among his 'boys,'" she said, "and yeah, they're keeping an eye on the door. Might want to park outside, unless you desperately want to be in here with us?"

I thought about it a second. "Nah, I don't need to be in there. Where is he?"

"Hall's only about half full," she said. "He's at the front of the room. First row. I'm in the back. Two bodyguards lingering at the rear of the room. Four with him."

"Hmm." I didn't know bodyguarding, so I don't know what to think of that. "Is that normal?"

"This hall has a lot of entrances and exits to cover. Too many for six of them to watch, plus cover him. It's pretty normal, I think." There was a sound at the other end, an audible gulp, and then Sienna said, "Oh, hell."

"What?" I asked, stiffening, thumping against the wall outside the room as I came back from where I'd started to sit down. "What is it?"

"The bodyguards," Sienna said, and I could hear her moving, rustling as she moved down a row, a clank as she hit a folding chair in her hurry to escape, "I recognize one of them. And if he sees me … or gets close enough … he'll probably recognize me, too."

17.

Sienna

"Don't panic," Jamal said coolly. I'd just thumped my leg against a chair in the row I'd been trying to escape. His invocation for patience was not exactly a huge help, seeing as I'd already inadvertently drawn attention to myself.

"Thanks for the tip," I said through gritted teeth, thankful I'd chosen the last inhabited row to plop down. It would have been even more embarrassing if I'd been in the middle of the audience.

"Who'd you see?" Jamal asked as I made my way calmly down the row toward the wall nearest the big entry doors to the hall where he waited. "Old friend?"

"Kindasorta?" I wasn't entirely sure. "I never got his name, only knew him as Soothing Voice—"

"He called himself that?"

"No," I said, "I make up names for people I fight, and that was his—"

"You called him 'Soothing Voice'?"

"Will you just let me explain?" I asked, snapping with impatience. "I busted him in Portland a few months ago for breaking into Palleton Labs, that place that was doing R&D into—"

"The meta enhancement formula," Jamal said.

"Right," I said, casting a look over my shoulder at Soothing Voice, who was standing there near the stage, looking around attentively. "He's an empath."

"Shit. That mean he can zero in on you?"

"No, he can't detect thoughts, only emotional states," I said. "I'm trying to keep mine calm—"

"You call this calm?"

"—in hopes that he loses me in the sea of people here," I said, trying to mine my natural irritation in order to mask my goal, which was obviously to watch this Caden Sims for trouble. "With—what, a couple thousand people in this room? I can't imagine someone who actually *doesn't* mean any harm to his boss is gonna stand out." I gulped quietly, so that Jamal couldn't hear me. I hoped, anyway. I really didn't intend this Caden Sims any harm and was actually desperate to keep matters from deteriorating ... as they tended to do.

"And now, without further ado," the speaker at the podium said, "I present to you—Cameron Wittman!"

I glanced back over my shoulder, and lowered my voice as the hall went down in thunderous applause. "Who the hell is Cameron Wittman?"

Jamal gave me a moment's pause, then answered in an almost stupefied voice, "How do you not know who Cameron Wittman is?"

"Because I assume he's not a criminal, and thus he's skated neatly under my radar thus far?"

"He's one of the biggest names in Silicon Valley," Jamal said, enthusiasm dripping from his voice like butter off scampi. "Founder of about five different tech startups that have completely changed the digital world as we know it. His IPO of—"

"Okay, I get it, he's a geek bigwheel," I said, rolling my eyes, as I frequently did in situations where I felt completely out of my element. "A geekwheel. Why is Caden Sims sitting in the front row for his speech?"

"Because Sims has the cash to be able to reserve front row tickets, obviously," Jamal said, like that explained everything.

"So ... what you're saying is that Cameron Wittman is the Justin Bieber of the tech world." I caught a nasty look from a woman I passed who overheard that analogy. Or maybe she was the one who I'd clashed with in the bathroom earlier. It could have gone either way.

Jamal didn't answer at first. "That's harsh. And unfair."

"To the Biebs?" I cast a look back at Wittman, who was like a bug on the stage, he was so far away. Fortunately there were two huge video screens positioned on either side that gave me a closer look at him. He was wearing his light brown hair in a Jack-McBrayer-style combover/helmet head, and I wondered how much he paid some Silicon Valley stylist for that look. Whatever it was, I had a feeling it was too much. Hell, if his stylist was paying *him*, he was still getting ripped off.

"That's so hateful, you have no idea. Wittman is a thought leader, and he has completely revolutionized—"

"Blah blah blah."

"He—"

"Blah."

"But—"

"Every word out of your mouth is like the teacher in Charlie Brown to me."

"Fine," Jamal grudgingly said at last, "but know this—the man has done things that no one else has. And he's a billionaire."

"Great," I said, turning my attention to the stage in time to catch some of Cameron Wittman's remarks, "because those guys never turn out to be trouble."

"—That we live in a world," Wittman was saying, "where communication is the key to our future success. Where misunderstanding must fall by the wayside in order to address the challenges ahead. Failures of understanding mean loss of opportunity—to connect, to serve, to lead. A truck filled with fresh produce unloaded in the Port of Los Angeles rots where it sits because the logistics systems accidentally lose it in the shuffle. It disappears, and by the time they realize their error on the ground, it's useless. A waste." He spread his arms wide, like he wanted to give the audience a hug.

"Where did this guy come from?" I asked, peering at him. "Other than Silicon Valley?"

"His great-great-granddad was a titan of industry," Jamal said. "Built up a family fortune during the industrial revolution. You know, robber barons. Well, the family fortune was on the wane until he came along and bet every dollar he had from his inheritance on his first venture. It went big, and the rest was history. Five IPOs later, and the dude prints money every time he has an idea."

"—but what if there were a way to make sure that nothing got lost?" Wittman asked from the stage. "Nothing slips through the cracks. History is filled with examples of things slipping through the cracks. The example I used before—it was two logistics systems failing to communicate, to share. One thought the cargo was off its books, the other failed to pick it up. Miscommunication resulted in a secret. The secret resulted in the loss of the produce. These things happen. There are shadows everywhere—a small company discovers a miracle drug, but they don't have the money to put it into clinical trials, because the disease affects only fifty people worldwide. No margin in that, right? It's practically a secret, because it can't escape the noise of everyday life. Company fails to raise the money they need to survive because no one knows about them, and no one high-profile has ever caught the disease, so …" He mugged for the camera. "… the company goes down and the drug disappears into the recesses of history, never to be heard from again. And over the next few years, fifty people around the world die of the disease when they could have been saved. Secrets. Failures to communicate."

I had to admit, he had a point there.

"Think about it," he said. "You go into a restaurant you've been passing for years but never stopped into. You order, and they have the best tikka masala you've ever had. Suddenly you're a fan, a fanatic, you want to go back over and over again. Where has this tikka masala been all your life? Right there, all along. Hidden in the shadows. Secret to you, at least. And what if they went out of business before you found them? Before anyone found them? That happens every day, and suddenly your favorite restaurant, it's gone. Never existed in your life. And that's what I'm really talking about—possibility. Communication. Peeling back the shadows, eliminating these secrets that occlude our vision …

that hamper our ability to live our lives, to do our best, to be our best."

"I think I'd be pissed if I had a favorite restaurant and it wasn't at least a little secret," I muttered. "But in fairness, I hate crowds."

"You're not really a people person, are you?"

"Just now getting that, huh, smart guy?"

"A secret is just a barrier between us and the information we seek," Wittman went on. "It sounds good, doesn't it? Mysterious? Alluring?" He was smiling at his audience, and his delivery was warm and inviting. "But these are the good kind of secrets. They're the ones that change our lives for the worse. They're the barriers between us and our goals, between us and the things that can make our lives better. They're even the barriers sometimes, between us and other people. Between us and the ones we love."

I frowned as I leaned against the far wall of the auditorium. It was reasonably dark in here, the light coming from the stage and the giant screens hanging from the ceiling. Where was he going with this, I wondered?

"In a future where communication triumphs, we need to reduce these secrets. Remove these secrets. Make them known. Whether it's a politician who's corrupt behind the scenes—"

"That'd be almost all of them," I muttered.

"—or a company that's playing dirty against its competitors or just a person who's playing outside the rules of fair play we've established as a society … what if we knew all these things?"

"I think in the case of the politicians, we have a pretty good idea they're all corrupt," I said, continuing my commentary track. Jamal responded with an irritated sort of grunt. I guess he was enjoying the speech.

"How much fairer would our society be if things were more transparent? If these backroom dealings were exposed? If companies had to compete on a playing field that was level, or risk being exposed when they cheated or gamed the system?"

"Oh, boy," I said, "I bet the arbiters of fairness in this

system are gonna make out like bandits."

"Has anyone ever told you that you are really damned cynical for being as young as you are?" Jamal asked, irritation finally boiling over.

"Why, thank you," I said. "The answer is yes, but I just can't hear it enough, frankly."

"It's not a compliment."

"I disagree."

"—a world without these secrets, without these barriers between us. A freer world, a better world, a fairer world—"

"I hate this guy already," I said, mostly to myself, "but I bet you woulda loved him, right, Gerry?"

Gerry Harmon stirred inside my head. *Well, he was a big donor,* Harmon said with a flash of amusement.

"Whoa," I said, "I think we might have found our King Daddy bad guy."

"What?" Jamal sounded like he'd stuck his finger in an electric socket. Uhh, if he'd been a normal person, anyway. I doubt sticking his finger an in electric socket would have done much to him. "Are you out of your mind?"

"He was a Harmon donor," I said with great conviction.

Jamal did not bother to conceal his opinion of my absurdity. "Annnnnd?"

"They have a track record of trying to kill me," I said.

"Gerry Harmon has gotten millions of different donations in the course of his political career," Jamal said brusquely. "I doubt every one of them, or even a statistically significant portion of them, have tried to kill you."

"I think you're underestimating how many people have tried to kill me."

"Either way," Jamal said, "that's not conclusive proof that this guy is in any way bad."

Not to mention it's insulting, Harmon added. *I publicly disavowed Buck Brock, remember?*

"What about Cavanagh?" I muttered in riposte.

Yes, it's a shame he didn't kill you. It would have made my life easier than it presently is.

"Thanks for proving my point," I said under my breath.

"What if this guy is ArcheGrey?"

"What are you on about now?" Jamal asked savagely. "Do you still have eyes on Sims?"

"Y—no." The crowd was giving Cameron Wittman a standing ovation, which prevented me from being able to see Caden Sims right now. "Seriously, though—what if Wittman is ArcheGrey? Which is why Sims is in the front row? Maybe they're going to meet afterwards."

"Yeah, probably not," Jamal said. "Cameron Wittman is a tech billionaire. Sims is a small fry next to him. If there were an exchange going on, I'd think it'd be the other way around."

"Maybe," I said. I was just spitballing anyway. "Still … every tale needs its villain, and until we get a better alternative, he's mine for this story."

"Yeah, okay," Jamal said, completely dismissing me. "Do you have eyes on Sims yet?"

"I'm five-foot-four, okay?" I huffed. "Unless you want me to start floating, the answer is no, I can't see over this crowd." That bothered me, like an itch in my mind, but it was just another reason I hated crowds. There was a lot of hustle and bustle in the place now that Wittman was done speaking. Not everyone was heading for the exits, but probably twenty percent of the crowd was. I guess it was all downhill after Wittman.

"I'd rather you not reveal yourself," Jamal said.

"In this, we are in agreement," I said, trying to at least keep a decent eye on my surroundings. It was tough, because I was constantly talking to him, which meant I was paying at least a percentage of my attention to coming up with witty repartee, and I realized that clearly I'd spent a little too much brainspace on that and not enough on my surroundings when I saw a familiar face staring at me from about twenty feet away, the crowd rolling around him as he stood there, staring at me. "Gulp."

"Whut?" Jamal asked.

"You remember what I said before about phones being bad for situational awareness?" I asked.

"Yeah …"

"I meant every word of it." Soothing Voice, the empath of my acquaintance, was cutting through the crowd directly toward me, at least two of his fellow bodyguards trailing along in his wake.

18.

Reed

"… I don't know where it even came from," Thomas "Call me Tom" Inglered was telling me, woozy and disoriented in his hospital bed in Orlando Regional Medical Center, a wavy, modern-looking glass building. Sun was shining in through his window, bright, blue, near cloudless hanging beyond. "I was just going along one minute and the next …" He shook his head.

Inglered was a man who looked like he kept in pretty good shape, though it was hard to tell through the hospital gown he was clad in now. He was wearing an immobilization sling on his left arm, pins and whatnot jutting out, with surgical bandages covering him to the point that he looked vaguely mummified. He had two black eyes and his nose was bandaged up, too, from the landing, his doctor had told us before we met him.

All in all, this man was fortunate he was still alive, but not looking too fortunate at all.

"Do you remember anything about the … incident?" I asked, mincing words.

"You don't really look like a detective with that beard," Inglered said, peering at me through half-closed eyes, like I was going to give him the secret of life in the next few seconds.

"Thanks," I said. "Can we get back on topic?"

"Seriously, the beard is weird," Veronika agreed. I shot her an antagonized look.

"Details, details," Inglered said, thinking about it. He had a roll of bandages around his skull, too; dark hair mingled with grey peeked out from between the gauze and tape. "It's all sort of blurry, you know? Doctor says the head trauma—"

"Yeah, we heard," I said, feeling like this was going to be a bust.

"There was one thing." Inglered sat very still now, no longer fidgety as he'd been when we arrived here. "When I was running up to—well, to where it happened—there was a woman …"

"Blaming his woes on a woman," Veronika said so softly only I could hear it, "typical. This is probably why he isn't married."

"Could you describe her?" I asked, ignoring the hell out of Veronika.

Inglered moved his lips around like he was shifting his tongue in his mouth. He hadn't heard her, luckily. "Maybe … she was … blond …"

"That really narrows it down," Veronika said under her breath.

"… kind of tall … leggy, I'd say … wearing like … what are those tight pants women wear all the time now?"

"Yoga pants," Veronika pronounced. She sidled up to the bed, cocking an eyebrow. "Tell us more."

"She had on a coat, but, like, a tank top underneath," he said, thinking hard. "I think she might have been jogging, too."

"So she was fit," Veronika said, before I could dive back into the conversation.

"I think so, yeah," Inglered said, nodding as he concentrated. "Yeah, she was in good shape."

"How tall?" I asked.

"What were her measurements?" Veronika asked, causing me to close my eyes and almost palm-slap my forehead.

"I … don't really pay attention to that sort of thing," Inglered said, staring at her, perplexed.

"Well, why the hell not?" Veronika asked.

"Can you tell us anything about her face?" I asked,

wondering why I was the one who had to bring this back around.

"Not really, no," Inglered said, shaking his head. "Honestly, I wouldn't have even taken notice of her at all if she hadn't recoiled away from me as I started to go past her."

Veronika and I exchanged a look. "Recoiled … away from you?" I asked.

"Yeah," Inglered said with a nod. He made like he was going to move his left hand and then stared down, remembering it was immobilized and mimed the motion with the other. "Like I was a burning stove or something. She just …" He yanked his hand back and cringed, probably from the pain lancing through his body at the violence of the motion. "Well … like that. Next thing I know, I'm flying through the air, and then I woke up here." He made a movement to shrug, and cringed at that, too.

"Well, that was interesting," Veronika said as we walked out the door a few minutes later, after having said our farewells to Mr. Inglered, wished him a good recovery, and thanked him for his time. I'd left him with a card, too, so that he could call us if he thought of anything else, but I suspected he was a dry well at this point.

"Yeah," I said as we made our way down the beige-toned hallway.

"What next, then?"

"Good question," I said, trying to think it through. "I guess we—" I paused as we approached the nurses' station.

There was a blond woman standing there with a bouquet of flowers, talking to the charge nurse. "I just want to leave them for Mr., uh … Inglered?"

"Why is his name a question?" Veronika asked, her nose crinkled up with a question of her own.

"Because she couldn't remember it for a second there," I said, staring at the woman in concentration.

"Deliveries are hard," Veronika said, then she, too, froze, catching it.

The woman standing in front of us wasn't a delivery person; she was way too well dressed for it. This lady was wearing a nice red blouse and black pants, like she hadn't gotten the memo that Christmas was last month. It was still a good look, especially with her …

Blond hair.

"Hey!" Veronika said, heading right for her, dark hair swishing behind her as she strode toward the woman with the flowers. She broke into a jog, then a charge, seeing the red and going for it, I guess.

"Wait!" I called at her, worrying that Veronika was about to do something terrible to Inglered's daughter or something. It wasn't like blond hair was a well-defined description of a suspect.

The woman spun in time to see Veronika coming at her in a full charge. Veronika's hands were glowing bright blue, her power fluorescent and almost pulsating with light. The woman recoiled, back thumping against the nurses' station, and her eyes went wide as Veronika closed in.

There was a blur, like the light around the two of them distorted as Veronika drew to within a couple feet of the woman. Veronika shuddered like a digital image getting scrambled, and then—

She launched past the woman and through wall behind the nurses' station, disappearing through the plaster and drywall as though she'd been hit by a truck.

19.

Sienna

"Hello, Sienna," Soothing Voice said to me over the crowd noise in the hall, warm eyes looking right into mine, voice just as deep and sonorous and, yes, soothing, as you might expect.

"Whussup?" I asked casually, eyeing the people around us to make sure no one took note of our conversation or, more importantly, me. We were good, because apparently people were in a much bigger hurry to flee the hall than they were to take notice of a random blond woman and a black man talking at the edge of the hall.

"Not going to bother with the pretense we haven't met?" He smiled as he slid in next to me and leaned against the wall. I kept an eye on his two associates out of the corners of mine as they stood off about ten feet, looking for any sign of motion or defiance from me.

"I doubt it would do much good since you already picked me out from across a crowded exhibition hall," I said airily, flipping my blond hair over my shoulder in a reasonable impersonation of Kat. When playing a role, you have to also use body language to your advantage, and flipping hair is something Sienna Nealon would only do when trying to be snarky. "But you should know—I have no ill intent toward you or your … uh … body that you're guarding."

"I think we both know that's not exactly true," he said.

"Different crew now, huh? How's Timothy?" I asked,

changing the subject to avoid getting into detail on that.

"I haven't seen him for quite a while," Soothing said. "Nor the others. Hopefully he's good."

"He came to see me after you got out," I said. "Seemed to think he was gonna be killed by some other party—President Harmon, I assume—for what you guys did in Portland."

"Things were a little worrying there for a while," Soothing said, sounding like he was agreeing. "Personally, I needed to find an employer who could help shield me from some of the potential … consequences … of those activities."

"And now you're protecting other people for hire," I said, chewing that one over. There was some metahuman bodyguard service powerful enough to stop whatever reprisals Timothy had feared following their break-in at Palleton? That was interesting. "With the meta version of the French Foreign Legion? Since they don't care about your background …"

"I'm not a felon," Soothing said with a shrug. "The SCOTUS decision came through at a good time for me."

"Not so much for me," I said.

"Yo, you gonna just talk with him all day or are you going to start putting these guys down?" Jamal hissed in my ear, probably hoping he could slip that message in without Soothing hearing it.

"I'm not killing bodyguards on a job," I replied in normal volume, pointing at my earpiece so that Soothing would understand. He nodded at me. "And I'm not really looking for a fight," I said, mostly for Soothing's benefit.

"You really shouldn't have come here," Soothing said, almost mournfully.

"Tell me about it," I said, shaking my head. "Crowds, noise, ten dollar lattes. It's not so much my scene, and that's not even delving into the fact that I'm at a loss when it comes to understanding tech—"

"I think you know what I mean," Soothing said with a knowing look.

"Didn't you learn anything from last time?" I asked. "Seriously … go on your way. Don't start something that we'll both regret. You because you have to go to the hospital for a lacerated everything, and me because I'm going to have to leave the city in a big damned hurry to avoid the heat."

"My boss hired me to watch his back," Soothing said. I had a feeling he was probably working on my emotions with his powers, though I couldn't detect it. "I wouldn't be doing my job if I just let you do what you're doing."

"What I'm doing is standing here, drinking an overpriced coffee and talking to someone on the phone," I said. "If your boss has a problem with that, I would suggest that his issue is with human freedom to move about and do things and not with me, personally. Unless he's vegan and upset this isn't soy, but I gotta tell you—screw that. Dairy-based cream just tastes better."

"We can do this loudly or quietly," Soothing said.

"Loudly is going to involve you screaming in agonizing pain," I said, "quietly means you leave me be and go on your way unmolested."

"I'm going to count to ten—"

"Really?" I asked, my face burning, "because I'm gonna count to three," I shot a glare at his two stooges, "and then I'm going to forget what I said earlier about not wanting to kill bodyguards, because I will—" I flared hot, my hair turning immediately into flame and disintegrating my wig. I set my eyes afire, too, for effect, and disintegrated my coffee as I lit off my hand and brought it up, "—scorch the earth of your bodies and leave your families weeping with nothing but a pile of ashes to show for you picking the stupidest damned fight of your lives."

"Uh, Teddy," one of the guys said nervously to Soothing, "our principal is out. We should leave. Now."

"Look at you, all smart and stuff." The crowd around me was chattering now, because your hair and eyes and hand catching fire draws attention, even of a jaded crowd of New Yorkers. Which most of them probably weren't. Tourists.

The guy who'd just spoken to Soothing swallowed heavily and waved a hand. "Let me just say, Ms. Nealon, I'm a huge fan. You're a real inspiration to those of us in the, uh, meta, uh, ass-kicking community, and uhm, if you feel the need to take action against these guys, I will tender my resignation right now, because this job does not pay well enough for me to die doing it."

"Finally," I said, puffing a little smoke out through my lips, "I've met a damned genius." I cast a flaming glare at the other bodyguard, this one a lady. "What about you? You want to spin the roulette wheel of fate, Slick? See if it comes up with your lucky number?"

She just shook her head. "Ahhhh, no. I can get a different job. A better one, probably. Less, uh … fatal."

I switched my glare back to Soothing. "Your call. Want to play?"

"You won't kill me," Soothing said, but he took a step back. "Probably."

"Are you willing to bet your life on that?" I asked.

"You've got quite a temper …" Soothing said. "Might want to put this on pause for a second before you do something you regret."

"I'm already a wanted fugitive," I said. "Honestly, most of the choices I'm going to regret are probably in the rearview at this point. Also … did you just tell me to calm down? Because you could just … make me." I almost spat the last two words at him.

"I, uh … can't seem to …" Soothing started.

That made me pause. "You can't?" I concentrated, remembering that last time when I'd had to overcome his power, it had taken a dose of furious emotion from my inner souls to do so. "Wolfe …" I muttered.

Not Wolfe, Wolfe said. *Wolfe is calm and amused, with a hint of bloodthirst mixed in.*

It's the new guy, Eve said, dropping the dime.

Yeah, Zack said, *he's even waving at us.*

I could imagine Harmon in my head, waving at me, smirking. *Calm you is the less fun you. Be angry you and burn this place to the ground!*

"You've absorbed a telepath since last we met," Soothing said, eyes narrowed as he looked at me.

"What?" I tried to keep from bristling in horror. "No!" That didn't even sound convincing to my ears.

"You have," Soothing said, peering at me and moving his

head around as though he could see into my skull, see Harmon laughing and causing his chaos within me. "I can't move you right now. I can't even see you. You've disappeared—just like one of them."

This is so much fun, Harmon said. Wolfe growled distantly in the background of my mind.

My mind whirled outside of all the stimuli it was receiving and trying to process—Harmon now arguing with some of the others in my head, Soothing still looking at me, waiting for an answer I couldn't construct skillfully enough to deceive him, Harmon still milking my thoughts to produce anger—probably not a tough task for the world's most famous fugitive/exile—and, of course, that thought in the back of my mind that I was supposed to be helping Jamal to collar this Caden Sims, to find out what scheme was afoot.

Which begged a new question …

Jamal had been silent for long minutes. That didn't seem natural, especially given everything going on my end of the conversation. "Uhhh, pal?" I asked, staring past. "Uhmm, buddy?" I didn't want to say his name and thus give anything at all to Soothing to work with. "Hey, yo!"

Soothing just stared at me, and I realized finally that Jamal, for whatever reason, had gone quiet.

And that worried me even more than the sound of sirens that I suddenly heard in the distance.

20.

Reed

I took off after the blond woman as soon as she started to move. She blew past a gurney in the sterile hospital hallway and without even touching it, it flew back at me like Veronika had, shot as though out of an invisible cannon. Its rubber wheels squeaked and rattled as it came for me, and I jumped, tucking my knees up to my chest as it shot under me by mere inches and the top of my head nearly hit the ceiling.

I threw up a wall of wind and the gurney squealed to a stop behind me before it had a chance to ram into anyone else. The danger averted, I looked back at my quarry, expecting her to be only a few dozen paces ahead.

She was already at the end of the hall, dodging around a corner and going blurry again, as though disappearing out of time or something.

I came around the corner and saw the staircase, empty. I blinked, trying to see down, to listen for her, but all I heard was the background noise of a hospital and a vague *skiffing* sound, like rubber-soled shoes on the tile floors.

Veronika's footsteps pounded behind me and she emerged around the corner, covered in dust. "Whoa!" I said. She had a big bleeding cut above her eyebrow and her hair was uncharacteristically mussed.

"Yeah," Veronika said tightly, "you should see what the other girl is going to look like. When I'm through with her, you know."

"If you know where she went, I'm open to—"

"There!" Veronika pointed out a window past the staircase. Sure enough, there was our blond-haired perpetrator, hurriedly walking out of the hospital, across a green lawn toward the street beyond.

"Okay, let's take this easy—" I started.

"Um, how about no," Veronika said, then grabbed me by the shirt and dragged me forward. She lit off her other hand with a plasma blast that scorched through the window and melted the glass to slag, leaving a wide enough path for us to step through. She then threw herself into my arms and I caught her by instinct. She turned her head and favored me with a glare. "Come on, Prince Charming. Carry me down." She batted her eyelashes at me, but I could see the twitch in the corner of her right eye that told me she was at least as angry as she was patronizing.

"Seriously?" I almost dumped her off, but it only took me a moment's consideration to realize that yeah, this was the fastest way to the ground, and really, we did have to go after this lady. Shaking my head, I stepped through the hole she'd made and wafted us to the ground lightly, carrying us forward with a tailwind at the same time, trying to close the distance between us and our quickly escaping fugitive.

"Good call," she said, and gave me a smacking kiss right on the cheek as she leapt out of my arms a few feet above the ground. She got tangled up in the winds and almost faceplanted, but she righted herself just in time, stumbling as she came back up, hands already aglow with plasma. "Hey!" she shouted, her voice crackling across the street. "Hey, bitch! I never call people that, but you—you deserve it!"

There were only a few people walking down the street, almost all of them probably hospital visitors. Every one of them looked at her, including our quarry. The blond woman was already halfway across the street when she stopped, her hair whipping around as she turned to see who would yell such a thing in the middle of a quiet neighborhood. Her expression didn't shift much, just enough to tell me she was beyond panicked about us coming for her.

Veronika heaved a blazing ball of glowing blue plasma at

her before I could tell her not to; it sped through the air toward the blond woman like a fast-pitched blue sun. It burned hot, I knew from experience: hot enough to melt glass, hot enough to turn metal to slag, and hot enough to reduce the woman we were following to a heap of ash. When it was inches from hitting our fugitive it blurred, warping, distorting—

And then it blazed past the blond woman, turbocharged and moving at least twice as fast as it had been before.

"Oh, sh—" Veronika got out as the ball shot toward a residential house across the street, burning, blazing, and streaking toward someone's home like a missile locked on target.

21.

Jamal

Sienna's talk-fest with the guys confronting her was sounding like it was going to explode into the kind of dramatics we had been looking to avoid when we'd come to the Javits Center. She'd lost the mission, and sounded like she was losing her mind, but I was only dimly aware of it, because more interesting things had started to crop up, as though intentionally keeping me from paying attention to her conflict with the new bodyguards of Caden Sims.

It was a little thing at first—a warning that someone knew I was in the surveillance camera system in the Javits Center. A gentle, digital slap to my face, and a hint that something was moving in the system to deny me access. Usually that was the sort of thing that took a while, so I ignored it, thinking I had time to deal.

Less than thirty seconds later, I was locked out of the surveillance camera feeds.

"What the hell?" I muttered. I doubted the Javits Center tech crew had the capability to deny me access. This had to be some sort of White Hat who was off site—or possibly on site, given that it was a tech conference, but one who was outside the employ of the Javits Center itself.

The next thing that happened was that I got booted from the Wi-Fi. No warning, no alarm, just a sudden and abrupt internet disconnection, giving me a lurching feeling like you get when you awaken unexpectedly from a nightmare where you suddenly miss a step. My stomach dropped; my part of this job required internet, and being connected to the Javits Center Wi-Fi was pretty key to my success. I couldn't let it rattle me, though; I switched to 4G LTE and bypassed, snaking my way back in. I snapped through the firewall the long way around and then burst back into the surveillance system in seconds, probably making a lot more electronic noise than I had up until now.

I didn't care. I had a job to do.

I scanned Hall A-1, looking for Caden Sims. I checked the most probable exit, which was the back of the hall, and then leapfrogged from camera to camera until I found him, being hustled along by three sturdy guys, his other bodyguards. They were moving to get him out of there, and I checked their route against the map. They were probably going to try and take him out on 12th Avenue. I pulled up the outdoor NYC traffic cams, searching for his SUV. I had tagged its plates, and sure enough, it showed up heading north up 12th Avenue, squealing to a halt by the curb.

I stood and bolted, grabbing my tablet so I could check the windows I had up on the fly, keeping an eye on Sims as I ran for the exit I was sure he'd use. If I caught him near it, I might be able to dump his phone before he left, and with the plate tagger I could watch his movements through the city's traffic cameras. Our plan may have gotten all jostled up by contact with the enemy, but it didn't have to die right here. This was the way I usually did things, after all, and now that we'd failed the way Sienna wanted to roll with it, there was no reason not to try it my way.

I came down a set of stairs a-leaping like ten lords, then vaulted down another set. The sun was barely peeking through the clouds outside the massive panes of windows that surrounded me. The Javits Center was almost all glass, and that made for a cool look, but I bet on a sunny day it was probably pretty bright and warm.

Fortunately today was neither sunny nor warm, and I shot into a door to the "backstage" areas that weren't part of the general public's routes through the Center. These were darker corridors, where the pipes ran, where the fluorescent lights were hung directly overhead, and there was no sign of glass windows anywhere.

I glanced down at my tablet and almost tripped over my own feet; meta balance was no match for the shock I got when I looked down.

I'd been disconnected from the LTE network, booted out of the cameras again, and kicked offline.

"What the f—" I hesitated, almost stumbled over myself again, and then realized it didn't matter. I knew where Sims was going, and I needed to be there in seconds if I was going to dump his phone before he left. It was all I could think about, getting the data, getting his info. I didn't want to confront him, didn't want to face his bodyguards—or worse, have to kill them—but if I could just get close enough …

I could win the information war, and get us everything we needed to know about who he was dealing with and where he'd been.

I turned around a corner to realize that Sims and his bodyguards were now rushing along behind me. I'd slowed down a little too much, and that was a problem. Because the minute I glanced back, I saw him—and he saw me.

"That's him!" Sims shouted, and his bodyguards stopped. They had him by the arms, physically carrying him along, but that stopped in a hot second as they came to a screeching halt. Seriously, I could hear shoes squealing against the concrete floors as they stopped. "That's the guy that killed my last bodyguard!"

All thought of dumping his phone was gone about a second after that came out, because his bodyguards formed an impenetrable line between us. Sims disappeared behind the line of their bulk, and now they started to advance again, more slowly this time.

At me.

22.

Sienna

"What's that?" Soothing and his two buddies all clutched their earpieces at the same time, like synchronized listening was suddenly a sport. They all had furrowed brows, concentrating hard, clearly giving their full attention to what was being said on the other end of the conversation.

"Trouble," I said, and threw a punch while Soothing was distracted. I caught him in the nose and it crumpled, he crumpled, blood went everywhere, and he hit the ground like a bag of gourds. I shot a look at the nearest of the two bodyguards who had already surrendered their pride to me in exchange for their lives and asked, "Where?"

He swallowed, comically, and threw his thumb over his shoulder toward a series of doors at the end of the room. "They hustled him out through there. They'd be heading—" He turned, pointing along the back of the room, "That way. Toward 12th."

Someone yelled something in his ear so loud I could hear the feedback, and he ripped the earpiece out and offered it to me wordlessly. The lady with him did exactly the same, like offerings to a goddess, and I snatched one of them as I went by. "Don't bodyguard for bad guys," I said, and they both nodded furiously. "It'll get you in trouble."

"Yes, ma'am!" one of them called as I burst into flight. "Thank you!" Sirens were still blaring outside, and I had a feeling the cops would be nigh pretty quick. I shot through the door they'd indicated, and zoomed down the hall until I reached a four-way intersection of painted concrete block. I froze there, listening intently, and jammed the earpiece the bodyguard had given me into my ear, hoping to hear a clue.

"—you give us away?" someone asked, sounding deeply agitated. "Lawrence! Answer me!"

"Lawrence can't come to the phone right now," I said breathily, giving him my most husky voice. "If you'd like to leave a message—or better yet, save your own life—please press one to surrender now."

"Press—what?" the guy practically shouted back. "There's no keypad on this thing! Who is this?"

"Sienna Nealon," I said flatly. "I'm coming down the corridor for you now." I picked a direction and hoped it was right, following the general direction of where my little helper had tried to guide me, trying to reconcile it with the map I had in my head of the Javits Center. Technically, I was off map at the moment, but that didn't matter, because I was pretty sure of my general direction. "Surrender your boss by the time I get there or you're going to surrender your lives when I do. Half your people are already out of the fight."

"SHIT!" the guy on the other end shouted. "It's her! She's here for real! Switch to channel twelve!" There was a little burst of static, then three others.

I pulled the earpiece out of my ear, and conveniently, right on the outside of it was a little dial. I switched it to twelve and put it back in my ear, just in time to hear them talking.

"Who is this guy standing in our way?" one of them said. "Looks like a geek."

"My accomplice," I said, just trying to get them to lose their shit now that they had no line of communication I couldn't tap. "Surrender now, or I will gut you with my bare hands when I get there." I wouldn't do that, mostly because getting guts on your hands is really gross. It's like playing in a bloody toilet, and who wants to do that?

Wolfe!

"Other than you. Nobody wants to do that other than you."

"What the hell?" A highly distraught male voice broke into

the line.

"Get this guy!" Another shouted. "We need to clear the area and extract the principal."

"Try it and I'm gonna extract your spleen," I said, my bag bouncing against my hindquarters. Annoying. "Might want to give that a thought before you try and extract Caden Sims from this area. Seriously, I have very short fingernails. It's gonna hurt a lot when I tear you open." I made a face, thinking it was lucky they couldn't see me, because I was grossing myself out as I was threatening them. Lucky thing Sienna Nealon had a reputation for horrific violence, even if it wasn't *entirely* well-deserved.

"Oh God, oh God!" one of them shouted, panic clearly setting in. "This isn't worth it!"

"It's really not," I added, chipper as hell. "I bet you don't even get a 401(k). Not that you'll survive long enough to retire."

"We have a job to do!" shouted one of them, clearly made of sterner stuff than the other guys.

"Unemployment line or gruesome death," I said, sounding extra contemplative as I zoomed around a corner. There was nothing ahead of me as far as I could see, just an intersection in the far distance. "I know which one I'd choose, but then, I guess I've always favored continuing to live over having my intestines pulled out of my still-living body—"

"I GIVE UP! I GIVE UP!"

"Cedrick, get back here, you pansy!" Stern Stuff shouted. Something thumped, and then retreating footsteps rang out somewhere ahead of me. A man in a suit sprinted through the intersection without stopping, and suddenly I had a very clear idea of where I needed to go.

I rounded the corner as a bolt of lightning surged past me. Far ahead I could see Jamal, electricity lancing wildly out of his fingers. There was a really big guy between us who had just flattened himself and two others against the wall. His chest was bulging, his shirt shredded, and I knew instantly I had a Hercules on my hands. He saw me coming and whipped a hand back, crushing his way through the block wall behind him. He disappeared through it, dragging Caden

Sims and another figure with him, and I heard a mighty smack as he slapped a hand against the wall above his impromptu exit.

Concrete blocks collapsed, along with the ceiling, and Jamal disappeared as the hallway came down between us, a cloud of dust billowing out, separating us from each other and our subject.

23.

Reed

Veronika's plasma burst streaked toward the house across the street from the hospital like a stray bullet, certain death heading towards unsuspecting souls. There might be nobody home or half a dozen people there; there was no way to tell except by the screams after it hit … and then it would be too late.

Something about the scene before me felt like the hard click of a gun's hammer being drawn back in my head. I was instantly breathless, as though I'd ripped all the air out of my own lungs. I couldn't think straight, couldn't see anything but the blitz of blue light streaking toward the house, toward murder, toward inevitable destruction—

I saw a little family in my mind's eye, a woman and an infant, imagined them disintegrated by the blast of blue, the mother covering her baby while the indifferent plasma burned them alive—

I didn't even realize I was screaming, wind blotting out the sound as hurricane forces descended around me. Without conscious thought on my part, my hand stretched forth and marshalled the winds. A curtain of air roiled and twisted, a miniature tornado assembled in less than a second caught the wavering ball of plasma in its swirling depths, absorbing the flickering ball—

Then bursting into blue flame, the heat dispersing over the body of the funnel cloud. It was a glowing tornado, coruscating like a living thing, its winds telescoping as it swirled, inevitably, toward the house. My unthinking, reflexive gambit had not stopped the blue plasma, it had only dispersed it, causing it to expand across the surface of my tornado. Now, instead of a compact blast of death, I had a blazing hot whirlwind of it, carried forward by momentum toward that house, that lone house, the arch of its roof seeming to invite death forward as my tornado sailed toward it.

"NOOOOOOOO!" My voice was scratchy, almost unrecognizable, and I jerked a hand skyward. The tornado took some small heed, churning its way across the street, leaving a scorching crater a foot wide in its wake, writing like the finger of hell across the asphalt. It jumped the curb, scorching the concrete and working its way across the lawn in a blazing swath as I pushed on forces inside myself.

I called to the clouds, the winds above, grabbed hold of everything I could. I was in pure panic, lashing out and reacting without reason or thought. My brain was not functioning on a conscious level but the need was clear:

I had to stop death. For death was coming to the people in that house, just as surely as any of the tornadoes I'd dispersed these last months would have wreaked havoc on the unsuspecting.

My body dragged along the lawn, tearing up divots in the earth as I tried to hold back the tide of this storm. The winds I was stirring were roiling wild, almost out of control, the plasma having heated them to the point where they were more difficult to handle than tame, cool air. Air infused with plasma heat seemed to border on the edge of my domain, and the resistance was stiff, dragging me physically across the lawn as I tethered myself to the tornado.

I shot off the ground, blasting off, leapfrogging up and above the tornado, above the conical top that blazed a bright and hellish blue. I felt like I was lifting it myself, trying to pull an impossible weight, as though I'd maxed out in the gym and could lift no more but HAD TO, because lives were on the line. I tugged hard, ripping my arms upward as though yanking a rope attached to a multi-ton weight. My muscles were puny, weak, their effectiveness at an end.

My power surged as I tapped the skies above. These were winds I could control, ride, hold. I drew their power down to me, used the sky as my anchor and pulled once more on the hellish fury roiling below. I couldn't see the house at this point, I only knew that it was down there, below the glowing blue tornado that spat ruinous blue washes of plasma as it tried to claw at the ground, to suck up anything into its cone of destruction that it could.

Sweat poured off my forehead, down my back. I shouted into the ether, the empty air before me, summoning everything I could, calling to every gust or possible gust or molecule I could hitch myself to. My head hurt like I'd pumped air in both ears, my body strained as though I was being torn apart. I lifted and pulled and tugged and warred with the tornado below. Blue plasmatic heat spilled out the top like a cup that ran over, the energy dispersing as it came out of the edges, convection carrying it off into the atmosphere.

I almost fell into its depths, I felt so weak. It was worse than any lift I'd ever done, worse than picking up a car and throwing it with my bare hands. It was a full garbage truck laden with lead bricks, and I was trying to drive it into the sky. I screamed and shouted and pulled and cried, watching the cone slow, the heat bleed. It was over the house by now, but I couldn't see what was left behind, couldn't see if I'd had any effect at all or if I'd left a wrecked home in my wake.

The goblet top of the tornado spilled its last blue, and suddenly it was just wind again, slowing and stopping, the funnel cloud vanishing just like the heated plasma that had turned it into a hellish vortex. I stared down, my brain so drained of energy that I couldn't even process what I saw at first. It took me a minute to realize what I was even looking at.

It was a house.

That was still standing.

And the burn trail left by the plasma tornado stopped halfway across the lawn.

There were people below, staring up, pointing up, but they

were all blurry to me. I took a breath, then another, air returning to my lungs like welcome visitors that I hadn't seen in some time. I fell six inches, then two feet, then another six, halting myself each time. I could not recall being this exhausted, not even when I stopped tornadoes. I couldn't recall being this likely to fall, either; I'd slept in the clouds these last two months, after all.

I slipped toward the ground in fits and starts, dropping a few feet at a time until I landed hard on the unscathed part of the lawn. Veronika ran up to me, ashen, relief all over her face. "You did it," she whispered, voice cracking with the fear that came from a very near miss. She caught me, threaded an arm around me, and I passed out in her arms, wondering dimly where the blond woman who started this whole mess had gotten off to.

24.

Jamal

When the roof came down and cut me off from Sienna, it came as kind of a relief. Not because of her, but because I'd been scrapping with those bodyguards of Caden's and it hadn't been going very well. I'd shot lightning at them, they'd dodged, and I was starting to worry I might have to actually hit one of them when she'd shown up and saved my day.

Then the big guy had ripped himself, Sims, and another one through the wall, and that was that, because the curtain came right down on our little play, and when the dust settled a few seconds later, there wasn't any obvious path through the debris.

"Sienna!" I shouted, touching my earpiece. I pulled it out and stared at it; I hadn't even realized I'd put it on mute. "Sienna!" I said, popping it back on.

"Yeah," she said, sounding a little irritated. "You there?"

"I'm here," I said. "You okay?"

"Dusty, but … yeah," she said. "You don't have eyes on these guys, do you?"

"No," I said, and turned around, looking for my tablet. I found it a few feet behind me, covered in dust but fortunately spared the fall of the ceiling. I turned it on and tried to get back online. "I know where they were going before, but … I can't see them now. Someone's locked me out of the system. Trying to get back online now—"

"Don't," she said. "The cops are probably in the center by

now. We need to get the hell out of here."

"What about Sims?" I asked, unable to fully surrender the idea of dumping his phone. I really wanted that data, wanted something, anything to make up for what had just happened here. Because all this had been for nothing if I didn't get his phone.

"What about jail?" she retorted. "Because I'm guessing the NYPD isn't going to be super merciful to either of us if we get caught here."

"Can you … I dunno, go through the wall after them?" I asked, looking back down at my tablet, trying to reestablish a connection. I was still getting blocked, and I figured it was at the local tower level. Maybe if I switched providers …

"Probably," she said tightly, "but given our luck today, I'd probably hit a load-bearing wall and bring down half the Javits Center on us. Not sure I should chance that."

"Damn," I said, mind already whirling to defeat whoever had locked me out. I was switching up, hoping Verizon would be my ticket back online. I turned and started to run back down the tunnel, taking a turn at the nearest intersection. Maybe they'd still go for the planned exit that they'd worked out before. Maybe I could still catch them.

"Yeah, it's time to scamper," she said, and air rushed against her microphone.

"We rendezvous back at the hotel?" I asked, turning the corner and bursting through a set of doors. I was back out in the convention center, daylight shining through those massive glass exterior walls, the metal holding them stretching up like a squarish geodesic dome.

"No," she said. "Too hot. I've got some of my stuff on me, and I left the rest in a duffel on the hotel rooftop early this morning. Once I swing by and grab it, I'm gonna bail on New York. We'll regroup somewhere else. Get out of town."

"But Sims is here—"

"Fine, stay if you want," she said, "but I have to go. I am not getting in a scrap with the NYPD." She lowered her voice and I heard hard resolve. "Because I don't think there's a way out of that where someone doesn't die."

I looked up from my tablet. "Them or you?"

"I don't know," she said, sounding a little more haunted than I would have thought. "Push comes to shove … I shove back pretty hard. I'd rather not find out what I'd do if backed into a corner."

"Yeah, well—" I stopped midstride as my tablet reconnected to the internet. There was a small but surging crowd still around me, people flooding trying to get out of the Javits Center. "Hold it, I'm back online and—"

I paused. Someone in front of me spun around in the crowd, tossing me a look. It was a woman, with brown hair and olive skin, eyes narrow, dark, and lacking the panic I saw on other faces. She was pretty, her hair wavy and her clothes looking a little formal underneath a baggy brown trench coat, which was a little retro. She wasn't freaking out, she wasn't worried, she was just going with the flow, and she'd turned around on me the minute she'd heard me say something about being back online—

Over a crowd.

In a convention hall where people were panicking and stampeding for the exit.

She'd *heard* me.

And she had a tablet clutched in her hand, too.

"Holy shit," I muttered to myself as she met my eyes, then dropped a finger on the screen of her tablet. Mine honked at me, and I stared at the words written across the screen—

DISCONNECTED

Again.

I looked her in the eyes and she stared right back at me, defiant.

I realized I'd just met ArcheGrey1819 in the flesh.

25.

Sienna

Chaos wasn't a good scene for me, but it was a pretty common one. I burst out of the Javits Center with the rest of the crowd, trying to lose myself in it. I was pissed that I'd let Harmon work me over like that, pissed I'd burned off my wig, but I was trying to keep my head down and about me, trying to blend in with the panicked people fleeing—well, I didn't know what they thought they were fleeing, but probably a fire or terrorists or metas or something.

"Ahhhh!" I screamed in a passable imitation of panic. My mascara had run thanks to copious amounts of sweat, and seeing another woman across the crowd suffering the same thing, but probably from tears of panic, reassured me that maybe I still had a thin veneer of disguise to keep me safe as I got the hell away from the Javits Center. After all, the last thing I needed now was to get cornered by some well-meaning member of the NYPD, which was why I was doing my best to lead the crowd surge across 11th until I could break away from them and get to an alley, then zoom out of there before they managed to lock down the crowds. I had a feeling it'd be a long time before they'd let everyone go, because it wasn't an uncommon tactic for criminals and terrorists to try and make their escape from a scene by hiding in among the sheep.

I needed to be out of the vicinity of the Javits Center long before they got things under control, and to that end I finally broke out of the crowd and started to run, feet a few inches off the ground in order to make it slightly easier on myself. I'd worn heels, after all, trying to match them to the disguise, and I wasn't that practiced in them. Wobbly would have been a good way to describe me, so floating while adopting the natural up and down bobbing of a run was a little easier, allowed me to mimic normal human speed as I ran between cars, bag still flopping against my back, heading up the street by dodging through the already jammed traffic.

I made it about two blocks and was ready to rejoin the crowd on the sideway when I heard the shout from above. I thought I'd gotten away with it, too, but the booming voice from above quickly disabused me of that clever notion.

"SIENNA NEALON!" the shout rang out, causing every head on the sidewalks to swivel toward me, and every eye to search me out.

Including one that was hovering overhead on a sled of ice, staring down at me with bitter anger born of our previous associations.

And he was still wearing yoga pants.

"Captain Frost," I called back, sighing. "Fancy meeting you here."

26.

Jamal

I didn't know whether I was more shocked by the fact that ArcheGrey was standing not twenty feet from me, or by the fact that ArcheGrey was a *girl*.

Err, I mean, a lady. A woman.

A very pretty, strangely dressed woman.

"ArcheGrey1819!" I shouted, my excitement bubbling over before I could contain myself.

If I'd wanted my suspicions confirmed, I couldn't have picked a better way to do it. Her eyes went wide, like the size of golf balls, and she leapt up out of the crowd in a metahuman jump, soaring twenty feet, and caught the steel skeleton framework that laced over the windows.

"Holeeeeee," I said as the crowd screamed. Now they'd seen a meta in the middle of this incident, and that did nothing for their calm. The stampede to the doors went wild, and I heard glass breaking somewhere over the heads of those trying to force their way out the doors.

For her part, ArcheGrey started running along the steel inner skeleton of the Javits Center, zipping around the vertical crossbeams as she made her escape. The sound of her feet against the beams did not register over the crowd as she hurried away from me.

I'd already lost Caden Sims, and now I saw my last thin thread making its escape. Something about it caused a surge of desperation in me. I wasn't normally the run and chase kind, but she was getting away …

I shoved my tablet down in the outside pocket of my bag and zipped it shut. Then I leapt into the air, grabbing hold of one of the crossbeams on the frame as I mimicked her move, and started to chase after ArcheGrey.

The crowd screamed again. Now they had two meta menaces to worry about as I ran and swung past a crossbeam. ArcheGrey was at least twenty crossbeams ahead of me—probably a hundred feet or so—and I was going to have to haul ass to catch up. It was like running an obstacle course, like running along the top of the monkey bars and dodging the poles that sprang up every few feet. My meta dexterity was the only thing saving me from a certain plummet to the uneven ground.

She leapt again, straight up, and I saw that ahead was the second floor, with escalators leading up to it. A sensible person would have just taken those, but I had lost all sense a while back. I had to catch her. She was my only lead now, my only chance to figure out what Caden Sims was up to with his dark plans and crazy rants about the grid and his connections to trouble.

I jumped after her, and ArcheGrey didn't stay on the upper beam for more than a couple seconds. She leapt lightly off and onto the upper floor as I started to follow. She cast a look back at me, and for just a second I thought she'd just run on and leave me behind to try and outpace her once I was on solid ground.

But she didn't.

I realized what she was going to do—and what she was—the moment that the lightning flared in her eyes. It lit her up like a thunderstorm, and she raised her hands, still hidden in her bulky brown trench coat, and pointed them at the metal crossbeams that I was presently holding onto.

Her hands glowed, and electricity danced from her fingertips, a thousand bolts of small lightning coruscating through the air until they hit the metal skeleton and electrified it, thousands and thousands of volts running through my body as I hung there, twenty feet in the air and with nowhere to run.

27.

Sienna

"Yes, fancy meeting you here as well," Captain Frost said, sounding a little like Nathan Fillion's Captain Hammer, "just a couple blocks away from a terrorist incident." He came gliding down on his ice, watching me without daring to look away, probably because we'd clashed before and he had presumably learned during that encounter not to underestimate me. "It's almost like you're wanted, criminal scum."

"'Criminal scum'? You're a sad man, Frost," I heaved back at him with minimal vitriol. I was keeping one eye on him and another on the sky, because my need to bolt was getting urgent. People were on their cell phones all up and down the sidewalk now, and at least some of them were probably reporting my presence to the cops, which was unlikely to defuse an already tense situation. "A sad, lonely-heart, groupie-boffing little man."

"I'm a hero," Frost said, sticking his chin out. "Which is more than I can say for you."

"You're an idiot, and you're going to evolve from that into a bloody puddle if you don't get the hell out of my way," I said. I had six different ideas in mind for taking him out already, but only a couple of them were non-lethal. As much as I disliked Frost, dislike was not sufficient grounds for murdering the bastard, at least not to me.

A principled, wanted fugitive. What a strange place I was

in, mentally. And physically, since it was New York City.

"I can't let you escape," Frost said, preening for the crowd, unmoved by my threat. "That's not what a hero would do." He stuck out his chin and struck a pose, and I barely avoided the vaunted double facepalm. For use when a single facepalm simply did not express the depths of one's disbelief at the stupidity on display.

"Okay, well," I said, and thrust out a hand without further ado. I blasted a net at him while he struck his pose and it caught him off balance, knocking him backward off his ice slide. He thudded against the hood of a taxi cab, his legs splayed wide and his head resting in a spiderweb of cracks on the front windshield.

"You can't *let* me do anything," I said as I lifted off, "because you lack the power required to make me do jack sh—"

Frost lanced out at me with an ice blast that caught me right on the shoulder. It stung like hell, like someone had burned my arm off (which had happened in the past), and suddenly my arm was buried in a ton of extra weight. I blinked in surprise at the sudden, tumorous mass that enshrouded my entire left arm, and sucked in a frigid breath. I went a little woozy, my brain chilled at the sudden freezing effect of ice-cold blood drawn from my capillaries and veins into the rest of my body.

I wavered and then crashed, smashing into a lamp post. Something shattered, and it took me a second to realize it was my arm. I crashed into the sidewalk as people gasped and jumped out of my way. My jaw made hard contact with concrete, and my already wavering consciousness flagged as I rolled.

My eyes fluttered, threatening to cast me into darkness at any second. I exhaled, and my breath frosted in front of me. "Shit," I said, barely getting it out, the pain in my numb shoulder like a distant thing, miles away, and my eyes fluttered once again and closed.

28.

Jamal

Ten thousand volts crackled around me, running through my body and into my skin, into me, and I held up my head and breathed in deep. It smelled like ozone, the glass darkened in the spots where the lightning hit it as it coursed through the metal frame that held the exterior of the Javits Center together.

The bolt found me, running into my heart, through my muscles, sparking across my flesh, and it felt like …

… like …

… Heaven.

"Ahhhhhh," I said, stretching where I hung on the frame. I opened my eyes to see ArcheGrey still standing there, only slightly more concerned than she'd been a moment before, when she'd cut loose with the lightning. "Mmm. That's good juice. Got any more?"

I leapt off the frame and landed a few steps away from her. She stared at me with dark eyes that still crackled with electricity. She burned, mouth all pouty, and I was all ready to go after her again when she flipped over the tables on me.

"I don't think this is gonna wo—" I started to say, and caught another flash of lightning at her baggy sleeves. Bolts started to snake out, but they looked different this time, less fluid and electrical and more—

Solid.

A snakelike lash of electricity jumped out of her sleeve and extended toward me as though it had a mind of its own. It caught me around the neck and flared, voltage dumping through my system. I absorbed that, no problem, but while I was distracted the coil finished wrapping around my neck and I suddenly realized that the sparking, snaking, dazzling electrical part of this show was just that, for me at least. A show.

The coil of metal underneath, the thing she was using to channel her power, that cranked me around the neck as she jerked and hauled me off my feet with metahuman strength. My shoes trailed the last hints of electricity as they broke contact with the grounding of the floor and ArcheGrey flung me with her coiled lash over the balcony and down.

I fell thirty feet and slammed into an abandoned coffee cart, breaking wood and what felt like my neck and back. It all came crashing down on me a second later, and a big pot of steaming coffee burned me across my chest and neck where the lash had just let go of me. I screamed and tried to brush it off, feeling the spikes of pain across my back and side. I hadn't broken my back, but I'd probably done in a few ribs.

"You shouldn't have come here." The soft voice came over me only a second before that lash wrapped, sparking, around my neck again. She jerked me up and I could hear the sound of hydraulic motors cranking somewhere up her sleeve. She brought me up so she could look me eye to eye, and I stared at her as she stared back at me. She reached out with her other hand and grabbed my knapsack. I heard ten thousand volts go through it, and if my tablet had survived her first attack, it damned sure didn't survive that.

I didn't know how to answer that, and I didn't get a chance. She punched me in the nose and it broke, blood rushing down my chin and in the back of my throat. It hurt worse than anything I could remember happening to me, including the scalding coffee and broken ribs. It wasn't just the hurt itself, it was the pride-deep wound I took getting manhandled like this.

"I don't ever want to see you again," she said, and I squeezed my eyes open enough to stare at her. She didn't look so pretty now. Now she looked terrifying, and maybe terrified, too, that I'd gotten as close to her as I had. "If I see you again …" Her voice drifted off, like she was contemplating the consequences for herself, "… I'll kill you."

She threw me, machinery whirring up her sleeve again, propelling me out of her hand at the end of the lash, which was flaring with lightning. I flew over the heads of the last member of the fleeing crowd, catching their screams as I went. I hit one of the big steel beams of the building's skeleton and flipped, smashing through the glass exterior of the Javits Center. It cut me all over, but I barely felt it as I plummeted down to the sidewalk below.

I was unconscious before I hit the ground.

29.

Reed

My nightmares all involved opening doors.

You'd think for a man that had lived in human society all his life, opening a door would be a simple thing. You just reach out, take hold of the knob, and turn. If there's a lock, you fumble with your keys and they rattle, metal clacking lightly against metal, until you find the right one, and insert it, wobbly, into its home, giving it a turn to finish things.

Doors were now my greatest fear, and the reason I'd spent the last two months living in the clouds, where there were no doors to be found, no great portals barring entry. No doors to knock on, no doors to kick in, no knobs to turn.

I hated doors. Which is why I wanted to live outside of them.

I imagined my own front door, dancing across my dreams as though unhinged, wavering, diagonal, off-kilter. It fluttered in the harsh wind that came its way, rattling as it hung open, then slammed closed with a sound of violence akin to a gunshot.

I shuddered inside; gunshots … those were my next least-favorite thing, after doors.

Ambling up my own porch steps, I paused at the closed door, eyeing the knob. Hadn't this been easy before? Hadn't it been simple? Most people never even gave this a thought, it was so ingrained in their routine. You simply … open the door. Could there be anything easier?

I reflected, standing there upon my own porch … that yes, many things were easier. Turning around and leaving seemed easier. Flying off to hang about in the empty clouds, where the sky was by turns blue and black and shades between, was a far, far easier thing than even knocking on this particular door, never mind actually opening it.

It was all about the doors. I'd gone through one in Cheyenne, Wyoming, that had changed things for me.

But I tried not to think about that door, or what happened behind it.

I'd been trying not to think of it for two months. But I dreamed of it every night, despite my best efforts, and my mind locked upon it several times a day, in spite of my intent.

I went through that door in Wyoming … and did something there. Something … horrific. Something … unspeakable.

And because of it, I couldn't even imagine walking through the door of my own house. Not now.

Not ever.

So I stood on the porch in my nightmare, frozen in time, staring at the door in front of me, willing it to open, and hoping it wouldn't, all the same. And I stood there in the darkness, caught between the two outcomes, as I so often was during these long nights in the clouds, wondering which particular outcome was going to be the one to cause me pain this time.

30.

Sienna

Losing a limb hurts quite a lot, usually. This time it didn't hurt quite so bad, probably because I was still dealing with the numbing pain of the ice that Frost had encased it in before I'd fallen. I'd clearly hit my head either against the lamp post or against the concrete, or possibly both, because my head was bleeding and aching like someone had rung my bell with a sledgehammer.

Pain lanced up and down my back, causing me to arch it as I squirmed against the concrete, people scrambling away from me like they'd lose their souls if they got too close (a not unreasonable fear). Screams of shock made their way through the thick membrane of darkness squeezing against my conscious mind, threatening to drag me back into painful slumber. Some of the screams might have been mine, but most of them were from the people around me.

"Wolfe …" I moaned, rolling from side to side, my back feeling particularly abused at the moment. Worse than the arm I no longer had, surprisingly. "… A little … help …"

Arm is coming back, Wolfe said, calmer than I was. *Hurrying.*

"Graci … as ," I said, that band of black unconsciousness fading as the healing kicked in.

De nada, Wolfe said.

This has been so much fun, Harmon said. *Why don't we come to New York more often?*

"Could use a … threat assessment …" I muttered,

focusing on Harmon with that statement.

He looked around theatrically in my head. *Who … me?* He looked around again, catching an ireful glare from all the other souls in my head. *Oh, you're looking for a team player. That's not me. I'm a solo act.*

Going to be solo in receiving a beating in a moment, Bjorn said, cracking knuckles he no longer had.

I would relish the chance to assault a former president, Eve said menacingly. *You are a soft, weak little man.*

Bastian was cringing. *Sir … please. If someone takes her out right now, while she's vulnerable … you're on the line, too.*

Harmon seemed inscrutable for a moment. *Oh, fine.* He nodded somewhere in the darkness. *That guy. Over there. He'll be a problem.*

"Talking about … Frost?" My eyes were at least half-closed. I wasn't much for writhing in pain, but something about all the damage I'd just taken had essentially shut down my body, and I was only now starting to get control over it again. Maybe it was the cold, maybe I'd fallen farther or harder than I'd thought, or maybe it was the head injury.

No, no, he's still fumbling about in that improvised mask you gave him, Harmon said. *That guy. There.*

"Wh—"

Someone kicked me in the ribs, which were already in a painful way, and it sent agony surging down my side. I let out a gasp and my eyes snapped open. A scraggly-bearded guy with an actual man bun and fearful eyes looked down at me, and then reared back for another kick.

Skin him alive in answer for this insult! Wolfe screamed in my head.

Harmon! I shouted as the next kick landed. It was human, which was to say not as bad as it could have been, but it still made me writhe in agony.

No, Harmon said. *Maybe you should make your shirtless Norseman give him a headache.* He sighed, deeply. *There I go, helping again. I truly am a generous fellow. You've all got the wrong of me.*

"Bjorn!" I said, and the bastard leaned back for another frenzied kick. He was way more panicked than I was, and was waving for other people to get in on the action of beating the shit out of me, brave soul that he was.

His agony will be delicious, Bjorn said with a big smile, and let loose a blast of the warmind that sent Beardo McMan-Bun ass over teakettle onto the cold sidewalk like he'd been punched in the face. He let out a pitiful moan and kicked me spasmodically, catching me in the shoulder I still had. It was a lot weaker, probably because it was an involuntary twitch of the muscles rather than a solid attempt to bust me up the way he'd been trying to a few seconds before.

Almost done, Wolfe said, still seething at an ordinary person taking liberties by trying to beat me down. *Then we can—*

Leave, I said firmly. I wasn't skinning anyone alive and eating their flesh. At least not today, and certainly not a man who smelled like he hadn't bathed this week. His man bun looked positively sticky. A sticky bun.

I sat up and then got to my knees. The rest of the crowd that surrounded me was easing back, probably fearing my wrath since I'd already sent one of their number to the pavement without word or action. "That's right," I grunted as I stood up, "keep your distance and we'll all just go on about our lives. Nobody has to lose life or limb." I glanced down at my arm, which had regrown to the elbow, where fingers were sprouting. "Well, no one else does, anyway."

You lost your bag, Harmon said, a little too gleefully for my taste.

"See? Now that's actually helping," I said, looking right at a woman in the crowd who got all wide-eyed and panicky when I looked at her. She looked around left and then right, as though she'd been chosen for attention by mistake. It might have been funny to watch if I hadn't been rapidly—and painfully—regrowing a radius and an ulna. "Where did my bag g—"

I didn't even get it out before another guy in the crowd turned and bolted, a very familiar bag slung across his back. He was hauling ass, too, vaulting over the hood of a cab stuck in the next intersection like he was a master of parkour.

"Sonofa," I muttered and started forward, taking a second to vaporize my severed arm, which had fallen about ten feet away from me. People screamed, cars honked their horns, and I lifted off into the air, shooting after the guy who'd stolen my bag.

I swooped down on him within half a block, grabbing him by the back of his coat and carrying him into the sky. He screamed and thrashed, then got real quiet after we got about five floors up. The cold wind assailed us as we rose, and I dropped him on the roof of a ten-story building and he rolled, finishing on his back and staying there, lifting up shaking hands.

"Give me the bag," I said, hovering a few inches above the rooftop and making the "come hither," gesture. My arm was almost regrown, though I was missing most of my sleeve now, which exposed me to the icy wind. The new skin was all covered over in goosebumps, and I shivered as I waited for this guy to wise up.

"A—anything you say!" He struggled and pulled the bag off, tossing it to me but coming a few feet short. I rolled my eyes and dropped down, snatching up the bag and opening it. I figured I'd grab my cell phone and try to call Jamal since I'd lost the headset somewhere along the way.

The problem was … none of my stuff was in the bag.

"What the hell?" I asked, pulling out a tiny Mac computer covered in stickers for what I presumed were bands.

"Please don't hurt me!" the guy said. "Just take it. My wallet's inside."

"I didn't—I'm not robbing you—"

He looked like he was trying to disappear into the rooftop. "Of course not. No. I'm *giving* you this—"

"No, you jackass!" I put his computer back inside and tossed his bag back at him, as lightly as frustration and my meta strength allowed. It hit him in the gut, prompting a "WHUMP!" noise as all the air left him. "I thought you stole my bag! Now I see it's not, so …" My eyes narrowed, and in my head I said, *Harmon …*

Oh, I'm sorry … did I give you the impression he stole your bag? My mistake. It was on the ground when we left.

"You truly are a son of a bitch," I said aloud, and the guy who I had just assaulted cringed, big, leaky tears coming down his cheeks. "Not you! Not you! I'm sorry for this. Do you want me to take you back to the street?" He shook his head, still crying. "I doubt this will mean much, but I really am sorry. This was just a huge misunderstanding." I was burning with embarrassment. "You sure you don't want me to take you back to the street? It's pretty cold up here." He shook his head again, still crying. "I mean, you could end up with hypothermia. You might lose a toe. Why don't we just—" He shook his head more fiercely and even bigger tears came dripping down his cheeks. "Dude, this is stupid. We have to get you off this roof. Really. Life or death. You can't just—"

I reached for him and he freaked out, not unreasonably, screaming and trying to whack me with flailing hands. I let him, grabbing him like I had before and making sure I held both him and his bag, snugly, and shot over the edge of the rooftop. He batted at my face and my chest and my arms, annoying me more than doing any damage, and by the time we reached ground level a few seconds later, it was taking all I had in me not to give him a smack across the back of the head that would probably do permanent brain damage.

"I was trying to help you, idiot!" I shouted as I dropped him off—gently—well, mostly gently—on the sidewalk. "And I'm sorry!" I shouted over my shoulder as I flew back to the scene of my unhappy landing. There was still a crowd, but they scattered as I came in for a landing. Cop car lights were flashing only a block up, and I knew I had to make this fast because the NYPD was probably pounding along the pavement toward me at this point since traffic hadn't moved one iota.

I paused just above my landing site, marveling for a half second because there was still one lady just standing there, utterly frozen, like Frost had encased her in ice. She looked too scared to move, but to her credit, at least she didn't appear to have a wet spot on her pants. She'd gone right past fight and flight and settled on freeze. It wouldn't have been a good instinct if I had been there to wreak havoc, but fortunately for her I wasn't a predator intent on preying on her.

"Excuse me," I said, as gently as I could, "have you seen my bag, by any chance?" She stared at me with horrified eyes. "It's black, and about yea big," I made motions with my hands, "probably fell off me when I lost my arm and came crashing down?"

She stared at me for a full second, and then her wide eyes went back to normal, like I'd broken her hypnotization. She raised a hand and pointed into the street, and spoke, calmly, even sedately. "Yeah, it's right over there, under that taxi cab."

I turned and looked, and sure enough, it had fallen under a taxi that was stuck in the gridlock. "Thanks!" I said and darted over to the car. The driver screamed in the confines of his vehicle and dove down in his seat, probably assuming I was there to murder him and curse his children or something. I ducked down and fished my bag out, re-slinging it over my shoulder.

When I stood up, a blast of ice pelted me right in the chest and sent me backward, prompting a sickening crunch as I landed on my back. The pain in my kidney area told me at least one of my burner phones had just bitten the dust, and I looked up to see Captain Frost incoming, rage all over the parts of his face I could see, along with a little blood. It looked like he'd ripped my light mask off along with a healthy dollop of his face, and his resemblance to some sort of half-assed version of the Red Skull was uncanny.

People screamed—this time, fortunately, not at me. Frost came arcing down, hand raised high, clearly prepared to deal me a fatal blow on landing. I stared at him, almost disbelieving as he came closer and closer, legs spread wide and knees bent to absorb the shock of his landing. He was going to land astride me, going to smash my head to pulp against the curb, and I suspected he thought there was nothing I could do about it.

Which was just another reason he was an idiot.

I lifted my leg coolly and angled it so my foot was ready to greet him. He came down as planned, encountered my foot with his yoga pants covered crotch, and his scream hit octaves reserved for calling dogs. The bottom of my foot smashed both of his testicles to paste, and I could feel them pop even through the shock of his body landing full force on the bottom of my foot.

He bounced off my greeting kick and smacked into the taxi cab that had sheltered my bag, cracking his head against the cab window (again). He whelped and cried, clutching delicately at his crotch, rolling in the street, covered in slush.

I stood gingerly and stretched, Wolfe's healing already doing its part to make me feel worlds better. I flicked a light net into his face again, trying to cover all of it but his mouth, and it worked, leaving him with a glowing look akin to a faceless man. It was going to hurt to rip that off, and I willed it to remain on his head as long as possible. He didn't seem to notice, though, because his attention was still fully on the damage I'd done to him below the belt.

"Jackass," I said, and cracked my back, trying to get it back into realignment. I looked at the small remnants of the crowd still lingering on the sidewalk, still cowed in fear except for the woman that had told me where to recover my bag. "Thanks, New York. You've been just great. See you again hopefully never." And I lifted off into the sky and blew out of there at top speed, heading for the cover of the clouds above and causing the buildings of Manhattan to shake as the sonic boom I trailed behind me hit them.

31.

Reed

"Hey," Veronika said as I came to in a darkened hotel room, the curtain drawn and her shadow obvious by its lustrous hair, even in the semi-dark. She sounded concerned but I couldn't see her face, and she smelled faintly of drywall dust and sweat, which suggested she had been too busy watching over me to shower.

"Hey yourself," I said, not trying to conceal the annoyance in my voice. I remembered what had happened, and my irritation at having to exert myself to the point of passing out because of her dumbass maneuver bled through.

"It was an accident," she said, a little more subdued than she might usually have been.

"Going through the wall in the hospital was an accident," I said. "Causing a stray plasma burst to nearly incinerate someone's home falls out of 'accident' territory and moves into the realm of 'blatant dumbassery.'"

"Ouch."

"Took the words right out of my mouth." I sat up gingerly, my body filled with a kind of weary exhaustion that closely bordered pain.

"Oh, yeah?" She moved comfortably into snarky defiance. "I didn't see you get hurled through a wall."

"Because I was smart enough not to rush in when we were plainly dealing with a meta that operates off momentum." I ran fingers through my hair and found it stringy.

"Yeah, I figured that out," she said. "Well, the second time. Channels the movement of things in her personal bubble to—"

"Not just movement," I said, delicately touching my forehead. It was damp, but didn't smell like sweat. I looked at the end table next to Veronika and saw a wet washcloth. I frowned. Had she been … mothering me or something? "She slung a gurney down the hall at me from stationary. I think she can channel her own momentum into other objects that get close to her, or at least accelerate them from near standstill."

"This is why I dropped out of physics class," Veronika said.

"Lemme explain it for you—"

"Thanks, Vox. Or are you more like a Meta Physics For Dummies?"

"She can make slow objects move fast and faster objects move—"

"Superfast?"

"Not a very science-y way to explain it—"

"I think you mean, mansplain it, but please, go on."

"—but that's the gist, yes," I finished. "You came at her quick, and she launched you into the wall. Thomas Inglered was running past her and she shot him into a tree."

"Great, we've solved the caper," Veronika said.

"No, we have the who and what."

"Ms. Mustard-hair in the park with the physics-related meta power."

"But not the motive," I said.

"Did you not notice she was bringing him flowers?" Veronika said with a shrug. "Because she dropped them at the nurses' station after we jumped her."

"I forgot about them, actually," I said. "Did the cops recover them after I—"

"Took a header into the lawn? Yep. They had an 'I'm So Sorry' note attached with no name. Guess Hallmark doesn't make a 'Sorry I Wrecked Your Ass With My Metahuman Abilities, Hope You Get Better' card."

"Shame," I said, "Sienna could raise their profit margins if they did."

Veronika blinked in the darkness. "So, anyhoo … I think this was an accident. She whoopsied as he approached and Tommy Boy went flying. She buys him a card to say, 'Sorry, shit happens.'"

"Not necessarily."

"Shit doesn't necessarily happen? I disagree."

I favored her with a frown. "I don't necessarily think it was an accident. Or at least, I can't conclude that based on the facts in evidence."

"Oooh, look at you, Sherlock, concluding facts in evidence." She folded her arms across her chest, causing a very small cloud of drywall dust to puff off her suit's sleeves. "What do you think happened, then? She tried to murder him with her slingshot powers and failed, then decided to finish him off under cover of delivering an apology card?"

"No, I think your original explanation is the most logical, but I can't rule out malicious intent because we don't know what she was thinking when she came to visit him. We need to investigate further."

"I like how you think I'm right but you're too stubborn to just cop to it."

"*I'm* stubborn?" I sat up straighter in bed. "Which one of us bull-charged the momentum shifter twice in a row?"

"I did not bull charge her the second time." Veronika shifted uncomfortably in her seat. "I shot a blast of controlled plasma at her." I waited, and she squirmed this time. "And … I am sorry for that," she said, more softly.

"Sorry," I repeated, more softly still.

"The house turned out to be empty anyway," she said, sloughing off any hint of contrition. "But you … you kinda freaked out back there."

"You almost destroyed the place. And you didn't know it was empty as you stood there, gawking, while your plasma burst kept going."

"It's not a boomerang," she said. "I can't call it back, okay?"

"Then you should really be more careful throwing your powers around."

"Yes, I let my anger get the better of me," she said, blowing air between her lips in a squealing hiss. "But you did the full-on scream of the possessed, and since you haven't cut off that cultist, crazy homeless person beard, you kind of looked like a lunatic as you vaulted into the air and started a plasma tornado. Which would have been way worse than the basketball sized burst I threw if it had hit. I mean, you damned near snatched total destruction from the jaws of minor destruction, that's all I'm saying."

"We make mistakes and people die," I said, breathing hard, my jaw clenched in a furious line.

Veronika sat there calmly, waiting a few seconds to reply. "Is this about me … or you?"

My face burned hot. "Don't—"

"Nope, you've opened this door," she said, causing me to blanch at her choice of wording, "so let's walk on through together. We all know what happened."

"I didn't—"

"You got mind controlled, Reed." She sat forward and the haze of light that filtered through the curtains behind her lit the edges of her face, giving me hints of her expression. "Whammied. And while you were being controlled, you did things. Terrible things. Augustus told us—"

"He would know."

"It would be very strange for a person of any decency to walk away from what you did in Wyoming without … doubts. Nightmares—"

"Did I have a nightmare just now?" I asked calmly, wondering. I couldn't quite recall what I'd dreamed, only that I had.

"Killing an innocent person is traumatic," Veronika said. "Hell, killing a guilty person is traumatic. Speaking from experience here. Killing at all … it's a tough business—"

"I've killed before," I said, flicking my gaze toward the foot of the bed where the outline of a TV rested in the darkness.

"Sure you have," she said. "And I bet every one of them deserved at least a little of what they got. You've had a pretty storied career hunting criminal metas, after all. But I doubt in all that time you ever once kicked down the wrong door and filled an innocent girl holding a baby full of lead. While under mind control," she said, making it sound like some sort of sick, repetitive, song lyric or limerick.

"I don't suppose, 'I don't want to talk about it' is going to make you stop until you're done?"

"Newp." She lowered the pitch of her voice. "You've been in the sky a couple months by yourself. How did that work out for you?"

"It dropped the nightmares to a manageable level," I answered. "Gave me time to realize that, yeah … I wasn't the one in the driver's seat when … it … happened. But I was a passenger, and I saw it all, and it felt like I was driving the whole time, which adds a wrinkle or two in my head. Makes it tougher for me to accept, to stomach it all." I rolled to the side and my bare legs fell out from under the covers. I finally realized that the hotel room was freezing. "Where are my pants?"

"They looked uncomfortable," she said, and cloth whipped across the back of my head, pants legs landing over my shoulders. "You were saying?"

I pulled my pants from around my neck and gave Veronika a salty look as I started to pull them on one leg at a time. "I'm fine, Veronika. I haven't finished making my peace with what happened yet, but I'm working on it. I'll get there."

"Didn't you have a girlfriend? A hot Italian cougar with legs up her neck and hair that a Medusa would be jealous of? Bosoms that make you want to—"

"You know the answer to that question already."

"Well, yeah, I was the one describing her bosoms after all—"

"I mean, you know I do—did," I said, standing and zipping my fly. It felt like a very awkward thing to do in Veronika's presence.

"You haven't seen her this whole time, have you?"

"You know the answer to that, too."

"I should know the answer to that. I thought about stopping by once I came to Minneapolis, see if there was anything I could do to comfort that poor, aggrieved, abandoned woman … anything at all …"

"FFS, Veronika."

"Did you just spell out FFS? Because you could just say it. I've heard the naughty word before. It's one of my favorites." She stood and straightened her jacket. "I get it. You're a rugged individualist man. Wanted to go it alone. But you're back now, which means … your days of going it alone need to come to an end, like, now. I've never been much of a team player, but if you're going to be team leader, I advise you to kill this desire to go solo, to bury your traumas and drink them away on your own time. Because there's being strong as a leader, and then there's being stupid and letting your psychological blisters become infecting sores that ooze—"

"Gross."

"—and cause problems at the worst times. Like, say, when you're trying to prevent a tiny ball of plasma from burning through a house."

I just stared at her. "I should have brought Kat along."

Veronika nodded. "That would have been way less fun for me. Soooooooo," she flopped down on the messy bed, resting on her elbows and looking up like a teenage girl. "Are you successfully out of your crisis? Your funk?"

"I'm fine, thanks," I said. The dark room around us was starting to feel claustrophobic, and I wondered why she was still here.

"Great. Because we have another question … what now, boss?"

"Now I'm going to shower, and I suggest you do the same," I said. She raised an eyebrow at me mischievously. "In your own room."

She clucked at me in a laugh. "I don't enable cheaters, Ace. You have nothing to fear from me unless you fail to get your crap together. And even then, like I said … Dr. Perugini is getting my first offer. You're the consolation prize."

"I so admire your relationship ethics," I said dryly. "Now go shower and leave me alone?"

"Gladly," she said, coming up, "but I wasn't actually asking about that when I wondered what now. I meant … what do we do about Momentum Lady. Momentum Queen?" She puzzled over it, her silhouetted finger touching her chin. "No, wait. How about—"

"Momentum is a fine name by itself," I said, "but it doesn't matter. Whatever her name, the play is still the same."

"Ooh, a play," she said. "Back to team sports. Your girlfriend would look great in a cheerleader outfit, by the way. Did I mention those legs—"

I ignored her and picked up the cell phone that was resting on the dresser next to the TV, and started thumbing through my contacts until I got to J.J. I called and Veronika just watched me, probably wondering who I was calling. She shouldn't have. "J.J.!" I said when I heard him pick up. "We've got a suspect, but we lost her after a fracas. We need your skills …" I looked right at Veronika, figuring I'd give her a thrill by going to another sports metaphor. "We need to go to the tape."

32.

Jamal

I woke up handcuffed to a hospital bed. This was easily one of the worst days of my life.

My face hurt a lot. I'd seen Sienna heal from getting busted wide open, but for me, healing took longer. Not as long as a normal person, probably a couple days even for some near-fatal wounds, but still … not seconds, either. And then pain stayed, a nice little casserole of agony to go with the clinking, cold metal wrapped around my wrist.

The steady sound of a heart monitor beeping led me to think I must have been messed up pretty bad by Ms. ArcheGrey before she put me down for the count. Everything looked normal on it now, but I wondered if it had been a lot worse when they'd brought me in. I suspected it had been, because throwing me through the glass wall of the Javits Center wasn't exactly a round of tickles and ice cream.

I blinked at the cuffs that had me trapped in bed, and rattled them again. They were light, not heavy, and I wondered if they were just garden variety human cuffs. I decided to try them and see.

I wrapped the chain once around my hand and pulled, figuring I'd just give it a test. The damned thing broke right where it met the bed, making a loud POP! that made me look around my private room self-consciously, as though some nurse was going to come busting in with an army brigade: *Ha! Caught you!*

There was no sound but the beep of the heart monitor, though, and a few seconds later, I realized … I'd gotten away with it.

Damn, freedom. That works.

I hopped out of bed and found my clothes in a plastic bag sitting on ones of those rolling feeding tables. My pack was there, too, complete with my fried tablet. Apparently they'd bagged my personal effects, so I grabbed them. My clothes were gone, probably sacrificed to scissors in the ER, so I dressed quickly in the spare clothes from my bag while I looked out the window. I was at least ten stories up, the city of New York all spread around me, so that exit was out.

I crept to the door, listening for sounds of footsteps or gurneys squeaking. I quietly pushed it about a foot open and peeked my head around.

There was a long hallway that stretched to either side. To my right, I could see an emergency exit sign, along with the staircase doors. I thought about going that way and decided against it. There was no way to know if it would set off an alarm that would bring every nurse on the floor running.

No, I was pretty sure going out the front door was the way to do it. I ducked my head down, snugged my bag on my back, and started down the hallway, acting like I belonged here.

All I could see at first were patients, but there was an empty nurses' station all the way down at the end where the hall widened, and I suspected there was an elevator lobby close by. It looked clear to me, so I casually sauntered my way down the hall.

When I was three doors from the nurses' station, the elevator dinged loudly and I froze. So I'd been right—there was an elevator right next to the nurses' station. Voices echoed down the hall as I held position and waited, listening.

"Our suspect is in room 1560," a strong male voice said. Cop, I figured. "Should be handcuffed, but we might want to make sure he's secured with metacuffs, because security footage suggested he was more than human."

I dodged into the nearest room and pulled the door closed

again, listening intently. I wasn't positive, but I was willing to bet I was the suspect from room 1560.

"Any idea what powers he's got?" another voice asked, this one female.

"Urnnnngh," someone said behind me. I turned and stuck my head around the corner to see an old man sitting there, breathing tube in his mouth and his glassy eyes on me.

"Hey, there," I said, thinking fast, "I'm a volunteer with the hospital. You need anything while I'm here? Magazine?"

"Unnnnnnh," he moaned, barely moving, a perfect example of misery.

"That doesn't sound good," I said, looking him over. He didn't seem injured so much as bandaged, maybe recovering from surgery. He had a tube down his throat, though, which didn't help communication efforts. "You want me to get a nurse?"

He glared at me, then lifted a hand with a long, white cord snaking to it. He dangled it, meeting my eyes, and said, "Unh."

"Oh, you got this, then," I said, nodding along. "I'll leave you to it, no worries."

I had just started for the door when he grunted at me again. I came back around in time to see him pushing the call button. A buzzing sounded at the nurses' station down the hall and I froze.

"Shit," I said under my breath. The guy in the bed frowned at me, clearly not understanding a damned thing.

I had no time for worrying about this, though. I looked out into the hallway and found it empty, at least for a moment. I ran down the hall, hoping I was right about the nurses' station being abandoned.

I burst out just as someone started around the corner—another nurse who hadn't shown herself yet. She started as I appeared in front of her, nearly dropping the phone that was in her hand.

"Ahhhhhhhhh!" I said, jumping almost a foot in the air.

She managed to keep a little more sedate. "Good grief! What are you doing!"

"Was just visiting a friend," I said, already backing away

from her. "Sorry. You startled me." I put a finger against my temple. "Lost in thought, you know."

She favored me with a look that said she thought I was crazy. "Sure. Don't run in the halls, okay?"

"Got it," I said, giving her the thumbs up. The elevator dinged behind me and an orderly with a gurney came rolling out just in time. I dodged in after he was clear and hit the button for the first floor.

I pulled my cell phone as the doors closed, thumbing open the Uber app, and summoned a car. There was one only two minutes away, and I figured I'd just stroll out the main entrance.

It took almost that long to make it to the ground floor, and by then I was sweating, expecting my paranoid fantasies to be fulfilled by a hundred cops waiting for me like a horde of Ultron robots. The lobby was quiet, though, and I walked calmly past the front desk and hopped into my Uber as he pulled up, just as the security guard got a call to lock down the hospital on his walkie.

Whew. That could have gone way worse.

33.

Sienna

I set down at the mall in King of Prussia, Pennsylvania, just outside Philadelphia, figuring I'd done enough to tempt fate for today. I used one of my more common means of dodging surveillance—finding someplace crowded, like a mall, setting down a little out of sight, going inside, changing my look in the bathroom, and then hoofing it out another entrance in order to confuse anyone watching satellite recon. A dedicated hunting party with unrestricted overhead satellites could definitely track me down, given enough time, but my job was to make it as difficult as possible for them.

Besides, I had a feeling that something was off about the searchers that had been assigned to me since Gerry Harmon—

President *Harmon, please.*

—since that giant, officious douchebag Gerry Harmon had gone missing. Because they'd gone a lot quieter in their search for me, maybe because I'd completely slaughtered and/or co-opted their last search team. I wanted to believe that maybe they didn't care about me anymore, but I had a feeling after this New York incident, they'd find their motivation again. There was no way I was coming out of this smelling like a rose, at least not in the press.

I stole a car and bummed around King of Prussia for a bit. It wasn't something I liked to do, thieving, but it was necessary in order to avoid flying, and I made sure to keep the "rental," as I thought of it, in pristine condition. I abandoned the car a few blocks away from a Denny's and headed over there to get something to eat.

My phone rang as I was huddling against the cold wind, walking along the road, the sky darkening around me. I answered it without questioning. "Hola," I said.

It was Jamal. "That's not how Spanish speakers answer their phones. They say, 'Bueno!'"

"You made it out okay," I said, breathing relief as the wind ran across the microphone.

"I'm in Jersey now," Jamal said. "I just rented a car. Where you at?"

"King of Prussia, PA."

"… Why?"

"I needed to get out of New York, but didn't want to get too far from where you were."

"So sweet," he said. "We need to get back in on this, like now. Immediate-amente."

"It would be a really bad idea for me to go back to New York City right now," I said. "Like … really bad. Catastrophic, possibly."

"Why's that?"

"Because they're going to be looking for me there," I said. "Full surveillance, facial recognition, everything. I need to lay low for a bit, stay out of sight."

"You think they're going to forget about you?" He laughed.

"No, but I think they're going to be looking harder in New York, and I don't want to have to—"

"Fight your way through the cops."

"To say the least."

He seemed to give that some thought. "Yeah, I can't guarantee that won't happen." Frustration bled through. "What the hell are we supposed to do about Caden Sims, though? He's plainly up to no good."

"I agree," I said, "and if you can get me a location on him, maybe we can drop in on him in a private moment."

"Like, right out of the sky?"

"And onto his head," I said. "But if you want me to linger

around NYC right now, while they're all in a tizzy and hunting me …? I vote no. I'll be more trouble than I'm worth, because I bet you they'll have me ten seconds after stepping foot in the city."

"I can shield you from the electronic part of their surveillance," he said, but he sounded uncertain.

"Oh, yeah?" I poked, trying to get to the bottom of the doubt I heard in his voice.

"Well …"

"Spill it, Jamal."

"I dunno, ArcheGrey just denied me access hard," he said. "Cut me right out. If that happened again … if she's watching … maybe I can't do that."

"Yeah," I said, "we just got punched. In the face. Hard."

"Tell me about it," he said. "I woke up in the hospital. ArcheGrey is a Thor-type, like me, but she's got some kind of wonky machine up her sleeve. Lets her throw electricity down a mechanical lash." I had a feeling he was rubbing some part of his body in pain. "It does not feel good, and I would not recommend it unless you can fend off a ton of volts."

"We should table this discussion for now," I said cautiously, "you know … just in case."

"Oh, you're talking in public, are you?" Jamal got it; I was worried about the open line, not anyone overhearing me as I walked down the shoulder of the road with cars roaring by. "Where can I meet you?"

"Come to town, we'll get together, have a Moons Over My Hammy at the local Denny's," I said. "Call me when you're close?" I threw that out there, not only because I wanted a Moons Over My Hammy, but because if on the very off chance we were being eavesdropped on, part of me wanted to redeem my failure to keep my conversational secrecy tight by setting a trap. I doubted it was going to be a problem—the odds were good that our burner phone conversation was perfectly safe and unlistened to by anyone, but just in case …

"I will," he said. "We got some planning to do. There's got to be another way here."

"There always is," I said, "but I hope it doesn't involve

returning to New York. Call me on the other line." I hung up and immediately dropped the cell phone in the snow and blasted it with a burst of fire. I had spares in my bag, and he knew to call me on the next one.

I couldn't believe I'd talked as freely as I had on the line. Stupid, really, but that was what happened sometimes when you forgot you were a wanted fugitive. I'd had a confessional conversation with him without even thinking about it. I didn't even know if I'd said anything incriminating. I'd certainly done a few incriminating things, like steal a bag from an innocent man, and mentally assault another who was physically assaulting me (though I doubted that last one would hold up to scrutiny in court).

"Getting sloppy," I said. I'd gotten too complacent on this gig, thinking I could just slip easily into New York City and do a little stealth mission. There was a reason fugitive Sienna was avoiding major cities.

Sometimes I forget that I cause chaos wherever I go. Soothing Voice being on the guard squad had been a damned inconvenient coincidence, but then, nowadays bad luck was pretty well following me always. Part of the fugitive gig, really.

It would have been nice, I reflected, to be able to be somewhere peaceful, without looking over my shoulder or worrying that my call was going to be intercepted and used to track me down. Imprisonment was the specter that always loomed over me, the thought that I'd get to spend the next years of my life like I'd spent the worst parts of my formative ones—in a tight, confined space, paying penance for whatever crimes I was deemed to have committed against my mom's—or the state's—authority.

The sad thing was, I wasn't even guilty of the crimes I was accused of. But because I'd done bad things earlier in my life, this was the price. My penance was to run, or else to go to jail for stuff I didn't really do. Well, I guess I did it, but there had been extenuating circumstances of the life-threatening variety.

None of that much mattered as I walked along the edge of a Pennsylvania road, heading for the Denny's. I wanted

Moons Over My Hammy and a chance to catch my breath. Hopefully the redhead wig I was wearing would offer some modicum of disguise, along with the purple contact lenses I'd put in (very distracting and made people focus on them rather than my face). Because I had a feeling that as soon as Jamal showed up, even if there hadn't been anyone listening in on our conversation … it'd be go-time again on this case of his.

34.

Reed

"I'm not Greek, but I'm bearing gifts," J.J. said when he called me back an hour or so later. "Don't fear me."

"Not a problem commonly associated with you, my friend," I quipped before realizing it was probably a little insulting. "But it should be," I added with haste.

"Quality save," J.J. deadpanned as I stood just outside my hotel's front doors, staring into the blue, cloudless Orlando sky. "Thanks for making the effort, at least."

"You mean, unlike others?" I asked, half-assing my swipe.

"You trying to backhand your sis with that one?" J.J. sounded genuinely puzzled. "Because you know she started acting different to me ever since Chicago. She makes the effort, too."

"That's great," I said, without really caring. My feelings toward my sister were so convoluted right now, I didn't even have the energy to even consider untangling them. You would have thought that spending a couple months in the clouds trying to get my head straight might have helped me sort out my reaction to the brainwashing that had turned me against Sienna.

You'd be wrong. Stop being wrong, wrong-head.

"Speaking of which, she just had an incident in New York City—"

"Fantastic," I said. "Anybody dead?"

"No, but she got into a scrap with Captain Frost—"

"Fantastic," I said again, trying to seal shut this particular conversation in a tomb that wouldn't be opened for ten thousand years. And maybe, if I was lucky, a rolling boulder would squash the person who tried to reopen it then. Like in *Raiders*. "I have a case, though."

"So, I've got some stuff here," J.J. said, clearly getting my "I don't want to talk about it" aural cue. "Tape reviewed and all that jazz."

"And?"

"And I see you're back on the job for like a day and already landing yourself in the same sort of crap you usually do," he said with a chipper laugh. "Some good vid of you going ape bonkers and making a tornado—an actual tornado!—in downtown Orlando. In January, no less. Wow."

"Tornadoes happen in January," I said darkly. "It's a naturally occurring phenomenon. Trust me."

"Yeah, no doubt," J.J. said. "Anyway, I got your perp lady, and I managed to catch her face in my recognition software web. Here's some bad news for you—she is not in the system."

I frowned, my feet squishing on slightly wet grass as I walked across my hotel lawn. "What does that mean?"

"No driver's license," J.J. said. "No passport. No photo ID."

My frown deepened. No passport wasn't that uncommon in the US. No driver's license, though? In a city like Orlando, where the mass transit wasn't exactly at New York or London levels? She'd certainly exhibited the ability to get around on her own, but if she was using her powers to whirl herself around Orlando, someone would be bound to notice the streaks of motion and hurled objects, wouldn't they?

"Here's some good news," J.J. said, "I managed to do the exhausting, painstaking work of using cameras to follow this dangerous denizen back to her, uhm … den, I guess?"

"Her denizen den? Good job."

"It wasn't easy, let me tell you. There were long minutes of stitching together different traffic camera shots. Perilous moments, filled with worry and concern. Would I manage to catch her in the next frame before she disappeared from this one? Would she off-road it and—"

"Yes, okay, I get it," I said, rubbing that furrow out of my brow as I relaxed and stared up into the cloudless sky. It bothered me, that lack of clouds, but not quite as much as J.J.'s fishing for compliments.

"—but I persevered and—"

"J.J.!"

"Oh, fine. I tracked her back to an apartment off Alafaya Trail on the east side of the city. It's a college area, and she looks youngish, so she's probably blending or something. GPS coordinates incoming to your phone."

My phone beeped in receipt of what he sent. "Got it," I said, glancing at the alert notification heralding the arrival of an address, building number and apartment. "Looks like an easy drive."

"At this time of day, maybe. Wait for rush hour and your happy ass is going to be sitting in the car with Veronika for eternity."

I shuddered. "Wouldn't want that. I'll collect her and get moving."

"By the way," J.J. said, with all the subtlety of a shotgun blast to the face, "have you talked to Isabella since—"

"Later, J.J." I hung up without dignifying his question with an answer. He knew what it was anyway.

I stared up at the blue sky above. I knew the answer as well, and knew what it meant—or what I thought it meant—to me. But I didn't want to go down that road. Not yet. I just wasn't ready.

35.

Jamal

I walked into the Denny's in King of Prussia, Pennsylvania, and found Sienna Nealon herself wearing a red wig in the corner of the restaurant, eating a sandwich on thick sourdough toast, with ham, egg, and cheese thickly piled between the slices, savoring it like it was the last meal she was ever going to get while subtly eyeing the room, probably for danger or possibly for a waitress to refill her milk glass, which looked to be getting low.

My life had taken a weird turn since I got the power to shoot lightning out of my fingers. Sitting down with fugitive superheroes while they eat sandwiches in a Denny's in Pennsylvania. Not exactly the stuff of my plans when I was graduating high school.

"Congratulations. Looks like you found me," Sienna said as I strolled up. Her voice was so low I could barely hear her, and her face was concealed behind half her sandwich. "You've managed something the FBI, the US Marshals, and countless other law enforcement agencies haven't been able to."

"Well, you did give me pretty thorough directions," I said, taking my phone out of my pocket and putting it on the table. It was the only electronic device I had going at the moment, since I'd lost my tablet in the fight with ArcheGrey. "That helped."

"Pull up a chair," she said, nodding to the booth seat

across from her. She had a light, pleasant expression on her face, as one might when sitting in a Denny's. It was uncharacteristic to the point of being a little unnerving. That and the red hair were making me think I was sitting in front of the wrong person, even though I knew it was her.

"That disguise is scarily good," I said as I sat, dumping my bag on the seat next to me. The tinkling of glass reminded me that I hadn't cleaned out that busted tablet yet, and probably should before I ended up with more gorilla glass fragments stuck in the corners than I could possibly get out without declaring the bag a loss.

"That's the secret of disguises," she said, taking in a huge bite of the sandwich and waiting until she swallowed to elaborate on that point. "You have to pick something so very different from who you are as a person, from everyone's expectations of you." She shifted a leg so that I could see she was wearing a dress again. It only went to mid-thigh, and I snapped my eyes up after a quarter-second because the point was made, and I didn't want to gawk.

"That's, uh, nice," I said, blinking away the image of smooth, silken legs that were like an afterimage in my mind. Girl had big thighs, but I didn't really consider that a bad thing. She also had a black dress on that met in a low-hanging V at the neck, giving a view that I fought to keep my eyes well north of.

"We need a new plan," she said, and thumped my brain out of heading in a direction where it could do no good.

I frowned at her sandwich. "Wait. Haven't you been here, like … hours?"

"Yeah, so?"

"You told me you wanted that sandwich back when I was still in Jersey. But you just got it now?"

She flushed under the spray-tan on her cheeks. "I came and got one, checked into a motel, then came back and ordered it again." She brandished the remaining half-sandwich. "It's really good. But stop trying to distract me from the business at hand."

"Because we need a new plan."

"Yes," she said. "Because the last one failed. Hard. Porn-star hard."

"Okay, yes. Thank you for that."

"I can go on."

"Please don't." I leaned forward on the table. "So … what do we do now? Because my vote is we go after Sims again—"

Sienna leaned back in her seat, putting down her half-sandwich. "I cannot go back to New York right now for a general visit. Cannot."

"But if we—"

"No. Get me a specific target I can drop on, and maybe. General wandering? Terrible idea, and you know it."

I hesitated. I did know it, but I was having trouble accepting it. "Man, we spiked this bad. We didn't get a clue about the code Sims was buying from ArcheGrey, I didn't dump his phone, and we landed you on the NYPD radar." I put my face in both hands.

"What do we know about Sims?" she asked. "Other than I still maintain that this Cameron Witless—"

"Wittman."

"Whatever. That this tech billionaire is his boss somehow. He's responsible for this in some way."

I kept my face in my hands but parted my fingers enough to look at her between the cracks. "Why do you assume that?"

"Because," she said, regarding her sandwich, like she was trying to decide whether to explain the way of the world to me or take another bite. "It's pretty much always the rich guy on these things."

"Because why?" I asked. "I don't get it. Don't you think it's a little discriminatory? I mean, blaming the rich for all your problems—"

"I'm not," she said tiredly, "I'm saying that whenever there's a grandiose scheme, there's always a rich person at the top of it."

I wrinkled my nose at her. "But that's—I mean—do you hear yourself, Vladimir Lenin? 'It's always the rich people at fault'—"

She rolled her eyes. "Jackass, listen to me." She brought

her gaze down and it burned with intensity. "This is not about your stupid political or economic filter, so leave that crap at the door. No, I am not smearing Cameron Wittman because he's a rich guy. No, I am not saying all rich people are criminals. No, I am not giving a blanket pass to all poor people and saying they're all innocent victims, because I do not live in a world of stupid stereotypes. What I am saying," and she leaned in, still speaking in meta-whisper, but with extra vehemence, "is that whenever there's a conspiratorial, grandiose scheme, there's always a rich person involved because," she slapped her hands against the table like a drum, "rich people have resources—i.e., money, connections—in order to put together the big deals."

I felt like she'd flicked me between the eyes. "Oh. And poor people don't because …"

"Yeah," she said. "But don't feel bad; middle-class and upper-class people don't have the bankroll to fund massive schemes, either. So, as a consequence, whenever I'm on a big case these days and a billionaire crosses my path, little bells ring in my ears, and I think, 'This could be the walking bank account behind all my current problems.'" She grabbed up the remaining half-sandwich and waved it at me. "That said, the second favorite answer for that question is 'Government REMF,' because while they don't have money, sufficiently-highly placed members of the government have power at their fingertips to cause problems as well." Her eyes narrowed into slits. "As evidenced by my most recent skull inmate."

"I don't know what a 'Government REMF' is. Still …" I said, "seems like an unfair kind of generalization."

"I'm not generalizing," she said. "Rich people, poor people, middle-class people, and everyone in the spectrum between … some of them get evil ideas, or grandiose plans that we'd class as evil. It's just that a wealthy person has the resources to carry them out without having to barter for the power to make it happen. Meta bodyguards like Caden Sims had surrounding him don't work for minimum wage. And if you're living on a dream and the sixteen cents you have in your bank account, you can't pay for armed mercenaries, metahuman bodyguards, political influence, explosives, assassins or any of the other rampant bullshit I seem to run across whenever some dickweed comes up with a dream of a better world that I have to defuse before it turns into a nightmare for the rest of us."

I listened to her irritable huffing and started to make a counterpoint, but a crack echoed in the restaurant and Sienna jerked slightly. She blinked at me a couple times and then looked down at her dress's neckline. I had studiously kept my eyes off it this entire conversation, which was not an easy task given that the contrast of the black dress against her pale (even with the spray tan) cleavage was pretty attention-grabbing.

There was a hole in the skin where a moment earlier there had only been the barely freckled curves of her cleavage. I stared at it and a little squirt of red shot out as her heart beat, splattering down her dress.

"Sonofa …" she muttered. Her eyes rolled, hard, and she pitched sideways on the booth seat. Glass shattered behind me as the next gunshot came, then another, and I dove for the floor. The world around me became a symphony of guns and broken glass as the suburban Denny's turned into a shooting gallery.

36.

Reed

Working our way down East Colonial Drive from downtown Orlando to the east side was a long and laborious process filled with about a thousand traffic lights, all of which seemed to be red when we arrived at them. The road was a long strip of old and new commerce, little strip malls with faded awnings, pawn shops, restaurants, and just about everything else you can imagine. When we got close to our turn, I saw a Walmart on our right, and it had possibly the most packed parking lot of any Walmart I've ever seen.

"This town's grown a lot since last time I was here," Veronika said. She'd been quiet for most of the ride, just looking out, eyes flicking over everything. I assumed she was keeping an eagle eye for threats and let her have at it. It was a blessing to not have to listen to her carping at me about Perugini and everything else, so I didn't bother to poke the bear. It wasn't like silence bothered me.

"Oh, yeah?" I asked, mostly out of politeness and a desire to avoid our earlier topics. I particularly wanted to avoid anything involving her making rude references to Isabella.

"I went to college here," Veronika said, and pointed to our left. "Just up Alafaya Trail."

I racked my brain. "Uhhh … J.J. mentioned a college … It's, uhm …"

"It was called Florida Tech when I went here," Veronika said, staring off in the distance like she could already see it.

"But I guess they changed the name after I left. Now it's the University of Central Florida." She shrugged. "I dunno. Broader-based education with a name like that, I guess."

I took the turn when the arrow went green and lurched ahead into a mess of stop-and-go traffic as Veronika sunk back into a pensive silence. "When did you go there?"

She smiled faintly. "Before they changed the name."

"When did they change the name?"

She looked sidelong at me with a smiling yet still sharp look, and I got the feeling once again that she was a lot older than her persona generally suggested. "Before you were born, sonny." She smoothed her flawless hair back behind her and straightened a wrinkle in her suit's grey skirt. "Turn left here." She pointed as we passed the grand entrance for the University of Central Florida, and I took the next left at the traffic light. I let her guide me through a couple more turns until we arrived at a grey, vaguely Craftsman-looking three-story apartment building with outdoor hallways and wooden railings. It looked like it might have been built with the school and refurbished a few times. There were some college kids hanging around along the sidewalks and the stairwells.

"This is a little too brisk for me to want to hang outside," Veronika said as we got out of the car, taking in a group of students on the upstairs landing with a nod. They all watched us curiously, a couple of them clutching beers in hand. One of them was a skinny girl in tiny jeans that hugged her barely-there ass, and I knew for a fact she wasn't twenty-one.

"Hey," I said, nodding at the kids as we hit the second floor landing. I glanced back at Veronika and saw her checking out the skinny girl's ass. I couldn't decide whether her shrug was one of indifference or affirmation, and she didn't give it away with her poker face, which was hidden behind black glasses like cops wear. I held up my phone to the skinny girl, who didn't seem at all abashed to be drinking underage in front of me. "You know this girl?"

"Yeah," the skinny girl said. Her hair was brown with a few streaks of blondish highlights, and it fell to mid-neck and curled a little, giving her hair a triangular look coming down from the small ponytail tip at the top of her head. She had a button nose and wide, innocent eyes which glanced up to the third floor. "She lives up there. Three thirty-four."

"Oh, yeah?" Veronika asked coolly, apparently not letting her opinion of the girl's ass, good or bad, color her attitude. "You know her name?"

"Uhmmm …" Skinny Girl thought about it a second, and then looked to one of her comrades questioningly. "Is it … Olivia?"

"Yeah," said a dude bro with her, no beer in his hand. He seemed a little tense at the sight of us, suspicious but still cooperative. "It's Olivia."

"You know her?" I asked.

He shrugs it off. "Nobody really knows her," he said. "She doesn't party or anything. Keeps to herself. I know her roommates."

"Yeah, she's weird," Skinny Girl opined.

"Weird how?" Veronika asked.

"Like, on rumspringa or something," Skinny Girl said, prompting a laugh from her friends. She sipped her beer in victory at making the funny. "Seriously. I think she's like, Amish or from a religious cult. She's got that vibe, you know?"

"What kind of vibe?" I asked, watching Skinny Girl carefully. This was important, because it dovetailed nicely with my assessment of this Olivia after meeting her for about two seconds. You form impressions of people at the gut level within only a second or two of seeing them, and there was something in her that I felt after seeing her, something that bothered me, if only for its familiarity …

"Her roommate? Brandy?" Dude Bro offered. "She says Olivia is super jumpy. Like, a loud sound will make her leap."

I knew the signs that they were talking about, the symptoms that they indicated. "You seen her lately?"

"Nah," Skinny Girl said, and nodded her head up the stairs. "But some other guys just came up a few minutes before you did. Big guys. Old, too." She giggled, and I got the feeling it was not entirely prompted by alcohol.

Veronika and I exchanged a look. "Cops?" she asked.

"I don't think so," Dude Bro said, shaking his head. "More uptight, no uniforms, no guns."

I narrowed my eyes at them. "They get into her place?"

"Might have," he said, shrugging. "Didn't see."

"Thanks," I said. They made way as Veronika and I hustled up the stairs to the third floor. We kept quiet to keep the concrete echoes of our shoes from ringing out over the open railings across the complex.

"Times like this it might be nice to have a pistol," I muttered to myself as I stepped up to the door frame. It was ajar.

"You could have brought one," Veronika said.

I lifted a hand and spooled up a gust of wind. "Nah, that's all right," I said, my pulse racing, and not just because I was about to go through the door. It was just sitting there, cracked open, green and foreboding, with who knew what kind of threats lurking beyond.

Or no threat at all.

I swallowed heavily, an acrid taste on my tongue, bitter and strong.

I didn't want to carry a gun anymore.

Ever.

I loosed the gust and blew open the door, charging in. It was a big, open common room with a few doors leading off to bedrooms, but the guys we were looking for were standing squarely in the middle of the main room. One of them was bald and thick, built like a brick wall, his pectoral muscles visible beneath his polo shirt like he was smuggling dinner plates under there. He also lacked eyebrows almost at all, as though he'd had them waxed off completely.

The other guy was thin, nondescript, the very definition of the old CIA appellation, "Grey Man." He would have blended in everywhere, wearing a polo of his own along with jeans—medium height, medium build, plain face and brown hair.

"I'm guessing you're not cops," I said, and the two of them exchanged a look. It was short and full of meaning, and I caught it. Hell, Veronika caught it, and she was still a step behind me.

The moment she was in the room, she picked up on the brewing conflict. Her immediate response was a mildly aggrieved, "Oh, dammit."

It only took another second after that for the two of them to come at us, at beyond-human speed, to confirm what I already knew—they were metas.

And they might have come here looking for Olivia, but now that they'd found us … they were perfectly content to settle for a fight.

37.

Sienna

Question: How many times have I been shot through the heart?

Answer: Too many.

I woke up on the floor of a Denny's with bullets whizzing over my head, staring up at the ceiling with my heels askew, my skirt torn, one of my legs hanging off the edge of the booth, and I realized that life had certainly gotten a bit worse since I'd involved myself in that damned love—err, lust—triangle in Menomonie yesterday.

"Wolfe …?" I muttered, partially deaf from the sound of rounds discharging around me. Blood leaked out between my cleavage, and I felt sticky all up and down my chest, like I'd spilled ketchup down there, only … stickier. Warm maple syrup, maybe.

Am working.

"I know you are," I said as sweetly as I could, "I was more wondering if all that shooting myself that I did before I got myself wanted had any effect at all on the bullet that just ripped through my chest."

Rifle bullet, Bastian answered for him. *High caliber. You're lucky they went for the heart instead of the head, or you might not be having this conversation with us right now.*

"Knew I should have advanced to shooting myself with rifles," I said. I'd worked up to 9mm or so, and could take those fairly well. Head-on shots still had the potential to damage me, but I'd been close to invulnerable to that caliber before I'd been forced to flee. I'd never really tested it with larger calibers, but if it followed the progression of my experiments with .22s and .380s, it probably wouldn't take too many more 9mm shots before I'd be ready to shrug off an entire street of cops plinking at me.

Unless they had a couple strays carrying .45 and .40 S&W. Sigh. This would have been easier in Europe.

"You okay?" Jamal called as a bullet spanged overhead and shards of wood spit down from the booth.

"Maybe." I lowered my leg from where it had been caught on the corner of the bench and reached up to swipe the remains of my Moons Over My Hammy from the table as I readjusted. "What the hell is all this?"

I caught a glimpse of a circular contraption with a camera hanging off of it along with a gun, and I barely got the time for my brain to work out what it was before Jamal yelled, "DRONE!" and knocked me back to the ground as the drone started shooting at where I'd been just a second earlier.

"You call these drones? I've been shot out of the sky by missile-wielding Reaper drones, okay?" The burst from the quadcopter drone blasted my plate and destroyed my Moons Over My Hammy, showering me with pieces of sourdough, egg and ham. I stared aghast at the wreckage of my sandwich. "Okay," I said, "this is now officially worse." I raised my voice to shout. "My Moons Over My Hammy! You motherfuckers!"

"You are a little too serious about that sandwich," Jamal said.

"You've clearly never had one," I said, rolling to my belly. Wolfe had healed my wounds, and now I was cranky. "Anyone else in the line of fire?"

Jamal made a show of looking around, but then ducked when one of the floating drones cranked a few rounds past his head. We were fortunate that they were seemingly afraid to bring the drone in through the windows they'd shot out. They weren't small drones, either; more like reinforced quadcopters with industrial engines in order to keep the affixed machine gun afloat. Machine guns weren't light, after all, though whatever camera equipment they were using to target them looked pretty small.

"I don't think so," Jamal finally answered, his face pushed into the carpeting. There was glass all around us, and bullets were still discharging in all directions at a pretty damned warzone-like clip. A few isolated screams suggested more panic than pain, and gave me hope that no innocent bystanders had been hit.

"What do you think the odds are that this attack is meant for anyone but us?"

"You hear of a lot of robberies of suburban Denny's involving gun-toting drones?" Jamal asked.

"There's always some asshole looking to revolutionize things, dontcha know." I shook the glass out of my redhead wig, which was askew, and tossed it onto my bag. I probably didn't need it now, since I was about to have to fly the Sienna Nealon flag. Which would probably be a boot being applied to an ass, if I were to be the Betsy Ross in charge of making it.

"You think this is because of our phone call?" Jamal asked. He sounded a little concerned.

"Yeah." It worried me, too, to be honest. This didn't feel like a government op, because they would have just sent the FBI or Scott or someone after us, not a bunch of hover drones with Uzis strapped to them. "I thought maybe I was setting a trap for this contingency, but …" Another hail of gunfire smacked into the bench where I'd been sitting, sending a fat wad of stuffing raining down on me. It landed on my eye and tickled, so I batted it away along with a stray piece of scrambled egg. "Okay, no more Miss Nice Badass."

Jamal just looked at me askance. "When were you nice …?"

I rolled to my side, broken glass catching me in the ribs and ripping through my already ruined dress. I held my hand up, index finger pointing like the barrel of a gun, and whipped it toward the drone hovering just outside the window across the restaurant. I couldn't hear anything over the rotors whirring, but I imagined the camera lens zooming in on me as the gun barrel moved to try and acquire me as a target.

Gavrikov, I said, and launched three quick blasts of flame as I kept rolling behind the counter. I caught a glimpse of my shots finding their target and managed to hear the quad copter spin into a crash outside, the sound of its rotors wailing hard against the asphalt, the sound of it busting to pieces like sweet music over the gunshots.

As I rolled past the counter, I came into view of another one of the quad copter drones, and hurriedly drew my finger down on it as it snapped to acquire me. We fired at the same time, and I was richly rewarded with the sound of two rotors combusting while three bullets caught me in the upper chest.

The wet smack of bullets through me was a pain I was long accustomed to. I hit the ground and lay there, taste of blood welling up in my mouth. One of them had gotten my lung, and I hoped—so hoped—that it had come out the other side, because otherwise it was going to get trapped in there. Never a fun prospect, leaving a bullet in your lung. Pretty damned painful, in fact, and I always ended up having to perform surgery on myself to dig it out again later.

You will be fine, Wolfe said, diagnosing the problem for me. *No bullet in the lung.*

"It's my lucky day," I said, not quite ready to get up again. You can only get so enthusiastic about getting shot when it's being done by a robot and not a person. At least with a person, I'd have the satisfaction of finding them and then showing them the sweet reciprocal feeling of having their lung violated by large chunks of lead. Possibly their rectum as well.

"Uhh … how you doing over there?" Jamal called. There was still an awful lot of ammo being hurled through the air over us, especially considering I'd just taken out two of the drones.

A tiny shard of glass came free of the window above as a stray bullet came whizzing through, and I closed my eye just as it landed on my eyelid. Ouch. It didn't pierce the lid, but it still stung. "I'm doing just grand," I said, trying to brush it free without worsening the problem.

"I think there are tripod-mounted machine guns set up outside," Jamal shouted as the noise quieted slightly. "Remote controlled or something, designed to mow down anything that moves."

"Who the hell does this kind of thing?" I called back as another gun fell silent. I was half-deaf from all the noise, but I could still differentiate that the heavy fire was coming from three distinct directions—basically from the three sides of the Denny's that had windows.

"Caden Sims?"

"Cameron Wittman?" I offered back. "These sorts of toys aren't exactly the cheap drones you buy off Amazon. They would tend to require—"

"Money, yes, I get it," Jamal said. "But Caden Sims ain't exactly broke, you know. He's a pretty wealthy dude on his own."

"There's rich, and then there's billionaire," I said. "You'll come around to my way of thinking, trust me." *If you live through this,* I didn't add. With all the bullets whizzing through the place, I doubt he needed to be reminded.

38.

Reed

The big, bald guy who lacked eyebrows came charging at me, and I responded to his move so quickly that it was almost subconscious. I sent a blast of wind at him so hard that it caught him and launched him into the kitchen with a ferocity that destroyed six cabinets and the stove hood before he disappeared through the wall into the next apartment.

"Whoa," Veronika said. "Punch to the face denied."

The Grey Man kept coming, though, skirting neatly around my riposte at Bald Bull's charge. I lifted my hand to send him back—maybe a little more gently than I had Bald Bull—when suddenly, he disappeared.

I don't mean he blended in like a chameleon, or activated a cloaking device from *Star Trek*. He didn't subtly adopt the colors of the wall behind him.

That sonofabitch disappeared, like he'd never even been there.

I was so stunned that when he punched me, it was doubly shocking. First, I watched a man vanish, and then secondly, thin air whacked me in the face with sledgehammer swing velocity, as though I'd just gotten slammed in the jaw by a Hercules. And it hurt.

My head slammed back into the wood doorframe, cracking it, and someone thumped me roughly. Veronika got knocked aside too, and the Invisible Man shoved past us and was out the door before I could do much to gather myself together.

I clutched at the back of my scalp, and when I brought my hand around, it was slick with blood. "Yeouch," I said, wondering what I'd done to deserve this—other than throw the Invisible Man's buddy into the kitchen cabinets.

"Tell me about it," Veronika said, pinching her nose. A thin trickle of blood marred her upper lip, and she was watching the door warily, like Mr. Invisible might come rushing back in any second.

"I think he's gone," I said, cringing as I clutched at the back of my head. The molding around the door was busted in two where he'd planted my skull into it, and I could feel where the wood had made a solid impact.

"Oh, you think so?" Veronika snarked, eyes blazing. "Well, your thinking has been wonderful so far, you should probably keep trusting it. After all, your thinking was what led you to deal with your problems by running away from everyone who cared about you for two months, so, yeah, you're a grade-A genius, let's listen to your instincts—"

I wanted to rebut her fierce words, but I couldn't. Not because I couldn't think of a reply, but because I was too busy grabbing her by the arms and shoving her through the doorway to the room just behind her. The look on her face was a cross between fury and restraint, the restraint probably keeping her from plunging a plasma-coated hand through my chest at this violation of her person.

I landed heavily on top of her, awkwardly, and knocked the wind out of her and myself on impact. She was pure anger now, glaring at me as she tried to catch her breath, offense about to leap back into action when she heard what I knew had been coming before I'd tackled her.

The doorframe exploded with the burst of buckshot as the Invisible Man returned, apparently having fetched his backup—a shotgun. Another burst echoed as the wall behind us exploded in a burst of plaster, and now when I looked at Veronika all that anger was gone, replaced with sharp fear at knowing we were cornered.

39.

Jamal

"Can we just go out the back?" I asked as the third prong of that machine gun ambush fired up again, hosing the Denny's with round after round. I was starting to harbor real doubts about how much longer the structural integrity of this place could hold out, because it looked to me like the volume of fire was doing some damage to the walls.

"No," Sienna said, chips of tile from the kitchen pass-through flying over her as she crawled back to me past the end of the counter. Her dress was a total write-off at this point, soaked in blood, and punctuated with white space where bullets had torn through. "What about the other people in here?"

I'd forgotten there were other people in here. There weren't too many, but I'd definitely passed a few on my way in. "Damn," I said, face falling. I thought we'd had an easy exit route.

"Don't fret," she said as she came back around, "I've got an idea."

"What's that?"

"Why, it's a notion that springs to mind—"

"Damn, you went full literal on me."

"Asshole move, I know." She hunkered down beside me, taking a few breaths in and out.

"What the hell are you doing?"

"Steeling myself," she said, closing her eyes again. "I'm

going to zoom up through the ceiling—"

"Uhm, and through *all the gunfire.*"

"Yes, all of that," she said, "and then I'm going to rain destruction down on the gun mounts from above. Hopefully before they, you know, catch sight of me and stitch me full of lead."

My eyes widened in shock. "I don't like this plan. This is a bad plan, right up there with jogging at night in a black jumpsuit on an LA freeway or bending over in the shower in prison."

"Ouch," she said with a cringe. "Well, with luck, everything I'm about to get shot in will heal." She started to push off the ground.

"Wait!" I said. "Let's go out the back!"

"I told you," she said, pausing to patiently explain it to me again, like the errant child I apparently was, "we can't leave these people beh—"

"No, no, no—let's go out the back and hit these gun mounts from the side!"

She calculated that for a second. "You know … that might not be a bad idea. I don't know what the hell they are, but I seriously doubt they've got a 360-degree turn radius, and … maybe if we're lucky, they don't have one covering the back door. This has been pretty ham fisted so far, after all."

I looked around at the completely destroyed Denny's, pieces of which were piling up on the floor from being shot off the walls, booths, tables and everything else. "Ham fisted. Uh-huh. Sure."

"What?" She glared at me. "They shot me in the heart instead of the head. That's an unbelievable screwup, okay? When you get one clean shot at Sienna Nealon, you don't aim for center mass."

"Duly noted." I motioned back toward the counter. "Now can we—"

"Yeah, yeah," she said. She floated about an inch off the floor and zoomed around the counter while I crawled after her. "I'm on it."

"Wait for m—" But she was already gone. I crawled after her as fast as I dared, catching pieces of glass in my hands, elbows and anywhere else I touched the ground. Blood was coursing down my wrists and forearms pretty quickly, and I batted my way through the swinging door to the kitchen, which looked like it had been sawed in half at about neck level by the extreme volume of gunfire.

When I got to the kitchen, I heard a lot more metal in contact with metal. Bullets were spanging off the surfaces in here, bouncing like mad off stove vent hoods and stainless steel freezers. I kept my head down and crawled for the back like a man possessed, thankful I didn't have to navigate any broken glass in here because there were no windows. I really couldn't hear shit at this point, the gunfire having receded somewhat and my ears probably having had their fill of incredibly loud noises for the day.

I made it to the back door in time to see Sienna glance back at me, smile, and then bring her hand forward in a hard punch. It blasted the door off its hinges and exposed the night beyond, giving me a clear view into the parking lot beyond.

No new sounds of assault cannons rang out in the night, just the same three running in the distance, slightly louder now that we had a door open to the outside world. Sienna shot out into the parking lot and ducked behind a white sedan from the eighties. She rolled and came up, looking around to see if anything was waiting for her.

Gunshots rang out and I watched her roll again, this time zipping under the car's trunk as the front tires blew out. Whoever was shooting at her—and I suspected it was another of those quadcopter drones—they were tracking way behind her quick, stealthy movements. She zipped up ten feet in the air as I came into the door frame and three quick blasts of flame shot out of her fingers.

I snuck a look outside as one of those big quadcopters came crashing down about twenty feet outside the door. I wasn't even done admiring her marksmanship when she flew around the corner, torn dress flapping in the breeze.

I went in the opposite direction, dodging over the still-spinning remains of the quadcopter, the blades spooling down even now, and looked around the corner.

Sure enough, there was a big damned cannon-looking thing sitting in the middle of the parking lot, just chipping away at this side of the building.

I readied my lightning, stuck my hand out, and gave it a toss.

My bolt was a bright, cobalt blue that sparked and hissed. It hit the end of the barrel, and the cannon stopped humming immediately. The barrel pitched toward the ground and went silent, steam smoking off of it in the suddenly quiet Pennsylvania night.

I opened my mouth and tried to force a yawn. I couldn't hear squat, like someone had dumped warm wax in my ears and let it harden in there. "Damn," I said, but my voice sounded muffled even in my own head.

"Nicely done," Sienna said, coming around the corner at last. She gave a look at the Denny's, which was completely wrecked, every window shot out and exterior surfaces covered in bullet holes. "We should go."

"Yeah," I said, and pulled out my phone. "You want to go grab my stuff? I need to do something real quick."

She cocked an eyebrow at me. "Sure. I'll play bellhop for you, I guess." And she headed back inside, stepping over the barely remaining partition between the parking lot and the restaurant. It wasn't much of a step, really.

I approached the cannon carefully, my phone in one hand and my other bared, cold night air tickling it. "Let's see who you're working for," I said softly as I sent a small, probing charge into the brain of the turret. Not enough to wake it up—assuming that was possible—but enough to interrogate the circuitry within in a way only I—and apparently ArcheGrey—could do.

The response was immediate. There was a little data on the thing, mostly the record of what it was seeing and transmitting out. I found the frequency it was operating on, dumped the small amount of visual memory and instructions that it had taken, and then uploaded all that to my phone.

I was plugging the frequency the turret operated on into my phone's homing signal as Sienna stepped back outside, duffel bag slung over her shoulder. "I've got a read on the person who was controlling all this. They are … two point four miles away and—" The signal disappeared. "What the hell?"

"What the hell what?"

"What the—they're gone," I said, shaking my phone. Like that would help. "Must have killed the signal when they realized their toys were all broken."

"Figures," Sienna said with a muted sigh of annoyance. "Just as well, we need to get moving, too."

"But—but—" I stared at my phone's display. "Maybe if I try and—"

"No time," she said, and for the first time I realized she was shouting. I started to ask her why, especially now that people were starting to emerge from the Denny's scared and timid, shaking as they looked out at us in the snow.

Then I heard it, that faint sound of a siren howling, and realized …

It was coming from a cop car that was right up the street and about to make the turn into the Denny's parking lot.

"Yeah," Sienna said, snaking an arm around my waist, "it's time to jet." I started to say I only needed another minute, but I gave it up before I even started. The cops were here; we didn't have a minute. She yanked me away from the wreck of the Denny's and into the cold night sky.

40.

Reed

"Is it my imagination," Veronika said as I lay atop her, the shotgun roaring again over our heads, "or is this case going a lot more violently than these things usually do?"

"It's not your imagination," I said, ears ringing, the stench of fresh gunpowder in the chill air.

"Oh, good," Veronika said, looking at me, her lips pursed in annoyance, "because my imagination usually takes me to way sexier places than this."

I looked her right in the eyes, my weight bearing down on her. "This isn't my idea of a good time, either." I pushed off her and rolled to the side. There was a window just to our left, a desk blocking easy access to it. "What do you think? Gunman just outside?"

The shotgun belched fury and noise again, peppering us. Veronika scampered my way, almost knocking me over as she moved to position herself in the narrow aisle between the bed and the desk. "Yep." She pointed diagonally toward the front door. "Right there-ish."

"Kinda what I figured," I said, and summoned up my powers.

I hit the window with a hard wave of air pressure. It bowed slightly, then burst, the glass ripping through the screen beyond and shredding it as the wind carried it forward. A scream lashed through the midday sun that spilled into the darkened room as my glass shards razored into the bad guy who'd been trying to fill us with buckshot. I kept pushing with the wind, and the scream changed pitch after a thump filled the air.

Veronika looked at me quizzically. "Did you just push him over the balcony?"

"I think so," I said, as the scream faded and a louder thump came from outside as the Invisible Man plowed into the hood of a car. "Yeah." I nodded. "I pushed him over the edge."

"I sympathize," she said, and when I gave her a questioning look of my own, added, "You're doing the same to me and it's only day two."

"Har har." I stood and started toward the door just as something whooshed toward the living room window and burst through. I saw Bald Bull charge out and over the railing, doing his own jump.

"Whoa," Veronika said, pointing at the hole he'd made in the wall. We both ran out the door to look; he'd definitely gone through the wall and over the edge. The fall hadn't seemed to have killed him, though; quite the contrary, he'd snatched up the Invisible Man over his shoulder and was running across the parking lot, shotgun in his free hand, hauling ass at a speed that looked a touch faster than a normal meta. "He is really motoring."

"Yeah," I said, wondering if I should give chase. He disappeared through a thick clutch of bushes, and I decided against it. He could have blasted me right out of the air like a skeet with that shotgun if I got too close. And I'd have to be close in order to engage these guys and bring them down.

"You not in a hurry to pursue?" Veronika asked, giving me that same curious look.

"I don't think we have to," I said, eyes searching the parking lot. "The cops are gonna be here in a few minutes, and they'll do a little searching for us, but I doubt they're gonna find these guys."

"Would we really want them to?" Veronika asked.

"No," I said, "they'd plow through the cops. But I don't think they'll do that. I think when they come back, they'll do it later tonight, all nice and quiet-like. They won't want to make any noise."

She raised an eyebrow hard at me. "You think … they're going to come back?" She swept her hands around as sirens wailed in the distance. Probably Skinny Girl and her friends had called the real-deal cops. "After all this?"

"I practically guarantee it," I said, and nodded at the parking lot. "Where do you think the Invisible Man went to get his shotgun?"

Veronika shrugged. "His car, I presume—" She paused, getting it. "Oh. You think they'll come back to—"

"Yeah," I said. "Criminals returning to the scene of the crime. And we'll just be sitting here, waiting."

41.

Sienna

We had to stop off to get Jamal a new tablet computer because, judging by his whining, hacking things with his phone wasn't that easy. I wasn't really listening, to be honest, because whenever he starts to go on about hacking, my eyes immediately glass over like death by boredom has reached out its hand for me. Big yawn.

I tried to act impressed, oohing and ahhhing when he placed an order for a new tablet and we dropped by a big chain store and picked it up without him actually having to pay any money for it. "Ahhhh," I said as we walked out, his hands clutching the bag bearing his ill-gotten prize. "Congratulations on your thievery."

"What?" He looked at the bag like he didn't understand. "I didn't steal this. They gave it to me."

"Because you—what, created a false order in their system or something?" I gave him my most amused expression, though I wasn't that amused. I was irritated and trying not to show it. "That's thievery. It's just slick, new-age thievery instead of the old kind where you'd grab it off their shelf and try to sneak it out. More brazen, I guess."

"It's their system," he said defensively. "Maybe they should upgrade it if they don't want to get hacked."

"That's like saying, 'Hey, if this guy doesn't want his house broken into and all his crap stolen, he should buy a better door and a heavier lock.'"

He sputtered for a second. "That's stealing from people, not a corporation."

"People own corporations."

"Rich people," he needled. "You know, your billionaires with their evil, grandiose schemes?"

"Comparatively few billionaires have evil, grandiose schemes. Also, a lot of average people own at least a piece of those corporations you steal from in the form of their 401(k) plans—"

"I need this," he said with an irritable hiss worthy of, well, me. "Otherwise, I can't bust Caden Sims." He must have figured out the inherent flaw in my pokes at him because he straightened like he'd gotten stabbed. "Hey! You've killed people."

"But I'm still lecturing you on thievery," I said, turning away as we strolled across the parking lot, "because stealing, like murder, is wrong."

We got far enough out of the parking lot to disappear, and I flew Jamal up into the air again and back to the King of Prussia mall, where we pulled that disappearing act again, wandering through the entrances and exits as I changed my appearance and then we "borrowed" another car.

"And *you're* giving me a talking to on stealing a tablet," he said with undisguised glee.

"Just until we get close to the rental car place," I said, shrugging as I indicated that he should start the engine. He did so a moment later with a well-placed zap of electricity right into the ignition. "Think of it as an Uber you don't pay for."

"Or a stolen vehicle."

"At least I'm returning mine when I'm done. I doubt you're going to take that tablet back to the big box store when you're finished with this little crusade."

I parked the car and left Jamal waiting in it, nervous as hell, looking like he figured the cops were going to bust him at any second, as I walked the mile to the rental car place and posed as a dumb, dumb, dumb brunette, ditzy as hell, needing to rent a car but not sure about anything ("Wait, there's a King of Prussia around here? Where is he? Or she?

I don't want to discriminate."). It did not amuse the clerk, but he didn't seem to tumble to the fact that I was a wanted felon using a fake ID, so mission accomplished.

When I picked Jamal back up at the stolen—err, borrowed—car, he looked pretty nonplussed, but he had his tablet out of the box and working, at least. "It's really cold out here," he said, shivering as he directed a couple of the heat vents toward himself and turned up the fan.

"Why didn't you start the car?"

He hesitated, then looked out the window as he answered. "I didn't want to steal that person's gas by running the car."

I cackled like a mad witch but let it go without further comment. "All right, so … where to? Somewhere with Wi-Fi?"

He looked out the window again, and when he answered, I could hear the shame. "No, uh … my tablet has 4G." He glanced at me, then looked at the console between us. "Which I am paying for from my own money."

I held in a chortle, mainly because I was a little amazed that my argument had actually influenced him. "Where to, then?"

"Just drive for a bit," he said. "Pull over when you find a parking lot that's got a decent crowd in it."

I drove. We went down a few major suburban thoroughfares, and I parked in a grocery store lot with bright lights that glared through the windshield at me as I sat quietly and waited for Jamal to do his thing. I almost didn't want to ask him what he was up to, figuring he knew better than I did what to do.

"This is interesting," he murmured after a few minutes of silent pecking on the screen. He flipped it around so I could see it before I could ask, and I was treated to color, if slightly grainy, security camera footage of what was unmistakably the Javits Center, with its sweeping glass windows. The security cam footage was paused, and I saw Caden Sims's bodyguard brushing past a woman who had somehow been allowed close to his bodyguard ring. "See the hand off?"

He clicked a button and the footage ran in a short loop, no more than seven seconds. One of Caden Sims's bodyguards was carrying something, and this woman, whose back was to the camera, did a perfect, spylike swoop and picked up the bodyguard's bundle when he set it down. Without acknowledging she'd done anything, both of them continued to move off. When she was about twenty feet past the knot of bodyguards, she stopped, turned, and— "What the actual hell?" I muttered.

"Pretty positive that's ArcheGrey," Jamal said. "Kind of impossible to tell for sure, because—"

"Because she's wearing digital clown-face?"

I agreed with Jamal; she was probably ArcheGrey1819. He would have known her height and build, but unfortunately, the face of the woman on the screen was completely and utterly obscured by some sort of bizarre, painted-on digital image of a skull that appeared when she turned to face the camera.

"Pretty slick bit of code," Jamal said, flipping the screen back around and pecking on it. He kept his other hand firmly anchored at the bottom of the tablet, where I could see small flares of blue light every few seconds, the product of him working his powers to interface directly with the tablet. "No big surprise that this isn't a naturally occurring phenomenon—"

"Realllly?" I snarked. "Because I was just thinking that someone wearing the digital equivalent of the *Saw* mask in the middle of the Javits Center wouldn't attract a damned bit of attention. I mean, don't get me wrong, New York is weird and its denizens allow for some weirdness, but this … is a bit much, even for NYC."

Jamal snorted. "This is a bit much for Mardi Gras in New Orleans. I'm trying to figure out if this is a real-time effect or if it's something she added later, after she knew she'd been exposed." He tapped the screen and did his little flashy light for a few minutes. "I think this is a program that works in real-time." He sounded vaguely excited.

"Meaning it … what? Searches out her picture in the video system and paints that garish pixelation over her pretty face every time it gets recognized?"

He blinked a couple times and looked at me. "How'd you

know she was pretty?"

I rolled my eyes. Guys were always thinking about one thing. "She kicked your ass, Romeo. Focus on catching her, not dating her."

"Uh, yeah," he said, and tapped a couple more times on the screen. "I mean, yes, I think you've got the gist of it, she's got a search program that comes in behind her wherever she is and just paints over her when it recognizes her face, thus invalidating any sort of ability for agencies to identify her wherever they look. Kinda tough to ID someone or launch a manhunt when this is your evidence. 'Be on the lookout for a digital clown.'"

I almost laughed again. "You really are thinking about her as a dating prospect, aren't you?"

He shrugged, clearly embarrassed that I'd called him out on this. "It's neat work. If I could ever get her to part with the program, it could have some uses, you know."

"I'm sure that's what you're interested in from the lightning-wielding, choke-chain dominatrix: a program."

Jamal ignored me, but I could tell it took some effort. "Seems like she's a dead end, at least for now. Maybe I could track her back to her arrival, but even so …" He ran a hand over his short-cropped hair. "She'd have to cover her tracks pretty well, and that'd be really time consuming … there's gotta be a better way …"

"I'm sure there is," I said idly, looking out the car window. My breath fogged it a little, reminding me how cold it was outside.

"Hey, here's something," Jamal said, flipping the tablet around again. This time I was graced with a screen showing Caden Sims and his closest bodyguards in the exhibition hall, Sims clapping wildly, and then reaching up to shake hands with Cameron Wittman, who nodded and listened politely to something Sims was saying. He replied, and then broke from the handshake to wave at the crowd. They both then parted ways, Wittman to backstage and Sims hustled out of the room by three of his bodyguards.

"So we've got contact between my new favorite billionaire suspect and our designated bad guy," I said.

"That could be totally innocent," Jamal said, pulling the tablet close in to his chest like it was a shield or something.

"Could be," I said. "Anything on where Sims has gone?"

"Nada," Jamal said, spinning the tablet back to work on it again. "I've got Wittman, though. He's got a midtown penthouse, and apparently he's in for the night. It might take me a minute to track down Sims."

"Is that an actual minute or a Los Angeles minute?"

He thought about it a second. "An LA minute."

"So, possibly hours, then?"

He nodded reluctantly. "Possibly."

I sighed, frosting the window again. "Why'd you look up Wittman's location?" I knew already, but I wanted to hear him say it.

He strained as he answered. "Mmmm, I dunno."

"Oh, you don't? Are you sure it's not because you think he's maybe possibly guilty and you want me to interrogate him for leads?"

Jamal opened his mouth and shut it. "Or it could be because I know I'm going to be a minute—"

"Hours. Just own it and say hours."

"—and I don't want you sitting here sighing and fogging up the windows like we're making out in here."

"We could make out. Then I'd have your soul and your powers, and you'd be more likely to come around to my way of thinking more quickly."

HAHAHAHAHAHA, Bjorn said, *the skinny boy would be my bitch in here. Mine, you hear? None of the rest of you will have him.*

Goodness, Eve said with an eyeroll, *suddenly we're territorial.*

"I almost got added to your cast of crazies once before, if you remember," Jamal said, eyeing me like he expected me to lunge for him, "and I didn't enjoy the burning sensation all that much."

"Oh," I said, "right." I'd forgotten that I'd almost absorbed him once, in the heat of a fight. "Well, if you change your mind, I know a Norseman who has an offer for you that I'd suggest you refuse." He gave me a bizarre look, apropos to my oddball suggestion, then shook his head and went back to work.

I sighed, and caught myself mid-sigh, and saw Jamal smile out of the corner of my eye. "Maybe I'll just … have a chat with Cameron Wittman," I said, pulling my phone out of my pocket and ditching my newest wig by tossing it in the back seat. "Text me the address?"

My phone buzzed. "Already did," Jamal said as I stepped out into the parking lot and the cold air rushed over me. "Good luck." I slammed the door, looked around to make sure there weren't any witnesses, and then shot off into the sky heading northeast.

42.

Reed

A stakeout with Veronika wasn't my idea of a good time, especially given how much sniping back and forth we'd enjoyed thus far with each other. Actually, saying we "enjoyed" it might give the wrong idea; she didn't seem to be enjoying it any more than I was at this point, which was probably why we were both stone-silent as we waited, watching the parking lot.

I was left with my thoughts, which I thoroughly disliked. I would have figured that returning to silence would be like a blessed respite, especially given how much shade Veronika had thrown my way.

Nope. Even though she was silent, old familiar thoughts were bumping around in my head and producing uncomfortable emotional reactions.

Thoughts like … what if Isabella was done with me? I'd been gone for two months without so much as a call, after all, and a month before that while I was working for the government and she was hiding from Harmon & Co. What if she'd found out what happened and assumed I'd used it as an excuse to bail out on our relationship? Or what if she'd gotten tired of waiting on me to get my head together? I had a feeling she wasn't going to be waiting terribly long if she decided to hang out her single shingle. Some guy would come along and snatch that up in a hot second.

Shit.

But I'd fled for a reason. I mean, I was the one who answered the door and let Harmon into the safe house in San Francisco, when we were hiding. It was practically impossible not to answer the door when the President of the United States knocks, especially when, I suspect, he'd sent out psychic feelers to induce me to do so. She'd left, she'd escaped, and I'd been in his thrall that entire time, doing terrible things at his command.

Or at least I assumed they were at his command.

The thing that was killing me was … how badly did he have to twist me to get me to do what he wanted? I honestly didn't know. It wasn't clear to me whether it took him turning my brain into a pretzel-like roll, with logic and cognition all turned up and conjoined with fantasy and bullshit, or if it was … just a simple thing, like flipping a light switch.

I was really, really afraid it was the latter. What if it was just that simple? Just a little push to get me to kill—

"I was about to say, 'Penny for your thoughts,'" Veronika said, "but now that I've seen your expression, I'm not sure I'd want them even if you were paying me to take them."

I stuttered a response. "It's not—they're—no, you wouldn't want them," I finally agreed so we could go back to silence.

What if all it took was just a simple little reversal of thought to get me to kill my sister? A little push, and I'd do it? What if all the moral principles I thought I had, everything I believed about myself … what if it was all just a flimsy little thread that didn't ultimately matter? That I was just putty in the hands of a telepath?

How much of this did Isabella know? How much did she suspect? Did she even know that I'd …

"Okay, discounted rate," Veronika said. "You pay me a dollar and I'll take a few of your thoughts." She was eyeing me uneasily.

"How simple do you think it is for a telepath to get us to turn on our family members?" I asked without hesitating.

"Ooh, okay, wow," Veronika said, cringing. "You took full advantage of that one, didn't you?" She settled into five seconds of silence. "I mean … if you want me to make you feel better, I had an ex who was a telepath, in addition to being really good at other, more human, psychological games. I learned some lessons about the human mind during that time."

I tried to decide whether I wanted to hear this or not. "Hit me with it," I finally decided. Because why not?

"Pushing the human mind around is kinda easy," she said with disarming frankness. Even now, on stakeout some hundred feet above the parking lot, hanging out in a cloud and talking in whispers, it felt more like we were at a bar with a couple drinks in front of us just shooting the breeze. "Think about how many manipulative people there are out there who don't have the advantage of meta powers. Getting people to do what you want isn't that hard, especially depending on the kind of hold you have on a person." She paused, eyes sliding around like she was trying to calculate whether she wanted to tell me something or not. She finally looked down and said, "That ex … was really good at making me think that I was the problem in the relationship. I walked out of it thinking that maybe I was asking to be hurt. We'd have an argument, and I'd be all spun around by the end of it, thoroughly convinced that the problem was totally in my head, that I was imagining it all."

"You got gaslighted," I said.

"They didn't call it that back then," Veronika said with the trace of a smile. "You kids have fancier words for things these days. Back then it was just playing head games." She shrugged. "How easy is it to mess with someone's head? By the time I was done with that relationship, I'd gone from …" She looked deeply uncomfortable. "Well, my mother was my best friend before it, and by the time I was finished … I hadn't talked to her in something like two years. Because I was convinced that my mother was one of the problems with our relationship. Of course, once I stopped talking to my mother, it was something else—something that hadn't ever been a problem before, but … it totally was, according to my ex." She smiled faintly. "The human mind is a malleable thing, Reed. Even before you throw telepaths into the equation. Everyday conversation moves our mind. We talk, we socialize, we persuade. We move in response to stimuli. This guy—the president—he didn't even have to do that. He had a finger on the button of your mind, took it and stitched it the way he wanted it to be, no need to engage in conversation or gaslighting, as you put it. Do I think it was easy for him? Yeah. Probably. And fun, too, I'd guess, getting people to do his bidding, which was why he wanted to get more and more working for him."

I opened my mouth and my teeth clamped it shut, rattling. "But Scott …" I said, closing my eyes tight.

"What about him?"

"… Scott got out," I said, forcing my eyes open. "He started to resist. To question—"

"He was also grabbed like … months before you, as I understand it. Months." She reached out and pinched my arm. "Months, you hear me? If you hate what he did to you in the short span of time you had with Harmon, imagine what that dude went through. He was hunting your sister from, like, April to November. We don't even know all the things he did in that time. She said something to me about how he made her watch her own house burn down. It's not shooting an innocent victim, but Sienna was his lover at one point. And he made her watch her childhood home burn to the ground. Can you even imagine?"

I pictured a woman with dark hair running, the barrel of my gun flashing as bullets streaked out to punch into her back, dropping her. She fell and slid in a lump, something caught beneath her body. The muzzle flared again, three times, and the front of her face blew off in a wash of red, occluded from view by the fortune of her back being to me.

"I can imagine a lot," I said, blinking the afterimage away. I bobbed my head as I stared down into the parking lot below. "Am I imagining, or is that our Olivia walking across the parking lot?"

I wasn't imagining it. There she was, our blond meta woman, threading her way through the parking lot, looking around for cop cars or suspicious people. She made her way between the cars, glancing around wildly. It made me wonder how long she'd been waiting for the cops to clear off. Probably quite a while—I guessed she'd lurked just a while longer at the fringes to be sure they were gone before she came home. I hadn't suspected she would come back; I figured she'd take one look at what had happened here and vamoose for somewhere else.

"She must need something from the apartment," Veronika said softly.

"She should have run straight from the hospital to here and grabbed her stuff." I lowered the cloud we were hiding in by about fifteen feet, subtly.

"Uh oh," Veronika said, pointing at the far end of the parking lot. I followed her finger and sure enough, there was Bald Bull and the Invisible Man. Invisible was hobbling a little, like our earlier altercation had taken some of the starch out of his sheets.

"They're not together," I said, frowning. "Olivia and our assailants."

"Then who the hell are these guys?" Veronika asked as Invisible Man disappeared with his power and Bald Bull kept moving toward his target—our perp, Olivia.

43.

Jamal

I sat there in the car, tapping and zapping, until I suddenly sat up ramrod straight, staring straight ahead out into the dimly lit parking lot. "Did I just make a huge mistake sending her out there?" I wondered aloud.

No one answered, because no one was there, but I thought about it for a few seconds, looking left and right in the empty car as I pondered that course of action I'd just undertaken. I'd let Sienna Nealon loose after Cameron Wittman, who she swore was the bad guy.

Turned loose the most powerful, feared woman in the world on a guy who might have been completely and totally innocent.

"She'll be fine," I said, but damn it did not sound convincing. "Just … fine …"

It took me a while to put the thought aside enough to keep working.

44.

Sienna

I wish I could say I entered Cameron Wittman's penthouse apartment with subtle grace, coming in through an unsecured rooftop vent or by ringing the doorbell. I imagined myself coming in and politely conversing with him, asking my questions to a receptive audience as he had his butler serve us tea and I carefully questioned him about his activities, leading to an admission of guilt produced with a flourish of the sort you might see from an old-timey villain in a mystery, "You have gotten me, detective! By the virtue of your wit, I am undone!"

But let's face it, I'm not world-renowned for my wit (though it's awesome, dammit); I'm known for my badassery.

So I blasted into Cameron Wittman's penthouse bedroom at high speed and practically triggered a sonic boom coming to a stop before I splattered him across the interior wall.

"WHOA!" Wittman screamed, launching out of bed like he had a spring-mounted ass. He was naked except for a really boring pair of plaid silk boxers, and his bare feet hit the cold, beautiful granite tile as his brain tried to lock on to the holy hell of horror that had just come through his window at the speed of a small airplane. His eyes met mine as he danced back and forth in the cold air I'd swept in with me, the balls of his feet making contact with the floor one at a time as he seemed to tiptoe from one to the other as I watched. He wasn't in bad shape, but I'd always heard these Silicon Valley guys took their health seriously.

"Hi," I said, smiling as I gave his brain a moment to process what he was seeing. "How's it going, Cam? Mind if I call you Cam?"

"You're Sienna Nealon," he said, voice still thick with sleep. It was almost like some ruffian had just rousted him from bed in the middle of the night.

"Yes," I said, "And you're not dreaming, just so we can head that thought off at the pass."

"I didn't think I was," he said, putting his hands over his bare, muscled, waxed chest. He'd stopped dancing from foot to foot, finally.

"Because this is too surreal for dreams?"

He looked at the person-sized hole in the window. "Something like that." He looked at me uncertainly. "I hope there's a reason for this that doesn't involve me going flying."

I nodded slyly. "I hope so, too, because I think we both know I've got enough felony warrants to juggle at the moment. Anyway, I'm here to talk. Do I need to worry about any household staff waltzing in and interrupting us?"

He blinked a couple times, then ran a hand through his bowl cut of hair. "Uh, no. The cook doesn't come in until six in the morning. I mean, building security might come up in a few minutes since *that* wasn't quiet," he nodded at the hole in his window wall, "but …" he shrugged, and I took it to mean that they were probably in the lobby, where most of their threats would come from. And it was a lonnnnng way down. He crossed his arms over his bristly, prickly nipples. "What can I do for you, Ms. Nealon?" he asked, sounding pretty composed for a guy who'd just been awakened so rudely and had little time to adjust.

"Caden Sims," I said.

Wittman just stared at me, then made a face. "Who?"

"He talked to you after your lecture at the conference this morning?" I asked. He stared blankly at me. "You shook his hand from the stage?"

He stared, like he was trying to remember. "Uhm …" He seemed to get it all at once, recognition flaring in his eyes.

"Oh, the weird guy. Yeah. I didn't catch his name. What about him?" His eyes moved wildly, like he was trying to keep himself under control, but failing slightly.

I stared at Wittman, debating how to play this. If his building had a fast elevator, security could be here quickly, like within five minutes or less. I had no evidence he had actually colluded with Caden Sims, and his reaction almost seemed sincere.

But the problem was … I never have been the trusting sort. It's a personal failing.

"Listen …" I said, dropping to the ground and dispensing with the ominous hovering. "I've just broken into your home, so you have no reason to trust me." I paused.

"Yes …" he said, hesitantly, as though voicing this thought to me might be enough to compel me to turn him inside out with my meta powers or something. "That did occur to me."

"I need info on this clown you shook hands with," I said. "I don't think he's up to any good."

Wittman frowned. "Well, yeah, that makes sense. He said something … really weird to me after my speech. Something about, uh … the system, bringing down the system …" He scrunched up his face in concentration. "I wish I could remember … not sure I even heard it all, because it was pretty loud in there … ovation and whatnot …"

"How attached are you to that memory?" I asked.

Wittman's eyes flared open wide. "Attached …?"

I waved a hand nervously in front of me. I hated stealing peoples' memories, but if he volunteered it … "Let's say it were to disappear from your mind—would that bother you?"

He adopted a pained expression. "Uhmmmmm …"

"It could be very surgical," I said. "Just a few seconds, and poof! No more memory of weird guy, and I'll maybe have a clue what he's up to."

"You want to … trim a memory out of my head … in hopes that it will help you … investigate … this guy?" Every word dripped with skepticism.

"I can tell that you're concerned about this idea of memory loss—"

"I think most people would be."

"—but it will be only the time around your conversation with him and nothing else. I promise." I stopped talking, because anything else I said was going to be nervous babble.

"You're a … wanted felon, right?" he asked. He brushed his hair back again a little nervously.

"Right," I said, "which means if I wanted to, I could just steal the memory while you screamed, and then turn you to pudding without even having to throw you out the window, and it wouldn't make a huge difference to the charges I'm presently facing." His eyes went huge at this, like shock and fear. "But I'm not really of a mind to do that, Cameron—err, Cam? You never did answer."

"Cam is fine," he said, looking pretty shellshocked.

"Look, if you want to run out the clock until security gets here," and his eyes widened again, "that's fine. I wish I could tell you that this is the last you'll see of me if you choose not to cooperate, but the truth is … it's probably not. Caden Sims is up to something bad—"

"You keep saying that, but you don't work for the government," Wittman said, sounding a little crazy and frustrated as he did it. "Why—why—why—"

"Why am I making it my business to stick my nose into trouble when I've already got a snootful of my own?" I asked, and he nodded. "Because that's the kind of stupid that I am, Cam. Instead of holing up somewhere and hoping these baseless charges will just disappear, I go looking to solve crises that other people are dealing with. And this Caden Sims? He's coding something with this hacker, ArcheGrey1819—"

If I thought Wittman's eyes had nearly exploded out of his head before, it was nothing compared to what they did now. His borderline terror gave way in a hot second to a flush of anger that reshaped his jawline into a point. "This Caden Sims is working with ArcheGrey1819?" He went past flushed, straight to glowing crimson. His phone rang and he snatched it up. "What? No, I'm fine. I'll need a window repair person at some point, but I'm busy at the moment. Send them tomorrow." He hung up without another word and when he swung back around to look at me, he had a hot glare. "Take the memory."

"That was … quick," I said, looking around, waiting to see if someone was going to come jumping out of the closet to tell me I'd been played, or shoot me, or something.

"My kid brother worked at the US Attorney's office in midtown as a junior prosecutor." His lips contorted in anger. "On the day it went down, he was one of the last to evacuate. He was in the lobby when the building came down." Wittman stared off into the distance. "He's got scars all over his body, and he'll never walk again. That's because of ArcheGrey1819."

I didn't want to point out that it was actually because of a meta they called the Glass Blower, because it would kindasorta defeat my purpose, and also, because ArcheGrey had been involved in the operation, so technically she was somewhat culpable, at least in the eyes of the law. "Okay," I said, instead, and stepped up to him, putting my hands gently on his jaws.

"Your hands are really cold," Cameron said awkwardly as I stood there in front of him, him in nothing but boxers and me cradling his face like a lover. With ice fingers. And fully dressed.

"Sorry," I said, and we passed the next few seconds in silence.

I made it into his memory before his pain really started, and honed right in on the moment Wittman finished his speech to thunderous applause. He was waving at the edge of the stage, taking his victory lap, and then I saw—

Caden Sims. Front and center.

He waved Wittman forward after applauding forcefully, with the kind of claps that turned his palms blood-red from trying to loudly register his approval for what Wittman had said. The volume in the room was explosive, the entire hall agreeing with Wittman at the loudest possible decibel level.

Sims reached out and grabbed his hand, shaking it furiously as Wittman reached down to him. It was a little embarrassing watching it. I was almost expecting Sims to start kissing his knuckles or something. "I agree with everything you just said," Sims shouted to him.

"What?" Wittman reached up to his ear, shaking his head slightly to suggest he couldn't hear. He really couldn't; I could get it, now, because I was just replaying the subtle impressions that had made their home in Wittman's brain, but at the time, with the thunderous applause? Wittman didn't have a clue what Sims was saying, he could only read the glowing, bordering on loving, expression on the man's face.

"We need to open everything up!" Sims shouted. "Too many secrets! Too many—"

"That's nice," Wittman said, nodding at him, and trying to pull his hand back.

"—too many barriers between people," Sims shouted. "I'm going to remove them. All of them." His lips moved so I could read them even with the faint words making their way into Wittman's memory, though unconsciously.

"Okay," Wittman said, patronizingly, and this time he managed to extract his hand from Sims's grip. He turned his attention back to the crowd and waved at them, already forgetting the strange man in the front row.

I skimmed the rest of Wittman's memories, but found nothing to indicate he'd ever met Sims before in his life. My mission accomplished, I made one quick stop-off in Wittman's most embarrassing memory, which was the time he'd gotten the bright idea to ask the prettiest girl in his high school to prom, even though he'd never spoken a word aloud to her and only worshipped her from afar. I checked, and it had no ties to anything useful, he didn't dredge it up for motivation (you'd be surprised how often people tied their worst failures to subsequent successes as motivators). No, he only used this one as a sort of psychological punishment, a way to mentally flog himself for being young and socially naïve, and so I quietly stole that memory as well, as a sort of payment for the kindness he'd done for me.

"Uff-da," I said as I yanked my hands off his face. My cheeks burned with the embarrassment from the prom memory I'd absconded with, as though I'd been the one who'd done it.

"Huh," Cam said, blinking as he came out of it. He put his hands on his cheeks and touched himself. "That was … that felt … I mean, there was like a burning feeling beneath it, but it … kinda bordered on …"

"Don't say 'sensual,'" I said, rubbing my hands together. They really were freezing.

Wittman blushed. "Heard that before, huh?" he asked to cover his own embarrassment at thinking it.

"I'm a succubus," I said, "I've heard it all before, but usually not from someone who's experienced my powers firsthand. Still, that was about as gentle as it gets. It starts to get more painful the longer I'm in contact with the skin."

"Hmm," he said, and seemed to remember he was nearly naked. He looked down and abruptly turned around. "Uh, sorry."

It took me a second to work out why he'd done that. "Oh." Like he said, sensual, I guess. "I really appreciate the help. I think this might have shed a little light on Mr. Sims's motives."

"Glad I could be of assistance," Wittman said, not daring to turn and face me. "Would you mind, uh …?"

"I'll leave you be," I said. "Sorry about the window."

"Thank you for not …" He started to say as I went to make my exit. "… Not acting like … everyone in the press seems to think you act. Not killing me, basically. Or just … ripping my mind apart, since it seems like you could have done that."

"I could have," I said, feeling beyond uneasy. "But I wouldn't. I never have, not to anyone. I'd rather kill someone who deserved it rather than tear them apart that way."

"Well … best of luck catching ArcheGrey," he said, still keeping his back to me. I tried not to stare—because he wasn't a bad looking guy, from any angle. That hair, though.

"Thanks," I said, completely ashamed. I'd busted into the guy's home in the middle of the night, scared the piss out of him, gone into his mind, and all I could do to thank him for his kindness was to steal his most embarrassing memory so he wouldn't fixate on it in shame in the future. I flew out the broken window before I could do anything else to embarrass myself, because right now I was feeling worse than he ever had when going through that old memory.

45.

Reed

"Look out!" I shouted down at Olivia as I dropped the floor of wind beneath my feet, sending me and Veronika tumbling to the earth. There was no chance we'd make it before the Invisible Man snookered Olivia, though, and hence, my warning.

Olivia heard my cry and froze in the middle of two rows of cars, as motionless as prey looking for the predator she sensed coming. She didn't move, but the air around her seemed to sparkle with near-invisible motion, and suddenly something launched past her the way Veronika had when she'd charged Olivia at ORMC.

The Invisible Man decloaked as he smashed into a car, headfirst into the windshield, his legs and ass sticking out of the glass, hood all dented in from his landing. There was a nice crease in the grill as well where his legs had smashed into it. I assumed there were going to be some broken bones from that little crash landing, but damn—I wouldn't have wanted to be the one on the receiving end of what she'd done to him.

Even after seeing what had happened to his partner in crime, Bald Bull apparently needed to learn this lesson for himself. He lit into a rhino charge, smashing an old minivan and bowling it out of the way as he screamed toward Olivia.

Veronika and I were still fifty feet above the ground, and Bald Bull was coming at her like a meteor, complete with a tailstream of air distorting around his motion. It looked like a glowing contrail, like he was burning through the atmosphere toward Olivia, sure to streak down and make her extinct.

Except she did have that power of hers, the one that allowed her to send people who came at her past like she was a bullfighter and they were a—well, you get the point. I expected it to kick in as Bald Bull came rushing toward her, expected to see that distortion, and then watch him blaze past like he'd done a slingshot around a gravity well. I figured he'd end up in China.

That wasn't what happened, though.

Olivia screamed as he got close and dove out of the way. Just a hair too slow, though, he clipped her leg as he blew past, and she spun, coming to a hard landing in the middle of the asphalt. It didn't look like her powers had affected him at all, but rather that he'd steamrolled her and she'd barely dodged in time.

I flared the wind beneath us and brought myself in for a guided missile landing, aiming for Bald Bull. For some reason, what he did spiked the rage in me. In the shadow of the parking lot, I saw Olivia's hair as much darker, almost ebony for a moment, as she lay splayed on the pavement.

Bald Bull came to a stop and started to turn as I came crashing down on him with a kick to the base of his skull. He staggered and I thumped off of him, feeling as though I'd hit a brick wall and abruptly stopped. I flared the wind again and caught myself before I landed on my ass, using it to flip over so I could land on my feet, catlike.

The thrum of the wind at my fingertips pulsed through my hands. I hovered a few inches above the ground, staring at Bald Bull as he turned around and seethed at me, his head catching the shine off a nearby streetlight.

"Guess nobody ever taught you not to bushwhack women in a parking lot," I said, doing a little seething of my own. "It kinda makes you a creep."

"And you stalking her from above makes you better than me?" Bald Bull asked, wearing a scowl that didn't do him or his eyebrowless face any favors.

"Have you thought about using an eyebrow pencil for that?" Veronika asked, coming up behind me and running her finger over her brow. "Even some guyliner would do worlds of good for—"

"Butt out," Bald Bull said, rubbing the sole of his shoe against the asphalt and making a loud scuffing sound. "This isn't your business."

"I'm not *your* business anymore, Tracy," Olivia snapped from off to my left. She was up on her feet, wobbly, but fierce. "I don't want any part of you—any of you." She wheeled to look at me, apparently including me in that blanket statement.

"I'd love to not be all up in yours, either, ma'am," I said, "but unfortunately you used your powers and a man ended up in the hospital, and then you fled the scene."

"I don't have time to explain myself to you," Olivia said, looking around like Invisible was going to pop out of the bushes and get her. (He wasn't; he was still splayed out on the hood of the car just behind Bald Bull.)

"You're coming home with us," Bald Bull—Tracy, I guess she called him, but I liked my name for him better—said.

"That's not my home," Olivia said tightly, and the air around her started to distort, suggesting to me that I wanted to avoid close proximity to her for the foreseeable future.

"Seriously, guyliner," Veronika said to Bald Bull. "Look into it. It'll change your life, redefine your—"

"Not now," I hissed.

"Right. Serious issues," Veronika said, and flared her hands into blue orbs of plasma.

Something about the light must have provoked Bald Bull. It glimmered in his eyes, and he flinched away from it just a second before the skin around either side of his sockets folded tightly into crow's feet. He bared his teeth and lunged, charging at Veronika, who looked mildly surprised as he distorted the air around him, not dissimilar to how Olivia had just done.

"NO!" Olivia screamed, but it didn't stop him. Not even close.

Bald Bull blasted toward Veronika, plainly set on running

her over. Veronika, for her part, set her feet and raised her hands, ready to meet him when he came. His feet churned up the pavement with each step, leaving little indentations, a ridged crater in the black asphalt that looked like shadowed hoof prints with every sprinting step forward.

I churned a hard wind just beneath him, lifting him off the ground as he approached Veronika. He swept upwards on a current for about three or four long steps before he even realized he'd run right over her head. The air around him was orange, glowing, like he was about to bust through and create a wormhole or something.

As soon as I saw that he'd cleared the top of Veronika's head, I dispelled the tornado I'd created beneath him. Bald Bull's eyes went wide and his mouth fell open in shock as the solid ground he thought he'd been running on dissolved beneath his feet. He hadn't even fully realized I'd lifted him up.

He crashed into a Volvo and both he and it flipped as though he'd t-boned it. Tangled up in one another, they rolled right through the shrubbery and small trees that had formed the small privacy enclosure around the parking lot of the apartment complex. A horn honked on the road beyond, and the squeal of tires filled the night.

"Olivia," I said, spinning in time to catch her starting to run, "don't."

She froze, her back to me, silhouetted by the overhead lights. "I didn't mean to hurt that man." I couldn't see her face.

"That's fine," I said. "If it was an accident, it was an accident. But you can't just run away from the problem and hope it all works itself out. You've got to talk to the cops. Explain things."

She came around slowly, and I could see the fear, the desire to run. I could easily imagine her bolting for it, her hair dancing as she ran away from me and all the trouble I brought with me. "What if they don't believe me?" There was real, raw worry in her voice, a thin cord of fear.

"They might not," I admitted, "but if you run now … you're going to be running forever."

Something about that caused her to tense. "I'm always going to be running anyway," she said, and started to turn away again.

"I was afraid you'd say that," I said, and shook my head. With one hand, I started a tornado beneath her feet. It swirled with fury, lifting her up unexpectedly the way I'd just done to Bald Bull, but much, much slower.

"What are you doing?" she cried as I picked her up off the ground. I let the wind buffet her endlessly, but without any particular fury. Just enough to lift her off the ground, and then form a spinning vortex cage around her to keep her from doing anything hasty. The air around her started to distort but all that happened when she triggered her powers was a sudden gust of wind that blew harder in the spin of the tornado, disturbing her hair.

"I can't let you go," I said, holding her prisoner right there. It wasn't the easiest move, but it wasn't the hardest, either. Once I had her off the ground, gusting it enough to keep her from breaking free was a simple matter of making sure that she simply had no tread for the bottom of her feet. Easy enough, because the wind had lifted her like a chair, right on her backside. I did the same to Invisible Man, and kept a weather eye out for Bald Bull, in case my tipping him over hadn't done enough to take him out of the game. "I'm sorry," I said to Olivia, as the first sirens started to sound in the distance.

"Please," she said over the roar of the wind, "you can't do this to me. You can't take me in—they'll get me." A single tear slid down her cheek, and was brushed off by the wind that held her captive.

"No, they won't," I said, not even really knowing who "they" were, beyond Bald Bull and Invisible Man. "I won't let them."

She didn't say anything else as the cops came roaring into the parking lot. She just stayed there in my little trap and stared at me like a frightened animal, and I back at her, as the red and blue flashing lights illuminated the scene around us.

46.

Jamal

"Whoa," I breathed to myself, staring at the screen. The words didn't blink, but I did, slipping my glasses up off the bridge of my nose and rubbing my eyes, making sure I had read this right. I slid my glasses back down and checked again.

I had it right.

"Now what the hell do we do about—"

The thump of someone smacking the window of the car caused me to scream unexpectedly, almost smashing myself through my own window in an instinctive retreat. The driver's side door opened and Sienna slipped back in, a few flakes of snow trapped in her hair, which was twisted and tangled from her flight.

She looked at me with something like grim amusement, and said, "You know … that wasn't a very manly scream."

47.

Sienna

"No shit," Jamal spat at me in reply to my little dig. He looked like I'd caught him in the middle of something deeply personal, red-handed, sweaty and frightened. He mellowed a degree, then asked, "How'd it go with Cameron Wittman? Is he … still alive?"

"Cam?" I asked, putting the car in gear. I didn't know where I wanted to drive, but I felt the urge to move a little, so I turned out into the parking lot, which was pretty sparsely attended now that the hour was getting late. "He's in fine form. We had a nice chat, and then he gave me permission to ransack his sole memory of Caden Sims, which was a very short encounter filled with very little insight save that whatever Cam Wittman was selling in terms of ideas, Caden Sims was buying in bulk and without reservation."

Jamal chewed that one over for a minute. "So that tells us basically nothing."

"Not nothing," I corrected him. "It tells us a lot about Sims, actually. He was totally fanboying all over Wittman up on the stage. I'm surprised they didn't need a janitor to mop up his seat afterward. He was insanely enthusiastic about what Wittman was saying, like a Beatles fan watching live or something."

"Beatles … fan?" Jamal looked at me blankly.

"I was raised by my mother," I explained, nudging the car out onto the frontage road and toward the freeway entrance.

"She was into the classics of her era and not terribly cool with me listening to the more modern stuff my peers might have been into. You know, during the forced internment in my house that we know as my childhood."

"Oh, all right then."

"Anyway," I went on, "if we know that Sims gets totally hot over Wittman's ideology, that gives us a direction to go on motive, and maybe even a direction to look in for his scheme."

Jamal's face was all screwed up in concentration. "So … what do you think his scheme is, then?"

"I dunno," I said, shrugging as expansively as I could with my hands anchored to the wheel. "He's into … open … stuff. No secrets. No barriers."

Jamal considered that. "In the digital world … that sounds like the mission statement of hacktivists like me. You know, free flow of information, exposing the dirty secrets of the great and powerful."

"That's how you read it? Interesting."

"You see it differently?"

"Yeah," I said. "Kinda scary, actually. Imagine no secrets."

"Was that a Beatles reference?"

"I don't think that's one of the verses, no. But really—think about it. All the things you have out there, exposed to the world."

"You mean like …" he raised an eyebrow at me, "… nude photos?"

"Pretty sure that's already happened to a lot of people," I said dryly. "And I'm sorry, but that's gross."

"Maybe they shouldn't have put their pictures on the cloud?" Jamal suggested.

"I'm guessing they know that now," I said, "but regardless, pretty sleazy and embarrassing and invasive."

"And emails? Because that's happened, too."

"Right," I said. "All that kind of stuff. We live our lives digitally these days—credit card numbers out there everywhere as we do, uh … online transactions—"

"It's called e-commerce, and yeah, it's kind of a thing."

"I have a pulse and an Amazon account, I know it's a

thing," I bristled. "I'm not some total relic of a bygone era, you know. Anyway, all our correspondence is online, we chat to other people, nude pictures, apparently—"

"But not yours, right? Turn here."

"I'm too paranoid and too self-conscious to ever do that," I said, and then perhaps flushed a little as I turned the car onto the onramp.

I didn't fool him. "You got scared off by it happening to all those celebs, didn't you?"

"As if I weren't paranoid enough because of all those upskirt video sites," I said, "they went and took all the fun out of the idea of sending racy photos to your significant other, the bastards."

"I'm seeing your point, I think," Jamal said. "There's a lot of talk in my circles about INFOSEC. Breaking it, mostly, but … there's some room in there for debates about whose information should be protected and whose ought to be gone after just for the lulz."

"I'm guessing the rich and the powerful are fair game on the lulz thing?"

"Anyone's fair game for the lulz," Jamal said with a shrug. "Some hackers have decency and principles, some of 'em just want to watch the worldwide web burn, for lack of a better way to say it. They'll troll anyone, anytime, just to get a rise out of them, and if it causes them genuine pain, that's even better." He shifted uncomfortably in his seat. "This one guy I heard about … he posted the chat logs for a couple teenage girls that went to his school because they made the mistake of logging in on a school computer where he had a keystroke logger. Boom, all their darkest secrets over the course of years of conversation, posted live for everyone to sift through at their leisure. One of them tried to kill herself with pills afterward, I heard."

"That's pretty dark," I said.

"Someone just set up multiple drones outside a Denny's and tried to gun us down remotely," Jamal said, "and you think someone releasing a teenage girl's chat logs is dark? Turn here, by the way."

"The consequences were dark, yeah," I said, steering the

way he'd suggested while focusing on the argument we were having. "People have secrets. They're entitled to some privacy in life."

"Apparently Caden Sims doesn't think so," Jamal said, "and—"

"Well, he's wrong," I said heatedly. "What the hell is the point if everything you are, everything you believe, everything you want for yourself just gets exposed to anyone who wants to know? What the hell is left of a person after their—their guts get opened to the world and sifted—"

"I dunno about guts," Jamal said with a healthy dose of jadedness. "Maybe heart."

"It doesn't matter," I said, trilling an ugly throat-clearing noise. "Whatever you want to call it, it's the essence of a person. Whoever we are, we have the right to share or keep to ourselves as we please. It's not healthy to just tell the whole world everything about someone without their permission. No one should have the right to do that to a person. It's a gross violation."

"Maybe," he said in a tone that suggested to me he meant "No." "But lots of people keep secrets that hurt other people, too."

I looked over at him as I kept my foot steadily on the pedal, the car going about ten above the speed limit. "You talking about yourself here?"

I could tell I caught him flatfooted. "Uh … well … I guess I have kept a secret or two that caused some hurt," he said. "Like … for example, the time I had to leave home for a while—"

"Because you had a secret girlfriend who got murdered and you avenged her," I said, trying to sound sarcastic but not snotty. I didn't have a lot of room to cast stones when it came to revenge murders. "Yeah. Imagine if that secret had gotten out."

"What if it had?" Jamal asked. "The whole reason I did what I did is because the guys who did it felt … untouchable. They had power behind them, and Edward Cavanagh was the man behind it—"

"AKA, Patient Zero in my 'It's always the billionaire

behind the grandiose scheme' theory."

"He would have walked, because the truth couldn't touch that man, couldn't stick to him. He had real power in his court—now imagine if instead of me having to take matters into my own hands—"

"You chose to do it, okay? No one made you. You could have let it go." Wow. I really swung wide on that one. But it was technically true. Some people could have let it go. Not me, obviously.

"You remember what it felt like?" Jamal asked quietly. "To—"

"To have someone hold me down and force my hands onto my first love's face, killing them slowly?" My voice sounded foreign to myself, hard. "Yeah. I vaguely recall."

"Yeah, I thought so," Jamal said. "Why'd you go after them yourself?"

"Because much like you," I said, "there was no accountability, no justice. Metas weren't even in the open then, and the idea that I could have proven in a court of law that these … people …"

I think she's talking about us, Bastian said in a stage-whisper in my head.

No duh, Eve said.

"… could get away with what they did, that there was no recourse …" I shook my head. "You know why. Same reason you did."

"If the truth had been out there, though," Jamal said, "you wouldn't have had to."

I rubbed at my brow, keeping a hand on the wheel. "This is all just a theoretical exercise, though. Every single secret known to man isn't just sitting out there, okay? There are secrets out there that are secrets of the heart, and teenage shit—who has a crush on who, who's talking crap about who. Oh, and credit card numbers. Routing numbers. We're not talking about murder confessions. We're not talking about justice." I looked at him hard. "We're talking about—"

"You're wrong," he said. "Everything's on it nowadays. Everything. Too many cameras out there, all tied together. Too many microphones listening everywhere. Too much digital memory, patterns waiting to be sorted into a coherent story by increasingly sophisticated AI algorithms. Nah, the truth's out there. Or—in here." And he brandished the tablet. "Which reminds me," and he tapped a couple things out on it, then flipped it around for me. "While you were out … I found our Denny's attackers."

I stared at the screen, which showed a van on a black and white image, heading down the frontage road next to the restaurant where we were attacked. It showed them turning in right at the parking lot, then skipped, and a few minutes later they hauled ass out of the parking lot, rear doors swinging wide as they made a hard turn. "Huh," I said. "I figured they'd be long gone by now."

"Indeed," Jamal said with a grin. "But they aren't. They laid low for a while, but they're on the move again now. Like I said … it's all out there."

"Fine and dandy," I said, "but where are they?"

"Funny you should ask," Jamal said, and he tapped something else out on his tablet, breaking into a grin, and I got the feeling that I might just like the answer I was going to get. "Because I just so happen to have their GPS pulled up right … here …" And a little blinking dot showed us, with a red one a few miles ahead of us.

48.

Reed

The Orlando police precinct that we went to after we got everyone rounded up was about what you'd expect from a long-in-service government building—faded paint that was due to start peeling soon and that lived-in smell that buildings tended to get after being around for a long time. It was also a little cool, probably because the temperature had dropped after the sun went down. Not nearly as chilly as Minnesota or Wisconsin in the winter, but cool enough to make me wish I'd brought a jacket with me.

The Invisible Man had been chained up and left bleeding in an extra-strength holding room at my recommendation. I'd made sure they used meta restraints to put him in his place and anchor him down good. The cops had all gotten instructions warning them that he could turn invisible as well, because the last thing we needed was a rookie getting freaked out and accidentally setting him free because he thought the room was empty or something.

"Please don't do this," Olivia said as I herded her down the hallway, my hand carefully clutching her arm. I hadn't wanted to chance touching her at first, but Veronika had threatened her pretty sufficiently while she was still trapped in my tornado cell. It had taken all the stiffness out of her spine, and now she was just going along meekly, both of us moving sufficiently slowly that I hoped she wouldn't be able to co-opt my momentum and use it against me, at least not without a heavy reprisal landing on her in the form of a tornado cell, part deux—with less kindness and restraint than the first one.

"I just need you to answer some questions," I said. "A man got seriously injured because of your powers. If you hadn't run, this might not have turned into what it turned into."

"If you'd had those guys after you … you would have run, too," Olivia said, but she sounded dead inside when she answered.

Bald Bull hadn't been there when Veronika and I went to check on him. The car I'd flung him into was still there, but ol' Bull was long gone. Disappeared into the night. I'd been looking at Olivia's face when we saw it, because I'd hauled her along in my little tornado cage … it wasn't a good look on her.

She was terrified of him.

"Hey," I said as we followed a cop down the hall. He opened a door, and I led her into the interrogation room with my hand on her elbow. It felt like a little much, but she was technically a criminal, in the same sense that someone who clumsily hit another person with a car while not paying attention was criminally negligent. "How are you doing?"

It was a stupid question, but she sniffed and answered me, though stilted. "Fine."

"I'm not exactly a genius—" I started.

"We know," Veronika said, covering it with a cough.

"—but I know that when a woman says something is 'fine,' it is not actually fine, nor even in the neighborhood or possibly same planet as actually fine," I said. "It's all right to be scared. This is scary stuff. But we're going to take your statement, and go through the process. What happened was an accident, and when the DA comes to talk to us, I'll make sure he or she understands that, okay?" I helped her to the chair across the table.

Veronika blew air out of her lips in a disapproving manner. "Gee, chief, you think maybe you should hear her side of the story first before jumping to the conclusion this was an accident?" She shut the door behind us with a thump, announcing with her scowl and irritation that she had picked the role of bad cop.

"You're suggesting she just launched that guy into a tree because … what? She was bored?" I fired back, trying to assert myself as good cop. "She didn't even lift his wallet afterward, and she was coming to visit him in the hospital with flowers."

"Maybe she wanted to finish him off," Veronika said coolly.

"I didn't—it was an *accident*," Olivia said forcefully. She had ramped up to righteous indignation at last.

"I know," I said, taking the seat across from her as I unlocked her handcuffs.

"Or she's a paid assassin who missed her mark hard," Veronika said. "Either or."

"I'm not an assassin," Olivia said, now sputtering with outrage. "I didn't mean to hurt him! He just—he got close and—when people get close and surprise me … bad things happen," she finished lamely.

"Maybe you should start at the top," I said.

"I was out for a walk," she said.

"With your name," I said, acutely aware that the cameras were running for posterity—and the courts.

"My name is Olivia Brackett," she said, the air seeping out of her like she was a balloon. She practically deflated in front of me, shoulders slumping as she spoke. "I was out for a walk. A guy came jogging by, got a little too close … he startled me." She looked at the table, couldn't take her eyes off it. "My powers … they're not easily controlled, and they just … activated. He went flying." She looked up and right into my eyes. "So I ran, because … who's going to believe me?"

"I believe you," I said. Veronika snorted, and I flipped her the bird. "Why did you come to the hospital?"

"I didn't want this guy to die," she said, her breathing picking up. "I wanted to see if he was all right."

"Absolve your guilty conscience?" Veronika asked.

"Come on," I said.

"Yes, I wanted to …" Olivia said, sounding increasingly

desperate. "Yes, I wanted to make sure he was okay because I felt guilty for running, all right?" She leaned into the table, and spoke directly to me. "But you have to understand … I only ran because—"

"You were afraid," Veronika said.

"Yes," Olivia said. "Of—"

"The law," Veronika said.

"Of Tracy," she said, and I mentally translated that to mean Bald Bull, "and his father."

"Is Invisible Guy his daddy dearest?" Veronika asked. She had a small lollipop in her hand and made a show of crinkling the wrapper to reveal a bright blue sucker that she popped in her mouth. When I caught her eye, she pulled it out. "Want one?"

"No, I'm fine," I said archly, and turned my attention back to Olivia. "Is Invisible Man—"

"No," Olivia shook her head firmly. "That's Howie. He's … an idiot, I guess, but he's not nearly as bad as Roger. Roger is Tracy's dad."

"Roger, Howie, and Tracy," Veronika said, "three names that seem like throwbacks to the 1950s."

"They were probably born then," Olivia said. "Howie, anyway. Tracy was born in the seventies. And Roger …" She shook her head, which turned into a full-body shudder. "He's … older."

"How much?" I asked.

"Don't know," Olivia said, finishing her shudder and keeping her shoulders hunched close, trying to retain heat in what was a pretty cold interrogation room. "I've known him all my life."

"Friend of the family?" Veronika asked.

"Yes," Olivia said quietly, staring straight ahead. "Or what was left of my family."

"Cue the sad backstory music," Veronika said through teeth clenched around her lollipop. She caught my scathing look and asked, "What?"

"What happened to your family?" I asked, shifting my attention back to Olivia again.

She hesitated, looked like she struggled with it for a

moment, then started to speak. "I was born and raised not too far from here. In a cloister."

I nodded. Cloisters were communities entirely of metas, a throwback to the times when our kind had been a total secret. Lots of metas had huddled together to raise our young in places where keeping the secret of our powers didn't matter quite as much. I nodded along.

"It was the worst parts of living in a small town," she said, back to staring at the pitted surface of the table. "I've never lived in a small town, though, I've only heard about it on TV. I've only ever lived in Orlando and in the cloister."

"But you had youthful dreams and wanted to escape cloistered life to pursue your heart's desire of tapdancing naked for strangers," Veronika said in a sing-songy voice. "'I know you're just here because of my prodigious dancing talents, gentlemen! Form an orderly queue and kindly respect my non-existent boundaries! Oh, you only have a roll of quarters? Sure, I guess you can shove them right up my—"

"Veronika!"

Olivia and I both glared at her. "Sorry," Veronika said without remorse, "I just feel like I've heard this tale before. The ending is always a bit predictable. It's not a roll of quarters, by the way, on the off chance you didn't already figure it out."

"I was a secretary," Olivia said, dripping with disgust, "at a dentist's office."

"And your boss never fed his roll to you like you were a jukebox?" Veronika asked.

"For crying out loud!" I said. "Veronika … just leave."

"Like I said, I was getting bored anyway." She made for the door, rapping on it sharply until it opened. "Wake me up before you head out?"

"Probably not, at this point," I fired back. I caught her smirk in the two-way mirror as she disappeared through the door. "Sorry about her. She had a rough childhood or something, maybe coped by drinking paint thinner, I dunno."

"I heard that," Veronika said through the metal door, loud enough for us metas to hear it, "and it was nail polish remover. Get your facts straight."

"You were telling me about the cloister," I said, trying to gently ease Olivia back into her story. Her eyes were red, and a little puffy. "About … Roger. About leaving."

"I wanted out," she said, settling her gaze on my chest. "I had dreams, things I wanted to do. Go to college like you see in movies."

I tried not to be snarky. "Like … which movies? Please don't say *Animal House*, or any of the lesser *American Pies*."

"What? I don't know, just … general ideas of college," she said. "A place that wasn't—that wasn't …" She hung her head in disgust. "A place that wasn't the cloister."

"What was so bad about being there?" I asked.

She looked up, and her eyes were rimmed with anger. "Everything. I was all set to leave a few years ago, had been planning it for years." Her tone was pure malice, buried anger repressed for years. "And then Sovereign came."

Whoa. I knew this story, all too well. Sovereign and his group, Century, had conspired to wipe out all the metas in the entire world. Outside the US, they'd done a pretty thorough job, too.

"Suddenly, Roger said we couldn't afford to have me out there," she said, still spewing her anger. "He said that this was how Sovereign's people were finding cloisters, by using telepaths to track down our kind in the big cities and then torturing them to find out where their home cloisters were. That it wasn't 'safe.'" She delivered the last word with such raw vitriol I almost wanted to scoot back from the table.

I didn't say anything, because Roger had actually been right on that one, and saying so would put a wedge between Olivia and me at a moment when I was trying to gain her trust. "Go on," I said, instead of correcting the record and metaphorically blowing my foot off in the process.

"They shut the gates," she said. "Cut off the satellite TV. The only thing we had to do, the only link to the outside world—" She put her head down. "They said we'd just hunker down until it was all over, and they got rid of the electricity, the water. They dug wells, did everything to take us off the grid. Roger said it'd be safer, that there'd be no sign that we were out there. No telepath could scan us as far out as we were, no records were left in any of the utility companies—they saw to that. And so our whole cloister just disappeared off the face of the earth.

"But we were still there," she went on, looking particularly haunted. "And anytime someone raised their voice saying they were gonna leave … Roger was right there, ready to shut them down however he had to. He put people in hotboxes in the middle of summer. They'd come out staggering, couldn't even walk straight. But they didn't act up again, didn't speak out again. Most of us learned from just watching it, knew we didn't want to go that route."

"How long before you escaped?" I asked.

"A year and a half," she said. "And when I got out, I learned that Sovereign had been dead for almost a year. I'd been stuck with them that whole time." She shuddered again. "You know what he did to me? Why I finally left?" She looked at the door, then at herself in the mirror. "Roger told me I was going to marry Tracy. Because he was the only one around my age in the cloister. 'It just makes sense,' he said. Me. With him." She spat disgust, as though Bald Bull Tracy was in the room with us. "As though I'd ever be interested in Tracy. Calling him dumb as a box of rocks would insult perfectly good rocks the world over."

"Heh," I chortled. "So … this Roger. How many people are in the cloister, and how many is he holding against their will?"

"I don't know," she said, and now she sounded defeated. "We didn't talk about it much, because if he overheard you … straight to the box. You ever even heard of such a thing, punishing people like that?"

I shifted uncomfortably in my chair. "I might know someone who went through something similar once upon a time. Pretty classic method of home imprisonment. Trying to control people, kenneling them like a disobedient dog."

"That's exactly what it was," she said, thinking it over. "Just like dogs." She made a disgusted face. "Roger … probably has five, ten people really on his side. But others go along with him because they don't want to get punished for speaking out. It's enough to keep the cloister in line."

"What kind of powers does Roger have?" I asked. "Like his son?"

"Tracy … his are like the complimentary opposite to mine," Olivia said. "Roger never said it, but I think he had it in mind that if we had kids, they'd be damned near invincible if they got his powers and mine." I did a little shudder of my own at that point; arranged marriages to produce desirable metahuman combo powers was not unheard of, especially in the old world of meta cloisters. Here in 21st-century America, though? It skeeved me out pretty bad. "Our … theoretical kid …" She made a face telling me in explicit terms what she thought of that, "… could redirect kinetic energy away from them with my abilities, or absorb hits and blows and channel it into charging or projecting it like Tracy does. He mostly does the charge thing, though, because he likes to hurt people up close. Doing it from a distance isn't cruel enough for him."

"What about Roger?" I asked again.

Olivia stayed silent. "Roger … he can …"

The table rattled a little, like the earth had quaked under our feet. "That's a little weird," I said, and looked back to Olivia.

She was pale like she'd had all the blood leeched out of her. "It's him."

"Roger?" My brain jumped. "Earth powers?"

"Yeah," she said, sounding like she was hyperventilating.

"I have a friend who can do that," I said, trying to be soothing. The building rattled again, and a ceiling tile fell and shattered into foam pieces on the table between us, prompting Olivia to scream. "It's going to be okay. He can only control earth and glass—"

"That's not all," she said, shaking her head. "He can move that, but he can also control elements ripped out of the earth like metal and sand—"

Augustus couldn't control metal; it just wasn't in his suite of powers. "Are you sure about the metal thing?" I asked.

"It's from his mom," she said, shaking. "His dad had the typical earth abilities. He bragged about it, how they all came through for him—"

"But didn't for his son," I said with a leer. Genetics were a funny thing, especially when it came to meta powers. I stood and turned, placing myself between Olivia and the metal door. If this Roger thought he was going to get her back without a fight, he was mist—

The door flattened me as it blew inward, and at the same time the two-way mirror shattered and shredded me from the side. I hit the ground, the metal door lying across me, and I looked down to see my chest bent horribly, a massive crease running sideways from one of my armpits to the other. As I watched, the door lifted up and hovered in the air.

A man stepped in through the door in casual jeans that rose an inch or so above his ankles, leaving his old, muddied dress shoes and white socks exposed. He was wearing a flannel shirt, the collar straight but the whole ensemble horribly wrinkled. He looked like he hadn't been to town in twenty years, but when his eyes alighted on Olivia, he smiled, surprisingly warmly.

"There you are, my errant girl," he said, maneuvering around the massive door that hovered over me. He made a move and it slowly swept across the room, bending and flexing as it wrapped a squealing Olivia up like a metal corn dog. She drifted over, kicking and flailing, trapped in the impromptu prison as it fell into Roger's arms. She was struggling to escape his grasp, railing and rocking at first, but her movements became feebler and more resigned as the seconds ground on. He pressed his fingers to her forehead and touched her delicately; she tried to throw his hand off with a sharp buck of her head at first, but he stroked her hair gently and the second time, she didn't bother to resist. "I was worried about you," he said, with utter sincerity.

Her reply was audible, the desperate choking sounds of a woman trying to contain her terror.

"I know you're afraid," he said with soothing calm. "But we're going to get you home straightaway. Get you looked after properly. Ol' Roger will see to it, don't you worry."

"You … can't …" I said, reaching out a flagging hand to

try and stop him. I wasn't even close enough to touch his pant leg.

"I think you'll find—if you survive this—there ain't nothing I wouldn't do for one of my own." He gave me only a momentary look as he said that; the rest of the time he was looking right at her, speaking right to her.

I passed out in a puddle of my own blood, pain searing every nerve ending in my body, before he even made it out the door.

49.

Jamal

I was staring at my screen, checking my Messenger and my usual forum for anything I'd missed while I waited for the GPS running in the background to alert me we'd gotten within a few hundred yards of our quarries, when Sienna said, "Okay, take the wheel."

I looked up from a message board thread about a particularly brilliant troll attempt, and said, "Whut?"

"I'm gonna fly out and wipe out their car," she said, pointing ahead through the darkened windshield as we passed under a street light. She was offering me the wheel. "Badda bing, badda boom. Bad guys in a soufflé."

"A … what?" I shook my head, hoping I'd just stared at my screen too long.

"I'm gonna go get 'em," she said, speaking slowly for effect. "Take the wheel."

"What are you going to do to them?" I asked.

"Smash them into tiny pieces, then smash those tiny pieces into even tinier, near-microscopic pieces—"

"And then lemme guess—smash those pieces into even tinier pieces."

"No," she said with amusement, "then we feed them to fish and let them digest the tiny pieces. It's a process, see, taking them from sneak attacking bastards to fish poop, and it takes like, three steps."

"Or," I said, holding up my tablet, "we could catch up

with them like we're doing now, and I'll use my powers to kill the alternator on their van as we pass. They'll drift to the side of the road and we can interrogate them."

"I don't love this plan," she said, stone-faced, "I don't feel like it's optimized to end with them in the ass of a fish."

"But it might get us some information on who sent them," I said, wondering if her straight face was hiding murderous rage or just an attempt to play with my head.

She blew a raspberry, but turned back to the wheel. "Such a measured response. Fine. We'll do it your way."

"Good," I said uneasily. I hesitated a minute, then started to ask, "Were you really gonna—"

"Probably not turn them into fish poop, no," she said, "but their faces would know they had been punched, and punched good when I was done with them. I'm not known for letting people shoot at me and get away with it scot free."

"No, you're not," I said, and hid my relief by looking back at my tablet. I pushed the tracker to the background, monitoring the updates to it via the electrical signals I was reading through the port, and hit refresh on my hacker forum. It had like, two new threads to read since I'd last refreshed it, and a half dozen responses on old threads I hadn't caught up on yet. I opened the first and started to read, feeling that cool rush of enjoyment and excitement at the relief that something new was there.

"You've got that look on your face again," she said, jarring me out of the moment. She was watching me out of the corner of her eye, and I looked away guiltily for a second.

"I was just reading—"

"Yes, I know," she said. "It's always on your face when you're reading. Like 95% intense concentration, 5% weird, zoned-out ecstasy."

"It's called internet addiction, okay?" I huffed, and tried to get back to the page.

She was silent for a minute. "Is it really?"

"Yeah," I said, more brusque than usual, because I was being interrupted, "it actually is. You get a rush of endorphins when you load up a page that's given you enjoyment in the past. Facebook, for example. People sit there and refresh it over and over again, hoping something new pops up to catch their interest. Sometimes people will toggle back and forth between multiple sites, or they'll have a favorite news page or forum they go to—and … you know, you just click over and over, waiting for something new to pop up. Feels like boredom, but then something hits and …"

"Huh," she said, like she was really thinking about it. "Is that the big deal about Facebook and Twitter?"

"And Snapchat and Instagram and text messages and everything else," I said, shying away from meeting her eyes because I was trying to skim one of the less-interesting threads that had popped up on my forum in my absence. "When you talk to people online, researchers say you get to know them more personally, more intimately, more quickly than in real life. There're fewer barriers to a heartfelt conversation, less inhibition in sharing because there's no physicality to worry about, no body posturing, no social cues to read or maintain. You'll confess things to people you don't know IRL because you feel more connected with them, and there's a perceived veil of anonymity even when they know exactly who you are. It makes people feel free to text or post stupid stuff that they'd never say out loud."

"I think I've heard about this," she said, "in relation to internet trolls. Anonymity brings a certain liberty to indulge the darker parts of your persona."

"It allows a certain liberty to speak your truth, though, too," I said, feeling a little swatted by what she'd said. "Yeah, anonymity can be bad. But it can also allow people who genuinely fear for their safety to say whatever's on their mind. Someone who lives in a dictatorship where they crack down on you for speaking bad about your country, or someone who lives in a theocracy where their very existence might bring them death—anonymity gives them a chance to speak to others like them without fear of reprisal. It gives people who might feel marginalized in the conversation a place to go and connect with others like them. To say what's on your mind, even if you know it'll be unpopular or bring down hell … and do it without completely wrecking your own life outside of the internet."

She snorted. "Pretty sure some people have taken that liberty thinking they were anonymous only to watch themselves get really famous, really fast, in the worst way."

"Yeah, well, there's downsides to everything," I said, and waggled my tablet. "I use this to feel connected, but hilariously …" I lowered the screen, "sometimes I feel more alone than ever, even when I'm hooked in and talking to some of my best friends online."

"At least you know what you're battling with."

"I'm not *battling* with it," I said with a forced laugh. "Why would I? What's the alternative? Since I got home, I'm just … sitting around. There's nothing out there to interest me, not now that Flora's gone. So … I stay online. Keep myself busy, because … what else is there?"

"Um, life?" Sienna asked, making it sound like it was obvious. "Life is out there. Real human contact."

"Internet life is like a microcosm of real human contact," I said. "The same dramas of betrayal, the soaring love stories—"

She laughed. Loudly. "There's no love like internet love, huh?"

"Laugh all you want," I said, "but welcome to the new day. People meet and marry from online relationships all the time. It's easier than going into a bar and striking up conversations with random strangers."

"Yeah, that's fine, I get that," she said. "But there you're taking your relationship from the internet into the real world. And you can talk all you want about the rewards and closeness of an internet relationship, but if you don't translate it into the real world at some point, move from the screen," she gestured at my tablet, "to out here … I don't want to say, 'What's the point?' because I get that there are actual, you know, chemical rewards in the human brain for that kind of contact, but … doesn't it feel …" She cringed, mouth twisting as she tried to get her thoughts into words. "… I mean, as someone who has had a world of trouble connecting with people even on the somewhat limited basis that I can … it just sounds to me like living online the way you're talking about is a pretty hollow way to go through life."

I didn't know what to say to that, because … what the hell could I say to that? I'd felt it, being up late, tied in with a posse that was after some mad hacking goal. We'd hit our peaks of triumph, kudos and congrats passed around before we'd all pass out in our individual houses, thousands of miles from each other. And I'd wake up the next day around noon, alone, the house quiet cuz Momma was out …

And I'd wonder what the hell the point of it all was.

Then, eventually, I'd get up and log on, and those feelings would recede for another day.

"Yeah," I said quietly. "You're not wrong." She didn't say anything, and after a minute I asked, "So, what gets you out of bed in the morning?"

"Punching people in the face," she said reflexively. It didn't sound like an honest answer, and I was about to push it when my tablet buzzed in my hand, the electrical feedback changing just slightly to allow me a warning of proximity, one that I'd set up.

"We're close," I said, and flipped the screen from my forum to the map. She'd been cruising about fifteen above the speed limit, heading into Philadelphia on I-76. I looked at the map and figured out we were less than fifty yards from the target. I raised my head and pointed when I saw it. "Right there."

"Cool," she said tightly. The van was just ahead and we were closing pretty quick. Snow was falling very lightly, and they were in the right lane, following the speed limit almost exactly. "How do you want me to do this?"

"Get in the lane next to them and cruise past," I said. "Not too quick. I'll hang my hand out the window, and when we're in their blind spot, I'll hit their engine with a targeted zap. Their ignition will click off, and they'll coast to the shoulder. It'll be quick."

"Will they know what's happened?"

"I don't know. I've never tried this before." I tried to keep the embarrassment out of my voice at failing to disclose this somewhat crucial information. "But it works in theory," I hastened to add.

"Oh, good, theory is a fine armor for warding off bullets to the head," she said, looking daggers at me. "Just in case …" She took a hand off the wheel and readied it, extending a pointer finger. "If you were driving, I could spike one of their tires with a fire shot."

"Good thing I'm not driving, then," I said, as we closed on the van, snow piled on its back bumper. "Because I'm really terrible at it, and I've never driven in snow."

She just shook her head. "Amateur."

"Well, it doesn't really snow in Atlanta—"

"It does in Minneapolis," she said, steering us over a lane gently as I rolled down the window and stuck my hand out. "Enough to make this look like a gentle spring rain. Let's get these douchebags."

50.

I let loose with my burst of electricity as we were about ten feet behind the van's driver-side door. Because our car was lower to the ground, I hoped that the driver wouldn't see what I was about to do. After all, it was night, it was snowing, and we were back a little ways in his blind spot.

But when that flash of lightning lanced from my hand to the nose of the van plowing down the interstate at 65 miles per hour … I had a feeling Stevie Wonder would have noticed the flash of blue that lit up the mirror and side of the vehicle as it coruscated into the engine compartment.

The van immediately slowed, its momentum killed with the engine. I'd done my part, but the van fishtailed, the driver trying to regain control now that the power steering was out. I drew a sharp breath.

"Damn," Sienna said. She applied the brakes gently, then sped up to rush us past the slowing van. The back of it nearly hit us as the driver fought to keep the back end from spinning out, and I watched out of the window, freezing cold air punching in like repeated slaps to the face as I craned my neck to look at the out-of-control van behind us. "Looks like this guy doesn't drive in snow, either."

I held my breath as I rolled up the window, watching in the passenger side mirror to see what would happen. The driver got it under control and started bringing the van to the side of the road. I half expected him to turn on the hazard lights, then I remembered I'd blown out his entire electrical system. His headlights were off, and the only thing allowing me to keep watch on him was the giant lamp posts along this stretch of the interstate.

"Well, you definitely got 'em, Ace," Sienna said, taking us to the shoulder and bumping along on the edge as traffic raced by to our left. "Now the question is whether they're going to realize we did it or n—"

A bevy of bullets tore through the back window. We both ducked, hard, and Sienna slammed on the brakes. She made a small, pained grunt, and I saw blood running down her shoulder, a cringe on her face, eyes squinted shut.

"I guess that's a not," I said, as the men behind us opened up again, peppering our car with another storm of bullets.

51.

Sienna

I took a round in the right shoulder and another in the lung. It had been a bad week for my lung, which is probably not something normally said by non-smokers. Blood slicked the steering wheel and made my grip dicey. What made it a little worse was that someone was chattering away at us with an AK-47 and I was stuck in my car, facing the wrong way.

I shouldn't have brought us around the van. I should have followed the same procedure I'd learned from the cops all those years ago, when I'd started to study with local law enforcement agencies and seen how they did traffic stops. I should have kept the threat in front of me, but I'd been afraid I wouldn't be able to stop on the snowy road in time, so I'd bumped around the target.

And given him a free pass to shoot up my car because of it. Dumb.

"You all right?" Jamal asked, hunkered over in the passenger side foot well. He was just about underneath the dashboard, which he could manage as a rather slight fellow. I'd have a hell of a time squeezing into that position, even if there hadn't been a steering wheel right above me, but then, I wasn't exactly petite.

"I've been shot twice, and that part of my brain that calls me stupid over and over is blaring hard in my head," I said.

You got shot, Harmon said. *Shot. With a gun. By people. Humans. Lesser beings. How did you ever beat me?*

"Shut up," I said, hoping he would. "We need to get out of this car because the trunk is not great cover against rifle rounds, and the seats are even worse." As if to illustrate my point, another burst hit the car and snapped Jamal right across the back of the head.

"Oh, shit!" I cried as he snapped a hand up to the back of his head. I shoved his head down and looked at the wound. The bullet had caught him right across the back of the skull, but fortunately, it had only left a shallow, grazing crater like a skidmark across the back of his skull, neatly bisecting the occipital notch. Blood ran out in a free-flowing torrent as I stared at it. "You're going to be okay," I pronounced.

"I got shot," he said, sounding horrified.

"Good news, 'tis but a flesh wound," I said. "Get out of the car before it's not."

"Did you just quote Monty Python to me?" he asked, dazed.

"OUT OF THE CAR!" I said, reaching over him, shoving it open, firing a blast of flame out the broken back window and then diving out my own door simultaneously.

My burst hit the front of the van with a WHUMP! as I spilled out onto the snowy shoulder with a thump of my own. My nearly-healed lung and shoulder wound protested my rough treatment, as did my shoulder blades. Pain was just survival reflex, designed to keep humans from doing stupid things that would get them killed. Most of the stupid things I did (probably) wouldn't result in my death, so the pain was just an annoyance, albeit one I still had to force my way through.

My vision cleared about the time a rogue snowflake hit me right in the eye. It tickled, but it also kept me from full visual acuity at a time when someone was trying their level best to transform me into a cadaver. "Sonofa—" I shouted as I fired a near-blind burst of flame backward toward the van.

It hit, and a blazing ring of fire took hold. It took me a second to realize I'd just caused their front driver's side tire to light up.

The sudden inferno lit a shadow around a figure that had been a little too blurred a second earlier. He hesitated, turning instinctively to see what had just sparked the sudden conflagration that had burst into existence just behind him, and I took advantage of his built-in threat response to blast him with one of Eve's light nets. He caught it sideways and was flung into the van, the momentum carrying him so hard that it indented the white, paneled side of the vehicle. He hung there, unconscious, strung up, legs dangling just a few feet from the burning wheel well. "I hope your underwear isn't combustible, you dick," I said, only a little vengefully, "because you're going to be there for a while."

"What did you do to him?" Jamal shouted to me from somewhere behind the car. I could see him moving beneath it in a thin coating of snow on the other side of the vehicle.

"Nothing he won't recover from as long as his underwear is flame retardant," I shot back, wiping at my eye and coming back to my feet with a hover push. I moved to squatting, because I didn't want to stick my head up in case the other guy in the van was also armed.

I saw motion at the rear of the car, and a guy bolted out with a pistol in hand, aimed right at me. I started to fire at him, just a reflex gesture that would have landed a flame burst up his nose, but a flash of blue light hit the tip of his pistol and he jerked as electricity ran down his body. The pistol fired and a bullet whizzed by me. My attacker jerked, spasming in pain, and then hit his knees, planting face-first on the rough, snowy shoulder, his butt stuck up in the air.

Launching into the air a few feet, I came down with a foot on his gun and ripped it away from him, sliding it under my car and out of his reach. He did not respond, so I kicked him in the ass for the crime of shooting at me a lot (not too hard, you wimps) and then lifted him by the elastic of his waistband and gave him a near-atomic wedgie. He did not respond, being unconscious, but it made me feel much, much better.

"You didn't get shot again, did you?" Jamal asked, wobbling toward me around the bullet-ridden trunk of the car.

"No," I said. "Did you?"

"Just the once." His hand went up to the back of his head

and came away soaked in blood. He stared at his wet palm and then got a very far-away look on his face.

"Hey," I said, snapping my fingers and dangling our prisoner by the underwear in front of him. "Focus on me, here. It's just blood."

"Yeah, I know," he said, trying to shake it off. Some people got weird at the sight of blood. I counted myself fortunate I wasn't one of them, because I'd probably spilled more of my own than anyone's.

"We need to get some detail on who hired these guys," I said, "if they're in-house thugs, mercs …"

"Why does that matter?" Jamal asked, blinking away his disorientation.

"I feel better about hurting mercenaries," I said, and gave my prisoner's undies another mighty lift. He grunted in his unconsciousness, and I had a feeling things were getting pretty darned snug down under. "They're not really people at all, you see. They're empty vessels who do whatever violence they get paid to perpetrate."

"That's a dim view. They're still people."

"So is Soylent Green, but at least it's not trying to kill me."

He squinted at me, clearly not getting it. "… Whut?"

"This guy could be out for a while," I said as a tractor trailer buzzed by and nearly splashed me with his wheel wash. I narrowly dodged it thanks to my metahuman speed. "Let's see if Mr. Underoos is a little more awake." And I tossed the guy I'd just wedgied into the still-smoldering grill of the van. He made a loud clunking noise that felt somewhat therapeutic.

"Wait … which one is Mr. Underoos?" Jamal wandered after me to the side of the van. I added a little fuel to the burning tire, which made him jump in surprise.

"This one," I said, pointing to the guy netted to the side of the van only a couple feet from the flaming wheel well. "Keep up with my sweet and obvious nicknames, will you?" I wanted everything to be nice and toasty for Mr. Underoos. I walked up directly behind him, admiring how bound to the van he was, his chest pressed against the side panel, and then poked him hard in the kidney with one finger. "Wakey

wakey."

"We are in the middle of the freeway here," Jamal said, avoiding the flaming wheel.

"We're on the shoulder, you big baby," I said. "Calm down."

"I mean we're kinda exposed," he said, still cradling his head and shivering a little. He wasn't wearing a coat. "People passing by probably called the cops already, you know? Gunfire and all?"

"Maybe," I said. "We are getting close to Philly, and it's not exactly a crime-free paradise. They might just think it's part of the local flavor." I could tell by his look he wasn't buying it, so I poked Mr. Underoos harder in the kidney. "Wake up. We need to talk."

I could tell that this time I'd pushed the button hard enough to stir him out of his torpor, because my prisoner immediately started squirming in the light net that had him bound from hand to foot. It was kinda like watching a baby squirm inside a blanket. "Unnnnnnnnh!" he shouted in frustration, cheek mashed to the side of the van. His eyes were wide, the sight of a flaming wheel only a few feet from him clearly inspiring a little worry.

"Oh, good, you're awake," I said, and poked him again in the kidney for good measure. "I was worried that fire was going to get to you before you had a chance to tell me who you work for."

"What?" he asked, his voice muffled by being pressed to the side of the van by the net.

"Who do you work for? Quickly, before that tire fire hits the fuel line."

"I'm not—why would I tell you that?" He squirmed against the bounds of his imprisonment, rather futilely.

"Because you don't want to die in a fire, duh." I poked him in the other kidney and that got him to grunt again. "I can tell you're not exactly the pick of the intellectual litter."

"I ain't sayin' noth—"

I coaxed the flames off the tire into a flare-up that lunged at him. For a little extra drama I shaped it into a lion, and had it open its mouth in a roar while also coming at him with a giant, flaming paw complete with huge claws. It was very theatrical.

Mr. Underoos must have thought so, too, because he immediately screamed and shit his pants as he struggled and failed to escape the net.

"Gyah!" Jamal said, covering his nose. "Is this why you called him Mr. Underoos?"

"No. But those undies are probably going to hold back the flames for at least a second or two longer now," I said, holding my own nose.

"Oh my gaahhhhhhhhhhhhhhd!" Mr. Underoos screamed as I let the lion of fire subside. "Let me ouuuuuuuuuuut!" His voice was so high-pitched it probably set off every dog in the tri-state area.

"Who do you work for? Or my flaming lion is going to leave a mark next time."

"Some guy, I dunno!" he screamed, top of his lungs howling. "He hired us over the internet! We were supposed to set up the ambush wherever he told us to, then meet him back at the Packer Avenue Marine Terminal for payment and debrief!"

"How did he contact you?" Jamal asked, chiming in with a useful question.

"Cell phone! In Barry's pocket! Ahhhhhhhh!" I brought the lion back and made it do a little jump, before having it rejoin the fire and lose its shape in the flames.

"Cool." I strode over to Barry and lifted him up by the wedgie again, then fished the phone out of his pocket. The screen flared to life and asked for his unlock code, so I tossed it to Jamal, who had it open in a few seconds. He stared at the screen, then finally nodded, looking up at me. "He's telling the truth."

"Now the bonus question," I said, walking back over to my new friend, "what else can you tell me about this guy who hired you?"

"I don't know him!" he screamed, hyperventilating. "I've never met the guy! He only used his handle to hire us!"

"What's his handle?" Jamal asked.

"ArcheGrey1819," the guy said, his breaths coming slower

now. I guess he'd hit peak panic and was coming down now.

"And …?" I asked. I didn't expect anything else, but figured I'd fish anyway. I brought the flaming lion back.

He squealed. "I'll tell you whatever you want to know! Anything! I wet the bed until fourth grade! I didn't lose my virginity until I was twenty-five, and it was to a hooker!"

"How many people have you killed?" I asked. A loser like this probably knew the answer off the top of his head.

"Twelve! Twelve!" he screamed, beyond all reason. "Until tonight, anyway. I don't know how many we got in the Denny's! Please! Just let me looooooooose!" He lost vocal control with the last little squeal.

"Oh, I'm about turn you loose—from life," I said menacingly, and Jamal must have caught the look in my eye, because he stepped up and laid a cold hand on my wrist.

"Please," he said, looking right into my eyes.

"Thank you and you're welcome," I said, completing the trifecta of polite phrases. Then I sighed when I saw the look in his eyes. "Fine. Have it your way." I aimed at the snow with my other hand and seared a message into it with light nets. It looked a little rough, but was legible.

"Denny's," it said, and I figured the Philly cops would get my meaning.

"Come on," I said to Jamal. "Let's get out of here before the cops actually do show up and end up dragging us out along with these losers."

"Sure thing," he said, probably relieved that I wasn't going to filet the guy right here. I hadn't planned do that, but he didn't need to know that. It was better to have everyone think you'd kill anyone, anytime, especially when you were already a wanted fugitive, than to need to dip into the badass credit account and find it empty. That was the sort of error you tended not to survive.

52.

Jamal

I breathed a sigh of relief once we'd trussed up both those bad guys and left them in the snow. The look on Sienna's face hadn't exactly been rich with mercy, especially once the dude who crapped himself had admitted he'd killed twelve people. She'd gotten this sort of hard-eyed look, like a veil of anger just fell over her, and I had a bad feeling he was about to become a human pig roast.

"I hope the cops have enough evidence," she said idly as she started the car and put on her blinker to get back into the traffic flow. There were fewer cars now, with the hour getting kinda late. "I'd hate to have to track these guys back down later and waste them if they end up walking from custody." The car, for its part, sounded a little rough but started right up.

"I wouldn't worry about it," I said, holding up Barry's phone and my own. "I recorded everything your boy Underoos said, and I'm sending it to the Philly PD in a minute, along with a record of correspondence from this phone. Should get their attention."

"Well played," she said, evincing a nod that spoke of grudging respect—or maybe just grudging. She was a hard one to read sometimes. "So … about our man Caden and his number one gal, who we seem to be on course to rendezvous with …"

"ArcheGrey, yeah," I said, thumbing through Barry's back-

and-forth messages with Arche. I thought it was funny that he thought she was a he, but then … I'd kinda made that mistake myself.

"Would have been nice if they could have shed some light on the plan," she said, and she gave me a long look. "You got any theories yet?"

"I dunno, exactly," I said, flipping back to my forum screen on my tablet. I had GPS on in the background, and we were heading toward the Port of Philadelphia and the Packer Avenue Marine Terminal right on the Delaware River. It was still a ways out, and the GPS was having a hell of a time calculating it, given that our speed was inconsistent thanks to the state of the roads.

"Come on, big brain," she said, hectoring me. "You've gotta have been thinking about it. You said something about bots earlier. How does that work?"

"Just a generic term for programs you put on someone else's computer that borrow some of their processing power and bandwidth for whatever you want to do," I said, explaining it without giving it a lot of thought. This was pretty basic stuff.

"Wait … how do you do that to someone else's computer?" she asked. "They let you do that?"

"Rarely," I said. "Usually it's a—you know, like you trick them into downloading a program, either on their phone or computer or tablet, and then—if the person doing the hacking is kind, like me, you only steal up their processing power when they're not using it."

"How often is the hacker kind?"

"Uhhh, best not to count on that," I said. "Just don't download anything you don't implicitly trust the source on. I mean, people get those email forwards from their mom, click the link, they download the program, and not only do they lose that processing power because of the bot, they also get a keystroke logger to soak up all the passwords they type in to the device, all the credit card numbers they store, they get their email, banking info … there's a lot of money to be made in that. Then, once the hacker has got the email, they can just turn around and use that person's address book to send out a whole new round of emails. Fun stuff." I shrugged. "There's a lot of damage you can do to a person's life if you really wanted to crawl into their digital world."

"Yeah, but everything you're saying sounds like—no offense—low-level shit. The stuff that ruins your day, but probably wouldn't thrill a guy like Caden Sims, right?"

"Probably not, no," I agreed. "If he's talking about busting barriers or opening up the world or killing off all the secrets or whatever … I mean, I have no idea. He'd have to hack someone big … like, one of the big providers of email, totally compromise their system … I dunno. Even still, that doesn't feel game-changing the way you say he was talking to Wittman. It feels like the same petty shit, except on a bigger scale."

She frowned. "Yeah. There's something here we're missing."

"Is this normal?" I asked. "I mean, I've been chasing this guy on a suspicion—"

"It's pretty normal for me," she said with a barely concealed smile. "I'm always chasing after someone with only a bare idea of what they're up to. I mean, Harmon was planning for years to create a super serum that would boost his powers to the Nth degree, and I thrashed blindly around the edges of that one all the way to nearly the end before I figured out what he was up to. Sovereign was this big mystery guy who was killing all the metas in the world through his organization, and I didn't even know that I'd met him—twice—and that he was my personal stalker until almost the end of the war." She looked over at me with sympathetic understanding. "Shadowy guys tend to, you know, operate in the shadows. This Caden Sims is no exception, and however much you might want to think you're crazy because of the evidence we have not forming a clear picture … don't. You're not crazy. He is acting very suspiciously, and he's associating with criminals and paying people to murder us. Law-abiding citizens do not do that shit, even when you follow them around a little. They actually look surprised that anyone would come after them. Only guilty people start paying off hit squads to buzz up a

Denny's in Pennsylvania." She broke into a frown. "How did they figure out where the hell we were, by the way?"

"I don't know exactly," I said, shaking my head. "My best guess is ArcheGrey and her mad hacking powers. You should ask her when we get there."

"I plan on it," Sienna said tightly.

"I don't think she's going to get all bent out of shape about the flaming lion the way that dude back there did. She's a serious customer." I remembered the look in her eyes as she vaulted away from me like someone out of *Assassin's Creed.*

"I'm sure I'll come up with something that'll make her sing loud enough to hit the notes I'm looking for."

"I hope you do," I said, as we kept going, cutting down the miles between us and Philadelphia. The darkness faded as the lights of the city cut through the cloudy night, but I felt more and more uneasy the closer we got to the confrontation I knew was coming.

53.

Reed

My phone buzzed me awake. I didn't recognize it as my phone at first; I just knew that there was an unnatural buzzing sound that I felt compelled to answer. I fought against the black drift of unconsciousness, coming to in a hospital room with dingy, drab walls and off-color paint. The TV was on a news station, but muted, and so I was left with only the bzzzzzzzz of an object on the little sliding cart in front of me, which I snatched up as soon as I realized what it was.

"Hello?"

"Mr. Treston," came a woman's voice. She sounded familiar.

"Yes?" I asked, mouth full of that cotton ball feeling, dry and scratchy.

"It's Miranda Estevez. I heard you were in the hospital."

I closed my eyes. Oh, right, Miranda Estevez. "Right. Ms. Estevez. My new boss."

"I'm just an intermediary, Mr. Treston. You're the boss."

"For my shadowy benefactor, yes," I said, and that statement was like an itch at the small of my back, one I couldn't get my hand around to scratch. "Yes, I'm in the hospital." I looked around my room. "We'd just caught the suspect and things … unfolded in a way I wasn't expecting."

"Yes, the Orlando police were kind enough to inform us that you were recovering after a run-in with an unknown meta."

"I bet they weren't real happy about their precinct getting trashed."

"I've taken happier calls," she said. "Fortunately, no one was killed."

I remembered something. "Veronika—"

"Is in worse shape than you, as I understand it—but she'll pull through."

I forced myself out of bed and felt the cool updraft of my ass being exposed thanks to this hospital robe. "Where is she?"

"Down the hall from you. Room 414, in case you want to visit."

"I do," I said, gnawing my upper lip. My clothes were in a bag on the table next to my phone, and I dumped them out. They were a little bloody, but they'd have to do. "Did the Orlando PD give you any other background on what happened?"

"They were kind enough to sketch out the incident, along with a forwarded request for more manpower." She sounded so calm about it. "Unfortunately, we're spread a little thin, though Augustus and Angel will be heading down to join you in about six hours, once they wrap up their current case."

"That's not quick enough," I said. "How about Veronika—"

"The doctors don't treat metas often. Our best guess is … longer than six hours."

"You're a meta doctor and a lawyer?"

"No," she said. "But I did consult a doctor familiar with metahuman healing, and that was what she suggested."

I froze, halfway through putting on my pants. "You talked to Isabella?"

"Yes." Her voice was so matter-of-fact as to border on maddening.

I shut down every instinct I had to bombard her with questions, but one slipped out. "Did you tell her you were working with me?"

The answer was eternal in coming, excruciating. "No."

Thank Zeus for small miracles. "Do we have any line

on—"

"I'm afraid you'll need to speak to J.J. for anything related to the case. I've forwarded him everything the Orlando police sent us, along with a request to dig into things a little further. He and Abigail have already reviewed the recordings from your interrogation of the suspect and her subsequent abduction. You'll find him a better source of answers than I could be."

I finished tugging on my pants and fastened my belt. "Thank you, Ms. Estevez."

"You're welcome, Mr. Treston. Do be careful. I doubt our mutual employer would be pleased to lose you so soon after you've rejoined us."

"That's good to know," I said tightly, and hung up, dialing J.J. immediately after I severed the connection.

I got an answer on the second ring. "Treston the Breast-man!" shouted a female voice that was most definitely not J.J.

"Abby?" I asked, trying to decide if I'd heard what I thought I'd heard.

"I've been holding onto that one for the perfect chance for like, so long," she said. "And I know, I know—Treston, breast man, they don't really rhyme, but—I just had to. It called to me, so I went for it. How you doing, Reed? How's the chest?"

"Aching," I said. "Is J.J.—"

"Right here in the background, bro!" J.J. shouted, his voice a little tinny. "Working the late nights for you, man, just like the old days. Except now it's a team effort." The distinctive sound of Abby and J.J. doing a high five stung my meta-ears. "Oh, yeah!"

"Go team!" Abby said.

"J.J.," I said, "have you reviewed my interrogation—"

"Of Ms. Olivia Brackett, she of the Blue Cloister Cult? Dental secretary by day, escaped cultist love bride by night? Yeah, we dug into it. Creepy stuff, huh?"

"Sounded like some counts of child imprisonment depending on how old she was when she escaped," Abby said. "And I'm not real clear on the law about keeping people in boxes, I'd probably defer to your sister for expertise on that one, but—seriously—gack. This Roger is gross. Seriously gross. I hope you introduce air into his bloodstream."

"I hear that's a really, really painful way to die," J.J. said conversationally.

"It is," Abby said. "Like, if you took a syringe and injected an air bubble into a vein, it would make its way to the aorta and—"

"Guys," I said, trying to bring them around as I fumbled to put my shirt on and finally gave up, tossing the phone down for a second while I did.

When I picked it back up again, I heard, "—and they would die screaming. At least until they passed out from the pain."

"Reed, you should totally try that on Roger the Cult Leader," J.J. said in something approaching awe. "I mean, he sounds like a eugenics hobbyist and a real controlling, 'Human slavery is a-okay!' kind of guy. You should test your new super ultra power upgrade by seeing if you can lance little needles of air into his skin."

"I'd rather go Big Bad Wolf on him," I said tightly, pulling on my socks, which were cool and slightly damp even after spending quite a while in a plastic bag.

"What does that mea—oh," J.J. said. "Like, blow his house down. I get it!"

"Yeah," Abby said, "I got it when he said it."

"You're so clever!" J.J. squealed.

"Guys!" I said. "I need a clear line of sight to these people." Something else nagged at me, and I spat it out before I could forget again. "And once this is over, I need you to look into our employer. This mystery has gone on long enough."

"Oh, we already did that," Abby said.

"Totally," J.J. said. "I did the legwork months ago, after we first got the offer, along with Sienna. The money to fund this place passes through a bank in Liechtenstein. They're kinda—well, really good, actually, at keeping their stuff hidden and secret. No backdoors in the system, no easy way in. Buuuuuuut—"

"But what?" I asked.

"But Ms. Estevez," Abby said with barely concealed glee, "chose a really, really weak password for her email, so … we got a name for the person she's corresponding with. Their traffic goes through a European server, and whoever handled their INFOSEC did a lot better job than Ms. Estevez, so we haven't had any luck hacking that email account, but we did get the name and a rough IP address—country, anyway, though that could be fake."

"The name she sent it to is 'Jonsdottir,'" J.J. said. "Very Norwegian. And passes through a Norwegian IP address."

"Sound familiar?" Abby asked.

"No," I said, racking my brain for any reference to a European named Jonsdottir. I couldn't recall anyone with that name from my Alpha days, not on either side of the playing field. "Mystery for another time, I guess. About—"

"Ms. Brackett?" J.J. asked. "We're on it. I'm searching utility records from just north of Miami to just south of Jacksonville for trace hits on a compound that went off the grid around the time of Sovereign's threat."

"Could be a while," Abby said, "or it could be quick. Hard to say."

"Keep at it, guys," I said, grabbing my jacket and slinging it on one arm at a time. "This woman … Roger and Tracy are keeping her against her will. This is straight up kidnapping."

"You don't have to tell me twice," Abby said.

"We're on it, boss," J.J. said. "And help's on the way. Augustus and Angel are hurrying, too. If you can wait—"

"I can't," I said, heading out the door. "I don't trust Roger. He sounds to me like the punitive type, and I doubt he's going to just forgive and forget that one of his animals strayed off the farm. He'll punish her, worse than he's ever done before, because she beat him. She had a terrible childhood, but at least she survived. I need to find her. Before something worse happens." I kept my head down, heading for Veronika's room. "Something she won't survive."

54.

Sienna

I parked the car along the side of a rough-looking road, just outside the Marine Terminal parking lot. It was pretty sparsely attended at this time of night, and I didn't need some rookie security guard phoning the cops about my license plate, especially given my back window was all busted out and my trunk had a few bullet holes in it.

"We should take our stuff with us and hide it elsewhere," I said. "Our car's a lightning rod for the cops right now."

Jamal just nodded and shouldered his bag wordlessly, putting the tablet inside. His nervousness showed. I got the feeling he hadn't liked getting his ass kicked back in New York, and I doubted he'd like it any more the second time around if he got into a real scrape here.

Fortunately, he had me, which meant that hopefully he wouldn't have to get his ass kicked this time around.

"She had a … something up her sleeve?" I asked, trying to remember what he'd said.

"Like a coil of metal that she could channel her power through," he said, looking around warily as we left our car and started across the parking lot. The wind was blowing small drifts of snow, and a long bridge stretched across the Delaware River just to our right. It looked like it might go for a mile, at least from here. "I could have taken her zaps, no problem, if not for that. With it, though …" he shook his head, cringing in pain, "… she whooped me like a redheaded step child."

"Well, let's not give her that chance again," I said, trying to act nonchalant as we strode through the parking lot. There was a heavy industrial building just to my left, and beyond it, what looked like a maze of container crates and cranes. There didn't appear to be many ships in the port.

"I'm all for that," Jamal said. "Where should we leave our stuff? I don't want to break this tablet."

"Yeah, it'd be a real shame if you had to steal another," I said, steering us toward a big F-150 pickup truck with a few feet of ground clearance. "Here," I said, and shoved my bag right under the vehicle. My duffel didn't even scrape the bottom, and I knelt down to check, because the last thing I needed was this guy driving off with it hanging from his chassis. His car was pretty thoroughly covered in snow, though, so either he was the night watchman or else he'd left his vehicle here and gone home with someone else. Longshoreman love was better than shortshoreman love, I supposed.

Jamal deposited his bag under the vehicle in the same way. "What if he drives off?" he asked nervously once he stood back up, rubbing his hands together.

"He's not going to back out, since the lot is empty," I said, directing us back toward the fence ahead, which separated the parking lot from the port itself. "Human psychology. He'll drive forward, and probably not bother to look in his rearview to see the two bags that someone's stashed under his truck."

Jamal nodded, seeming a little impressed. "Not bad. But what if he—"

"Then we lose our bags, and you have to resort to thievery again," I snapped and then quieted him with a look. "Now come on. You have Barry's phone?"

"Right here." He flashed me the screen, which activated as he lifted it, showing me the time. Damn, this had been a long day. I was also severely pissed I hadn't gotten the second half of my Moons Over My Hammy.

"Know where we're meeting Arche?"

"In there," he said with a nod toward the fence. "I guess

our would-be assassins weren't supposed to be intimidated by the fence."

"Fences are for people who can't leap ten feet straight up," I scoffed.

Jamal looked a little shamefaced, and I immediately regretted my choice of words. "I don't … know if I can jump ten feet."

I sighed, grabbed him around the chest, and launched into the air. I set down on the other side of the fence before my powers had a chance to work, because I'd had to put a hand over his mouth to keep him from squawking. "Whispers only from here on out."

"Okay," he said, louder than he needed to be, but fortunately, not loud enough to be heard more than about ten feet away from us.

"Lead on," I mouthed, and he nodded, taking us toward the container stacks.

I didn't want to ask him where we were going, because he seemed to have a GPS coordinate for the meet-up from Barry's phone. So I followed behind him as he crept, taking his sweet time. I couldn't complain, because he was actually doing a wonderful job of muffling his footsteps. Part of that was the thin layer of snow, which would be bad for us if someone tried to follow, but in combination with the wind, it did a reasonable job of keeping our footsteps from echoing between the corrugated cargo container stacks.

There were mountains of containers, too, the kind that they double stacked onto trains and transshipped across the country, or put on tractor-trailers singly to move across states. I counted three rows of them, about thirty or so feet between them, like towering high rises, a city of cargo containers.

"We gotta go through there," Jamal said when we reached the start of one of the canyons. I stopped him at the edge and stared down the long row.

"In there?"

He nodded, pointing straight ahead. "A couple rows in. Might be in one of the containers, actually."

I surveyed the dark rows, looking for any movement in the

shadows. I didn't see anything, but that didn't mean there was no one there. "Hold here a second," I said, then lifted off the ground a foot and slid across the row to the container pile to our right. Beyond it was a massive crane, the long boom secured up at the top for the night.

I stopped at the edge of the container row and looked out, trying to see if anyone was lurking beyond. There was a huge concrete dock that extended out into the river a few hundred feet beyond, and in the well between it and the next one over waited a container ship that was utterly dark; not a single light on the bridge mast was lit, nor did anything shine in any of the portholes. It looked as though it had been abandoned at anchorage.

Staring down the row of cargo containers, I spied another crane. The row of cargo containers was at least four long, though it was hard to see the end of it from here. I thought about flying up and circling, but I doubted the thin layer of snow falling would do an adequate job of masking a flying woman from the sight of any watchers.

I snuck back over to Jamal and went past him, looking up the next row of containers, then the next. No one was visible, though I felt certain if someone was hiding, they'd probably be doing it in the cross gaps between the rows, where I couldn't easily see them.

"What are you thinking?" Jamal asked, teeth chattering, when I came back to him.

"We circle around on the dock side," I said, indicating the direction I'd gone to scout the first time. "Enter the container maze closer to the rendezvous point. It's not wise to give ArcheGrey any more chance to ambush us than we have to."

He nodded and followed me as I stalked back around to the right, skirting the edge of the container city. We walked under the shadow of the nearest crane, the one tasked to work the dock immediately to our right. I couldn't see anybody hanging out in the cabin up on the superstructure, but that didn't mean someone wasn't there, quietly peering down at us.

A shiver ran up my spine, and not just from the cold. It

was probably only thirty degrees Fahrenheit or so, which wasn't bad considering that where I came from, it would have been in the single digits or lower right now. I ignored the very faint crunch of snow that Jamal's steps were producing; I still hovered, but I didn't want to carry him like a bride. Guys tended to get weird about that, for some reason.

We reached the intersection of the first set of containers and he gestured to our left. "Yep, in there."

I looked around the corner. There was no one in sight. "You sure?"

He nodded, then gritted his teeth to control against the chatter. Poor lamb.

"Wait here," I said, and he nodded again. I headed into the warren of containers, leaving him behind. I didn't want to expose his more vulnerable self in what I was increasingly starting to believe was an ambush. After all, why would Caden Sims or ArcheGrey want to leave behind the Denny's assassins as possible connections to their criminal malfeasance? They'd just orchestrated a massive act of violence that couldn't be overlooked and might even make the national news. Anyone cold-blooded enough to plan the kind of attack that could have resulted in the death of dozens of innocent people wasn't very likely to balk at tying up a few loose ends.

I reached the intersection between the four container stacks. Intersection of Ambush Road and Cornholed Way. I looked around, circling slowly, waiting for someone to speak, for someone to move.

As it happened, I didn't have to wait long.

But nobody said anything.

And nobody moved.

With a hard crunch and the sound of metal buckling, the container stack immediately to my left came crashing down. From the time I heard the metal crunch to the moment the container came tumbling down was less than a second.

A second during which I only had time to raise my hands as tons of metal and cargo came crashing down on me.

55.

Jamal

The containers came down like a falling building toward the center of the maze where Sienna had disappeared, and there wasn't a damned thing I could do about it.

Bending metal makes a sick, squealing kind of sound, but it wasn't very long in squealing. The crash came after only a few seconds, and I got a sick feeling of my own as the tall container stack smashed into the one nearest me and sent four stacked containers crashing my way.

I pushed off the corner where I'd been lurking, watching Sienna until she'd disappeared into the shadows ahead. I took the landing on the back of my neck and got stunned. Gracelessly, I sprawled there, pain radiating down my back, as the container stack came down less than ten feet away from me.

The container exploded at the seams upon impact, cargo smashing its way out of the corrugated steel box. Wood dust burst out along with packing foam, and I scrambled to try and get away from it before some stray projectile from the crash impaled me.

The next container crashed less than a second after the first, rolling diagonally toward me, and I twisted, kicked and clawed against the snowy pavement trying to escape it before it came to a rest. It broke at the seams as it rolled as well, the sides of the container coming apart like an apple being peeled in one long strip. Pieces of widescreen TVs broke out of cardboard packages and shattered in the wreckage of the container tower.

I managed to make it clear before the next two containers came down, and they rolled toward the crane and the docks, the last smashing against the steel superstructure. It rattled and railed in the night, the still and quiet snowfall shattered by the violent avalanche of the containers before me.

There was movement in the stack beyond the wreckage. The container tower that had originally fallen was still standing a couple containers high, held up by some invisible force hidden behind the one on the ground where I'd been hiding.

Sienna.

"Are you okay?" I shouted, and thought the better of it a moment too late.

"Better than you're going to be. Run, you idiot!" Sienna shouted over the sound of shattered metal containers and consumer electronics settling across the asphalt docks.

I started to turn, but something moving beyond caught my eye. A stray bit of voltage crackled in the night, lancing along a length of coiled metal. I could see the individual links in the flare of blue light as it surged out like a fallen power line, dragged from the sleeve of a woman standing atop the container above Sienna, looking down with cool disdain, as though she were observing a scene of no particular importance instead of an attempted assassination.

ArcheGrey was here, and as she looked right at me, I got the feeling that she wasn't at all surprised that we were here, too.

56.

Sienna

Steel containers weigh literally tons. Packed so they could be hauled by trains, they tended not to skimp on the weight, because, after all, why transship it across the ocean in small, feather-light containers when you could package them into steel boxes large enough to crush a human being if they fell out of their stacks?

Also, they really, really hurt when I caught them. My wrists broke instantly, my shoulders nearly got sheared off as I lowered my head to try and absorb the impact with something other than my skull (not that it would have done any damage to the brain of the absolute IDIOT who had just wandered into the middle of an ambush), and I stood there, trying to keep from crying and dropping to my knees, or curling up in a ball and saying, "To hell with it!" and giving up on life while the tons of weight on top of me deprived me of it.

"Are you okay?" Jamal's voice called over to me as I struggled under the weight of the entire damned world, and probably a few ancillary asteroids that had joined the mass of the planet in the last few minutes just to spite me.

I couldn't believe he was wasting his time asking. "Better than you're going to be. Run, you idiot!" The thump of heavy boots on the container above me would have drawn my attention if I'd had x-ray vision. As it was, I was laboring really, really hard not to drop the immense weight I was struggling under. Crackling electricity cued me in to exactly who I was dealing with, even without the benefit of seeing her myself.

ArcheGrey. Lovely.

"Don't kill her!" Jamal shouted, voice echoing in the anything but calm night.

"I'm not going to kill her," ArcheGrey said. She had an Eastern European accent, and sounded like she smoked a few packs a day of unfiltered.

"I wasn't talking to you," Jamal said.

I looked around, rather futilely, trying to scourge him with a glare through all the corrugated metal and wreckage, but instead I caught motion at the end of the row of containers, the opposite end from where we'd entered.

Guys. With assault rifles that looked like SCARs (Special Operations Forces Combat Assault Rifle) based on their shadowy outlines under the lamps.

"I'm not that worried about me killing her at the moment," I said to no one in particular, gritting my teeth and trying to lift. As the gunmen opened up, a few things ran through my mind—I hoped that they were carrying the SCAR L (Light) rather than the H (Heavy), because the bullets were nominally smaller. I also hoped they were really lousy shots.

And mostly, I hoped that I wouldn't get hit at all, because I wasn't sure I could survive dropping the containers on my body.

But as the first bullets tore into my chest and arms, none of those hopes mattered one damned bit, because the containers came crashing down, slamming me to the rough, waiting asphalt ground, and everything went black.

57.

Jamal

ArcheGrey lashed out at me with one of those metal tentacles, and I dodged it by a matter of inches. Even though she hurled it at me like a lasso, there wasn't much telegraphing. It just came shooting at me and I was forced to dive and roll, mainly because I lost my footing on the slippery ground.

She descended behind me as I got to my feet and broke into a run, the sound of gunshots once again chattering behind me as I dodged toward a distant crane. I didn't want to get too far from Sienna, but I didn't have a lot of other options right now. Trouble was coming, and hiding in the container stacks looked like suicide based on what I'd just seen happen to the strongest person I knew.

The cold air stung my cheeks as I ran. I needed cover, I realized as the lash came whipping at me again. I threw myself sideways. The only good news with her and this weapon was that she couldn't pull it back to swing it again very easily, which gave me at least a short span of time to pick myself up again after dodging it.

ArcheGrey was coming after me, her face a solid mask of disapproval. She kept throwing the lash and striding forward, barely breaking a sweat as she came at me. I scrambled for the crane, hoping I could hide behind its steel legs, maybe find a moment of respite from the constant attacks.

I was so close—only a few more feet and I'd be clear

behind the steel leg of the crane. It wouldn't protect me entirely, especially given the damage she'd done to the shipping containers, but it would at least give me a couple seconds to think, to come up with a plan other than sprinting and dodging my way down the cold Philly docks.

The whipping sound of her lashes suddenly grew more intense and I looked back to try and judge my next dodge. I saw one coming for me, right for the face, and I lunged to the side—

Missing that she'd sprouted a second lash out of her other sleeve, and she waited until I was committed to my dive to sling it at me.

I hit the ground and started to roll, but the lash slapped me hard, like a club across the face. It belted me to the ground and I thudded, skull-first, against the pavement. Stars flashed like the night sky had suddenly lit up in a thousand supernovas above me, and suddenly she was there, her lash wrapped around my chest and squeezing me like a steel boa constrictor.

She didn't even look at me. Instead, she reeled in her other lash and stared off to her left, back toward the chaos where the containers lay destroyed and spread all over the shipping terminal. Two guys were approaching with rifles slung across their chests, barrels smoking in the cold air.

"We got her," one of them called. "She's got to be dead under those containers. We'll dig her out and—"

A brief flash of fury ran across ArcheGrey's face, and suddenly I saw a long, vicious-looking rifle in her left hand, extended toward them. "No, you won't," she said, and four shots rang out, adding additional flashes to the stars I'd already seen in my eyes.

When my vision cleared, the two gunmen were dead, shadowed shapes with a purple tinge to their silhouettes from the sustained brightness of ArcheGrey's muzzle flash. "You killed them," I said numbly, suddenly remembering her threat to do the same to me if we met again. I braced, readying myself for death.

She whipped her head around and looked at me with steely calm. "Better them than her, the useless idiots," she said, and

I froze, my brain trying to reconcile what she'd just said. "Now come along," she said, and dragged me, struggling, from the docks, "because we don't have much time before she digs her way out, and we have things to do."

58.

Reed

I found Veronika's room without much difficulty, but seeing her lying on the bed, unmoving, the heartbeat monitor beeping slowly in the gloomy atmosphere, was a studied contrast with the woman on the bed, who was usually annoyingly vivacious.

It was disturbing to see her like this, black bruises around her eyes and a grey pallor to her skin that bordered on deathly. I gently closed the door behind me and slipped across the room, studying her as I approached.

Her eyelids were closed, a little dried blood still on her lips. Her hospital gown rested loosely around her, giving hints of her rising and falling chest beneath the blankets. She twitched slightly in her sleep, and I wondered if maybe, just maybe, I should wake her.

"Stop gawking at me at me like you're going to kiss me out of my sleep, wuss," she said, and her eyes sprang open. "It's creepy."

"Veronika!" I said, taking a step back and clutching my chest to stave off the heart attack I felt like I was about to have. I almost did a high jump in surprise, one of those numbers where you jump unwittingly, knees to chest in shock.

"Haha, got you," she said, and then weakly coughed. "You look like absolute hell, Reed. Worse than when you showed up at HQ with that beard that looked like it was about to have birds fly out of it." She rustled against the pillow. "That takes doing, man. Lighten up before that stick up your ass breaks in half and you get splinters."

I didn't know which part of that to even respond to, so I ignored all of it. "The medical experts at our … employer … seemed to think you were still out of it and bound to be for a while yet."

"Well, I heal fast," Veronika said. "I'll be fine in a day or so, back to near full capacity and ready to put up with your bull again." She locked eyes with me. "But you don't have a day, do you?"

"I have a day," I said, "but I'm not sure Olivia Brackett does. That guy, Roger …"

"Was that his name?" Her eyes narrowed into angry slits. "I haven't had my ass kicked like that in a long time, and I haven't missed the feeling." She gestured at the foot of the bed. "He broke my back, Reed. On purpose. Crippled me with a filing cabinet from behind while he was talking to my face. It zoomed out of nowhere and cleaned me out. Then he played piñata with my skull until I went unconscious, apparently because pulling a remote-control Bane on me wasn't enough."

"Good reference," I said.

"Olivia Brackett is cooked," Veronika said, "and I'm not going to be able to walk for hours yet." She jerked a few times in the bed, as though trying to compel her body to action without results. She drew a thready breath and looked at me with fire in her eyes. "You need to go after that girl. This man … he's cruel for fun. Because it suits him. Not the forgiving sort."

"That's what I told J.J.," I said, easing back up to her bedside. "He's working on location. Throwing everything at it, actually. And Augustus is on the way with—"

"They'll never make it in time," she said, shaking her head. "Whatever this guy professes to his followers about being a benevolent ruler … it didn't show in his encounter with me. He's pissed, and he's nuts. He's going to put Olivia in a world of hurt, probably a world she'll never recover from."

"That was my impression as well," I said, tightening my

grip on the bed rails. "That he was the vindictive type."

"He sent his son and Mr. Invisible to track her down the minute they got word of her," Veronika said. "Yeah, he's not letting go of this. He probably views her as a threat to his authority, and I think we both know what impotent weasels do to people who threaten their authority. The emotion he's going to let loose in her direction is going to be like …"

"Vesuvius," I said. "She's been gone for years, and I bet he's never gotten over her defying his control. He sees that like a direct challenge."

"Safe bet," she said. "But …" Skepticism fell over her face. "I don't know if you can handle this, Reed. He's strong. He's got the kind of powers that harmonize together to make him a real bad dude. He didn't just throw the filing cabinet at me. He busted through concrete block with his mind and heaved pieces at me, broke glass—" She pointed to a few lined scratches on her cheek that looked like a cat had gotten her, trace lines of scabbing. "He's got it all. I don't know if you're ready for this fight, even if you do find him."

My phone beeped, and I pulled it up to look. A text message on the screen read, "Think we've got it," followed by an address that I clicked, activating my GPS.

"I don't think I have a choice," I said, staring as the screen pulled up a map. The location was about an hour away, northwest of Orlando and up near the Ocala National Forest. It looked isolated, out in the woods and away from easy access by civilization. "And it looks like we did find him."

Veronika stayed silent for a minute. "I don't want to tell you not to go after him, because I know what Olivia Brackett has got to be going through right now, and it's hell. Someone needs to get out there and save her, because they are not going to give her even a fraction of a chance to save herself." She closed her eyes. "But—and don't take this the wrong way—but I wish your sister were here instead of you."

I took that in without reaction, internalizing the insult. "Because she wouldn't hesitate to deal out … what? Death and pain?"

Veronika's eyes sprang open and she found mine. There was a hardness there that was antithetical to the lightness with which she usually spoke. "Because she would know the kind of cruel son of a bitch she was facing and act accordingly. You … I don't know if you're ready to deal with the mad dogs of the world. You think everything's a puppy, that maybe you can talk your way through everything. You can't. This Roger … he doesn't care about what he's doing to Olivia. She's an object to him and his ilk, and he will crush her gladly to remove her as a thorn in his kingly paw."

"I've dealt with psychopaths before," I said softly, thinking of Anselmo Serafini in particular.

"Oh, yeah?" Veronika asked. "How'd that go?"

"The last one … I tossed his ass on my sister's flaming, unconscious body and watched him cook like a hot dog that fell into the coals," I said without an ounce of remorse.

Her eyes widened, and she almost looked … impressed. "Well, if you find a way to do that again, now … you might just be ready for this."

I leaned forward and kissed her on the cheek, and she rolled her eyes. "I'll be ready," I whispered in her ear, and then turned around, heading for the door.

"Maybe you are ready," she said. "After all, your fly is down."

I stopped and checked, then corrected the problem. "Whoops," I said with mild embarrassment.

"Go turn that controlling bastard into an alligator dinner, will you?" she asked. "And if you're not back in six hours, or whenever I get feeling back in my toes …"

"It'll all be over by then," I said, looking back. "One way or another."

"Make it the good way," she said, and I nodded as I left.

59.

Sienna

My skull was a pretty hard thing, according to those who knew me best, and very difficult to get much of anything through. I would have thought that this bit of hyperbole about my stubbornness did not extend to steel shipping containers.

Tragically, I was right.

My head hurt so bad it felt like it had been detonated from the inside by a hydrogen bomb. There were metal pieces crushing into the bone from above, and my jaw was pinned against the freezing, snow-covered asphalt below. I was fortunate in that there was a very small gap between those two locations still, mostly owing to the uneven nature of how the shipping containers had fallen together. It was a space of less than a foot, which allowed my skull to be slightly crushed but not fully gone to splat.

And it felt like my face and head had been put in a blender switched to puree.

That's a new feeling, Harmon crowed. *Everything is always so exciting with you. We get to experience the sensation of massive skull trauma without actually having a skull to traumatize anymore.*

Wolfe, I thought, since my jaw was so thoroughly broken as to prohibit speech. I made some guttural noises in my throat, though.

The impotent liar is right, Wolfe growled in my head, *you don't make this easy.*

The weight of the containers still rested on my broken shoulders. *Easy is for tourists and amateurs,* I said as my jaw grunted and strained to pull itself back together against the weight of tons, not us.

None of the rest of us would be insane enough to constantly walk into trouble the way you do, Eve said. *This is why I stuck to mercenary work.*

And that's why mercenaries keep dying at my hand, I said, surprisingly gleeful for someone whose face probably looked like roadkill. My jaw finally reformed itself, and the container wreckage groaned above as the strength of my jawbone outmatched steel. That was the Wolfe power of resistance and healing at work; the next person who punched me in the jaw was in for a nasty surprise, and probably a broken hand. I'd never fractured my skull intentionally in order to strengthen it before. Maybe I was a little too squeamish for it, maybe I preferred not to cause that particular sort of unspeakable damage to my body on purpose, especially since so much came my way without having to try very hard.

My shoulders reset, and the container above me squealed again as it shifted. I placed my hands up, palms flat, against the bottom of the surface. Surprisingly, my arms hadn't been broken. There was just enough space between the container and pavement to spare them the crushing destruction. Lucky me, I suppose. Lucky for the next person I backhanded, too.

My ribs stitched back together again, though they were easier, knitting themselves whole and allowing my poor, pummeled internal organs to finally heal. I had felt my liver lacerate, my heart was pretty well smushed, and I'd just ignored my hobbled ability to draw breath because … why worry about what you can't change? I mean, other than the excruciating pain, which I'd mostly shielded myself from by retreating into the soul sanctuary in my head.

I came out now, completely, and although I was accustomed to much, much pain, what was waiting for me was more than I typically dealt with. I lifted, directing my shoulders and back and arm muscles to pushing the damned load off of me. It was much easier now, now that—presumably—the weight of four containers wasn't stacked on top of me. I suspected the tower had fallen the moment I'd dropped, probably rolling off in various directions and splitting open, because what I was lifting now felt a lot like it had broken open and even lost some of its cargo.

I threw off the destroyed container, the steel sides flapping a little as I tossed it. As soon as I was clear of it, the full pain of my organs healing themselves came back to me and I had to take a knee. *Easy,* Wolfe growled.

"There is no easy with me, okay? Just be ready for everything to be maximum hard."

I used to say something similar, Bjorn said in that sick, gloaty way he had.

I ignored that. The pain of the cold air hit me, my nerves finally singing out that they were mostly whole again. I looked around, expecting to see … something. Anything.

All was quiet on the dockside. I hovered into the air and went high, looking for any sign of Jamal, of ArcheGrey—

All I found was two dead bodies just past the container field. They'd both been shot in the head, and they were carrying SCAR assault rifles. Out of curiosity, I dropped down and grabbed one. Yep, they were SCAR H's. It would have been an exceptionally bad idea to shoot me with a lighter round.

Still, these guys had ended up dead anyway, and the entry plus velocity of exit wounds suggested a rifle. Lots of mess. Accurate, too, which ruled out Jamal.

I felt a pang of guilt. Jamal wasn't here. This was an extremely bad sign. "Jamal!" I shouted, figuring that after dropping me with shots under a container pileup, sniping my head off probably wasn't priority one.

There was no answer.

The Marine Terminal was quiet.

There was no sign of him or ArcheGrey.

That hollow feeling, the sick one, laced with a feeling that I'd failed hard at something really important—that feeling settled in my belly as I drifted back toward the ground. I waited for a shot, a sign, anything.

Nothing came.

That feeling in my stomach kept getting worse and worse.

The whole point of being on my own in crisis was that I didn't have to worry about watching someone else's back, I didn't have to worry that someone else couldn't take the heat that was coming. But I'd gone and gotten myself into trouble again by taking on a partner, trying to save the world from troubles it didn't see coming.

And now, maybe it had cost Jamal his life.

I looked around again, one more time, and saw that truck in the distance, the one we'd hid our stuff under. With nothing else to do, I headed that way, clearing the fence and then returning to the ground so it didn't look like a girl was flying all around the Philadelphia waterfront. I dropped under the truck and retrieved my bag, and Jamal's.

He hadn't come this way, then, or doubled back to retrieve his things.

That meant he was either still being chased …

… Or she'd gotten him.

I opened my bag and grabbed my new cell phone, thumbing the screen. It lit up, and there was a text message from an unknown number. I read it, my eyes getting wider and wider as I stared, taking it all in. It was simple enough, just a few words, and yet every one of them chilled me more than the January air:

"If you want him back, come to me." And following that was a set of coordinates for GPS, ready to click through so I could follow them straight to my next ambush.

60.

Jamal

ArcheGrey wasn't the talkative type, I figured out pretty quickly after she dragged me off. She'd kept me wrapped up in those lash arms of hers, like a half Doctor Octopus, not even bothering to speak to me. Like I barely even existed. Enough to keep me confined, but not enough to worry about what I was up to. I tried to fry the boat's engines, prevent escape, but even when I directed my electricity through a part of my body not wrapped up her in lash, it still discharged into the lash, sparking it bright blue.

I gave up on that pretty quick, figuring I'd better save my voltage for when it might make a difference.

She got us on a speedboat and drove it herself, sprinting it down the Delaware River and out toward the open ocean. I could tell when we hit the ocean because the bumps of the swells became maddeningly more pronounced. I was soaked from the spray and shivering within a few minutes, even covered as I was from shoulders to ass by her lash.

She looked back from her place at the helm, coolly indifferent, her hair soaked to her forehead by the same freezing spray. "You'll be fine," she said disdainfully. Her knee-length coat, already completely doused, hung limp and open, and she didn't seem too bothered by the freezing cold. "Your meta endurance will keep you from dying."

"That's a real consolation." She didn't react to my reply, didn't even turn around again. She stayed over the controls, focusing on them with all her attention, keeping her back to me so I couldn't see what she was doing.

We rode like that for what felt like hours, the boat bucking up and down as I lay against the wet, thinly carpeted deck. I kept expecting my ass to freeze to the decking, but instead my teeth just chattered madly. It was the cold that distorted my sense of time. I wondered if I was freezing to death, or if Arche was right and my meta endurance was strong enough to protect me against frostbite and death. I wanted to believe she was right, but the cold was bitter and painful, and it seeped into my fingers and joints like dull knives being inserted into the skin. It was miserable, and I wondered if I'd ever be warm again.

Finally, Arche stopped the boat, killing the throttle and bringing it back to idle. The speedboat coasted, buffeted on a couple of swells, and she finally turned around. Her hair was crusted with ice, like a crown, and the city lights of Philadelphia were barely visible in the distance. We were out to sea quite some ways, and I wondered if she meant to toss me overboard and test how long it would take me to sink, unmoving, beneath the waves.

I suspected it wouldn't be long, because it felt like I couldn't even move my legs at this point.

She regarded me with a practiced sort of indifference, like she was calculating whether it was worth saying anything or whether she should just stare at me. She probably had something in mind, but she was so damned inscrutable I couldn't tell what she was thinking. I gritted my teeth together so they didn't rattle, and stared back, my thoughts running in their own direction, less malicious but far more predictable: *Cold! Cold! Cold!* And so on.

Arche reached behind her in that long coat, and came back with that weird rifle. Her fingers looked slick on the grip, but she kept it pointed at the deck. I didn't know how long we'd been going, just that it had felt like forever. There wasn't much light except for that shed by the instruments, and the seas were lapping hard against the hull. I didn't even know if this kind of boat was supposed to be out on the ocean, and definitely not on this kind of rough night. We rocked sideways against a hard wave, and frigid water rushed over us, streaming down my body and into my clothes.

Also, I made a sound like a squealing kid. Not proud of it, but it happened.

"We just gonna … wait here … to freeze?" I asked through chattering teeth.

Arche lifted me up, staring at me like I was a bug. "No," she said, and no more. Like that answered anything.

"Why don't you just … kill me, then?" I asked, mustering my last ounce of defiance, but honestly so cold by that point that a tiny part of me actually wanted her to. Just so it would be over, and maybe I'd be warm again.

Here she showed a slight flicker of surprise. "I'm not going to kill you," she said, very definitely.

"Oh, yeah?" I asked, teeth rattling. "Why not?"

"Because she wouldn't like that very much," Arche said, and she stiffened, looking around.

"She?" I asked, and it hit me. "Oh, you mean—"

"She means me," Sienna said, her hair lighting on fire like a torch in the night, illuminating her hovering just a few feet away, holding a nasty-looking rifle in her hands, pointed right at ArcheGrey's chest.

I looked at ArcheGrey, and she actually smiled.

Then she dropped her rifle, put her hands up, jarring me slightly, because I was still wrapped in one of her lashes. "So glad you could join us," she said.

"Whuut?" I asked between chattering teeth.

"She sent me a text message with this location," Sienna said, not letting go of her rifle, staring down the barrel at Arche. "And if you think I won't shoot you because you're unarmed—"

"You won't shoot me because I sent you a message for a reason," Arche said stiffly. That elusive smile of a moment earlier was already gone and she was back to indifference. "You need my help, and I need yours."

"For … what?" I managed to get out, still hanging in her lash.

She turned me loose, and I hit the ground with a thump. I didn't really feel it, probably because I was so numb. "With

Caden Sims, of course," Arche said, as though it was completely natural. "We have to stop him."

Sienna just stared hard at Arche down the barrel of the rifle. Finally she let it drop, a little at a time, millimeter by millimeter, until she said, with a kind of jaded surprise:

"Huh. I did not see that coming."

61.

Sienna

I was waiting for a trap, but it kept not springing itself at the logical moments. I had thought about just blowing ArcheGrey's head off from a quarter mile away with my purloined SCAR H, but that seemed unsporting, even for one of the FBI's Ten Most Wanted. Well, at least for this particular member of that elite (mostly) fraternity.

Then she dropped her weapon and told me she wanted to stop Caden Sims.

I kept waiting for the sucker punch, but the obvious moments to spring it were already gone. There weren't any boats nearby, and I doubted any choppers were operating in the area given the harshness of the winds, but I half expected a sniper shot to ring out and some SpecOps guy in the distance to claim an amazing kill over bucking seas.

It kept not happening, though, so I finally started to let my rifle sink toward pointing at the water.

I wondered if maybe Arche had loaded the boat up with dynamite or something. Of course, that would kill her, but I'd faced crazier enemies, ones who were perfectly willing to kill themselves to kill me.

Finally, I came to the point of conclusion that if this was a trap, it was a) a dumb place to spring one, because she didn't have any reinforcements easily accessible (unless Scott was hiding beneath the water. He could have been hiding beneath the water) and b) it should have happened already.

Ergo … maybe she really did want to talk about defeating Caden Sims.

"Okay," I said, drifting closer to the deck, ready in case she decided to zap the shit of me with her powers or try to lash me up like she had Jamal, "tell me why you want to defeat your boss, and try to keep it to thirty words or less."

"He's not my boss," Arche said, "and I didn't know what his plan was until after I helped him." Then she clammed up.

I waited, then waited a little more. "Is that it?" I asked.

She shrugged, her frosted hair unmoving as she did so. "You said thirty words or less."

"I admire your economy of phrasing," I said. "But—"

"What the hell—is Caden Sims—up to?" Jamal butted in, sounding like he was yelling and half-dead at the same time.

Arche gave him a somewhat disdainful look. "You don't know?"

"Some of us can't read minds," I said.

Some of us can, Harmon said gleefully, *and we just choose not to share that information with the plebes.*

Wait, I said, *you know what Sims is up to?*

Of course, Harmon said with malicious amusement at my expense, *we were in the same corridor with him in the Javits Center, and I don't need your permission to use my power. It's passive, unlike most of these schlubs.*

Hey, Gavrikov, Bjorn said, *I think he's talking about you.*

"This would have been useful information earlier!" I said, probably sounding a little outraged.

ArcheGrey stared at me like I'd come unhinged and she was considering taking a step back. "I didn't know earlier. I only found out in the last couple hours when my program finally broke through into his hidden server."

"Wasn't talking to you," I said. "What is he up to?"

It's quite simple, really, Harmon said, *he's going to make sure that there are no more—*

"Secrets," Arche said. "He's going to reveal all of our secrets."

"I don't get it, and both of you are talking at once," I said, causing Arche to frown again and look at Jamal, who was similarly staring at me in befuddlement, albeit completely covered in a thin crust of ice where the seawater he'd been doused with was now frozen. "I'm sorry, can we get this man a blanket?"

Arche looked at him for a second, then turned loose her snaking, metal arm appendage. I heard the faint whir of the machinery as she did so and wondered at its origin. It was sturdy, according to Jamal. It had to be in order to keep a meta under its control by strength—and in order to split steel, as it had back at the docks. It conducted electricity but didn't get zapped out by it …

All in all, that gear made Arche a formidable foe, at least to everyone else. Me, I'd just zap her between the eyes with a blast of hot air and watch her brain evaporate as her blood boiled. But to everyone else? Very formidable.

Jamal kept his arms wrapped tightly around himself the moment she let him loose, and I beckoned for him to come closer to me. He did, crawling his way across the deck until I could stoop down and lift him to his feet. I lit off a bright flare of fire, hot enough that he ducked back involuntarily, but I caught him before he went overboard. "Stay still," I said, "I'm drying your clothes."

"Th—thank you," Jamal said, looking like he was going to shake apart.

"Now, someone explain to me what's going on," I said. "No more secrets? What does that mean?"

It's simple enough, unless you're a simpleton, Harmon said.

Hey, Bjorn, Gavrikov said back nastily, *I think he's talking about you.*

I'm actually talking about all of you, Harmon said smugly.

"He asked me to craft some code for him," Arche said, "to which he attached something that he'd gotten from … someone else. I don't know who. But it's a processor with more computer power than anyone has ever seen."

"What … did your code do?" Jamal chattered.

"It processed encryptions and broke them more quickly than had ever been possible before," Arche said. "Which is how he brute-forced the cell phone companies and managed to track you down in that Denny's."

"You wrote a hacking script," Jamal said, still shivering,

but less now.

"No," she said, and here she evinced a glow of pride. Not a glow by most standards, but this lady's emotions were on mute, so the smug look she gave now was practically a glow by her standards. "I created a program that verges on AI, but with one function—to seek out all the unencrypted data on the net for common usernames, and then to apply that to other data that the program can intuit by creating profiles of every user—"

Because I know you're confused by this, Harmon said, *let me boil it down—she wrote a program that can break any encryption. At all. Every email. Every medical record. The criminal justice system. Government databases. If it's hooked to the internet, it's fair game for this program.*

"No more secrets," I said quietly.

Arche blinked at me. "Well, yes. Because he's mated the algorithm to this processor … yes. As it was, my program could have been used to stalk a few people and assemble full profiles of their information, wherever it might have been on the internet. But with this … with what he's got …" She shook her head. "No. No more secrets. Every email account, every server on the planet. All our passwords, every social media post, everything that there's a record of out there … it will become public. If you think any hack in history—the Sony email, Ashley Madison, if you think any of those were bad … wait until you see what happens when there are no more secrets online. Every credit card number will be exposed. Every bank account. Every dirty secret."

"The whole banking system will crumble overnight," Jamal said, sounding a little like himself again.

"Every medical record," she said, "every prescription. If you've been treated for syphilis, everyone will know it."

"Boy, that's going to be embarrassing for unfaithful spouses," I cracked.

"All of that will come out, too," Arche said. "Every single text message ever sent will be fair game. All the information will be out there for the sifting." She got a slightly haunted look. "All the national security information that's not stored on black servers."

"A whole lot of spies are gonna get burned," Jamal said. "Every classified weapons system is gonna go public …"

"And the plans and fate of President Harmon are going to get out of the realm of speculation and all the evidence is going to come out," Arche said, looking at me very knowingly.

Jamal looked between us. "Uhhh, what do you think that's going to show, exactly?"

"The truth," Arche said, staring right at me. "That the sitting President of the United States was a metahuman with the power to read and control minds. That he had co-opted the machinery of the government and private enterprise in a scheme to make it possible for him to control the minds of every person on the planet." She looked right at me. "And that he deployed every single asset at his disposal, both inside government and out, to destroy the one person he viewed as the impediment to his plans."

And succeeded, at least in that regard, Harmon said, but he didn't sound gleeful about it. It was sort of a pyrrhic victory for him, after all.

"How does it feel?" Arche asked, staring at me, a little smile turning up the corners of her lips. "Hearing speeches every day?"

It's absolutely wonderful, isn't it? So enlightening, Harmon said. *You're really quite fortunate.*

Zeus was less of a narcissist than you, Wolfe said. *And he was an actual god who ruled two empires.*

Odin, too, Bjorn agreed.

"I'm sure I don't know what you're talking about," I said, trying to stay noncommittal.

"I'm sure you don't," Arche said.

"This doesn't sound so bad, in a way," Jamal said, looking right at me. "I mean … don't get me wrong, there would be nasty consequences for the world, but … if the truth about Harmon comes out, you might be the only person who comes out of this smelling like a rose. Everyone knows about the murders you did commit, and, if, like she says, there is evidence out there that you didn't attack those people in Eden Prairie unprovoked … your name would get cleared,

Sienna." He smiled faintly. "You could go home."

"The truth is out there," Arche said, her amusement gone. "But don't think it would do everyone in this boat any favors." She looked hard at Jamal. "The truth of her past might come out, but so, too, would the truth of yours." She paused, and here she looked uncomfortable. "And mine."

Jamal's reaction went to stricken in a second. It wasn't hard to imagine why; the actual murders I'd committed had already been blown open to the public and had been pardoned years ago. Legally, if a determination could be made that Harmon was acting to take over the world, only a few die-hard nutbags would be able to argue that I hadn't been justified in trying to fight back against him. Well, maybe more than a few, but it'd still at least provide a path to clearing my name.

Jamal, on the other hand … the people he'd killed, both in revenge for his girlfriend's death and on the plane when he'd had to fight back against Caden Sims's bodyguard … those would almost certainly land him in massive trouble.

"We can stop this," Arche said. "Before it's too late."

"Sienna," Jamal said. "You don't have to stop it, if you don't want to." He looked a little sick, his dark skin slick with melted water now that I'd helped heat the ice that had covered him. "You'd be crazy to. I mean, unless she can come up with a way to expose the truth of what happened to you—"

Arche shook her head slowly. "That bit of truth is being actively covered up."

"By whom?" I asked, feeling oddly cold (literally and figuratively) about the whole thing.

"I might tell you if you help us," she said. "But not before. Call it payment for services rendered."

I stared her down. "Why not just … do it yourself? Take him out, if you know where he is and what he's up to?"

"I don't know that I can," she said. "He has meta bodyguards. You saw them at the Javits Center."

"They were creampuffs," I said. "Half of them quit when I threatened them."

"There are more of them now," she said. "Guarding his

estate. And I'm not as impervious to bullets as you are. So, yes, I could storm the beach myself—or cliff, actually, because his hiding place is a cliffside mansion in the US Virgin Islands, but …" She shook her head. "I don't wish to die. And I don't want to be exposed in the way his plan threatens to do. Which is why, when I found out … I changed the ambush plan back there."

"You still damned near killed her," Jamal said, sounding more upset about the ambush at the docks than I honestly was.

"The gunman did not work for me," she said, but she didn't sound very apologetic about it, "and I couldn't call them off at the last minute, when I found out what was happening. I am adapting as quickly to this new information as I can. I encourage you to do the same."

I stared at her, the flame still burning bright in my hand, though now Jamal had stopped shivering. "I could just drop in and destroy Sims's house."

She shook her head. "You could, but … he has servants. I anticipate you would not want to do that, though I would not have a problem with it if you did."

"That's cold," Jamal said, "and I'm not talking about the weather."

Arche shrugged, clearly indifferent to the plight of Sims's employees. "People die. I expect you want to minimize that, and I will work with you to do so."

"It's like you know me," I said, staring at her through narrowed eyes. I got the feeling based on her approach that this was Arche's version of throwing herself at my mercy.

"Sienna," Jamal said, "think this through."

I'd been thinking it through all along. Jamal was right, maybe the truth would come out for me.

But since the first time I made the decision to be a hero, to come out and confront evil when it reared its ugly head and threatened other people, I hadn't made my decisions based on what was right for me. Caden Sims planned to unleash havoc. Whatever good he thought was going to come out of opening up the floodgate of secrets, I didn't think he actually knew what was going to come of it. He'd embraced

Wittman's idea about opening up the barriers between people.

Taking away their privacy wasn't going to make for fewer barriers between people. It was going to create more, once the exposure of all those secrets happened. People would take these conversations, their banking, everything—offline. The damage to the economy would be catastrophic.

The damage to trust between people? Probably also disastrous. Chatrooms would go vacant, e-commerce businesses would die off, social media would become a lot more stilted for a while.

Secrets wouldn't go away. People just wouldn't trust their information online at all anymore, which would carry a set of consequences that would change the world for at least the foreseeable future.

All the pain he'd cause, all the mess he'd make, the fallout … would be for essentially nothing. Humanity wouldn't be drawn together by this sort of event.

It would be ripped apart, at least for the short term.

"I'm in," I said, nodding slowly. I just couldn't see any good coming of this, at least not for anyone but me and maybe a few others. And the mess would be … incalculable. "What do we do?"

Arche nodded once, and tilted her head to the front of the boat. "You'll find a set of thick ropes up there. If we're going to get to the Virgin Islands quickly, you'll need to—"

"Unghhhhhhh," I said, bowing my head. "Are you serious?"

Arche met my annoyance with the ghost of a smile. "You are faster at flying than this boat is at propelling itself."

I sighed, and looked at the dark sky, the snow falling gently down, and the dark clouds on the horizon. "All right, fine." I pointed my finger at them both, and I could tell Jamal hadn't quite gotten there yet. "But you two better make damned sure I don't take a bolt of lightning to the head while I'm up there playing Rudolph."

62.

Jamal

The boat rattled and protested against the speed at which it was being pulled through the water. I was soaked once again, but fortunately now it was with warmer water, though I still felt pretty chilled. The sun was up, we were somewhere south of Florida, and had been traveling most of the night at a pace that was, frankly, frightening, given we were in an open-topped boat doing speeds that were usually reserved for planes, not watercraft.

Sienna was out ahead of us, the tow ropes secured to the front of the boat as well as the rear. She was harnessed up, and the boat was just flying through the water. I was keeping a very wary eye on the cleats that secured the ropes, knowing that if any one of them gave out, we'd go cartwheeling into the waves at several hundred miles per hour.

I was watching very, very carefully for any movement in those suckers.

Arche, on the other hand, had her head back, leaning against the carpeted speedboat's deck, looking as though she were blissfully sleeping. Her coat was wrapped tightly around her, and she'd secured her rifle on her belt with a hook once Sienna had started pulling us along. It hung under her trench coat, almost unnoticeable under the bulge of the rest of her gear.

"We will be there soon," she said, not opening her eyes. "You should sleep some."

I had watched her through the night because, well, I still didn't exactly trust her. Clearly, she didn't care. "They say if you can't get at least three hours, you might as well not bother," I said, instead of what I was really thinking.

She opened her eye just a slit to look at me. "That is stupid. Some sleep is better than none."

"Scientifically … maybe not," I said with a shrug. I didn't care either way. I wasn't going to sleep while we were traveling through the water at hundreds of miles per hour. Or was it knots since we were in a boat? I had no idea. "Can I ask you something?"

"No," she said firmly, and the slit at her eye disappeared as she closed it.

I hadn't expected that response, and already had my question out before I realized she'd shot me down. "Why do you do go to work for people like Caden Sims all the time if you—oh," I said as my brain caught up with her comment.

"Why do you sit around on forums and talk about hacking like ordinaries when you can use the power of electricity to do things they never could?" She didn't stir as she posed the question.

I thought about. "Because … it's what I do. It's who I am."

"There is your answer," she said. "Life would be boring if I didn't do anything."

"Yeah, but that's not much of an excuse when it comes to working for bad people," I said. "I mean, Nadine Griffin used you to destroy a woman's life, to wreck her own prosecution."

"I just do the jobs," she said. "I don't get emotionally involved."

"Even when it hurts people?" I asked. "Or kills people?"

"Then you definitely don't want to get emotionally involved." She cracked an eyelid again, perhaps to assess my response. "The people who hire me … they would do these things anyway. This is not my problem."

"Wow," I said, "that's harsh."

"Is hard world out there," she said, her accent playing up her words. "Why do you think Sienna is so dedicated to this idea of taking down Sims?" This time her eye opened all the way. "When you see that Sims may be the only answer for her proving her innocence?"

I didn't have an answer for that, but I speculated anyway. "Because she's trying to do the right thing for me—"

Arche shook her head. "It's because she knows people. How they react, in a way that Caden Sims—or you—don't. Secrets fuel our world. Without them, people feel exposed, frightened, helpless—stripped bare. If word gets out about Harmon, about what he did … well, things have gone well so far after the world learned about metahumans. It hasn't always gone so well. But if this secret gets out, the one where the US president was going to take over the world with his mind …" She mimed an explosion with her hands. "She knows how people will react. Fear. Chaos. And that's in addition to all the other secrets coming out."

I didn't have an answer for that. Maybe she was right—about Sienna and what would happen. I scanned the horizon; there were islands popping up now, and Sienna seemed to be slowing down. She eased off as we threaded between a couple of volcanic-looking islands that jutted out of the sea, and came in for a landing in the boat a few minutes later. "I can push from in here if need be," she said, looking windblown and wet, not to mention tired. She made her way to the back of the boat and shrugged out of her coat, wringing it out and tossing it next to the duffel bag she'd brought aboard with her.

"We can use the engine from here," Arche said, pulling up phone and waggling it. I saw the flare of her finger at the bottom port and knew she'd been tracking our progress all along. "Ten minutes away from the house, maybe." She pointed in the direction we'd been heading. "Can probably see it from here."

"Do we have any ideas how we're going to do this?" I asked, my stomach roiling with nerves.

"She should fly us up the cliff to the pool deck," Arche said. "We assault the house, make for the basement server room. If worst happens, blow it up." She was looking right at Sienna.

I looked right at Sienna. "You're not actually going to—"

"It'll be fine," Sienna said, running hands through her hair as she wrung it out and put it back in a ponytail. "Nothing's getting out, okay? No need to call for the destruction of this guy's entire house. We'll get this server, and then we'll—"

"Go home?" Arche asked, her amusement returned.

"Well, you will," Sienna said to me. She ignored Arche completely, and the other woman stepped over to the helm and started the engine. It hummed a little, and then she put the motor back in the water and straightened out the rudder. We were underway a few seconds later.

I could see the house sticking out of the side of an island in the distance, looking a little like Tony Stark's house in *Iron Man* perched on the Malibu Cliffs. I held my breath for a second, knowing that what happened in that house would determine whether I actually would be going home after this—or going someplace much worse, like jail, or maybe even to a grave of my own.

63.

Reed

I set down just outside the compound in a grove of pine trees. I could see some long-frond palms ahead, and a lowland patch that looked like a small swamp. The compound was situated out of sight of the main road by a couple miles, an isolated property of small cottages that looked like they might not have ever had air conditioning, even before Roger took them off the grid.

I'd surveyed the compound once from the air, maintaining a safe distance in a low-flying cloud before deciding on my course. I needed to get close and find Olivia. She hadn't been visible from the air, which, theoretically, meant I might have the wrong place. It wasn't like I saw Roger, Howie, or Tracy from my pass, either.

But somehow … looking that the place, I knew it was the right one. Call it intuition.

Or it could be because I saw the row of swamp boxes that they used for punishment over in the far corner of the yard. That kinda gave it away.

Once I was down, I took the path toward the tall, wooden fence that circled the place. It had a strange look about it, this place, like something out of the 1800s that had been left to decay out in the woods. Part of me had hoped this would have been easy, that Olivia would have been … I dunno, tied to a tree where I could just swoop down and rescue her. No such luck, which meant I had to do this the harder way:

infiltrate the compound to make absolutely certain I was in the right place (those swamp boxes could have been chicken coops, I guess—it was hard to tell from the air), find Olivia, then free her, probably beat Roger and Tracy, along with Mr. Invisible Howie, and …

Yeah. Not a small series of tasks I'd set before myself. Fortunately, I was motivated by a burning anger that didn't seem to be going anywhere. That and a burning desire to save the day for Olivia Brackett.

I leapt the high, grey, decaying wooden fence with a wind-burst-aided leap, then flaring the air beneath me again as I came down. The excess churn rattled the fence down its length, making an eerie kind of clanking noise that sounded out of place even in an isolated compound in the middle of the Florida woods.

I paused, waiting to see if anyone responded to the noise I'd just made. Maybe no one heard it. Maybe they just thought it was a normal wind.

When the first door to one of the decaying shacks opened and Tracy stepped out, his shoulders tense, I knew I'd blown it even before he set eyes on me. Which he did a second later. It would have been hard to miss me; I was standing right there, dressed in my black suit and looking very out of place against the backdrop of grey, washed-out fence.

"You," he said, snarling as he started toward me at a trot, "you shouldn't have come here."

"I know," I said, heading toward him, "but you shouldn't have kidnapped Olivia. That's a class A felony, punishable by life in prison." I held my ground. I'd just had it confirmed that I was in the right place, after all. Why would I leave now?

Sanity?

Reason?

Desire to not get attacked by multiple metas with strong powers?

Lucky thing I was crazy enough to ignore all three of those, I guess.

Other doors were opening around the compound. People had heard Tracy's shouting. He was charging at me, now, that burning fury in his eyes. I guess I'd given him a little hell last time, what with pounding him and causing him to get struck by a car. Olivia had said he absorbed kinetic energy, and though she hadn't said it explicitly, it suggested to me that if he absorbed it, he did something else with it later.

Like turn it loose on me.

I stood my ground, though, figuring …

Well, figuring I didn't care to get pushed around by this loser.

He was just a bully, the kind of guy who would bum rush anyone who pissed him off, expecting they'd just move. Sane people probably would. Who wants to get bowled over by a guy who can just absorb all the energy of your clash, after all? Who wants to punch someone who'll just take the power of your punch and turn around and batter you with it?

The thing about wind power, though … it relies less on the kinetic energy of an object hitting another object, and more on the resistance of something—a sail, a flag, a human body—catching it across its surface area.

And Tracy? That guy had a lot of surface area.

I blasted with a several-hundred-miles-per-hour gust that lifted him up and carried him off at a rate of speed that was mostly reserved for airplanes, speedsters, and my sister. For a split second, I saw his eyes get huge, then he was swept off into the clouds above and sailing off on a journey that I hoped would take him to enlightening places. Or the ocean, at least, which was where I hoped to drop him, far from where he could do any harm.

"Oh, goodness," a guy said from just inside the circle of should-have-been-abandoned houses. There was a crowd gathering now, people exiting the decaying structures. They were poorly dressed in old clothes with holes in them, a ragged people who were clearly less well taken care of than Roger, Tracy, or Howie.

"I'm looking for Olivia," I said, trying to keep my voice even, but hard as a diamond as I walked casually forward. Tracy was just a dot in the distance, now, fading rapidly as my winds carried him off to the east and his rendezvous with the cold waters of the Atlantic.

Someone pointed toward a house in the distance, a bigger one than the rest. I'd noted it on the way in, the one that looked slightly better—a few newer planks that replaced some old ones, a roof that had all its tiles. It was a subtle thing, because it still looked like hell. It also felt like it was at the head of the circle, if such a thing was possible. First among equals, except obviously someone wasn't equal.

The door to the nicer house opened, and out stepped Roger, fastening on his jeans and looking around. "What's all this hubbub about?" he asked, sounding pretty damned crabby. He scanned his flock and his eyes alighted on me as I stepped into the circle of crumbling houses. "Well, well," he said, his jaw tightening and his face losing that cranky old-man look and going straight to raw, angry threat response. "Looks like we've got an interloper, come to meddle in our business. Seems we're going to have to show him …" his expression darkening to a savage, feral, intensity, "… how we do things around here."

64.

Sienna

"Okay, team," I said as Arche pulled the boat up underneath the cliffside dwelling of Caden Sims, "let's all try not to kick the hornet's nest here."

Arche looked at me curiously, her hands loose on the helm's silvery wheel as she jerked it sideways slightly and cut the engine. We were still a hundred feet from the cliff. "How do you anticipate this going?"

I gave it a second of thought. "Well, we're going to fly up to the pool deck there for insertion," I pointed to the concrete pool deck that overhung the cliff by a few feet, probably giving a primo view of the ocean and the sun, which was rising behind us. "Then we're going to locate and destroy Caden Sims's secret superserver with the fury of a descending horde of Luddites—"

"Luddites form hordes?" Jamal asked. "Furious hordes?"

"You'd be pissed, too, if you saw the world around you consumed by cell phones and the internet," I said. "Anyway, after we take out the server, we'll be greeted by Sims's house servants with hugs and mixed drinks of the daiquiri variety, and we'll party the day away up on the pool deck, taking in some of the sun, SPF 50 our only precaution. Because everything will be peaceful and awesome and fine."

Arche's lips twitched in a thin line of amusement. "I hope you are right. But I doubt it will be so."

"Oh, it will be so," I said as she dropped the anchor

overboard. "We will make it so by virtue of our flailing fists and lightning shots. The lightning's on you guys, though, because all I can throw is fire, nets, and shade."

"Can confirm on the shade," Jamal said, easing closer to me, probably anticipating that I was going to grab him in just a minute. Which I was, since this plan hinged on me flying him and Arche up to the pool deck to start the party.

Once Arche had tossed the anchor, she walked toward me with that same studied indifference. She had the whiff of a long life about her, a feeling I got from metas who typically had lived a few hundred years and grown a little jaded about all the things we young humans got so excited about. Janus had a similar vibe about him, but a little less muted, probably because he could feel emotions. I doubted Arche had felt much of anything in years save for a fear of being exposed.

Which brought up an interesting question that I'd been pondering for a while—what secret was she dreading getting out? Because there was no way she was undertaking this mission out of a vague and generalized concern. Everything about this woman, from the program that shaded her face over on security cameras to defeat facial recognition to her apparent reluctance to let the world's encryption die in a fire suggested that she had at least one big, juicy secret of her own that she was hiding, which was why she was all in in on this particular crusade.

Personally, I didn't much care what her crusade was. I was planning on beating the boss level with her, and then I was going to knock her ass senseless and turn her over to the local authorities so they could sort her out. She'd committed what I would colloquially refer to as an assload of crimes, including allowing a truly vile woman named Nadine Griffin to carry out serious subversions of the justice system, and I liked the idea of her swinging from a yardarm for it.

Too bad they got rid of that yardarm thing long ago. I'd settle for seeing her be one of the few metas to go to jail since they turned loose the tide of criminals I'd put away. Still doing my job, even while a wanted fugitive. That said a little something about me, but I tried to ignore it, because it wasn't really a great time for patient self-reflection.

Also, I was feeling just a little sea sick, and was thankful that the boat ride portion of this mission hadn't been longer.

"Come here, you sexy bitches," I said, and grabbed Jamal around the waist. He let out a yelp of surprise, even though he knew it was coming, the big baby. Arche leaned in close enough to me for me to grab her without having to reach out for her. She didn't try and cuddle or anything, just put herself in a position that I could snake an arm around her carefully. Underneath her trench coat I could feel the machinery that allowed her to control those mechanical lashes, and it was surprisingly compact; I wondered who was designing her tech, because it was a neat little accessory for the woman who felt like shooting lightning from her fingertips didn't make her quite dangerous enough. The fact that her utility belt had an attachment that allowed her to clip on a Steyr Aug (European assault rifle) made me curiouser and curiouser about both the woman and her garment maker.

"Up we go," I said, lifting them into the air at a much slower pace than I usually would have. We weren't directly below Caden Sims's cliffside lair of evil genius, because his house had two stories, both with a magnificent view of the sea, and you could have easily seen us flying up. Instead, we were off to the side with the pool deck, the right side of the house, and I took us up at about twenty, thirty miles an hour, in order to spare my compatriots the head rush associated with my usual flying style.

We crested the fence around the pool deck, which separated it from thick woods that meandered off in the distance of the cliff, and settled down on the far side of the pool. It was a glorious aquamarine, and looked awfully inviting after I'd spent a whole night pulling a boat from the freezing, storm-plagued coast of the Eastern seaboard down here to the Caribbean. It was kind of sad, but the last three months of hiding out and being a fugitive was prompting me to want a vacation much more than the last few years of just doing my normal job ever had.

I set my two companions down gently, staring at the glass doors that led into the house, watching for movement behind them. One was wide open, propped with a doorstop to allow the lovely, pleasant breeze that was coming off the ocean into the house. It was starting to get warm already, and cool shade beckoned inside the house.

"Well, that's easy," I said.

"Yeah," Jamal agreed, "no breaking and entering required."

We circled around the pool and headed for the door, treading quietly. I kept my eyes ahead and off the inviting pool. I had a brief image of myself, sitting next to one of those, in this warm and pleasant air, a sweet beach drink in my hand—

Later, I thought.

Yes, later, Wolfe agreed. *Hunt first, relax after.*

I think you mean, 'Kill first, kill always,' Zack said, a little sourly.

Wolfe likes beaches. And a drink called a Blue Hawaii.

"Well, that's informative," I said. Arche gave me a look that told me to shush up, so I did, and headed into the shaded interior of the house a couple steps ahead of Jamal and Arche.

I didn't make it more than a few more steps inside before I realized that this thing wasn't going to be quite the cake walk I was hoping for. "Damn," I said, looking around the open-concept kitchen and living room stretched out in front of me.

Three very big guys and one very hard-looking woman were standing there watching us from in front of a commanding, room-length plate glass window, and not one of them was Caden Sims. One of them was clearly a Hercules, swelling before my very eyes. Another was hovering a couple feet up, hands glowing with light nets, nearly invisible wings fluttering over his shoulders. The guy beside him had two massive, boa constrictor-sized snakes growing out of his shoulders, with their mouths open and fangs the size of my index fingers glistening at me in the morning light. And finally, the woman …

Well, she had what I can only describe as a red lightsaber extending out of her right sleeve, like it grew out of the back of her hand. "That is so cool," I said, staring at her. "My brother would absolutely shit to see that."

"Um, Sienna," Jamal said, with none of my enthusiasm, "there are … kind of a few of them …"

"Yeah, but I mean, look at that!" I gushed. "She has a *lightsaber* sticking out of her hand. A lightsaber, Jamal!" I turned back to her. "I've been doing this for a while, and I've seen a lot of stuff …" The woman I was talking to had started off a little standoffish, but she was actually melting a little bit, her RBF disappearing as I complimented her, "… and your power? Totally one of the coolest I've ever seen."

"Thank you," she said, sounding pretty sincere about it. Then she caught some harsh looks from her buds, so she hardened back up. Shame.

"You're trespassing on private property," the Hercules said. He looked familiar, and it took me a moment to realize he was the same guy who had pulled Sims through the wall to make their escape in the Javits Center.

"Well, duh," I said. "I didn't just wander into Caden Sims's house in the Caribbean by accident. I came with a purpose." I stared them down. "And that purpose is to wreck his servers. No one needs to die for that to happen, but I think you all know …" And here's the part where I lowered my voice to reflect the full menace of Sienna Nealon about to do her Sienna Nealon thing, "… I could kill every last one of you right where you stand, and walk over your flaming corpses to get my job done." I watched the visible discomfort creep across the face of Snake Shoulders, and my friend with the lightsaber's eyes darted questioningly to the side. "I'd rather not," I said, catching her eye, "especially to you, because—seriously, that power is lit AF." She flashed a nervous smile and caught looks from her friends again, so went hard again immediately. "Please … your boss is a bad guy, and he's planning to do bad things with that processing power in the basement."

Four out of the five of them looked nervously toward a staircase across the room behind them. "The server farm is downstairs," I said under my breath to Arche and Jamal. My opponents had just confirmed where the servers were.

"You're a liar and a fugitive," the Hercules said, projecting strength.

"I'm a fugitive," I said. "I'm not lying, though. Caden Sims is up to absolutely no good here, guys. Please … don't turn this into a massacre." I was actually both of those, but not in a way that they would have appreciated—I had a deep and serious desire to avoid killing these bodyguards, who had clearly been hired to do a job that involved protecting a person's life and property. It wasn't like they were assassins, or mercs hired to kill me. I'd worked with bodyguards before, and while there were certainly shitheads in the profession, just like with any others, and I might be able to find fault with their choice of protectee …

… But their unease told me that they didn't know about Sims's illicit activities, despite their knowledge that there were some sort of servers downstairs. They probably just thought he was another weird tech mogul or something.

"We're not standing aside," the Hercules declared, and I saw the faerie guy, Snake Shoulders, and my new friend the Jedi nod. "You can't just come into someone's house and say they're bad, then bust their house up just because you're tougher than anyone else."

"Actually, I can," I said, as calmly and pleasantly as I could muster. "That's kind of the point of might making right. I can do it, and I choose to, when the cause is just, as it is here."

"I'm not stepping aside," Hercules said, sticking out his noble, well-chiseled chin. He looked like something out of a Mr. Universe competition. "If you have to kill me to do it … then I guess that's what I'm standing for." He set his feet, and the rest of them sort of pulled together in a little human wall arrangement.

"Well, damn, you guys," I said, a little humbled. My bluster had worked pretty well in New York. "I'm not going to kill you, because that would be wrong, but I'm totally going to have to kick your asses—"

A screaming, piercing pain ripped through my back as something like a knife of cold razored into me just below my left shoulder blade. It missed my spine by a couple inches but I dropped to the ground anyway like my legs had failed, hitting the cold marble floor with a thump and cracking it with my newly-hardened jaw.

As my vision blurred and fuzzed before me, I saw my new enemies coming at me while I was down, and something told me that in spite of what I'd just said about not killing them … that they might not show the same mercy to me.

65.

Reed

"Where's Olivia?" I called as I summoned up a barrier of wind around me, low intensity, just a basic one that wouldn't keep much out—yet. It was my precursor, my readying stage for things to come, and it carried the bite of the Florida air, filled with a surprising combination of humidity and chill.

"We got us a little aeolus that's wandered out among us," Roger said as he sauntered toward me. I was looking around the circle of houses carefully, because with his power he could pretty much deck me from any direction and I wouldn't have a lot of warning. "I've known your kind before. You can't do much of anything here, fella."

I gave a quick glance around. The crowd of Roger's "followers" was notably mellow. I counted three faces that showed any kind of defiance. Out of about thirty. Not a great ratio for him, which told me a lot about the kind of loyalty he inspired. "I don't see any brick," I said, acting like I wasn't really paying attention to what he was saying.

"Why does that matter?" Roger asked, squinting his eyes as he assessed me in a very lackadaisical manner. I could tell he believed what he'd said, that I wasn't much of a threat.

"Because I'm not like the aeoluses you've met before," I said. "Because I'm not going to bother huffing and puffing." I set my jaw, trying to keep from clenching my teeth. "I'm skipping straight to blowing your damned shanty camp right the hell down."

I boosted the power of that precursor wind shield I'd put around me, turned it gale force, and swept it out in a hard circle as I lifted off the ground. I saw the invisible man out of the corner of my eye, blown away in a forced cartwheel, his mouth open in shock at his rude, unplanned departure from the earth.

In the years since I'd met my sister, I watched her go from a pale, scared teenager who had been kept down by her mother for most of her life into a preeminent badass whom pretty much no one went out of their way to mess with. Even the government hadn't been able to bring her down, and they'd damned sure tried to hit her with everything they had.

I'd watched that transformation, from the girl no one had known about, a person hidden in the shadows, to the deciding factor in a war that would have resulted in the enslavement of humanity …

… And I'd been quietly jealous the whole time.

Jealous of her power.

Jealous of the way she used the hell that had been thrown at her as heat for the forge that made her into an even badder badass, tearing through unstoppable enemy after unstoppable enemy, upending the whole damned world.

I'd been jealous of her that whole time, because I'd lacked the forging hardship she'd faced, and I lacked the power that allowed her to turn loose harder than anyone else on the planet.

But now … I'd tasted the hardship. The trauma. I'd been mind-controlled by a megalomaniac, and loosed on an innocent girl. I'd pulled the trigger and watched a woman die, by my hand, but not my will, because my will was twisted to someone else's ends. I'd had my body played with like a toy, turned against me the way Sienna had been played with by Old Man Winter. Fortunately, I had not had to destroy someone I loved. That fate I got spared.

But I had still been used by someone else to cause pain, havoc, death.

And I had gotten stronger.

Because that was the price of my power.

Now I wasn't even quietly jealous of Sienna anymore, because now … I had an inkling of what she'd been through, what she'd had taken away in order to make her who she was.

A stranger had to die to turn me into what I was now.

And what was I?

"I am the wind," I whispered, but there was no way in the hurricane of hell I'd summoned up that Roger heard me.

My power blew out in all directions, and the little ramshackle village just disintegrated like toothpick houses, as though I'd hit them with a bomb, they shattered and flew. The metas who were grouped around were bowled over as well, but I kept my wind a foot off the ground, so once they hit, they stayed down, watching everything fly over them in a storm of epic proportions, hurricane season come early to central Florida.

Roger was on his ass, too, keeping low, his eyes a hell of a lot wider than they had been a moment earlier. The earth was starting to swallow him, and I couldn't have that, so I blew him right out of the ground with a sweeping wind that dug him out like a steam shovel. He looked shocked at the force of my power. I doubted he'd ever been yanked out of his earth before, and certainly not by any aeolus he'd ever encountered.

"Where is Olivia?" I made the wind howl my words, something that felt so instinctively right. The skies were dark; I'd conjured clouds out of nowhere, and the sky was now black.

Roger tried to look away from me, his hand twitching as he lined up power of his own. I saw what he was going for before he fully got it.

A bevy of pipes still stuck out of the earth in the wreckage of his house. He had ripped them free, and they were shuddering their way through the storm winds toward me, like a glistening spear he was going to turn loose at any second. They were flying against the wind, edges sharp where my attack had sheared them, and he plainly had some impaling in mind for them.

I hit them with a gale, and they stopped in midair. They

weren't just sharp at one end, either. Because of how he'd been forced to rip them out of the earth, they were definitely pointy at both ends, which seemed like delicious irony to me.

Roger looked at them, then me, eyes wider and wider as his attack got foiled, obviously, in front of his eyes. I was acutely aware of the currents of air, how everything was moving around me right now. His other "loyal" subjects were staying down, keeping under all this. Invisible Guy was good and gone; Tracy was still on his way to the ocean for a swim.

Then I saw Olivia. She'd been staked to the earth under Roger's house, apparently in a crawl space. Her face was bloody, her clothes were dirty, but she looked … more or less all right. She was watching me, and smiled in relief, her clothes whipping as the storm blew over her, her eyes closing and her smile widening as she lay there, head back, laughing into the storm.

It was just Roger, my bubbling anger, and me, the howling void of my storm between us, and fighting our little contest of strength—the force of my wind against his control over metal and earth elements.

He tried to raise the ground beneath me, but my wind swept it away in clumps of dirt that became dust in the intensity of the gale.

He tried to blow sand at my eyes, but it was just as gone, just as quickly, unable to match itself against the force of my storm.

And then … he did the last thing he probably could.

Something broke out of the ground from the ruin of his house, reaching out of the ground about ten feet from where Olivia lay. Something sharp, something heavy. A stake, a pipe, something. It lanced into the air and held as Roger and I stared at each other over the pipes he'd tried to ram through me. He was shaking, concentrating. I'd been holding him up in the air, and still, in the middle of the chaos and he just stayed there, because … what else was he going to do? He was in my power, and he was fighting back with his pipes—that had been stopped by me—and his last, other gambit … the thing that was hovering to the side where he'd raised it, the end dangling, twisting slowly like a missile tracking toward me. He was getting his aim right, and then I knew he'd be sending it my way, as surreptitiously as he could.

I doubt he knew I could feel it there. I doubt he remembered in that moment that if I'd really wanted to hurt him, or kill him, I could have just run him forward into his waiting pipes. I actually could have overpowered him, and I started to show him that.

But then he tried to bring that secret weapon, the one hovering, ready to drive it through me—

And I whirled to the side and gave it a hearty shove with my wind.

Roger's reaction was one of surprise, probably because he'd had to drive it hard to fight against the buffeting shield of wind around us. He'd let it build pressure, force, enough of it to skewer a wild boar, as Aragorn might say.

Instead … I redirected it about ten feet to the side, hoping that Olivia, watching all this unfold, would be ready for it.

She was.

The metal length zipped at her like a projectile, entering her personal bubble as the air around her distorted. She saw it coming, and closed her eyes, concentrating, as I gave her the chance to exercise some control over her powers and her life.

It sat there for a fraction of a second, hovering around her, then twisted, distorted—

And came flying at Roger with five times the speed and force.

The piece of metal he'd intended to hurl through me like a javelin came at him faster than he could react at its sudden, improbable change in direction. I gave it a little extra push with the wind to make sure it stayed on course, and it did.

It sang through the windstorm and found its mark in Roger's chest. His jaw dropped in shock as he was skewered on a length of rebar that made me feel like I needed a tetanus shot just from looking at it.

I could have moved him out of the way at the last second, I suppose. Could have saved his life when I saved my own, hoping he'd learn a lesson from watching one of his own use her chance to hurl a weapon at him with lethal force.

But for some reason, all I could think was … someday this guy would escape that underground prison. He controlled the earth, after all; how could he not?

And on that day … I didn't want to feel guilty for whoever he might hurt next.

The rebar sailed right through him, ripping his heart clean out.

I let the storm die down. The lengths of pipe hit the earth and bounced with a thump.

Roger hit the ground with a thump, too. His eyes were already glassy, staring up at the sky as it started to clear. He had that smell of death about him, I could tell as I landed, the chaos around me clearing.

No need to kick down a door this time, I thought, as I hurried over to let Olivia loose from her imprisonment. And no need for a gun, either. She was lying flat, her clothing still stirred by the wind, but a smile plastered on her face.

"Looks like she wins," I said, leaving Roger's corpse behind me and not looking back. He didn't look anything like that girl in Cheyenne, and I doubted I'd feel an ounce of guilt about letting him meet an ugly end.

66.

Jamal

"Get downstairs. Now," Arche said, shoving me roughly as Sienna hit the ground, bleeding from a wound under her shoulder.

I hadn't seen the attack coming, and I barely saw it now.

There was a semi-solid hand formed out of the hazy shadows at Sienna's back, like a limb sticking out of a black puddle.

Except it ended in what looked like a knife blade.

I stumbled under Arche's semi-shove as the enemies that had formed their little line started toward us as well. Arche deployed her lashes and charged them with electricity in a crackling burst.

She whipped her left lash toward the shadow that had stabbed Sienna, the blue, flickering light illuminating a shape that seemed to become translucent under the glow, and then she whipped the right one in a hard swing that went over Sienna's fallen form and drove the other four attackers back. "Move! Go stop Sims!" Arche shouted.

She didn't have to tell me twice. I pounded past them as they shouted shock and dismay at Arche's unexpected attack, and I vaulted over the edge of a spiral staircase rail and landed roughly, then jumped down the last few steps. I found myself in another open-concept room, this one with a bar, and another living space capped by a desk that looked out over the waves.

Nope. No Caden Sims here.

I sprinted down a small hallway with a couple of doors. One had the look of a closet, butted as it was against a short wall, so I threw open the other door. Immediately, I got hit by a wave of freezing cold and the faint blue glow of LED lighting in an aqua color that pretty much matched the pool.

"Found it," I said, realizing that the door I'd opened was heavier, insulated like a freezer door. It really was colder in here, frosty air sneaking out. There was ice all around the room, which I couldn't see very deep into because of a low-hanging fog over it, like it was filled with dry ice or something. Server towers ran in front of me like skyscrapers sticking out of the mist.

I wondered how there was mist in a room that seemed like it was subzero, but I didn't have time to ponder on it while Sienna and Arche were scuffling upstairs. I could hear the clash of battle, Arche's lash crackling and ripping into something as someone yelled.

No time for debate. I held out my hands, targeting the nearest server tower, and lit the damned thing up with all the voltage I could muster.

Electricity ran over it furiously, blue sparks twisting and diffusing through the cylinder. When it all died away, the blue LED that ran the length of the server … was still aglow.

It was still running.

"What the hell?" I asked, slipping further into the room. I'd expected my electricity to zap through it and go to the next, then the next, like chain lightning, until they completely fried out the entire place. I damned sure didn't expect my electricity to just spark off, like I'd shot it at a rubberized surface.

The door clicked closed behind me. I tried to push it open again, but there wasn't a handle. It took me a second to realize that there was a keypad. Which was weird, because I hadn't noticed one on the other side.

"So you found me," a voice came from down the row. There must have been twenty, thirty servers in this frozen room. The cold was to keep the processors from overheating, but this was taking it to an extreme I hadn't quite seen before. I'd read something about cold being used to reduce the resistance of electricity in a processor, but … that was pretty bleeding edge stuff. I couldn't remember the context of the article, but I would have sworn it had something to do with quantum computing.

Then again, Arche had said that Caden Sims had come up with a way to put more processing power to work than anyone had ever seen. Enough to decrypt the whole damned internet. Quantum suddenly started to look a whole lot more plausible.

"Yeah, I found you," I said, trying to figure out where Sims was, exactly. "Why don't you come on out here and we can talk about your crazy plan to open the door to the bathroom while everyone's got their pants down?"

Sims just laughed. "Most people are going to thank me when this is over. It'll be embarrassing at first, sure … but they'll get over it. The truth is going to be out there, and it's going to be … beautiful." He sounded a little in lust with himself, or at least the idea. "Imagine it, Jamal! Maybe people will finally see you for who you are … instead of seeing your brother and not noticing you at all. Then again," Sims laughed, "your brother never murdered anyone, so … maybe them seeing you isn't such a good thing after all?"

"You have no idea what you're going to unleash with this," I called back, easing down one of the rows, trying to figure out where he was. I was cold, again, and this time I was in the damned Caribbean. If I stayed in here too long, I was going to end up covered in ice again. "You think people will just go along with you exposing their secrets, their private conversations? You're going to make doing any kind of business online impossible."

"I'm not worried about business. I'm worried about truth. I'm worried about people being kept in the dark by the powerful. About secrets big enough to destroy us … because they're out there, Jamal. You have no idea what secrets are being kept. Like the ones about your friend upstairs, for instance."

"Yeah, those are harsh," I said, looking down the row. He was close, I was pretty sure. "But you could just reveal some of the worst of them, you know. Go through, pick out the truths that you think need to be told, let them loose on the world? You don't have to expose every credit card number on the web, every teenager's text messages, every Snapchat, every nude selfie, every person who's ever supported terrorism by buying a Justin Bieber album … Imagine how family members are going to look at each other when they find out, especially the Bieber thing?" Easter lunch would be tense in my house this year. "There's a lot you're letting out that you don't need to. You're opening a door that can't be closed again, and it ain't a small door. There's a lot behind it."

"You'd rather live in the half-truth," Sims said, and I heard a footstep a little ways to my left. "You'd rather not know what others are saying about you, when they're talking about you behind your back. You'd rather live in the uncertainty. Well, I'd rather *know.*"

"But you won't!" I shouted, and my voice echoed in the frosty chamber. "You'll expose all these people, all their secrets, all the feelings they've put on line—but all they'll do is have new ones. Life will go on, people will just be more suspicious of what they say online."

"Not just online," Sims said. "In view of a phone. In range of a computer. The microphones could be listening at any time. Think how many people have one of those talking things from a major conglomerate that responds to voice commands. Everything they say in range of it, everything they do near a computer camera … it's always been possible that they could be seen, heard, but they've never thought of it as a threat. Technology was our friend … but people need to start thinking of how it can be our enemy. How it can be used against us. Because I promise you … those companies that you're so worried about saving, that business that gets done online … they're preparing the means to exploit it. They're readying the weapon to use it against us. And nobody has a clue. This thing I'm doing? The truth will get out there. All of it. People will finally see. And hopefully … they'll walk away while they still have a chance."

"What is this really about?" I asked, walking down the side

row where I'd heard him walk. "I know you worked in tech … but—"

Something blindsided me, sending me headfirst into the nearest server tower. My head hit plastic and I bounced off, spinning and barely catching myself before I hit the cold ground. I shook my head and saw Caden Sims standing there, wearing nothing but a freaking speedo, his skin blue and frozen, cold radiating off of him.

And suddenly it made sense why the room was so cold.

Caden Sims was a frost giant. Except medium height. So… a frost medium?

"It's about the truth, I told you," Sims said. "The truth I saw firsthand. And now … the one I'm going to show everyone else … after I kill you."

67.

Sienna

Damn, but the hits I was taking just kept on coming. My resolution not to kill the bodyguards just doing their jobs took a hit, too, when that stabbing pain got me right in the back. I didn't get a glimpse at my attacker until the other four bodyguards I'd been standing off with came charging. Arche shouted something that I lost in my pain—yes, the agonizing sort, which hit me right in the lung AGAIN, and a flash of blue cast a pall over me as I found myself again in my own head for a few seconds while I hoped and prayed that Wolfe would heal me.

You ask for miracles, Wolfe said, looking at me with a sort of fatherly disappointment that I found extremely disquieting.

I keep getting bushwhacked, I said. *Did anyone else see anyone behind me when I came in? There was no one there, right?*

Could be a shadow-melter, Eve suggested. *They can absorb into the shadows, slide out, make knives and other weapons of the darkness.*

I just stared at her. *Well, that's a useful skill, too. Between this shadow-melter—if that's what got me—and the lady with the lightsaber hand, I just saw two new meta types today. Two.*

Plus you've got a Snake Shoulders— Bastian started.

I think that's called a Zakkahn or something, I said. *I ran across a couple of those in Eau Claire one time.*

And a fae, Eve said snidely.

Oh, yes, I said, *who could forget one of your peeps?*

You can't forget us. We're unforgettable.

And a Hercules, Zack said.

J.J. calls those them the Rattata of metahumans, I said.

What … does that mean? Gavrikov asked.

I'm not exactly sure, I said, checking back on my body, which was still on the floor. Maybe a second or two had passed, probably less.

It's an exceedingly common Pokemon, Harmon said, and when everyone looked at him, he shrugged a little defensively. *The lady with lightsaber hand knows; I learned it from her.*

Sure you did, I goaded, deciding I should probably plunge back into the pain waiting for me. I didn't really want to, because my body wasn't close to healed yet, but this was what I did. Dove into pain, fought through it, and beat the ass off of people.

I shot a net of light blindly behind me, turning my head in time to see it make contact with a person whose body was half-shadow, lit by the crackling electricity that Arche had channeled through one of her lashes. She was whipping the other around in front of us, trying to hold back the tide of trouble coming our way in the form of Sims's bodyguards.

I honestly figured she would have bailed on me and gone to get her own task done, but I suppose leaving me down would have just left her back open to attack from any of these clowns. Jamal disappeared down the stairs in a jump as I started to force my way back to my feet.

"Time to go all Oprah on these people," I said, trying to ignore the pain of my back and lung stitching the gaping hole in muscle and tissue back together. I raised my hands, targeting the enemies that were already dodging Arche's attacks. "You get a light net!" I fired one that hit the Hercules in the face. "You get a light net!" The next one took Mr. Fae in the head and flipped him over in mid air. He crashed down through a glass coffee table, struggling to get rid of the impediment to his continued sight and breathing. "Everybody gets a light net!" I fired one at the lady Jedi, but she cut it neatly in half with her weapon.

"I applaud your generosity," Arche said, swinging for the fences at the shadow-melter, who had already disappeared again from the light net I'd snared him in somehow, "but may I suggest you instead offer free flaming corpses to everyone?"

"Request denied," I said, blasting at Hercules again a few times with further light nets. I pinned him against the far wall, hands and feet all bound. I didn't expect it'd keep him down forever, but I hoped it'd get him off my back for long enough that I could put down a few of his fellows for the count.

Mr. Snake Shoulders caught an electro-lash square in the center of his bare, bronzed chest and jerked comically, like he'd just had someone plug a severed TV cord into his ass. His eyes rolled back in his head, the snakes swayed, their eyes rolling as well, and they all pitched over together, his chest moving in a steady, albeit slow, up and down motion.

"You could have killed him," I said to Arche as I wheeled around, jumping at the reaction of a voice in my head, crying of danger impending.

"I tried," Arche said, "but I lacked the voltage to spare." I didn't really doubt her, but I didn't have time to call her on it because I realized exactly who had spoken up warning me of the shadow-melter coming at me again.

What the hell, Harmon? I asked as I dodged a bladed attack from the shadow-melter and fired a light net right at him again. *You joining the team?*

Harmon's eye roll was worthy of Robert Downey, Jr. *No, I'm just sick of pain for the day. We might not get to experience it in quite the same way you do, but be assured, there's no lack of secondhand feeling for it on my part, and I'm quite tired of it.*

Cool, keep me alive, I said.

Light up the shadows with the nets, Wolfe said before Harmon could vent another sour comment, which I could tell was coming. *Give the shadow-melter nowhere to flee.*

"Okay." I fired three hard light nets into the shadowiest parts of the corner behind me, and they hung there, casting a brighter light than I usually allowed for them. Then I lit off a torch in my other hand, a long blaze of fire that swept all the rest of the remaining shadow away.

I was left looking at a skinny guy who was desperately, desperately seeking the darkness he'd been melting into and out of just a moment before.

"I see you," I said, and punched him in the jaw hard enough to hear the crack as he flew back and slammed his well-lit head into the well-lit wall. I netted him hard a half dozen times just to make sure he didn't come surging back late in the game.

I swung around in time to see Arche under attack from the Lady Jedi and Mr. Fae. She threw up a lash and Jedi Lady cut through it like it was mushy pasta and she was a fork. The lash went flying, stray voltage surging off of it, and Arche staggered back, worry showing on her face as she tried to hold Mr. Fae back with the remaining lash. He was doing a pretty good job of dodging it, but Arche was also managing to ward off his light nets.

"Nobody likes a cheap knock off," I said, and sent my biggest net yet flying at Mr. Fae. It caught him facing sideways and hurled him across the room into the brick fireplace, shattering it and destroying the big-screen plasma hanging above it. He stuck there, like he'd been caught in fly paper, and I hurled another couple nets at him to truss him up like the Hercules. The last one snapped his head back into the stone good, and I saw his eyes shut and his body go limp against the nets.

"You're not exactly the original," Arche said, hobbling back, her remaining lash defensively positioned in front of her. Lady Jedi was standing off from the two of us, and Hercules was ripping himself out of the wall where I'd bound him, so we didn't have a ton of time before things got interesting again.

"You should go help Jamal," I said, ignoring her quip—for now. "Because I haven't heard his triumphant scream followed by his triumphant return yet, and that worries me."

"You sure you can handle these two by yourself?" she asked as Hercules brushed the last of the clinging drywall from his elbow and flexed, hulking as he stomped his way back over to me.

"Easy peasy," I said, "go on."

Arche apparently didn't have to be told twice. She hurled herself toward the stairs at a breakneck speed, disappearing down the spiral while Lady Jedi, Hercules, and I just stared at each other.

"You guys really sure you want to do this?" I asked. "Because …" I looked at the havoc around us, "… I mean … it could be going better for you. That stab in the back thing was pretty key to your winning, and it kinda didn't work. It's all downhill from here, see."

"I like my odds," Hercules said, flexing again. "You bind me to a wall, I'll rip right out again. You can't stop—"

I blasted him six times in less than a second, peppering him with light nets to all four limbs, another across his sprawling chest, and one across his massive thighs just for good measure.

Except this time, instead of binding him to a solid wall, I bound him to the giant, floor-to-ceiling window that looked out over the ocean.

"Go ahead," I said, "rip out of that." His eyes were platelike, darting around as he considered his predicament. If he tried …

As if to highlight his quandary, the glass around his hands and midsection spiderwebbed, the cracking sound audible under the silence that Lady Jedi and I were leaving. "Ooh," I said. "It's a long way down," I taunted, and for her benefit, "People who live in clifftop houses should not piss off those of us who can throw them like a stone."

"I can't let you do this," Lady Jedi said, composing herself right there in front of me. She raised up her glowing blade, and I saw the tip shake a little.

"You're a good egg," I said, readying my response, which was going to be a dose of the warmind from Bjorn followed by a hard cross to the jaw. "And for that … I'm going to hurt you as little as possible … though if you follow the pattern of everything else in my life lately, I doubt you'll appreciate it very much."

68.

Jamal

I shot lightning at Caden Sims and he hurled frost at me and our two powers met in the middle, electricity running through the spikes of ice that came at me in a storm. The two passed each other more or less harmlessly and I was forced to dodge behind a server tower to keep from getting impaled on a big icicle.

"The truth is going to come out, Jamal!" Sims said over the crashing sound of ice frosting the server behind me. I scrambled, running to the next one in line, because I didn't need to become a Jamal-cicle for no damned reason at all. "You can't stop it!" He got a little more sober, serious. "You don't have the power."

"Oh, the irony," I said, putting a hand against the server and cranking up my juice. It did nada, the electricity harmlessly running over the damned thing and grounding right down into the floor beneath my feet. If I'd been susceptible to it, it probably would have given me a good jolt.

"You could have frosted my cupcake on the plane, you know," I shouted down the aisle as I started to make my retreat. I wasn't loving the chances I felt like I had against this lunatic. He was on a committed mission, and apparently had rubberized his room, which made using my powers harder but didn't seem to do much to inhibit his.

"No, I couldn't," he said. "These powers of mine? They're

new. And fortunate, because the ice man I was using to fulfill this function before quit when he heard Sienna Nealon came after us in New York. That cost me almost all my bodyguards. Forced me to explore alternative treatments. Just like what exposing the truth will do to a human race bound in digital purgatory."

"You should take a big bite out of a block of ice," I whispered to myself, wishing he'd stop explaining himself. Whatever reason he had in his head to do this thing, it wasn't something I understood, and I doubted anyone other than he did, either.

"There you are," Caden said, appearing at the end of the row next to me. He extended a hand and shot a frosty blast at me, which nicked me in the leg as I dove behind another tower for cover. I hit the frosty ground and mewled in pain.

He'd frozen my leg, and not just a little. It was covered in ice in a way that I hadn't been even after my boat ride with Arche. A solid chunk of frost grew out of my leg like a diamond sprouting from a rock. It might have been a little beautiful, refracting the blue LED strips in the server room, if it hadn't been so damned painful.

I started to crawl, hurrying to drag myself away from Sims. I made it around another corner before he caught up with where I'd been. I waited, in ambush, figuring maybe if he stuck his head out—

He peeked, smart enough not to expose himself even though he'd plainly done some damage to me. I saw him, and held deathly still, hoping he wouldn't see me. I needed him to stick his head out at least a little ways, or else his damned server would just absorb my electricity when I threw it at him.

He eased out, taking his sweet damn time, eyes flitting from underneath the blue sheen of his frosted eyebrows. Sims was being cautious, and the pain of my frozen leg was stealing my focus minute by minute. I was leaning against my tower in a sitting position, curled against it, only one eye and part of my hand sticking out, ready to shoot him.

Sims didn't say anything, not now. When his head was exposed three-quarters of the way, he saw me, finally, and started to throw out a hand of his own.

It was now or never.

I hurled lightning at him, electricity jumping the gap between us—

And dispersing, uselessly, against the server he dodged behind.

Now I was stuck, with nowhere else to go. I couldn't move, couldn't run, and he knew exactly where I was.

"Hah!" he crowed, and it was the sound of a man who knew I was done. He stuck his head out again, framed by the exit door, which was just down the row. This time he hurled ice back at me, and I couldn't quite dodge behind the cover of the tower in time. It hit me in the face, knocking me over into the aisle and giving him a clear shot at me.

I sat there, ready as I could be for death given I didn't really want to die. There was a splitting pain in my forehead where he'd caught me, an outgrowth of frost from my skull like an icy tumor.

"The world will be a better place for what I'm about to do to it," Sims said as he stepped out. He blasted my hand, anchoring it to the ground in a sudden block of ice. I gasped at the pain and stared at him when I managed to pry my eyes open again. "I'll—"

The door behind him blew off and hit him squarely in the back before he had a chance to turn. It smashed him into a server tower, cutting through him and burying itself in the case a few inches. His body was neatly partitioned just below the shoulders, his chest sliding down, now separated from his head and everything above his collarbones.

"Holy hell," I managed to get out between chattering teeth as ArcheGrey stepped into the room, coat trailing behind her and hair curled, like some sort of cowgirl from the Wild West. "I got froz—"

"I don't care," she said, and swept her lash around above me in a hard, swinging motion that wiped out five servers by cutting them neatly in half. She drew back and whipped again as she strode into the room, and fuzzing static crackled through the air.

I pried my frozen hand from the floor. It was painful, but

doable, especially now that the temp in the room seemed to be noticeably rising with Sims dead. There was still a block of ice around it, and I slammed it against the ground, carefully chipping pieces off as Arche strode through the room, wreaking havoc with her lash. A few of the servers she'd devastated were now burning, acrid smoke filling the room.

"Jamal!" Sienna's voice filtered into the room, and she appeared in shadow at the doorway, backlit by the daylight streaming in from the glass windows out in the downstairs living area.

"I'm right here!" I raised that frozen hand, and she came over with fire in her own, melting it in seconds. It didn't really help me with the pain, but at least the ice was gone now.

"Where's Arche?" she asked.

I paused, realizing the sound of exploding servers had stopped. I looked over my shoulder as Sienna held me up, and I nodded past the sparking debris and wreckage. "She went that way."

Sienna gave me a look, and I could see the analysis on her face: I assumed it was the debate between, "Do I ditch him politely to chase her down, or drop him like a leper's foot and explain later?" Politeness apparently won out. "Can you stand on your own?"

"Yeah. Be careful with her," I said, and Sienna was gone in a flash, zipping around the ruins of the server room to the back corner. All was quiet for about thirty seconds, and then she came back, looking like she wanted to punch someone, hopefully someone who was not me.

"She got away," Sienna said, eyes narrowed in a barely contained sense of fury.

"What? How?" I asked.

"She used her lash thing to carve a hole in the foundation and crawled out," Sienna said, lips pursed tightly. "She's gone. I flew out to look for her and there's not a sign of anything except sirens, and there's kind of a lot of woods around the house, so …" She grabbed me under the arm and started dragging me along. "We need to vacate the premises."

"You don't think she grabbed our boat, do you?" I asked as she carried me out and kicked a chair through the window overlooking the sea. We were flying out before it even hit the water, and I breathed a sigh of relief as we set down in the boat and Sienna pulled up the anchor. "Guess not."

"My gut tells me that she didn't want us to find her, so she had an escape plan before we even set out last night," she said, settling behind the wheel and pushing the boat, subtly, with her flying power. The boat turned and started to move without her even needing to start the engine. "That said, I'm not starting the motor, just in case she set a bomb or something to be sure."

I sagged into one of the seats, feeling the slow burn of the sun, which had risen into the sky, warming me after that damned freezer server room. Hallelujah. I was damned sick of the cold. "Well … I guess we did it, huh?"

Sienna didn't smile. "I guess we did. Except for settling ArcheGrey's hash. Unless you can …" She gave me a nod.

I fished for my backpack, which I'd stowed in one of the watertight deck crates at Arche's behest when Sienna brought it aboard. I pulled it up and had a connection to the cellular network in a few seconds. I did a quick search, dabbled in a couple of areas, seeing if I could find her via her cell phone, but … I looked around and opened the livewell built into one of the boat's benches.

Arche's cell phone, the one she'd used to text Sienna about me, was sitting right there, on the dry bottom.

"She planned it all out," Sienna said when I showed it to her. "She's gone already. That lady's a ghost. If she can hide her face from cameras on the net the way she does, what are the odds you can track her down?" She sighed. "And what are the odds she kept her bargain about the source of this cover-up relating to Harmon?"

I frowned as the boat skipped on a little swell, throwing a dash of spray up into the air. It might have been cold if I hadn't just come out of the freezer, but as it was … it was kind of refreshing. "Probably not good." I thumbed her phone and it lit up, instantly, which made me almost swallow my tongue in surprise, and a little touch of fear. "Or not."

There was an app, plain as day, right in the middle of the desktop, like she'd left it there as a present, labeled, 'For Sienna.' It was even named, like a little note, and I'd clicked on it before I'd finished thinking things through—like it could be a bomb or something.

It wasn't a bomb.

It was exactly what I'd thought it was when I saw it.

69.

Reed

"You know that saying about how you can't go home again?" Olivia asked me as the doctor in the ER dabbed at a cut over her eye with a long, Q-tip looking swab. "They nailed it."

"I'd say you went home again all right," I said, trying to keep things as light as she had. She'd exhibited mostly relief at the sight of me rescuing her, which was, I suppose, a good thing. I expected whatever else she was feeling would probably come springing out later, maybe in the form of nightmares. I had it in mind to tell her doctor to recommend a psychologist before she got discharged.

"Okay, yeah, I made it home again," she said, staring off into the distance, "and I guess … yes, I made it out. And I suppose it's worth it, because now at least Roger is done being a controlling jag to people." She looked right at me. "How did the others take it?"

I didn't know quite how to answer that. Olivia had been a little out of it once I'd gotten her unstaked, and so she'd missed the rush of people hovering around me after they'd seen her feed Roger his own rebar spear at warp speed. The reaction had been … well, pretty much gushing excitement.

"They took it well," I said. "Some of them were worried about you. You'll probably get visitors."

"What about Tracy?" Here a hint of terror peeked out in the strain around the corners of her eyes.

"You know," I said, feeling him still in the grip of the wind, somewhere over the Atlantic. I hadn't let him loose yet, and I wasn't convinced I would. Maybe I'd let him sail the world without a bite to eat for all eternity, or maybe I'd drop him in the Arctic. I wasn't sure. "I don't think you'll have to worry about him."

"And Howie?"

"Dosed with suppressant and in custody. Extra chains, and all the right precautions. He's not going anywhere but jail, then to trial, then to a meta prison. For a long while. But I get the feeling that Roger being dead probably took a lot of the wind out of his sails."

"Good," Olivia said, nodding as the doctor finished disinfecting and started to put together the suture. "That's … good."

"Yeah," I said, shuffling my feet a little, ready to make my exit. "You're going to be all right, okay? The police have it from here." And I started for the door.

"You really did it," she said, halting me in my tracks. "I didn't think anyone could protect me from him, but you … you really showed me the way. And … thank you for letting me be the one to …" Her voice trailed off, but I knew what she meant.

I pasted a smile on my face and turned around to show her. "You're welcome. Glad I could … help," I settled on, after searching for the right word. It was probably the best one, I reflected as I opened the door and stepped out into the hall. It wasn't exactly the word I meant, but she had enough on her mind without me hitting her with my baggage.

Because the word I'd been thinking of wasn't "help." Not by a long shot.

What I'd done here … was atone. Or at least start. And I had a feeling I needed to do a lot more … of both helping and atoning … before that feeling of guilt that weighed down my insides would even come close to feeling like it wasn't a ten-thousand-ton weight.

70.

Sienna

We pulled up to a dock in Charlotte Amalie, St. Thomas, one of the US Virgin Islands. It wasn't terribly crowded, and I was already gussied up in a fresh wig, this one black as pitch with some bangs that framed my face in a way that I deemed unflattering but effective at hiding my identity. I was also wearing a bikini, which was another choice that I deemed unflattering—bordering on mortifying—but would again be unlikely to identify me.

Jamal was doing a pretty shit job of keeping his eyeballs in his head, but I ignored him because it was mildly adorable and flattering in a way that the bikini wasn't. He even tried to offer me a hand out on to the dock, but I ignored him because I can fly, and because my character for today was the strong, independent sort, who wouldn't have taken a helping hand from a dude even if she was about to fall into a vat of acid. The haircut kind of said so, but the black sunglasses I was sporting? They sold it.

"The airport is just down the road," Jamal said, dinking around with his cell phone again. "Flight to Atlanta leaves in two and a half hours, and apparently I have to clear customs."

"Yeah, it'd be a shame if you snuck in some sort of imported vegetable," I deadpanned, my bare feet slapping along the boards. Jamal was carrying my duffel for me because girls wearing bikinis don't usually carry duffel bags.

"That could be super dangerous."

"How about if I snuck you back in?" He waggled Arche's phone at me. "It's theoretically possible."

"I'll pass." I stared at the phone with my usual, practiced cynicism. When he told me Arche had left her app on the phone with my name on it, I had been pretty sure it wasn't for any good reason. But as it turned out … she'd left him the software that allowed her to block facial scanning … and the other part of our bargain.

She'd keyed the facial block software with my picture. Supposedly running, according to Jamal. So that if I chose to wander into a big city now, one with a web of cameras tied together, they'd end up getting a scrambled face for me just the same as they did for her.

I didn't particularly care to test it right now, but … it was a little interesting to know that in spite of her being a completely unemotive person … ArcheGrey1819 might just have done more for me than almost anyone else had in the last few months. Albeit for motives that were an utter mystery to me.

But the message she'd left about who was covering up for Harmon … I shook it out of my head. It shouldn't have been a huge surprise. I had been hearing about the nation of Revelen quite a bit lately.

"I think there's more to her than meets the eye," Jamal said, looking at me staring at the phone. He'd failed to look the gift horse in the mouth on this one, which was fine. In spite of what he maintained as a more quiet, reserved exterior than his brother, I'd kinda figured out Jamal was almost as optimistic as Augustus was. He just hid it better.

"Maybe there is," I said, shrugging as we kept walking down the concrete pier toward a road ahead. I saw a few taxis waiting a couple piers away, where a small cruise ship was pulling into port.

"You don't sound convinced."

"No evidence for it," I said. "Whatever Arche joined our side in the fight for? She kept it to herself. So yeah, maybe there's more to her. Maybe she's a deep and compassionate soul beneath it all, someone who's been burned enough to develop a deep layer of scar tissue that prevents her from connecting with people." I hid the smile I felt bubbling to the surface, and took the opportunity to prod Jamal. "Maybe she's just been cut off from humanity for too long, living in cyberspace, surfing the net … and clicking the refresh button is the only way she can feel good, or normal, and to keep doing it over and ov—"

"I see what you did there," Jamal said, letting the phone hand fall down to his side.

"I'm not subtle when it comes to my practice of psychology," I said. "And you've got a flight to catch, so … you should probably go." I gestured toward the nearest cab.

"What are you going to do now?" he asked, the wind coming in off the ocean swaying him a little. Poor guy still looked a little like hell. Me, I'd used the ocean water to wash the blood off.

"I think I'll take a vacation," I said, looking out over the crystal blue seas. I thought about my plan from a few days earlier, in Menomonie, to head south for the rest of the winter. You probably couldn't get any further south in US territory than the Virgin Islands, at least not in this hemisphere.

He looked like he wanted to ask if I was staying, but he must have thought the better of it. If he really wanted to know, he knew how to track me. He finally settled for saying, "You deserve one."

"So long, Jamal," I said as he got into the taxi. "Stop clicking that damned internet button, will you? Go live your life. Go camping or something."

He smiled at me as the cab pulled away. I waited until he was almost out of sight along the crowded road before I grabbed a cab of my own, and told the driver, "Take me to the most expensive, secluded resort on the island." I fell asleep a few seconds later, rocking gently in the back of the cab.

71.

Reed

"You did all right, Treston," Veronika said as we took the offramp in Eden Prairie, Minnesota. It was some pretty grudging praise, but I'd take it, especially coming from a woman as stingy with her compliments as she was free with her innuendo.

Night had long since fallen, and flying back from Orlando had been a chore and a half. TSA cut us no breaks, since we weren't government employees, and the security line at the airport was like the Bataan Death March but with helpful ropes to guide you to your eventual probing by a bored blue-shirted TSA employee.

We were almost back to the office, and I felt like once I got away from Veronika, maybe I could take a breath and plan my next move. Sure, I'd had hours to do it, but I still hadn't quite come to a conclusion.

Check into a hotel …?

Return to the friendly skies, without a constricting metal encasement this time?

Or …

"You don't want my advice, do you?" she asked, as if she could read my mind.

"I could probably live without it."

"No one appreciates my wisdom." She shook her head. "At least they like my bawdy jokes."

I didn't have the heart to break it to her that I didn't, so I said, "Well, no one's perfect."

"Whatever, dude," she said as we pulled into the parking lot of our new office. "My watch has now ended. I hope you make the right choice, but I've been around long enough to know that most people can't stop sabotaging themselves long enough to hold on to anything good, so …" She turned and offered me a hand. "Good luck. That's all I'll say."

Why bother pointing out she'd just said a hell of a lot more than 'good luck'? "Thanks." I shook her hand and we got out of the car.

The lights were still on inside, and the receptionist smiled at us as we came in, nodding us back through to the employee area. The place was pretty quiet, what with Kat and Colin still on assignment in California and Augustus and Angel still working their way back here. I didn't see any sign of J.J. or Abigail, but thinking about them made me recall their findings about our mysterious benefactor, Mr. Jonsdottir.

I saw movement inside one of the offices, and looked to the nameplate: Miranda Estevez.

"You good?" Veronika asked.

"Yeah, I've had all the advice from you I can handle."

"I meant, do you have a ride?" Veronika fired back.

"I'll just take a company car," I said, waving her off. She shook her head and headed out, a big purse slung over her shoulder. "See you later, Treston."

"Hasta," I said, making my way to Miranda Estevez's office.

I found her behind her desk, nursing a drink and twirling her hair around a finger as she stared at papers on her desk. She looked up when I darkened her door, and for the first time since we'd met, she smiled—just a little. "Mr. Treston. I hear things in Florida netted out favorably for you."

"It all worked out in the end," I agreed, wondering just how to play this.

"How do you feel after your first mission?" She held up her glass, and I could smell aged Scotch. Expensive stuff. She rattled the glass. "And … hm?"

"Yeah, I'll take some," I said, and she spun around quickly

to pull an ice bucket off the desk behind her. She put a scoop into a glass, then poured a rush of Lagavulin on top of it and gingerly slid it across to me. I held it up, gave it a long sniff, and sipped. It burned nicely on the way down.

"How do you feel you did?" Miranda asked again, leaning back in her seat. She was more relaxed than I'd seen her yet.

"I got the job done," I said, still standing.

She surveyed me, and I couldn't tell if she approved of my guarded answer or not. She smiled, but only faintly. "You did."

We waited in silence for a few minutes that would have felt a lot more uncomfortable if I hadn't been sipping whiskey and looking around the room. "Who do you work for, Ms. Estevez?" I finally asked.

She didn't react, not a whit. "Don't you know?"

"You know, our last lawyers—"

"Rothman, Curtis and Chang?" She quirked an eyebrow at me.

"Yeah, them," I said, and set down my glass on the bookshelf behind me. It was filled with those bound volumes that seemed to populate the shelves of lawyers the way lice populated preschools. "I got the feeling that our contact man there never actually knew who he was working for. That he was just a middleman the whole time." I turned back around to look at her, snagging my glass. "Is that the case for you, too? Are you in a double blind, wondering who you're working for while you're feeding the marching orders to us?"

"I don't think that's what a double blind is."

"But do you know who your boss is?" I asked, pressing harder.

"Of course," she said, not breaking eye contact. This should have been horrendously uncomfortable. "I work for you. You're the boss."

"Then where's the money coming from?" I asked. "Cuz I know it ain't coming from my bank account."

"No," she said, "but your benefactor … I'm afraid wishes to remain safely anonymous."

"I'll just bet. Running a team of metahuman contractors that work like a legal consulting version of the Avengers …

I'm sure our backer is doing this purely out of altruism."

"How do you know for sure?" Ms. Estevez asked, still carefully neutral. "So far we're profitable, albeit only slightly. Or perhaps it's someone who's suffered at the hands of a rogue meta, and knows the value of having people with experience helping the police."

"And maybe it's someone with an agenda of their own," I said, "one that's darker and more self-serving than they'll admit to."

"If that were the case," Ms. Estevez said, "there doesn't seem to be any shortage of powerful metas willing to do terrible things for considerably less money than you're now being paid."

She had me there, but my natural suspicion just didn't want me to give up. "What happens on the day when Moneybags decides the team needs to go in a different direction than I do?"

"What makes you think that day will come?"

"I like to be prepared for every contingency."

"I expect on that day, if it comes," Ms. Estevez said, "loyalty is bound to win out over money, isn't it?" Her eyes showed a glimmer of amusement. "And Moneybags, as you called our benefactor, isn't anywhere to be seen. So … what do you think will happen if the day ever comes when you want the team to go in another direction?"

"I have a feeling we'll find out," I said, setting down my unfinished Scotch on her desk, leaving the last of it. "Good night, Ms. Estevez."

"Good night, Mr. Treston. I trust we'll see you tomorrow?"

"Count on it," I said, leaving her in the office, alone, with her Scotch.

72.

Sienna

I'd checked into this palatial resort under another of my fake names. I'd switched to a blond wig and put a silken wrap on before I stepped out of the cab, thankfully clued into our inevitable arrival by a severe bump in the road that dragged me out of my slumber.

It was a beachfront place, as befit the most expensive resort on the island. I had a balcony that overlooked the whole resort, blue water stretching out just past the white, sandy dunes. I was laid out on a chaise lounge, my wrap shed, enjoying the shade. I had fallen asleep for a while, but now I was awake to see the day start to come to a close, the sun sinking toward the horizon ahead.

"Beats the hell out of Menomonie, Wisconsin, doesn't it?" I asked no one in particular. I'd brought the room service menu out with me in anticipation of being hungry. I was planning to order a drink with dinner. Maybe a Blue Hawaii, whatever that was.

Mmmm, Wolfe said. Blue Hawaii. *Very good.*

"Or maybe something else," I said.

You're awfully quiet, Harmon said, doing his usual probing. It wasn't like he couldn't read my mind, unlike the others.

She's always most dangerous when she's quiet, Zack said.

"What is there to say?" I asked. "Another scheme, another fight, another can of whoopass opened on a horde of unsuspecting bodyguards and mercenaries."

Oh, you're so *strong,* Harmon said.

Don't be a dick, Zack said.

"Let him spout off," I said with a shrug. "I kicked his ass, too. Whining and sarcasm are all he has left."

Arrogance is a dangerous quality, Gavrikov said. *And it always flees just as you fall.*

"Arrogance," I said, almost snorting. "Did you ever consider … that maybe … just maybe … no one can really beat me? That maybe no one can stop me?"

But they can kill you, Zack said.

And for most people, that would be enough, Bjorn said.

Yeah, killing Sienna Nealon is a pretty big get, Bastian said.

Your head would look nice in a trophy case, Eve agreed. *To many people. I never kept heads as trophies. Too much rot.*

"My point is … everything I can lose, I've already lost," I said. "They can kill me, but that's about it. And most of them can't even do that."

All it takes is one, Wolfe warned. *Trust us in this.*

"Because I was your one?"

It is a bad idea, tempting Fates, Wolfe said.

"Screw those dead ladies." I lay my head back on the padding of the chaise lounge.

It's going to be fun watching that overweening pride lead you into the fall, Harmon said. *I'm going to enjoy it all the way to the end.*

"Have fun with that."

Oh, I will.

"Maybe that'll make two of us."

Sienna, Zack said.

"Yes?"

I think you're losing your way, he said. *I think you've lost … hope. Perspective, maybe. I don't know. You're lost, though, out on your own like this.*

"I'm not lost." I looked at the fading sun, turning the sky orange as the waves darkened below. "I know exactly where I am."

You've lost yourself.

"I know who I am," I said. "I'm the idiot that keeps throwing herself into the path of every stupid, world-ending scheme the crackpots of this planet can concoct. And a bunch of lesser knuckleheaded plans, too."

So why do you keep doing it? Zack asked, and I stared out into the setting sun. *It's cost you your friends, it's cost you your life … but you keep risking all you have left every time something like this comes up. So … why keep doing it?*

"Because it's my job," I said, and my voice cracked. I covered my mouth, and sat there in silence, tears streaking down my cheeks for a long while after that. "Because it's almost all I have left, really."

73.

Reed

I didn't take the car because I'd been drinking, and because screw the FAA. I could feel a plane in the air better than they could sense them with radar. Hell, if I wanted to, I could tell them the position of every plane in the air over North America right now, military and civilian, and maybe even the location of all those stupid little drones that they sold in stores nowadays, too, if I concentrated really hard.

I stared down on the house from a low-hanging cloud. The truth was … I'd been here a few times in the last couple months.

I'd just never come down.

She was probably watching TV, but I wasn't delusional enough to believe that Isabella Perugini would wait around for me forever. She wasn't that kind of woman, the kind who would just sit around, waiting for her man to return.

Especially when that man was pretty much busy doing nothing but being a shithead.

Why was it so damned hard? The door was right down there. I didn't have to kick it in.

All I had to do … was knock.

What was the worst she could say? "To hell with you, you *maledetto cazzo*!"

That … that would actually be pretty bad, if you knew what it meant in Italian.

She might say it, too. But I'd never know if I didn't go up

and knock.

I thought about Olivia, unable to go home for all those years, unwilling. And even when she got there, Roger was waiting, standing between her and any kind of life with the people she'd grown up with. Fear paralyzing her, like a permanent wall between her and the people she'd known at the cloister. They'd lived in it; some had probably died in it, too afraid to take action to change things.

There was a lesson in that.

I barely realized it when my feet touched down on the lawn. I'd never done that before, resting them on solid ground, here.

The front door loomed ahead of me, big and white and shining under the front porch light. It felt a thousand miles away, and yet there it was … waiting for a knock.

What would she say? What would she think of me after—

The sound of a footstep behind me caused me to spin, and I saw her standing there, frozen in the street, bundled up tight in a heavy jacket, her arms folded in front of her like she was trying to hold in warmth.

"Isabella," I said, and my breath caught in my throat like I'd lodged it there with my power.

She didn't say anything, staring at me stone-faced, her eyes fixed in that hard gaze she usually reserved for my sister.

"I'm … sorry," I said, "I—"

"Shut up, you idiot," she said, and strode toward me. I caught her and she kissed me, her fingers caressing my bearded cheeks, her leather gloves smooth against my bare skin. We kissed, and kissed, and kissed again, and I held her tight.

"Come inside," she said when we finally broke, and she walked toward the door, her hand on mine.

I stared at the brightly lit white portal to my old life and let her lead me up the steps, shaking gently as we approached. I stopped on the porch as she unlocked the door, and it cracked open as she looked back at me.

She stared at me questioningly, waiting as she stepped over the threshold and our arms reached maximum extension as I paused outside. "Are you coming?"

I closed my eyes for just a moment. The desire to let go of her hand, to leap back into the sky, to let the wind take me off …

It died right there, like a tornado under my attention.

"Yes," I said, and came in, closing the door behind us.

74.

Jamal

"Hey," I said as I came in. The lights were on, and I could hear noise from the family room. I wasn't sure what I was expecting—maybe Momma and Taneshia watching something on TV together, like they tended to do. I was always the third wheel in those situations, content to go to my room and log on while they laughed and watched, talking and enjoying themselves.

Normally I didn't even stop as I passed by that archway into the family room.

But tonight, something stopped me.

"Hey, brah," Augustus said, popping up off the couch. He caught me in a hug that surprised me as much as him being here did, lifting me up a little to show me how my little brother wasn't so little anymore. "How you doing?"

A long answer formed in my head, something about how I'd been on an adventure with Sienna Nealon, how we'd saved the INFOSEC of the whole damned planet …

But I tossed it all out in favor of, "Fine. What are you doing here?" I looked around. Taneshia was on the sofa, clearly next to where Augustus had been sitting. "And where's Momma?"

"I'm just in town because I had some business in Alabama that wrapped up today," Augustus said casually, like I was supposed to know what that meant, even though he hadn't told me. I actually did know what it meant—more about it than he did—but I didn't feel like I needed to show him up, so I just adjusted my glasses and listened politely. "Oh, I didn't tell you, did I? I got my old job back."

"That's good," I said. "I know you were all worried about that government mess screwing things up for you."

"Yeah, but it all worked out," he said, and clapped me on the shoulder. "Hey. Me and Taneshia are going out in a bit. You want to come?"

"I … just got home," I answered reflexively and pulled from his grip. I held tightly onto my bag, carrying it with me down the hall toward my room, ignoring the clutter and the fact that Augustus followed me. I set it down on the bed and pulled out my tablet, setting it up on the desk and clicking the button to wake it.

"That's not a no," Augustus said, hovering at the door, sounding hopeful. This was how he always was.

"I don't want to be y'all's third wheel." I stared at the screen as it lit, and tapped the browser open. It started to preload my home page, the forum I always visited. The Messenger icon lit up and went green.

Online, it declared. Eighteen new threads to catch up on.

"You won't be," Augustus said. "Come on. I ain't seen you in months. Come out with us. It'll be fun."

"Nah," I said, shaking my head. The threads were calling to me. I wanted to click 'em all, open them in a new tab, refresh and see if there was something new that popped up between now and the last time I clicked it.

I stopped myself just before I hit the refresh button.

This wasn't what I wanted. Not really.

I looked over my shoulder and saw Augustus there, earnest as ever, still lurking in the door, waiting on my reply.

"You know what? Yeah," I said, nodding along. "Yeah, I'll come with you." And I flipped my status on Messenger to offline, and went to go out with my brother.

75.

Sienna

My cell phone rang a few minutes after I'd finished dinner, succulent fresh lobster dipped in butter. I answered it, because it was one of only two numbers I had memorized at this point. "How are you doing this evening, Ms. Estevez?"

"Not as well as I expect you are," Miranda Estevez answered. I would have felt a little bad for her, sitting her ass in an office in snowy Minneapolis while I was here in St. Thomas, but she was being paid well for what she was doing. "I have an update on your brother."

"Oh?"

"He performed better than expected," she said. "And he's back home now."

"Thank goodness for small miracles," I said, stepping off my balcony into the chill of the air conditioner. I hadn't realized it had gotten a little warm out there until I stepped inside. "Pride seems to be a common genetic component between us."

"The others are also doing well," Ms. Estevez went on. "Everything is set up here. The operation is running smoothly in your absence."

"Excellent," I said. "Do some good. And keep an eye on them for me?"

"You're the boss, Ms. Nealon."

I hung up and looked out my window.

Damned right I was the boss. I had been all along, though

it had been my secret the entire time.

I have to admit, Harmon said, sounding grudgingly admiring, *if I'd known that you had a half a billion in secret money hidden away in Liechtenstein with which to just start your own quasi-government agency and continue to meddle, I probably wouldn't have had you fired from the FBI. It just made you more troublesome.*

"You're the one who forced my hand," I said, covering back up in my wrap now that I was cool again. I flopped onto the comfy, king-sized bed. "I went to bed after our conversation on Election Day thinking … man, I hate being out of control of my own fate. And when I went to bed, I just happened to remember that half billion I 'inherited' from Omega the last time I went to London …" I shrugged as best I could lying down. "It just sort of called out to me, the idea of starting my own shop."

Yes, well, Harmon said, a little more snottily than usual, *I still managed to turn you into an outcast and a fugitive, so, I guess we're drawing closer to even.*

"I don't think we're even," I said, "since I'm stuck with you, and you've ruined my life. It feels like I got a pretty crap deal there."

The feeling is mutual. So, he asked, *what now?*

"Now … we wait," I said, laying back on the bed. "Just like we always have."

Sounds like a pretty empty way to go through life.

I blinked as I stared at the ceiling. I didn't like him, but I liked it even less that he was right. "Shut the hell up, asshole," I said and closed my eyes.

Maybe sleep would help pass the time more quickly.

Sienna Nealon Will Return in

TOXICITY

Out of the Box
Book 13

Coming March 14, 2017!

Author's Note

Thanks for reading! If you want to know immediately when future books become available, take sixty seconds and sign up for my NEW RELEASE EMAIL ALERTS by visiting my website. I don't sell your information and I only send out emails when I have a new book out. The reason you should sign up for this is because I don't always set release dates, and even if you're following me on Facebook (robertJcrane (Author)) or Twitter (@robertJcrane), it's easy to miss my book announcements because...well, because social media is an imprecise thing.

Come join the discussion on my website:
http://www.robertjcrane.com!

Cheers,
Robert J. Crane

ACKNOWLEDGMENTS

Editorial/Literary Janitorial duties performed by Sarah Barbour and Jeffrey Bryan. Final proofing was once more handled by the illustrious Jo Evans. Any errors you see in the text, however, are the result of me rejecting changes.

The cover was once more designed with exceeding skill by Karri Klawiter of Artbykarri.com.

The formatting was provided by nickbowmanediting.com.

Once more, thanks to my parents, my in-laws, my kids and my wife, for helping me keep things together.

Other Works by Robert J. Crane

World of Sanctuary

Epic Fantasy

Defender: The Sanctuary Series, Volume One
Avenger: The Sanctuary Series, Volume Two
Champion: The Sanctuary Series, Volume Three
Crusader: The Sanctuary Series, Volume Four
Sanctuary Tales, Volume One - A Short Story Collection
Thy Father's Shadow: The Sanctuary Series, Volume 4.5
Master: The Sanctuary Series, Volume Five
Fated in Darkness: The Sanctuary Series, Volume 5.5
Warlord: The Sanctuary Series, Volume Six
Heretic: The Sanctuary Series, Volume Seven
Legend: The Sanctuary Series, Volume Eight
Ghosts of Sanctuary: The Sanctuary Series, Volume Nine*
(Coming 2018, at earliest.)

The Girl in the Box

and

Out of the Box

Contemporary Urban Fantasy

Alone: The Girl in the Box, Book 1
Untouched: The Girl in the Box, Book 2
Soulless: The Girl in the Box, Book 3
Family: The Girl in the Box, Book 4
Omega: The Girl in the Box, Book 5
Broken: The Girl in the Box, Book 6
Enemies: The Girl in the Box, Book 7
Legacy: The Girl in the Box, Book 8
Destiny: The Girl in the Box, Book 9
Power: The Girl in the Box, Book 10

Limitless: Out of the Box, Book 1
In the Wind: Out of the Box, Book 2
Ruthless: Out of the Box, Book 3
Grounded: Out of the Box, Book 4
Tormented: Out of the Box, Book 5
Vengeful: Out of the Box, Book 6
Sea Change: Out of the Box, Book 7
Painkiller: Out of the Box, Book 8
Masks: Out of the Box, Book 9
Prisoners: Out of the Box, Book 10
Unyielding: Out of the Box, Book 11
Hollow: Out of the Box, Book 12* *(Coming January 2017!)*
Toxicity: Out of the Box, Book 13* *(Coming March 2017!)*
Small Things: Out of the Box, Book 14* *(Coming May 2017!)*
Hunters: Out of the Box, Book 15* *(Coming July 2017!)*
Badder: Out of the Box, Book 16* *(Coming September 2017!)*

Southern Watch

Contemporary Urban Fantasy

Called: Southern Watch, Book 1
Depths: Southern Watch, Book 2
Corrupted: Southern Watch, Book 3
Unearthed: Southern Watch, Book 4
Legion: Southern Watch, Book 5
Starling: Southern Watch, Book 6* *(Coming Early 2017 – Tentatively)*

*Forthcoming

43688657R00189

Made in the USA
Middletown, DE
27 April 2019